CAN YOU SEE ANYTHING NOW?

A Novel

Katherine James

PARACLETE FICTION

BREWSTER, MASSACHUSETTS

FOR RICK

2017 First Printing

Can You See Anything Now? : A Novel

ISBN: 978-1-61261-931-6

Library of Congress Cataloging-in-Publication Data
Names: James, Katherine, 1965- author.
Title: Can you see anything now? : a novel / Katherine James.
Description: Brewster, Massachusetts : Paraclete Press, 2017.
Identifiers: LCCN 2017026688 | ISBN 9781612619316 (paperback)
Subjects: LCSH: City and town life--Fiction. | Motivation (Psychology)--Fiction. | Desire--Fiction. | Life change events--Fiction. | Psychological fiction. | BISAC: FICTION / Christian / General. | RELIGION / Christianity / Literature & the Arts. | GSAFD: Christian fiction. | Christian fiction.
Classification: LCC PS3610.A4436 C36 2017 | DDC 813/.6--dc23
LC record available at https://lccn.loc.gov/2017026688

10 9 8 7 6 5 4 3 2 1

Published by Paraclete Press
Brewster, Massachusetts
www.paracletepress.com

Printed in the United States of America

PART ONE

Who's lived his whole
ruddy bloody cruddy life
in five-walled rooms?

—DAVID FOSTER WALLACE,
INFINITE JEST

1.

Margie: early in the morning

Of all of the ways that Margie Nethercott could kill herself, she found it hard to imagine a better way than fading out of the universe with the help of a palmful of pills. Preferably of the white, chalky type, chunky disks of tiny particles forced together via mechanical arms and metal plates in some factory deep in South America, where the coca leaves shading the whole affair smirk from the jungles. Yes, but, with the Brave New World comes a certain ease in offing oneself, and with this ease comes monotony. Suicide should contain a bit of drama. Something. Pills were anemic, and guns were terrifying. Drowning, on the other hand, had stood the test of time. Smooth, simple, and metaphorically appropriate in light of the lungs filling with liquid and air bubbling upward like packets of life that pop at the surface.

And so it was that very early in the morning on September twenty-third, Margie tied a large stone to her ankle and let it pull her to the bottom of the lake.

The plan was well thought out. The rock, in fact, was predetermined, having been chosen by Margie weeks earlier as she walked by the water contemplating her latest diagnosis of multiple sclerosis and feeding her escalated state of sorrow with tidbits from remembered misfortunes of her youth. The rock itself was a comfort. It had the slightest green tint of algae, one side hugging the mud and slop of the immobile water. She spied it on her evening walk, coming down the hill and around the lake. The size was right. The placement and color. The tone.

The time—she had left her bed at 3:07 according to the glo-green digits of her alarm clock—was random. Margie, lying in bed, stone still herself, listened to the tiny wheeze exiting Nick's too-small nostrils for more than fifteen minutes before she was satisfied he was asleep. Sometimes Nick worked through the night on his thinly imagined magnum opus, a work that called on much obvious material to state what was already obvious to those inclined to reflect on such things as the obvious emotional manifestations of *imperfections*—ours, theirs, or some abstract combination thereof. She often came downstairs to find him on the couch with his laptop, hunting and pecking the keyboard, a hungry determination on his face as his small dark eyes darted about in sync with the hasty movements of his fingers.

She had some rope and a section of fishing net. The silty gray hue (Margie pictured everything in colors and hues) of her life was just the plain fact of it. Being alive was not an off or on thing, it was a spectrum, where death hovered somewhere mid-ambit and she'd been a flickering thing for years. Things that made her feel real: art (her own, not someone else's), sometimes reading, sometimes music, physical pain. This time she would end her life with an appropriate last breath in the middle of the night in the quickening breeze of early fall, giving way to the Weekeepeemee Lake like a soldier on his own sword.

She dragged a canoe across a patch of sand and pushed the bow into the water where it wobbled atop the tiny waves, lifting the load from Margie's arms as though in gentle affirmation of her intention to kill herself. She set the rock—with the rope and the net—into the bottom of the canoe and pushed hard so that it slid off the sand and into the water and the darkness toward an old swimming raft floating on oil drums forty yards out. Back straight, she sliced a paddle into the water, gliding quietly forward, stars across the sky.

Once on the swimming raft, she shoved the canoe away with her foot—a kick with a bit of lazy anger behind it—and set to wrapping the rock in the net and tying the rope to the net and then her ankle. The sky was dark but for the stars. The water was black. Still, there wasn't the void that she had imagined—she knew the edges of the lake, the sloping hill beyond, the soft haze of certain light across the sky that hinted at the more nocturnal part of town, and these things felt to her like intruders. She sat at the edge of the raft.

Gripping the rope tightly, she slowly lowered the rock into the water, stalled for a moment, and let go. The rock tugged her ankle down first, then her leg, and she tightened her lips. She felt the firm tug in her leg and then also in her torso, as though the rope was tied to her heart and gently yanking it, the way she remembered the placenta, after Noel was born, finally easing out of her as the doctor pulled at the umbilical cord. She gripped the edge of the raft, and the rough wood dug a fierce line into the back of her thighs, one leg sunk deep into the water, the other floating near the surface and ready to follow. Small swells of water flapped cool around her half-sunk leg, and a breeze only strong enough to muss a few strands of hair touched the side of her face. She stared at the waves. It was entirely possible to feed oneself with sorrow to the point that, above or below the water, a turning would happen. A redirection. The canoe wandered alone, a dark oblong shape now nosing the shore. Margie looked up at the stars. The stars were her friends, she thought to herself, before slipping into the water and letting the rock sink down, tugging her body in one very fine movement with a solid, hapless jerk.

As she slipped into the water, the rock sank into the slop of mud at the bottom and yanked her under. She felt the tiny pings of rough mud and sand hit her legs as the rock kicked up debris from the bottom. And then, in a way that she understood as her natural, her *instinctual* desire to live, she found her head above water after all, her Puma-clad feet balancing on the very rock that was supposed to bring her demise that dark finger of a morning. It was unclear whether the lake was low because of high temperatures and the recent short-term drought, or whether her memory had simply failed her. She hadn't been in the lake for five years. It was not as deep as she had remembered.

SHE STOOD ON THE ROCK with her chin tilted up for two hours, cavernous air above, half floating, half standing, her arms bearing nothing but the waif-like currents of the lake as the stars faded and a low fog settled over the water as per its morning routine. A group of ducks squawked, winging over her, and splashing a wake as their thin legs reached forward, guiding them into a synchronized landing. She relaxed, making threads of her limbs, and slipped under the water to rest her neck and arms and then came back up, face wet, blinking water from her eyes.

A few early walkers and joggers began to appear, coming down the short hill and rounding the corner and back up the other hill. She could see Cecilia Henley, the woman with the twins and the backyard strewn with Little Tykes playthings, her thick thighs jugging left and right, large feet pointed slightly out as she began the climb, as though the street was the large trunk of a tree and here she needed to wrap herself around it, grip it between her legs, and keep her focus on the sky. Cecilia Henley tilted her head back as she ran, gasping, knees out, feet out, pavement passing slowly beneath her. It was a funny thing to watch.

Margie let herself pee and felt the cloud of guilty warmth around her for a moment before it gave way again to the cool water of the Weekeepeemee. Her limbs were by now sucked clean of any vitality, their structure loosening—bone, muscle, and nerve dividing into a useless, rubbery mass. She had no choice but to call out.

"Hello?" She tilted her head back farther when she called, and the white morning sky blinded her. "Hey!"

A jogger stopped and hesitated, turning toward the lake. He put his hands on his hips, breathing hard, and walked curiously to the edge of the water. It was James O'Neil. She could tell because of his stocky size and—even from far away—the purity of his face, that look of wonder that he always had—eyebrows up toward the middle of his forehead like he never could quite figure out something or like there was an element of surprise for him in the most mediocre things. He wore a green shirt with white lettering and gray athletic shorts. He stretched his head forward and squinted, peering across the water. "Hello?" he called out.

"It's Margie Nethercott!"

"Margie?"

"I'm stuck!"

"Margie?"

2.

Margie: these complications

Margie was still weak from the morning. She sat on the edge of the bathtub. Outside, down closer to the river, men hammered shingles into a roof deck, and the scatter of muffled thumps became oriented somewhere in her diaphragm, a pounding at the inside of her chest that seemed to touch at her throat and jaw with every beat. What a failed suicide felt like was a hangover.

She ran a hand through her hair, pausing at the base of her neck. She was familiar with beauty but cursed with its expectations—her body had already begun its revolt in the usual ways: five pounds here, a certain sag to the upper eyelids, the skin at her elbows chalky and loose. Her jaw line was firm, though, and her face had yet to lose that perfect symmetry and form that could still turn a head.

She ran the water into the bath hotter than she was used to, and slowly lowered herself into it. A pile of wet clothes lay beneath the towel rack. She looked up at the small window above the tub and watched shadows from the Japanese maple in the backyard flutter across the sheer of the curtains.

James O'Neil had been kind and understanding, paddling the canoe out and getting into the water and feeling down into the deep for the rope and tugging on it and going under and seeing the difficulty of the tight knot and, yes, he would need a knife, something sharp, so just hang tight (no pun intended—or at least these are the thoughts that Margie had) and he would be right back—are you doing all right? Are you getting tired? The ducks bothering you? And what the hell were you thinking? These last two, again, just thoughts. There was, in the end, a small group of neighbors—Mary Sommerfeld, Al Carson, and then Nick, finally, tired-looking and drawn and wearing those fricking shoe-slippers that he insisted were meant to be worn in or out of the house. Finally. He had showed up. Having been called. The irritable scrape of the aluminum canoe, the spot of wet rope still at her ankle, the fog gone and then the terrible, terrible blue sky.

It was easiest to be silent but then the silence began to own her, pressing an invisible palm over half of her face as she walked with Nick to the car and he said the things to the others that needed to be said. *We'll have to figure things out. Thank you for your help.* Nick was very, very good at these things. People expected it of him. *I'm so grateful that you were there.*

She turned the hot water off, ran the cold for thirty seconds, and sank deeper into the tub. She looked at her feet, half afloat above the drain. Under the water they looked so young, like a child's feet, white and soft and honorable. Nick knocked on the door and came in.

He stood there.

"I'm sorry and I'm sorry and I'm sorry," Margie said.

"I could be very angry." He pinched the bridge of his nose, and his glasses popped up half an inch. He crossed his chest with his other arm. "You know."

"I am . . . *sorry*. I am."

He leaned back against the sink and gripped it with his hands. He stared at the floor.

"My work looks like crap and my hands shake. I'm tired, Nick. My symptoms are getting worse. Everything slants, at least in my head."

Nick stared at her without seeing, his mind at a specific place. "Then we call the doctor and we discuss it with him."

"And it's not just about that anyway," Margie said. "You're always marginalizing things. You of all people. Sometimes I just . . . I'm just so tired."

Nick stared at her in the tub. A few pieces of grass floated under the faucet. He looked at the grass.

Nick had a degree in psychology and studied forms of vascular resting therapy. Vascular resting therapy was something he thought up himself. Everything is connected to the blood, he said. Like plant life, the physical body is only as alive as it is receiving nutrients; air, soil, sun, water. He told her these things eagerly, enthusiastic, and went back to work before she could comment. Sometimes Margie imagined veins that were all leathery and shriveled from being outside the body. She imagined pulling at them like shoelaces, dragging a fetid heart or a shriveled kidney across the floor. The organs would make a scratching sound since they were dry and lacked blood.

There was a large leather chair in Nick's office, purchased from Blackstone, where his clients sat. Nick let what was left of his graying hair grow a good two inches below his ears where it curled outward. He wore jeans with a rip under one knee and moccasin slippers that were smooth on the soles like dog paws. His glasses were thick, black-rimmed circles. He crossed his arms and nodded, still staring at the grass floating under the faucet.

"Sometimes I just feel so tired, and then I had this strange energy that came out of nowhere and had to be used or it would disappear. It would get wasted and disappear if I didn't, I don't know, *act* somehow."

"Of course, what else could you do?" Nick looked at the floor.

"Don't be like that. I want you to know what it's like."

"Productive ways to use energy," and here he hung his head a little bit forward so that it bounced with each word as though attached to springs, "go for a run, make dinner, clean out the goddamned shed. . . ."

It wasn't the first time Margie had done something so stupid. There was the depression and then there were fits of something like rage, an energy that could, they both knew by now, express itself by locking itself into bathrooms with razor blades and pills, opening car doors on interstates, courageous almost acts of violence that never quite made it to the next level. "Never" being the key word here, for some form of this same scenario had happened enough times to squeeze the danger out of them. Nick had other things going. Still. Still, even with every razor blade and open door on the interstate, the lake was a sure shot toward something, being so fundamentally deep and shallow all at the same time, and she had never, *never* intended it to be so public. She should do something with this, Margie thought, a retrospective of suicide attempts, so fucking meaningful and so fucking stupid and so fucking futile. "Let's just not tell Noel, okay?" She tilted her head back against the tub. "And I'm really sorry."

"Sure Margie, no, I won't tell Noel," Nick said, and left the bathroom, but not before taking a swipe at a toothbrush next to the sink. It flew off the vanity and hit the wall, landing in the toilet.

Mary Sommerfeld showed up at the house with a casserole.

"It's a spa-ghet-ti cas-ser-role," she said in a slight lilt leftover from a childhood in Georgia, "baked spaghetti." She set the Corning Ware down on the kitchen table. She wore oven mitts with culinary terms printed on them in green Italian-looking script and olives and sprigs of basil in between the words. Her extra weight was keeping her young, Margie thought to herself, filling in potential creases around her eyes and mouth. Her neck, which should have been crêpey and ropey, was risen dough, giving her the advantage of having the look of someone to be trusted. "It's one of Julie's favorites." Julie was Mary's granddaughter. Margie had spent a frustrating week painting the girl, working to make her mouth less static. The girl had been like a corpse to paint: eyes, mouth, nose, everything flaccid. No brain in that girl.

Mary stood in the kitchen with her gloved hands on her hips. "Last week I made eight of these. Eight." She rolled her eyes halfway before continuing. "That was for Julie's soccer club. I don't know much about soccer, but at least I can cook. She's on the traveling team this year and they decided to make her captain. She's worked so hard at bringing that team together—last Saturday we put together sixteen pairs of flip-flops with the blue and yellow team colors braided around the straps. The girls loved them!" And then she stalled, sweeping an oven mitt through the air as though to erase her words. "Margie, you need to get more rest. Forget the art for a while, it will always be there."

She then bustled about, opened the oven door, closed it, turned the temperature up, glanced into the dark living room for Nick. Margie watched her the way a camera sees a city at night with the shutter open, light trails interspersed with fixed moments. She had barely seen her at the oven before she was over at the sink, turning on water, running a thick thumb through the flow. Time felt slow and fast at the same time and could only be tolerated if Margie kept her distance.

"There are many people who have difficult things to deal with. Just take good care of yourself. . . ." Her tongue was visible between the sounds coming from her mouth as though it were necessary to push them out.

Margie began to smell the spaghetti warming in the oven and felt sick. It was dusk outside. Nick appeared carrying a small paperback book. The back of the book said in large yellow letters that moved in stages into smaller black type, "The Higgs Boson lies dormant as far as its identity, but this book will. . . ." Nick set the book on the counter and placed a hand on Mary's shoulder. "It was very kind of you to come," he said. "We'll enjoy the spaghetti, I'm sure."

"I'll stop by tomorrow sometime for the dish. I'd say you could keep it, but it's honestly, it's my favorite one for baked cas-ser-roles."

"Noel will be home for the weekend," Nick said, walking her down the hall to the door. "I'll have her run it up to you. And thank you. Thank you, Mary." Nick opened the door, and she stepped to one side and strained her neck so that she could see back into the kitchen. Margie stood with her back to the sink. She raised a hand goodbye. She smiled.

"Well I'm happy to be of help. You let me know if there's anything you need. Anything at all. *An-y-thing*," and then yelled, "I mean that!" She padded out the door, oven mitts under one fleshy arm like two dead fish.

"Thank you!" Margie called weakly from the kitchen.

Nick closed the front door, glanced at Margie. "Sorry," he said, and walked back down the hall to his office.

Margie poured herself a glass of wine from a box that Nick kept in the fridge and went into the living room. There was a plaid chair, a relic from her grandfather's apartment. She sat down and stared straight ahead for a moment before snapping back to life. The house was old, worn, charred even—the sort of house that appeared inherited, cushions with tassels and linen curtains bleached by the sun. Sometimes there seemed to her a sort of purgation working the corners and walls, a blanching somehow, in the way the floorboards continued to grow lighter in the high traffic areas, the carpets more threadbare. She took a sip of wine and leaned back into the chair. Nick came out of his office and walked past the living room on his way to the kitchen, looking for the book he had left on the counter. As he looked, his mouth turned down at the corners, and his round, black-rimmed glasses, along with the loose skin of his neck, made him look like a turtle.

"Do you know when you talk you personify everything?" Margie said half to herself. Her feet were crossed on a small ottoman, and she compulsively shook one of them as though to distract herself. "More than most people. You say things like, 'the couch is beginning to barf stuffing' or, 'the rain is eating at the picnic table.' You have an oral thing too. It's all about the mouth. It's *always* all about the mouth."

Nick came around the corner holding a mug of something. "I've never been all that Freudian, Margie, if that's what you're getting at," he said, taking a sip. And then, "I can't explain you to people."

He sat down across from her on the ottoman. "You remember the Aesop fable? The one with the wolf?"

"Oh, god no . . . are you serious?"

"I'm not being mean. Listen, it's not that I don't understand. It's just that there are appropriate ways to struggle with things."

"Struggling by definition is not something you choose. How does one appropriately struggle?" She tilted her head for emphasis.

Nick looked past her, out the window, and shook his head the tiniest bit.

"I'm just. I think . . . I get overwhelmed."

There was a silence.

Margie continued, "I think sometimes that I'm okay and even though I've got issues, problems," she shrugged her shoulders, "I've got it together, but then there's all this shit that comes out of nowhere."

"Right, I get that."

"No, Nick, you don't know anything about *this*!" She started to spread out her arms to indicate herself and then let them fall, dropped her head, and began to cry quietly.

Nick stood and went to her. He put his hand on her shoulder.

She looked up at him and said through her tears, "It is true—that you personify everything. It's something I've been meaning to tell you," but she didn't say it with much heft, for she had been struck by something in his eyes and barely heard her own voice. Nick was a fake, he had to be. Either he was a fake, or she was.

ALONE IN BED, she held the morning's events at arm's length. She couldn't bring herself to think about them. If she allowed a thought—such as the fog and James O'Neil swimming around down near her ankles trying to untie her knots—she let out a stale whimper of shame.

When Nick crawled into bed, she remembered how she had lain still in the dark of early morning, waiting for the slow movements of his breath so that she could sneak down to the lake. She inched away from him, closer to the side of the bed, and let her chin rest on the edge.

And then she laughed. She laughed quietly by herself—a slight breath impossible to hear. Of course, how foolish. It was a ruse. She must not self-sabotage anymore. And yet that was the point, no?

She looked into the dark at the floor. She smelled the musk of the worn Persian carpet, a smell she associated somehow with love, a stale musk that reminded her of her grandfather, his studio, his cigarettes, the soft wool of his worn jacket. Her grandfather. Lee. Seventy-eight and done with his own special suffering, he had left her his paint and his brushes. A trio of palette knives tied with a blue ribbon.

3.

Etta: the five languages

Etta Wallace sat on her front porch in a white rocker she and her husband had bought at a Cracker Barrel the last time they made the trip down to her sister Sarah's house in Chattanooga. She tucked her short blonde hair behind her ears, unzipped her aqua-colored windbreaker, and slipped it off. She hung it from the back of the rocker before settling back into the seat and breathing deeply. Even in a small town like Trinity, things happened. She was sad, truly sad, when she'd heard about Margie Nethercott. So far most of the talk had been gossip, really, disguised panacea because everyone decidedly knew what would help her. This inpatient program, that counselor. Even gluten-free diets and that sort of foolishness.

From her perch she could see most of Trinity. The wood-frame house sat three streets up from Maple at the corner of Rosetree and Fourth, the sharp incline of homes created a strangely beautiful landscape of asphalt shingles and brick chimneys—an evening shock of sun whitening the ruddy surfaces for half an hour before sneaking west. Etta liked that she saw the beauty in the rooftops.

Etta was an artist, a local celebrity really, although she hated to think of herself in that way. She painted tomatoes. She had learned to paint them from a book she purchased from Carlino's, *Painting the Primitive Plumb*, that had various fruits, vegetables, vines, and leaves featured on the glossy pages with step-by-step instructions as to how to dab on a swipe of light reflection and simplify or "suggest" the curve and tone of a particular organic item. Her attempts at most of the fruits and vegetables had been failures—her vines had looked stiff and Crayola green, bananas too half-moon, but the tomatoes, the red red and uncautious curve of the brush indicating a tomato, had worked, had definitely worked, and Etta kept painting them. She painted them on furniture, on small canvases she framed and matted, on the backs of rockers, on old slabs of peeling wood and antique washer boards she found in the basement of Aaron's Antiques. She attached rusty nails and twisted wire to the backs of things to hang them. She had an Etsy page. She sold her pieces at the May hospital fair. "Etta's Tomatoes," her burlap sign read. She and Edward lined up the pieces for display. There were forms to "order now" for Christmas—20 percent off. More than once she had sold out of her paintings and had to introduce preordering. She felt a special attachment to the world in light of her gift, a comradeship of form; humanity sought out beautiful things and Etta created beautiful things. Now she wanted to create something uniquely beautiful, something others might not notice, and she was beginning to believe it might actually be the rooftops. The rooftops. What a challenge.

She stood up from the rocker and leaned over the railing of the porch to adjust a painted sign that said, "Harvest Blessings." She wanted it hung off-kilter. A leggy rose bush touched the porch railing here and there in yellow blooms that were quickly drying up. The leaves were pockmarked by beetles, the holes making a scattered mess of the shiny dark green petals. She needed to spray them. Etta looked out at the angles of roofs reflecting the setting sun and heard the beginning beats of the high school marching band practicing. The snare drums launched into the cooling air a frenetic rhythm buffeted by the distance and the fading day. She saw the lights of the football field in the distance stutter and blink on. She looked at her watch. Edward would be home in half an hour. She unzipped the quilted floral cover to her Bible and opened it to the book of Romans, where she had left off, her purple ribbon bookmark with the stitched ichthus keeping her place like a kind foot in a closing door. She would learn to paint the rooftops, she thought, they were so pretty in the evenings, and began to read her Bible, one finger under each sentence as though to stabilize it.

Etta had begun to make Hunter Style Chicken in her Crock-Pot, which was a great success, freeing her up to paint her tomatoes or garden or go to TCC (Trinity Community Church) wives Bible study without worrying about what she and Edward would have for dinner. He was always a good sport no matter what, but she did feel the need to apologize when she threw together sandwiches or warmed up spaghetti sauce for dinner. It had been an adjustment to begin cooking for only the two of them once Tyler had left for school. She honestly didn't want to do it anymore. At first they just fended for themselves, but then readjusting was, she felt, a constant necessity in life to assure there was a time to connect at the end of the day. *The Empty Nest Marriage* had been a book with such helpful suggestions. Chapter three had included suggestions on how to continue to cook well for two people—low cholesterol needs, foods rich in fiber, and then the section on the Crock-Pot. Etta had used Post-it notes to mark places of interest and hadn't bothered to take them out when she loaned the book to her neighbor, Christine, who had a girl who was a senior in high school and two tenth-grade boys—they could have been twins, they looked so similar, but Bradley had been held back, which was difficult but probably necessary. And then of course Larry, already in college. Not much longer and Christine and her husband would be going it alone too . . . Etta hoped she'd leave the bookmarks intact—there were sections she wanted to read over again. The dynamics of a marriage change, the book said. There would be new circumstances that would require a couple to encourage each other in a different way.

There were five love languages, Etta liked to remember—gifts, touch, serving, communicating, quality time. Most people communicated through their *own* love language and not the love language of their spouse. Etta's love language was *serving* and Edward's love language was *touch*. *The Love Languages* was a book she had not passed on to a friend as of yet. She should have, she thought. It was on Edward's nightstand, unread as far as she knew. But she'd read out loud the important parts to him—and then talked about their particular love languages—and he'd seemed interested. Saturday she'd brought it up again, the ways they could love each other better, and Edward, was he irritated? Spent the day digging up a patch of yard to add more room to her garden.

Etta had secretly gone to the mall and purchased a red teddy from Victoria's Secret. Edward's fingernails were filled with dirt when he entered the bedroom and found her in a red negligee powdering between her breasts with a violet smelling puff of cotton, something that another book, *Secret Intimacies*, had suggested. *Secret Intimacies* went so far as to provide step-by-step instructions to spice up your sex life! The book came sealed in a foggy vellum that revealed only a hint of the purple floral cover of the jacket underneath it. Edward's dirty fingernails hadn't bothered her—it actually aroused her—thick hands, rough palms. It was a lovely afternoon. He would remember it. It reminded her of earlier years, before Tyler was born, when he had worked scrubbing out pools while finishing up his MBA. He would come home exhausted, in a good way. They would lie together for hours.

She turned the Crock-Pot to low and began to set the table for dinner. It had been a full day—she had cleaned out the pantry, weed-wacked, and then talked with Christine for quite a while. Christine was worried about Bradley—who had reluctantly given her a slip from two of his high school teachers requesting a conference with her and her husband. Spanish and English, Christine had said sadly. And then they'd talked about poor Margie Nethercott. Christine remembered Margie's grandfather, an artist as well, who had his own issues, painting in that tiny garage all day, the one window cracked, coming out to sit on an old vinyl lawn chair to smoke a cigarette, and then back into the garage again, walking so slowly it was almost a limp, as though the last thing in the world he wanted to do was continue working. It almost seemed like he *hated* to paint. Etta had felt a special connection to Margie as she talked with Christine about her although they had only met once. She imagined the two of them would enjoy each other if they ever had the opportunity to get to know one another. She told Christine how difficult it could be to find the time to *create*, something Etta explained was crucial to an artist's emotional well-being. And here Etta had felt slightly deceptive, as though her point in saying this was somehow rooted in pride. *Oh Lord, forgive me.*

When Edward came home, Etta was sitting on the leather ottoman with her knees touching and her feet apart, pigeon toed, the fat of her stomach accordioned under her breasts, in front of the TV with the remote. She was flipping between the six o'clock news on channels 7 and 10, two versions of a New York City subway derailment. Channel 7 had blurry cell phone pictures; a dark confusion of people exiting a train car, walking next to the curved cement wall hugging purses, briefcases, phones, books, shopping bags, smart phones with cords snaking out of hooded sweatshirts. Channel 10 showed a man in a yellow rain jacket on the street next to the subway entrance, a slow line of people exiting the stairs behind him, turning their heads to the camera and then down again, aware somehow, for a moment, that they had come up from the deep according to some outerworld grace deposited in their favor that then dropped quickly out of view with the light of sky and bust of the subway crowd up from the stairs.

Etta pressed mute. "I can't imagine this," she said, looking at Edward as he dropped his keys on the small table next to the front door. He seemed distracted. "Did you hear about it? The subway? All the lights go out, the train stops, people don't know where they are. It would be terrifying. The confusion. . . ."

"Yeah, the derailed subway." Edward walked over and stood in front of the screen, rubbing the back of his neck with his hand. "Someone died, I think. That's what I heard. It might be why it derailed—someone was on the tracks." Etta turned the volume on again.

"Five-thirty in the evening. It was packed." On TV the reporter in front of the stairs stepped aside to allow the camera to get a shot of the crowd of people slowly coming up from the subway. He stretched an arm out to indicate the large amount of commuters affected by the derailment. He said, "It's been a slow ride for the west side," and then, "Back to you, Monica."

Etta and Edward went to the kitchen and sat down for dinner. Outside, a man called sharply to his dog, "*Pepper!*" The dog barked twice. Edward took one of Etta's hands in his, and they bent their heads to say grace.

4.

Margie: art and a kind of love

The deeply yellowed newsprint photograph of Chris Burden with blood running out of a neat and precise hole in his upper left arm—his face profoundly absent of either pain or fear—was taped to the dirty and gesso-splattered wall above Margie's drawing table. Pieces of yellowed, half-removed tape blitzed the space where she had posted sketches and works in progress and then ripped them down in irritation or boredom. The picture, taken in 1971, showed Burden standing with his back to a wall, fifteen feet from a friend who held a .22 caliber rifle tucked up to his face, one eye almost squeezed shut.

Margie tried to forget the morning at the lake. She spent the rest of the week up in her studio, the picture of Burden visible in her mind's eye as she worked—the physical picture itself hanging on her wall, as well as the whole moment sucked back into time when Burden's head and heart, she imagined, stopped for one-eighth of a millisecond as the bullet—intended only to graze Burden's arm—plowed into skin, blood, and muscle, making the most precise and lovely hole and then exiting toward the blank white wall behind him. She thought about it. Maybe he and his friend had an unsaid agreement that the bullet would hit him that Burden didn't want said out loud or he would have acquiesced to fear. Maybe the hole in his arm was planned in some silent way, some agreement between the two of them to go deep into pain literally and metaphorically without either of them actually saying it—for that would have been true art. Maybe it was advertised as performance art and the bullet was to skim past his arm, barely missing it, that way when the bullet actually hit him it would be viewed as an unfortunate mistake and his friend couldn't be indicted for any kind of attempted manslaughter or that kind of thing. It was courageous. Or was it. She had no idea. Burden was also an idiot—he began his career, just a kid, naked in a locker, a water bottle above him, a bottle to piss in below him. After the performance of *Shoot,* he was taken to a psychiatrist. Later he appeared hugging Volkswagens on film and spending time naked in white rooms lit with fire and gasoline, somehow ending up with the stigmata—he held his hands palms up for more black and white photographs. There was something particularly awful and defining about a black and white photograph of blood.

The attic felt cavernous because of constant light coming through two skylights cut into the east and west slants of the roof. In fact her studio wasn't that large. Margie had always thought of the expansive ceiling as being held up by a bent elbow, weary but determined, holding watch somehow. It was the same personifications she gave to her paintings, attributing to them more life than they deserved. She went to one of three dirty attic windows and watched two girls and a small boy playing in a yard across the street. Noel would be home in a few hours.

She leaned into the glass. One of the girls had a nest of knotted blond hair at the back of her head from rolling in the grass. Noel's hair at that age had already started to deepen from red to auburn.

As a woman with short blonde hair, wearing an aqua windbreaker, walked past the children, she smiled widely and picked up her pace, swinging her bent arms as if tiny propellers on each elbow were giving her bursts of energy that propelled her on. Margie couldn't imagine being a woman like that—she probably had her own hairdresser and a schedule that included a date night with her husband. Margie pitied her, but then she pitied herself more.

She bent down and tugged a large sheet of plastic across the floor to a corner of the room next to a group of prepared canvasses that lined the wall. She used the plastic when she gessoed canvases. There were white streaks at right angles, skipped sections where wrinkles in the material pulled together. The plastic was pointless. The plank floor was covered with the white stuff, swipes and smudges. There were lines of oil paint like candle wax down the legs of the largest easel where she had tried encaustic but failed—thick and soft and never dry, the paint had added to leftover smudges and swipes from her grandfather's brushes. Nick used to come and sit while he ate his lunch. This was before he had built up his client list, when he was seeing only four or five people. She played Van Morrison then, in the little black CD player with the detachable speakers. "On Hyndford Street." Margie would listen and feel the movement in her shoulder as she sketched a quick wipeout for a painting and react to his voice with a zeal she felt would be more justified had she been a photojournalist or *New York Times* correspondent, someone who chipped away at history. She said this to Nick one time, that she wanted to be someone who chipped away at history, and he hadn't understood. "Stop being so abstract," he said. But it hadn't really bothered him, because he was turned on by her—hair up, T-shirt, jeans, more than likely barefoot, but it wasn't a convenient union; Margie at work and Nick horny, she couldn't be bothered when she was painting. "It could be very technical, painting," she told him, "like rewiring a lamp."

"I could get distracted rewiring a lamp," Nick said.

In her work there was a more potent sexiness.

Nick used to model for her. He was a wonderful model. Slim, tall, a fine facial structure with full lips and then his neck and clavicle—he laughed when she said clavicle—and then of course a very clear torso, muscle movement, everything. She liked to paint him in his glasses, the round dark circles. He would get turned on. But she was painting.

Margie absent-mindedly squirted a spot of linseed oil on a waxy palette sheet. Taking a brush, she dipped it into the small mouth of a tube of cobalt blue and twirled it in the linseed, creating a wide oily bloom. She looked at the canvas, gessoed except for two corners where the khaki thread of the material remained. She liked a very thin coat on her canvases, liked the texture of the canvas or every once in a while linen to absorb the paint a little. Sometimes her heart ached mysteriously when she painted. She tried to establish why but couldn't.

MARGIE WAS SENT TO LIVE with her grandfather three years after her mother died because her father didn't know what to do with her. When he was alive, her grandfather painted humor, part realism, part animation, leaving his own studio in the little wooden garage with half-finished paintings of detailed half-eaten sandwiches and fruit, half of a pear, half an apple—sections done in painstakingly literal form and color using the grid method—with the rest animated, like James Basket in *Song of the South* strolling through the unnatural countryside, fictional butterflies landing on his thick black hands. Zip-A-Dee-Doo-Da Zip-A-Dee-Yay. Sometimes he left the lightly penciled grid intact, painting to either side of the lines so that there was a thread of space without paint, a Chuck Close type of reality, and then comically giving way to the cartoon as though he could care less. Left as they were, the paintings revealed the process of painting, the technical process of measuring, sketching, blocking in. Her grandfather Lee never intended to sell them, but they lent him their personalities long enough for him to complete a commissioned work for someone intent on coupling their Springer Spaniel with their children, a doctor husband with his stethoscope, rubber tubing making an upside-down, half-formed heart next to the buttons of his white coat.

Back then there wasn't much to the town of Trinity, or even now really. Hill met hill at the low seam of the main street—Maple Avenue—where you could look out from the attic of one house into the kitchen of another. Grandfather Lee had lived in a space above a converted garage, a one-bedroom apartment with two dormers and an old cast-iron stove. He was a walking archive of midcentury aesthetic. Margie remembered his smell. Wood paneling and disks for ceiling lights, smoke out from lungs and back in, creating a leather patina deep in his chest that, if visible, would have matched perfectly the Naugahyde lounge and ottoman that was tucked into the little space with the dormered window.

The day he told Margie he had cancer, she had been working on a small painting of a magazine image she'd found on her grandfather's desk. This isn't something he would have approved of. Always paint from life. She bent her head over the image on the table and then looked back up, squinting at her work propped up on a small easel.

The side door to the garage was open and the sun was low in the west, sneaking through the trees and hitting the wooden ceiling joists in a stutter of light. The garage wasn't insulated. There were nails from the exterior siding that punctured the walls between the wood studs so that if you weren't careful, you could lean into one and get a bite. In the winter they used two kerosene heaters and draped a quilt at the top of the stairs to keep the heat from escaping to the apartment upstairs.

Her grandfather held a small white paper bag and a sheaf of papers in one hand. A cigarette was snug up against the thumb and index finger of his other hand like a sixth digit. He put the cigarette to his mouth and drew in deeply. "I have cancer, peanut." He let the smoke leak from the side of his mouth as he spoke.

Margie looked up. He put the paper bag and the papers on his desk and began to leaf through a few of his sketches, smoke floating into the light from the sun. "I have to start choosing my projects carefully. This one, you think?" He held up an oil sketch of General Tso's chicken and then brought it to his easel. "I should be working on something for Saturday." He crushed out his cigarette and lit another one. He went to Margie and ruffled her hair before slowly climbing the stairs to the apartment.

Margie sat looking at her little painting. She bit her bottom lip and continued to touch the brush to the canvas. She squirted another spot of turp and oil on the pallet sheet, swirled the brush in it, and went back to the painting as tears pooled in her eyes.

HER GRANDFATHER DIED before he was truly appreciated. The partially dark, baroque-looking paintings he had collected of half-eaten food began to sell only after he became sick. People, like ants at a crumb of cookie, eager to appreciate art, began to purchase his paintings. Before long they bought anything he had painted. When he had become too sick to paint portraits, he brought out the unfinished half paintings and sold them, giving the money to Margie where she was to walk to the bank and deposit it into an account labeled, simply, Margie. The liver cancer killed him, but it saved Margie. He did, for a few short months, paint from an old wheelchair, doped up on OxyContin, the wheels of the chair smudged with prints from his stained hands where he pressed them forward, moving the three feet necessary to get to the small sink. People came to see him, crazy Mr. Baldwin, speech slurred but paintings crisp with colors straight from the tube on one half and then the dark purple-based forms on the other. The two months in his wheelchair with OxyContin proved to be his most prolific, perhaps honing in on the visual mysteries of his own narcotized mind.

Two Saturdays after he told Margie he had cancer, his skin and eyes had already given way to the disease. A dull residue seemed to fit over him like a net. His watery eyes receded farther into his head and appeared to be searching for something uncomplicated. Some untroubled space that had disappeared.

People began to show up early that day. They pulled slowly into the part-grass, part-gravel lot next to the garage and parked, tires popping on the gravel as they slowed. Car doors slammed shut and people laughed. Inside, he directed Margie as they prepared to pull open the door.

Margie looked out the side window and into the lot. There was a Jaguar and a Volvo, as well as a handful of other cars. A man got out of the Volvo wearing a plaid vest and aviator sunglasses.

"I'm going to need my mahlstick, peanut. I'll need you to hold it for me. I'm having a bitch of a time with the tomato seeds." His voice had grown even more gravelly, and strangely, it reminded her of a woman's voice, like the Billie Holiday record he used to play for her and make her sit and listen to until he was satisfied she'd *really* heard it. On a small table was a cutting board, and on the cutting board was a piece of white bread with a slice of baloney. Margie cut a tomato in half and then sliced another section off. She held the tomato piece up with her fingers and settled it onto the baloney. She pushed the table closer to her grandfather and then went to get the mahlstick.

"There's a bunch of people from the city out there," she said as she set the stick down, leaning it next to the easel.

"Good." He didn't look at her. He was mixing colors. Every once in a while he stopped and rested his wrists on the arms of the wheelchair and looked into his lap. She could see him breathe; it was his back that rose and fell with each breath.

"Do you want me to open the door?"

"Two more minutes, peanut." He went back to the paints and then, using his feet as much as his hands, maneuvered himself closer to the easel. Margie jumped up to try to help him. "That's good. I'm fine . . . Go ahead, open the door."

The large garage door rattled on its tracks as Margie pushed it up into the ceiling. There was a small group of people gathered at the end of the driveway with Styrofoam cups. They sipped at their drinks and talked among themselves. One man was gesturing with his hands. He kept moving one palm left to right in front of him as he laughed. When the door opened they broke apart and looked hesitantly toward the garage.

"Do you guys want to watch Lee Baldwin paint?" Margie half yelled to them as she walked out onto the driveway. This was how the scenario went on Saturdays. This was how it all started; *do you want to see Lee Baldwin paint?* And then there was the guy from *The Atlantic* who came. And then others. *Do you want to see Lee Baldwin paint? Do you want to see Mark Rothko paint? Do you want to see Jackson Pollack paint?*

Margie held the mahlstick for her grandfather, grasping it tightly with one hand on the top of the canvas, the other end of the stick supported by the easel's brush tray. She kept it as still as possible. Her grandfather's hand shook slightly. He drew a dark curve with a liner brush. The paintings were about things that people consume.

In the attic the sun revealed smudges on the dirty windows. Noel coming home. Noel, her smart daughter. Arriving via carpool with someone—Ingram, a Barnard girl—who advertised in Butler Library for weekend rides upstate once a month. There were cars out of the city every weekend, but this could mean ditching a ride in Brewster and grabbing a bus the rest of the way up to Mt. George where Margie or Nick would pick her up. It was a progression worth noting, the effort of returning home, as though having finally left, making your way back required a certain skill, a tacking to port and then starboard.

Margie left her painting and took the steps downstairs one by one, allowing a moment of indecision about halfway down, during which she considered hastily sketching out the Bridgestone children before Noel got home. But her body ached and felt crazy like it was defaulting to some middle irritation that had always been there, slightly hidden in some half-dark corner, full of hate and waiting for the moment to jump. She would be defeated, but how much to give way and how much to stare it down? Had she ever stared anything down? She was a weak soul, always had been. And now, she was less and less energized by portraiture. The precision was taxing, her thumb, fingers, and wrist she imagined becoming less accurate, and the separation of colors that was so appealing in her twenties and thirties was giving way to a numbing ochre, as though she was growing indifferent to light. She found herself feeling the same about painting as she felt about the indolent medicated people downstairs, hopeful for a breakthrough, gently closing the front door and walking quietly, as though not to wake the sleeping, to Nick's office.

5.

Noel: calculations and a fire

Precious Perfect Number One. Somehow these words had inched their way into Noel's conscious state, maybe at the point of waking or of falling asleep, some halfway place where she must have been fishing for resolutions. She was resilient in the matter of marriage. One guy, monogamous, eternal. It was bold of her, and her friends rolled their eyes, but still she persisted. Humans were meant to mate for life and there was a human out there just for her. What she didn't let on about was that she was feeling pressure. Now in college she'd need to see things begin to happen—every guy she met went into one file or another. Viable or Out of the Question. Her great fear was to have graduated and be working at Enterprise Rental Car, wearing pantsuits and drinking from a travel mug. Oh, god, she was so glad she wasn't a business major. Being back at home made her feel like she could stall forever, never go back to school, always wake up with the sounds of her parents' movements in other parts of the house giving her that mellow, I can fall back asleep if I want, feeling.

She felt the muffled buzz of her phone vibrating under her pillow. She pulled it out and held it above her head to see who it was. Owen. He was always up an hour before she was and she tried not to be irritated. The most irritating thing about Owen—his happiness.

"Hello."

"Hey hey," he said quietly as though feigning laziness, aware that too much pep so early would bother her.

Noel dropped her head back onto the pillow. "Owen, I'm so hung over."

"You are not."

"No." She sat halfway up in her familiar bed, not like the one at school, "but it's more dramatic. Like a rockstar."

"Yeah, like Amy Winehouse."

"That's not funny yet. She died like last month." Noel pressed a finger to the wall next to her bed and drew a figure 8.

"Like Marilyn Monroe, or Betty . . . um . . . the eyes one, the one with the big eyes. . . ."

"Bette Davis. Probably more Judy Garland, someone really troubled. I would say Marilyn Monroe but I'm not sexy like her."

"Shut. Uuup," he said loudly with a lilt. "You are definitely sexy."

"Mm-hmm. I guess I'm more skinny-sexy. My thoughts aren't sexy though. I think I was dreaming about brain chemicals. Reuptake inhibitors, in case you were wondering. They take the place of dopamine so it stays in your brain longer and makes you happy. Wait. I think—maybe it's serotonin that does that. . . ." She ran a finger along a puckering seam of the floral wallpaper. The pattern was tulle, she thought. Navy tulle. No, it wasn't tulle—toile? She couldn't remember the spelling or the name. Her thick comforter was bunched at her feet. So much of her room and life up until she left for school was about the physical state of things around her. "Psychopharmacology is a bitch," she said, "an hour and a half of hexagons and chemical abbreviations. I don't understand most of it. I think that maybe drugs should be designed like lipstick colors, shades for personalities like deep mauve, flirty pink, a purple that leans left, toward blue." She sat all the way up in bed and bent forward to stretch her hamstrings, her free hand reaching toward her feet. "And yes, I think I'm pretty great for making that connection." Her roommate had turned out to be an odd assortment of emblematic drama. Black on black clothing and hair chopped almost clean with paper scissors so that you could see patches of her milk-colored scalp. The girl—Pixie—kept the TV on constantly, turning the volume up for commercials and down for programs, and she folded paper towels into neat cushions to place her collection of ear studs and lip rings on after washing them in a dish of Palmolive.

"Drop it and take British Literature."

"Mmm . . . I don't know. My roommate is unwholesome."

"Do you mean she eats crappy or she does stuff with the door closed?"

"Unhinged. It's not clear yet. I base this only on her looks at this point. She's grungy, which by the way requires a certain preciseness. I think she cuts herself with razor blades or scissors. Maybe just her nails even." The roommates were a computer-generated match based on a lengthy questionnaire sent to them with their housing packets back in June, which was disconcerting to say the least.

"She wears tutus and long sleeves. Two rings on her lower lip, one on each side, like fangs." *Cutting*, Noel had learned on the internet, was referred to as self-injury, or SI. In college there's a proper way to say everything. "And she has these metal studs in the back of her neck. And there's some bar holding them together so that it looks like it's going all the way through her neck, really painful, but she says it's only going through skin. Her name's Pixie. *Pixie.*"

Noel needed coffee. The coffee in the cafeteria at school was Starbucks. Each carafe had a label that said so like it was such a big deal and it was extra generous of the school to use Starbucks coffee, which kind of sucked actually. Noel got out of bed, went to the window, and looked out.

There was a silence.

"Owen?" Noel said.

"Yeah?"

"I really don't feel like going downstairs. It's my mom. Actually, it's both of them. It's my mom and my dad. You know, right? About what happened?"

"Yeah. You all right?"

"It's just so stupid."

"Yeah."

"I feel so stupid."

"*You* do?"

"Yeah."

"*You* feel stupid?"

"I just feel dumb."

Owen didn't say anything.

"Really, really dumb."

"Because of her?"

"Like *so* dumb."

"Because of your mom?"

"Mm-hmm . . . I guess so." She sat back down on the bed and leaned against the headboard. "I hate this whole thing."

"That makes sense. That's understandable."

"I mean, what am I going to say. What should I say?"

"Don't say anything. They'll talk to you about it at some point."

"So what, like, act like I don't even know?"

"Pretty much. For now anyway. You should go out for a while, go someplace. Let's go play tennis."

Noel paused, then said, "Hells yeah, gimme half an hour."

She hung up. The shade of one of her tall windows was halfway down. It was kind of invigorating to wake up in a room with ten-foot ceilings. Her tiny room in the city had a drop ceiling with a pipe creeping guiltily out from a hole cut in the insulated material and then back up into another hole on the far side of the room. It had dark, urine-looking stains seeping through an old coat of off-white paint.

Noel went to the window and yanked the shade—it went all the way up and then fell with a loud bang.

NOEL HAD PULLED HER THICK, mahogany-colored hair back and wore a wide gray band around her head to keep the strands from coming loose. She sat at the kitchen table, a bohemian thing with scratch marks and carvings. There was the spot where, at thirteen, she had gouged into the wood with a dried-out pen, lost track of her letters, and misspelled her name N, O, L, and then squeezed in the missing E, which looked as though it had fallen—filthy and tattered—from some beatnik purgatory to rest fiercely between the accommodating O and L. Her mom came in wearing pajama bottoms and a T-shirt without a bra that said *Autotech*. She sat down on the other side of the table, crossed her legs, and then recrossed them the other way before picking at one of her nails.

"I made coffee," Noel said. "You need to get something better than that San Marco stuff."

"It's cheap. Did your roommate go home this weekend?" One of her mother's knees bounced lightly, up and down.

Pixie lived in New Jersey but told Noel she decided early on that she would live as though home was California, pacing visits out if she went home at all—Thanksgiving, winter break. She lived with her father, who worked with steel, soldering joints and tresses here and there in New York City. "He spends afternoons under bridges hanging from a strap of canvas and chain, sparks springing from his hands," Pixie had said in monotone to counteract her lyrical sentence. Her dad lived with a woman Pixie hated. "The woman," she said, "eats cow tongue sandwiches."

"She doesn't really go home," Noel said. "Owen's home from Boston though. I'm meeting him at the courts."

Margie stood up and poured herself a cup of coffee. She took a bottle out of a cupboard and shook a pill into her hand. "It's a beautiful day."

Noel watched her chase her pill with a small glass of water. "There's a lot of pills at school. It makes me want to be under the influence of nothing. There's a lot of Adderral. I might even give up coffee actually."

"That's honorable. I should be so disciplined."

"Kids are taking pills to study better and then to party better—they take a pill for, like, the different parts of their day."

Margie slowly sat back down. She put her elbows on the table and put her head in her hands. "Hmm. I think our generation may have something to do with that."

They were silent. Margie said, "My medicine cabinet could pay next semester's tuition."

Noel went to the sink and rinsed out her mug. "I should go meet Owen."

When she left, Margie dressed and went upstairs. She looked out the window, expecting to see either the children playing or the woman in the aqua windbreaker. She saw neither, turned around, and went to her easel where she took her favorite three brushes and gently pressed the tips of them on the table to loosen up the bristles.

The courts were already warm from the sun, the painted green pavement emitting tiny deceitful sparklets of light at the cursory glance. Noel squatted at the fence, letting the chain links painfully support her back as she retied her shoes. Across the street, Carlino's was opening up. A man carried out giant tins of baby's breath and statice flowers and placed them under the window. Noel stood up and bounced a tennis ball with her racket as she watched The Mayor—a homeless man people called The Mayor—walk by Carlino's, then pause, turn, and put his face up to the window, his nose almost touching, slap at the glass, and then turn away again and walk down the street as he yelled over and over something impossible to understand. The old man was timeless. He was thirty, he was sixty. Something needling at his brain coincided with the ugly state he perceived the town of Trinity to be in. He complained loudly, in a rough crane of a voice, that the benches were coming apart, the trees were losing their leaves too soon, the doors to the old Tivoli movie theatre were sticking in the open position, and why, he said, did the garbage come on Tuesday, it's always Wednesday, Wednesday, it's always been Wednesday when the garbage gets here, in a smaller and smaller voice, perhaps now tripping down the sidewalk in a mumble and an angry half-bop step. The high school kids would wait for him to approach and pull him into conversations. They knew the things that would get him going. *I thought they were going to fix that bench,* they would say, and eventually he'd launch into something, muttering Mayor this or Mayor that and—*why, thenwhythehell did you vote for me—I'mthemayorgodfuckingdamnit. . . .*

The Mayor gave up on the wide glass of Carlino's and walked down to the corner of Maple and Fifth. He stopped to light a cigarette. He didn't live anywhere.

Noel watched as a couple took to the far court, tennis balls in the guy's pockets. He lobbed one to the woman. The woman missed the ball and bent over laughing. A tan Camry swung quickly into a parking space in the small lot next to the courts.

"Noel!" Owen raised a racket toward the sky in greeting and slammed the car door. He wore jeans and an avocado-colored T-shirt with a rip at the hem. Owen was lanky, and while his hair was dark, his face was milk-toned. He was a talented musician. It was his music that had persuaded Noel to officially go out with him for three short months in their junior year of high school.

The night she heard him sing at Vincent's, the high school venue in North Junction, fifteen minutes south of Trinity, he had stood on the small stage with his Martin, shifting back and forth a little bit, eyes down at the frets and then up for just a moment like he was shy of the world. Noel was near the back, next to the women's bathroom, and every time a girl opened the door the loud sound of laughter drowned out Owen's voice. Noel had pushed through the crowd to get closer. She knew him from her gym class. Pasty legs. But there was something about him.

She got within five feet of the small stage, where she was able to hear, and it wasn't long before she felt herself begin to cry, a catch in her chest, as though life was just an afterthought and the world was really music.

When he stepped down from the stage, she went up to him. "Hey, Owen, that was really good."

"Oh, hey, Noel, what's up? Thanks. I was nervous, but thanks."

"It was really good."

"Thanks."

"Did you write it?"

He was putting away his guitar. He slipped a pick in between the frets. "I did. With a touch of plagiarism. Here, for the sake of honesty. . . ." He took an iPod out of his pocket and began unwinding the earphones. "Come over here." He led her to a quieter area next to the front window. They could feel the cold coming through the wide glass that was beginning to fog up. He handed her an ear bud and she put it into her left ear. He put the other bud in his own ear and tapped the iPod a couple times. "Hope There's Someone" by Antony and the Johnsons began to play.

Noel pressed the earphone in her ear with two fingers and looked at the floor as she listened. She looked up at him and smiled. He smiled back and nodded.

"It's beautiful," Noel said.

He kept smiling.

"It's really beautiful. But it's not like yours, you didn't plagiarize. . . ." She started to remove the earphone, but he took her hand and gently pressed it back to her ear. They stood next to the window and listened—*who will take care of me / when I die / when I die . . .* Owen stepped closer to her, as though to reunite the two ear buds. A second song began and Noel listened. *You are my sister, we were born / so innocent, so full of need / there were times that we were friends, but times I was so cruel. . . .* The music was delicate. The voice ethereal. Noel leaned her head against the cold glass of the window. Owen looked into her eyes, moved closer, kissed her on her forehead, then took his own ear bud and put it in her other ear. He lifted a strand of her auburn hair and placed it further back on her shoulder as though rearranging her for a photograph and then left, picking up his guitar before he walked out the front door. She saw him glance over his shoulder at her in the window before continuing down the street.

When they broke up, the issue—as though it were an engagement ring—was who would keep the iPod. Owen wanted her to have it. She said it was his. Owen worked out at the school gym. Noel would see him at the equipment, weights on pulleys, clink of steel, sweaty vinyl cushions and the long crossbar swinging from its cable, rubber grips at either end where Owen's long arms were slung over the bar like a persecuted Christ. Sometimes she would feel a whirring in her lower stomach after a glimpse of him in the gym, a quick hormonal dip that rode her insides and then disappeared. They never slept together. They broke up standing next to the Abenaki River, feet bare on stone, Noel looking down at the water, convincing him things would be better, and they were. They stayed close, emotions and pressure easing into what for the most part became a comfortable friendship. They had made a loose pact not to talk or text during their first month away at school.

"Hey," Noel said, unhooking the latch to the chain-link fence and swinging it wide. She gave him a hug with one arm, racket in the other. Her cheek pressed momentarily against his chest. "So . . . Gordon?"

"Sweet. Columbia?"

"Columbia. It's in New York City."

"No good?"

Noel tucked a loose strand of hair behind her ear and bounced a tennis ball off the pavement and smack into the palm of her hand. "No, I like it. It's in New York. It's more than I expected though. The subways shake the glass in my one tiny window—it's the size of a dinner plate, the window is. I live above an ATM queue—there's a constant line of people, a narrow hall underneath me that's filled with porn, and a tiny little ATM that I don't understand, because how does all that money fit in there? Honestly, it scares me. I'm afraid someone will kick the door and wander up. Someone with, like, a knife and a fresh twenty-dollar bill. This is all embarrassing. I've always thought of myself as adventurous. Oh, and then my roommate. Absolutely freakish."

"You should have just got a dorm room."

"Not that I didn't expect these things though," Noel said. "It's cheaper this way—the apartment. But yeah, hindsight."

"What do your parents think?"

"Everything's fine. They haven't met Pixie. My roommate." She lobbed a ball over the net. "Pixie," she repeated. "Plus, it's not like I'm going to bring it up now, after everything."

Carlino's was full of things excessive and tipping over. "A true fire trap," Owen said, as he carefully turned sideways to fit between a card display and shelves stuffed with things like bandages and calamine lotion. Two cards slipped out of their wire racks and fell to the floor. Owen bent to pick them up. Carlino's was hard to define. Most people called it a deli, but its section of drugstore things like Benadryl and Dr. Scholl's, ace bandages and saline spray, had grown over time and now occupied a good half of the store on the opposite side from the deli counter. The section seemed to grow exponentially—one bottle of cocoa butter purchased and two new products would appear. There were items hid deep within the shelves that had little yellow price tags coated with years of grime that still read "98 cents." And then there was the part of the store that Carly Carlino called the Home Décor area: dried flower wreaths, doorstoppers in the shapes of dogs, and cloth-covered jewelry boxes. Owen's shoulder brushed a wreath hanging on a pegboard, and it came off its hook and started to fall. He grabbed it.

"Why, exactly, are we here?" he said, carefully setting the wreath back on its hook.

"I don't know," Noel said, "it's not Mother's Day. I usually only come here on Mother's Day or Father's Day. These floors are uneven." She shuffled up a carpeted section to demonstrate. "We should buy some candy or something."

They went to the deli counter and looked through one of the glass cases at small chocolate and vanilla things set in pink fluted paper cups. There were yogurt-covered pretzels and nubs of chocolate pebbled with nuts and marshmallows.

Owen rested his hands on the display case and looked through the glass. "I like your mom," he said.

"Yeah, me too."

Carly Carlino, a woman Noel had met once when she'd showed up for a group session with Nick, had her back to the counter and was wrapping up a basket of fruit with cellophane. She primped at the edges, carefully pulling a red bow out to improve its shape. Her hips bulged under her tight jeans, and she wore high-heeled clogs with leopard fur on the edges. Owen stared through the glass at the chocolates.

"I wish I was allergic to peanuts," he said. "It would add drama to my life—and diabetics live on the edge I've always thought, in a good way. Their lives depend on a needle and insulin. How adventurous is that? It adds an element of risk to everything. You wouldn't need paintball or bungee jumping."

"*People* with diabetes," Noel said. "You're not supposed to call people 'diabetics.' I learned that in my psychopharmacology class." She traced an invisible square on the glass with her finger, indicating which piece of chocolate she would get. "I think the insulin thing would get old really fast. Like if you bungee-jumped every single day—if you bungee-jumped two times every single day—it would become irritating and not be something you looked forward to anymore. You'd think to yourself, 'Oh, crap, I still have to jump today.'"

"You're right, I think," Owen said. "I wonder sometimes, though, if we don't make our lives hard on ourselves sometimes just out of boredom. You know, the obvious things, like drugs, but also family drama and partisan politics. Sometimes I think that these things we complain so much about are really just because we're really freaking bored. Middle school is the perfect example. Middle schoolers discover boredom and then do all that stupid middle school stuff."

Carly turned toward Noel and Owen, and Noel pointed to the peanut clusters. "Can I have one of those?" she said to Carly. "I'm glad I'm not allergic to peanuts."

Carly Carlino opened up the glass and reached in to pick up a piece of chocolate using a little square of waxed paper. "Just one?"

Noel nodded and then changed her mind. "No, two." She looked at Owen. "You get one too."

Carly slid the door on the case closed and opened up a tiny white paper bag. "You're Dr. Nethercott's daughter, aren't you?" she said, looking up from the bag.

Noel nodded and smiled. "Yes, I am."

Carly leaned close to the two of them as she handed them the bag and half whispered, "He's very good. I've been seeing him for some time." She tilted her head toward the back of the store, referencing her husband in an invisible office somewhere. "Some of us need a little extra help, a second opinion if you will, when it comes to living with pain, with the people we love. I've grown so much, you know. Anyway, tell your father I said hi. Tell him Carly said hi."

"A little weird," Owen said as they stood on the sidewalk and took the chocolates out of the white paper bag. "Do you know you have the cutest butt ever? Really. Out of all the butts in Boston, yours is cuter than all of them."

"And that's not weird at all," Noel said. "Quite the non sequitur." She slipped the black elastic band off her head and let her hair fall free. She looked at Owen and half smiled.

He shrugged, tossed his head back, and put a chocolate in his mouth. "I'm glad I'm not allergic to peanuts either, actually."

Two times the sirens had gone off in Trinity indicating tragedies that ultimately changed the town forever. The first siren was in 1978 when four high school kids in a Camaro tried to get air off of the hill on Turner Road coming out of town and lost control, all four killed. Through the windshield. All four. One girl landed on a fence like a rag doll, hair up and over her head like you could see the stitching if you looked close enough. The four of them had been drinking, had not been drinking—who could tell at that time—but the town argued for a year over who to blame. That was when the bright yellow sign indicating the approaching hill and curve was installed, as though this would prevent another accident. Margie moved to Trinity a month after the accident and people were still talking about it. Now they knew when to punch the gas, more than one high school kid said, secretly horrified that it was possible to die.

The second siren was when Mr. Scayr killed Mrs. Scayr and then killed himself, Mrs. Scayr in the kitchen, head half propped up by the old Admiral stove, Mr. Scayr in his mustard-colored armchair like he had sat there and thought about what to do after killing his wife, before going ahead and pulling the trigger on himself. The whole scene was on the evening news. It was 1979, only one year after the car crash on Turner Road and before things like real blood and real dead people were politely excised from the media. There was, of course, the expected responses to the horror of the event in light of the name Scayr. Stories at slumber parties and circles with Ouija boards, Mr. and Mrs. Scayr fed kids adrenaline from the other side, haunting memories and hosting dark bathroom visits in front of mirrors—*Donna, Donna, Donna,* they would chant Mrs. Scayr's first name, holding candles and ready to run toward the light when they felt her on their skin. The supernatural scared Margie.

When the Scayrs died the town added an addendum to the mandatory health screening at the high school that already included an eye exam, blood pressure, and height and weight check. "Do you feel safe at home?" the nurses were required to ask after Mr. Scayr killed Mrs. Scayr and then killed himself. They looked down at their sheets of paper with boxes to be checked and paused. So many kids said no as a joke that it would have been hard to know if a kid was telling the truth. They sat on the paper-covered examining table and swung their legs a little and said, "No, ha, ha."

Noel and Owen walked to the lake. Owen had crumpled the paper bag from Carlino's into a ball and was tossing it from hand to hand. The yellowing and reddening of the trees appeared to magnify the water, each tone wiggling into elongations like many hands and fingers entwining. The water rippled with a breeze and Noel's hair blew forward, splitting a part onto the back of her head. She tried to hold her thick hair down with her hands, finally grabbing the majority of it in one hand and holding it to her shoulder. She laughed, and her lips widened, and Owen looked at the dimple on the side of her mouth and looked away. He tossed the crumpled paper bag into the water, and Noel gently bumped his side and said you're not supposed to litter, and then they watched it bob, lifting and falling in the small waves. She's right, he thought, but he liked the look of the bag before it started to sink.

THAT EVENING, OWEN AND NOEL sat with their high school friends around a fire, smoke following the breeze, two six-packs of Yuengling, cold with condensation and covered in pine needles, tucked under the bushes. The southern part of the Abenaki River, down near the old brick warehouse with the faint, snowy "Bunk & Hill" still visible high on one side under the eve of peeling rubber roof, widened into a small pond for a short moment where younger kids had dammed the water with branches and rocks, before it narrowed again and emptied into the lake. There was a makeshift fire pit. Flames sparked into the dark, drifting and floating away with the heat.

Jason Vanderwaal showed up late and sat down next to Noel, who was sprawled on a colorful blanket staring trancelike into the fire. Jason was not tall, had a thick torso and a very round face, with eyes so close together that it almost looked like he had a genetic defect—some disease called Owl Syndrome, or Marpelier's Disease. He tried hard at everything. Noel forced her eyes away from the fire, elbowed him kindly, and said in a goofy voice, "Hey, Jason, whatcha been up to?"

The fire lit faces around the circle with a flashlight-under-the-chin effect. Owen sat on across from her, his palm resting on the mouth of an open beer that he had gradually been pressing deeper into the dirt.

The group talked about music and art all the time. Noel wasn't sure she was even creative—at least not in a visual way. Apart from her voice, which was pretty good and didn't need to get louder to hit certain notes, she was more at home with the rumbling drawers of her father's file cabinet, Nick's pages of notes with questions and answers and examples like "let's say that so and so," or, "for the purpose of clarity I'll refer to her as Nancy." It was a conglomeration of word problems reduced into equations that fit into paradigms for pain correlations he hoped would one day be used in references and manuals, touched on in lectures, folded into therapy, and passed on through generations. He would pinch the bridge of his largish nose and imagine future models. This, all so that he could solve the problem of pain. If chronic pain, he liked to say, was the result of reformulated pain receptors, then reformulate the vascular pathways, whatever that meant. Sometimes Noel imagined one of her dad's counseling patients as a child huddled under an overbearing mother or giving way to the narcissism of an abusive father, stuffed into closets, fed saltines, the light of day nothing but a rumor.

"Hey, Noel," Jason responded, elbowing her back. "Not much. Just bored again at home. Only one day and I'm ready to go back to school."

Owen looked at the thin layer of foam in his beer and took a sip. A handful of Trinity High grads. Jocelyn, Miriam, Owen, Jason, Noel. Jocelyn had rushed a sorority and Jason had rushed a fraternity. They came home with sweatshirts. "Living proof of the natural corruption that occurs as one ages," Owen said. "It's necessary if you plan on living in a corrupted world." Half of them going Greek would threaten to split the group up, as though the group wasn't already at the divide of reason and sentimentality, where the determined rush of familial blood again takes over and pushes them back into the specific tastes of the homes they were raised in. Noel thought about these things. She knew she would be like her parents—both, or one of them. Jason lit a cigarette and rested his elbows on his knees, cigarette dangling next to his bare foot. Miriam looked at the cigarette and rolled her eyes. The conversation was about the new social order that exists in college—the kind of thing that happens, Jocelyn said, when you put so many people of the same approximate age together. It was inevitable.

"Hierarchy *has* to happen when there's no natural delineation—like age—to 'place' people in a society." Owen almost hooked his fingers for quotation marks, but refrained. "People feel uncomfortable when there aren't obvious boundaries. Like the kids on the playground who huddle in the middle when the fence is taken away."

"Who's in charge?" Miriam said.

Jocelyn looked at her. "What?"

"Who's in charge?" Miriam repeated. "I mean, if there isn't a social order, then we don't know who's in charge and so we force hierarchy." Miriam was thoughtful, but had a tendency to take the back way into conversations and could at times appear stupid. "It's scary," she said. Miriam liked Arcade Fire and Andrew Bird and wore gloves with the fingers cut off. She was a soft voice and managed her opinions by stating them as oddities, but Noel still called her Angry Girl because she wore so much black. Miriam lived with her mother who was a hoarder. Everyone understood that she took care of her mother, but in a way that allowed her mother to maintain the appearance of authority. In some ways Miriam was a true genius, living with a woman who kept cantaloupes until they floated in their own muck, juices fermenting into an orange mucus, and yet still allowing her mother the self-respect of telling her daughter to be home by two AM, a comment stated as Miriam left the house and that they both understood was meant to be taken nebulously. Their home was filled with items of value to *someone*, the litter creeping out of the living room and kitchen and into the small hallway to the two bedrooms. Clothing and blankets spilled from kitchen to basement stairs and down to where the old washer and dryer were piled with empty Tide cartons that could be of use as mailing boxes or helpful carrying containers or even something to start a fire with. Miriam had perfected the art of appearing well-adjusted ever since fourth grade when a teacher had tipped off a social worker to her living conditions. And the home wasn't as bad then as it was now. Back then Miriam got it in her head that as long as she seemed okay, she and her mom wouldn't get split up.

Her mother would occasionally be willing to part with an item if she was convinced it would go to good use. She would track its progress, an old curtain rod that she would give to Miriam to give to someone who might need it. She would get a number and call for updates. *Well it really was of no use to me, I'm so glad you can use it. You'll need to be careful though, I think that one end is slightly bent and I'm afraid that it could double in and bend even more if you're not careful.* This happened once when she had reluctantly given a curtain rod to Noel to give to her mom. Now garbage was piled on tables and against walls. From outside, the dirty windows were pressed with old boxes like suckers on a squid, towels, dirty plates, unopened mail. There was a snow-shovel-wide path through the living room to Miriam's room that had the occasional shoe or paperback book that needed to be kicked aside like a stray clod of snow. Miriam kept her room clean. She used a baby gate when she was home with her door open, but when she left she managed to close the door, kicking back blankets and paper cups before leaving the house. Miriam handled a lot and seemed pretty normal, but Noel was pretty sure she sometimes tried to vomit up her food.

Jason jumped into the conversation. "Lord of the Flies," he said, agreeing with Miriam. He squinted as he took a drag of his cigarette. "We. Is. Kids. We're let loose too soon in my opinion." Smoke leaked out of his mouth and joined the stuff rising from the fire. "They keep us infants with schedules and rules and stuff and then it's like they're so tired from watching us they practically shove us out, go figure things out, nothing we can do for you now. The Greek system provides structure. I need structure. I'll be the first to admit it."

They were quiet for a while. There was the issue of Noel's mother. There was the fidgeting *uncenteredness* of it, like it was all well and good and it was *Margie* of course, so nothing new, but if they really talked about it, it could get weird.

"It's been strange coming home," Noel finally said, "after everything. It's like they're always waiting for me to talk."

"It would probably be better if you had brothers and sisters," Miriam said. "It's like life goes on and there's always someone there who appears to have it together. You could be doing this or doing that, and even though it's different from other people, there's still stuff to talk about, I think just because there's *more* of you." Every once in a while everyone would look her way like, *Wow, what the hell, Mir, that's good*, but then plenty of times they didn't.

"There's something wonderful about being under the same roof with people you connect with," Jocelyn said. Jocelyn had already brought the conversation around to sororities one too many times and now could not be trusted. No one said anything, and she looked up, becoming defensive. "I'm just saying. . . ."

"So what the hell, Noel?" Jason said. "What's up with Margie?" This was Jason letting Noel know that there were fingerprints from

Trinity all over her mother's moment last week of early morning eccentricity. It was sort of honorable, but she hated him for it.

"Yeah," she said with a little laugh, looking into the fire and then coughing. "Nick's pissed, I can tell. He's been riding his bike a lot."

Miriam shrugged her shoulders. "My mom once locked herself in the bathroom for four hours. I think she wanted me to *think* she was going to kill herself. It was a timing thing. Sometimes she was so quiet in there, as though she'd already grabbed the razor blade, but I could see the shadows under the door. Actually, I could see her feet, either side of the toilet, and figured she must of sat there freaking bored to death just so I'd *think* she was a danger to herself. This is the best she can do to prove I care about her? Shit."

"I don't think she *wanted* to kill herself," Noel said.

"Your mom or my mom?"

"Margie." Noel didn't look up.

"Margie's cool," Jason said.

"I don't know." Noel took two long swigs of beer and leaned back on her arms. "Maybe it's performance art." She smiled and laughed a little.

Jason grew excited. "Chris Burden shot himself. There's a picture of it."

"Yeah, in Margie's studio. We've all seen it, Jason," Owen said.

"Chris Burden didn't shoot himself," Noel said, taking another drink.

Owen looked at Noel. "You think your mom was doing a Chris Burden thing?"

"No," Jason interrupted enthusiastically. "Yes. She *was* probably trying to—yeah, Burden shot himself but it was in the arm. Couldn't go through with it."

"Burden *didn't* shoot himself," Noel repeated, "An assistant shot him. At close range. And the bullet was supposed to just graze him but it hit his arm. The picture's above my mom's drawing table. It's been there since I was, like, I don't know, five." Noel turned her beer in her lap, held it up to the fire, and looked through the remaining liquid at the foam. "I don't think he knew at first what happened." She shrugged. "Even though, I guess, he planned the whole thing. He has this glazed look. In the picture."

Jason raised his beer toward Noel in respect, and nodded. Up above the little gathering next to the Abenaki, in the area cleared of trees and imbued with their scattered voices, heavy smoke from the fire dispersed into the dark, invisible but for the melt of heat that rippled the air—it would have been possible to feel it and see its movement in the air like an oil spill even from forty feet above. An early October breeze caught the fire and turned it counterclockwise, causing Owen to stand up and cough, take his beer, and walk to Noel's side of the fire. He stood behind her and then sat down and rested his cheek against her hair. The water in the little dammed-up pond wrinkled into a million tiny waves with the wind and then grew still. Distant drumbeats from the high school marching band gathered strength. "Pa, da, da, da, padadadada. . . ."

Noel raised her drink to the group before finishing it up, and then broke into exaggerated song, "*We went down. to. the rivahhhhh. . . .*"

6.

Pixie: getting the most out of life

There was never enough money. Her roommate was something out of a Whole Foods, like a gluten-free rice cake. She was sick of Asian people. At school Pixie found herself back where she started, reading books. She had grown up that way, because the TV was nothing but static and there wasn't a yard to play in. Not that she would have played outside, by herself, fifty feet from an interstate, with no trees and the sun hitting everything. Books created space like a yard would have, only without the *all by herself* sort of thing, which she assumed was important for a kid, not being alone. Pete, her dad, had paid Mrs. Giannoppolis a small amount of money every Sunday to watch her, keep her down in the restaurant at a booth with crayons or a book, or to stare at the little TV without the static hanging in a corner up near the ceiling, but she was comfortable upstairs at the window, where she would be able to see Pete's sun-baked Honda pull into the lot at the end of the day, the familiar sight of the car with its left rear window duct-taped halfway up. Pixie would leave the restaurant and go upstairs to the apartment when Mrs. Giannoppolis was busy with customers and not paying attention.

Once, when she was nine, she went upstairs to read and wait for Pete to get home. Out the window of the little dormer, above the air conditioner, she could see the red lights of the Grand Union across the parking lot, flat in the hazy sun, and then brighter as it started to get dark. She stood next to the window and let the cool air from the air conditioner hit her chest and the air seep under her collar, billowing her shirt. It was getting late. A UPS truck turned into the parking lot of the dry cleaner's next door. She held a small book that she had found in the school library, already checked out by someone else. She had seen it in a study carrel next to a notebook and pen, and had lifted it quietly and slipped it into her book bag. That was a week ago, and she had forgotten about it until that afternoon, when she was downstairs with Mrs. Giannoppolis, eating pizza. She pulled it out of her bag and read the first few pages, improvising when she came across words she didn't know. *Mezzanine.*

She stared at the Grand Union sign. It was an image scored into her mind so fiercely sometimes she saw green on her eyelids as she fell asleep. She looked at the cars going past the store, every one of them, until her eyes began to hurt, then went back to the small couch, sat down, and curled over the book, pressing the thin spine into her bare thighs.

There were sentences that didn't make sense but she kept reading. *Wilhelm saw a pigeon about to light on the great chain. . . .* It grew darker and she crawled to the other side of the couch, reached over, and turned on the table lamp. She continued reading, and there were sections that caught her attention; *Fair-haired hippopotamus!—that was how he looked to himself. He saw a big round face, a wide, flourishing red mouth, stump teeth.* She stood up and walked to the window again. The cars had thinned out. Only a few went by. The UPS truck was gone. She placed the book upside down on the window unit, open to her page, and went into the bathroom. Her father's ragged toothbrush was still resting on the side of the sink where he had left it that morning. There was a glob of toothpaste still on it. She stuck it under the faucet and rinsed it off. She opened the medicine cabinet and it squeaked. She closed it. She went back to the couch and then got back up and went to the door to secure the chain. She sat down and read. It was night and she was tired. She got up again, turned on every light she could find, looked out the window one last time to see if Pete was pulling in, then lay down on the couch and placed the open book under her cheek to keep the scratchy material of the couch from touching her face, and fell asleep.

When she reached fifth grade, Pixie learned that life didn't have to feel the way it did—flat and undeveloped—when a boy from the middle school gave her half of an ecstasy. When Pete came home the night she had taken the ecstasy, she had nothing to say to him, she just picked up his arm and kissed it, she loved him so much. Her life quickly became books, and pills, and then sex. The one-third and one-third and one-third fighting the shit out of each other for dominance, and it looked for a while that the books would win—high school awards and scholarships for college. Sex pretended to be dormant, a slow leak of oil, but it would change her direction—boys with power, boys with peaceful smiles and weapons hidden behind their backs. It wasn't just a lack of self-esteem, it was a lack of *life*.

Something had numbed her—the little apartment perhaps, no mother, Pete with nothing but his dirty forearms, New Brunswick—and so, anything that would give her a nudge and remind her that her pissy life did actually exist, because she wanted to be real, became medicine. Books worked at first, then pills, then boys, and finally cutting. Cutting was the simplest and most easily accessible, the only downside being the unpretty line of scars up her arms, part of her back, her thighs even, like a human diary. And there was nothing so immediately wonderful, in Pixie's fuck world, as the relief that came when she pressed into her skin with a blade and felt that first ease of blood. And there was most certainly nothing suicidal about it. She took pains, in fact, to avoid the high-risk areas—never going near her wrists in a certain way, for example—so that there would be no confusion as to her intentions if she were ever to be discovered after death in a crumpled car or an emergency room or on some kid's living-room couch. She assumed a bleak future, but not knowing any better, she observed the bleakness as a formation on the horizon not worth thinking about. It was her normal and could actually be her comfort.

Some small part of her brain was rooting for her, though. Those tests were just so easy. She felt that lightness when she took them—energizing—like a flippered pair of Jovian feet were at work pushing her toward some surface. In the end, as she took more and more, pills became her biggest enemy, threatening to muffle that active part of her brain. The relief of sex and cutting didn't put her in danger like pills did. But pills, in the end, worked because they made the numbness benign. School, she was beginning to realize, well, fuck. Pills were easier than cutting, so easy to swallow with even just the tiniest dribble of water. If she had enough spit, they went down just fine.

7.

Etta: friends forever

Life, Etta was used to saying and didn't bother to deconstruct anymore, was best lived by "Laughing as much as you breathe and loving as long as you live." Many of her books stood by her on this, *Stick a Flower in Your Hat and Laugh*, *Secret of a Love-filled Life*, *Moment by Moment*, and the *Joy of Humor.* Erma Bombeck stood fuzzily up in Heaven at Etta's personal finish line, rooting her on, reaching over the tape at her waist in an act of physical encouragement, long nose and laugh lines secured into her face after years of, what Etta understood as, making women happy. Erma Bombeck stood in Heaven flailing her hands in circles imitating wheels—*Speed up, keep it movin', life's a race to be won by love and laughter.*

It wasn't that Etta never had a bad day—she certainly did. There were days, she told the women in her Bible study, when she couldn't figure out why God didn't just make things easy. He could if he wanted to, she knew that. She didn't have much to say when people she knew suffered. When David McMillan had melanoma—and then both of his parents had died that same year. Awful timing, she would have said to God, given the chance. But where else are people going to go? It's like the disciples, when Jesus asks, after he says some things that don't seem to make sense, if they will desert him too, and they—at least one of them—John or Peter, say, "Where are we going to go to?" The truth is there's nothing else out there. Not that Etta had really looked. But she knew there wasn't. She just knew.

If she could be of any encouragement to Margie Nethercott, she wanted to know. She would bring down some muffins. She would introduce herself to Margie, nothing big, just, when people are struggling, it seemed to Etta, the people around them run away—embarrassed, uncomfortable. She would do the opposite and introduce herself. She had a recipe for raisin-bran muffins that required soaking bran in milk for half a day that she thought the Nethercotts might enjoy. Baking—even if there is no *need* for the food—at least expresses kindness, and who doesn't appreciate kindness? She was aware that they were health-conscious. One of them, she thought she remembered, was a vegetarian, and bran muffins of course are always nice anyway. She poured the batter into twelve muffin cups and slid them into the oven before taking off her apron and washing her hands one last time. She would bring them down warm. In her basket with the wooden handles and wrapped in a light blue linen napkin.

She made her way down the hill with the basket, enjoying the unseasonably warm weather. The morning was still and the river echoed a soft rush up the hill. Perhaps after her visit she would get out her paints. Etta tried to think of a way that she could let Margie know she was an artist too. Not to brag of course, but so that Margie might feel some sense of connection with her. There was a chance that Margie was already aware of this—some of her recent work, five tomatoes on a board with weathered brass hooks attached—was in Carlino's store. She had decided not to call first, only because it was the sort of day people were usually okay with people dropping by. A call would only be awkward. These were days that you'd hear screen doors swinging open. People *emerged* on unseasonably warm days like this.

The Nethercotts' house was well landscaped. A beautiful wooden fence, painted white and left to peel—with bare rose vines that Etta remembered blooming wonderfully all summer long. The house was peeling a bit too. It was a burgundy color. Etta stood on the front porch with her basket of bran muffins, looked for a doorbell, didn't find one, and leaned forward to use the door knocker—a curved porpoise that arched over the hinged knocker like it was mid-jump—that had a slight green patina. She wondered if the peeling fence paint was intentional. She doubted it. No one came to the door.

She knocked again, louder, and heard someone coming down the stairs. Margie opened the door. She was wearing a sleeveless floral housecoat with pink piping along the edges. There were snaps that were covered in the same floral print down the front. The smock went to Margie's knees, where Etta could see she wore a pair of faded jeans that were chewed up at the bottom. She had a long-sleeved black shirt on underneath the housecoat, which was covered in paint.

"Hello, Margie?" Etta smiled, holding her basket somewhat awkwardly.

"Yes?"

"Uh, I'm Etta. I live up the street."

"Oh," Margie looked a little relieved. "Hi."

"Hi. I know this is sort of abrupt, but it was such a nice day and I've been meaning to drop by and introduce myself." Etta changed directions. "Actually, we met this summer at the outdoor concert. We sat next to each other. Your daughter, a beautiful girl, was so engaging. . . ."

"Oh, yes, of course. . . ." Margie opened the door wider. "Excuse my mess," she lifted her arms from her sides for a moment, indicating her paint-covered clothes, "I'm working upstairs. . . . I actually thought you might be a client of mine."

"Oh, I'm so sorry, if you're busy. . . ."

"No, I'm not expecting them. I got confused, that's all."

"Yes," Etta said, "You paint. This was one of the reasons I thought we should know each other. I'm an artist too." Oh, the foolishness. If she'd only left it alone. . . .

"Really?"

Etta held out the basket. "Well, kind of." She laughed a little. "It's a good day for baking. I hope you don't mind a visit."

"How nice. Thank you, would you like to come in? I can take a break . . . nice to have a break."

Margie showed Etta to the kitchen and turned the flame up under an already hot kettle of water. "Would you like some tea? Do you drink tea?"

"I'd love some."

"Mary Sommerfeld stopped by too. The other day. Do you know Mary?" Margie appeared to relax. The tea kettle began a hazy whistle.

"Oh, yes, we go way back. . . ."

"It's kind of you to come by." She pulled mugs out of a cabinet and two tea bags from a box on the counter. She poured the tea and set a red mug in front of Etta.

There was a silence. Etta self-consciously lifted the tea to her lips, feeling a bit of a tremor in her hand as she did. She'd had too much coffee that morning. Hopefully the tea was decaffeinated.

Margie sat down and traced Noel's name that was carved in the table with the tip of her finger. "So, you live up the street?"

"Yes, three blocks up. 102. Twelve years now. My husband's name is Edward. You met at the park, but of course you wouldn't remember that. We have a son, Tyler. He's a sophomore at Villanova."

"The paper boy."

"Oh, yes, the paperboy," Etta laughed. "He hated that job. Always wanted me to drive him so he could just throw them out the window. They would land on the sidewalk."

There was another short silence.

"I admire your work," Etta said.

"Thank you. What sort of art do you do?"

"Silly little things really. I have a few things in town."

"I'd like to see it. Representational stuff?" Margie looked over her mug at Etta.

"Um, tomatoes mostly." Etta laughed, embarrassed.

"Tomatoes?"

"I know. Funny, but I do sell quite a few of them. I've wanted to begin doing landscapes, but people in Trinity love tomatoes. They *love* tomatoes here. I honestly don't know why." She laughed again.

"I feel like there should be a term for art that works because of its environment," Margie said, looking into the middle distance. "Some art, you hang, and then everything around it has to kind of submit, but then there's the art that fits right in, like it was created to fill a specific need. A red picture that makes a room look better, that kind of thing."

Etta looked puzzled.

"It's just that some things are right for certain spaces, but nowhere else."

"I guess maybe my tomato paintings are more of a craft," Etta said.

"Would you like to see what I'm working on?" Margie was grateful for the break and, right then, another person. She wanted to move away—farther—from that certain part of herself she'd been paying so much attention to. "I'm putting the last touches on a portrait right now."

Upstairs in the studio, Etta, taken aback by the clutter, tried to appear nonchalant about the chaos. She tipped forward a canvas leaning against a wall and looked behind it at what appeared to be a portrait abandoned halfway through. It looked kind of gray, or even blue, with dark shapes not yet distinguishable.

"Sorry about the mess." Margie kicked a stray piece of wood under a table.

Etta looked at the newspaper clipping of Chris Burden tacked onto the wall over the drawing table. She leaned across the table to get a closer look, saw the bullet wound with the trickle of blood down Burden's arm, and stepped back.

"That photograph intrigues me," Margie said. She was sorting through a pile of charcoal sketches. "Burden ended up being a jerk, really, but still, I've never been able to get away from that picture—it does something for me."

"You must spend quite a bit of time up here," Etta said, looking at a piece of canvas that was stretched out and nailed to another area of the wall. There were spots of mixed color, the colors of skin in somewhat neat rows, squareish strokes from a wide brush. A large painting of two children and a dog was on a very large easel in the far corner of the room. The south wall, without windows, was covered with unframed work. There was a male nude at eye level. Etta looked at it hesitantly.

"Nick," Margie said, "in his twenties. Don't know that he would model for me now. Probably for good reason. His skeletal structure's the same, but I certainly wouldn't have access to it like I used to—he's put on at least twenty pounds, probably thirty. He was actually pretty thin, too much so, but he was wonderful for painting. He really was."

Etta glanced quickly at the genital area and looked away. She couldn't imagine painting someone like that. There were two or three others—of women—why did a nude painted now seem so much more, well, *pornographic*, than nudes done by the old masters? The portrait was one of Margie's favorites. The bone structure was visible almost in a grotesque, stretched way. She hoped Etta hadn't been offended. The colors bordered on disturbing—purples, blues, and the holistic effect of the flesh tones blending together when back from the canvas five feet or so. It was a translucent skin—she'd worked to make it look that way—that seemed to pulse with the blood barely depicted beneath the surface.

"I've never taken a figure drawing class," Etta said. "I don't paint people."

Margie looked at her. "It's essential. Take the Saturday class down at the art center. It's a good class. Sometimes I drop in. You can pay a sitting fee—twenty dollars—for three hours, or take the whole course. Find out what model they plan to use ahead of time. The model is important." Was this a sympathy visit? It didn't even matter. "I'm picky."

"Perhaps I will. Maybe after I work on my landscapes. I have a view out my front window of the valley. . . ." Etta was going to describe the myriad of roofs visible from her deck that she wanted to paint, but suddenly the project seemed silly.

Etta and Margie stood in a clouded connect somewhere within a polarity that threatened to take over the room, holding on to what each knew, the mountains of surface and odor and color and dimming light threatening to bind and also rip at some vague infrastructure supporting both of their lives.

When she left, Etta glanced over her shoulder at the Nethercotts' house as she walked up the road and felt a little like Lot's wife running from the flames. She quickly thanked the Lord for her time there, grateful to have been able to visit with Margie. Hopefully, she helped lift her spirits.

IN BED THAT NIGHT, Etta lifted Edward's T-shirt up to expose the indentations of his stretched-out rib cage. The moonlight was in their room. She felt the undulations of his ribs with the tip of her finger and then kissed him on the mouth, knowing that he would understand her touch to be a sort of wifely foreplay, this precursor to sex, the way the book *Secret Intimacies* had taught her.

8.

Pixie: in sync with something

Pixie woke up with half of a paperback book in one hand. The last one hundred pages or so. At the top of the right pages it said in bold letters: Final Approach. On top of the left pages the author: Jason Freeman. She held it open for a moment, focused on a page, and read, *the sound of the engine whined into steely high decibels.*

Her sheets and blanket had bunched up between her bed and the wall, where she habitually shoved them when the heat kicked on, quickly cooking her little room into a dry, irritating space of recirculating air. She sat on the edge of the bed and flipped through the book, noticing a smear of brownish blood on the back page where there was a section of glossy cover still clinging to what was left of the binding. She tossed the book on the floor.

Noel was in the little kitchen rinsing out a mug for coffee. There was no food in the apartment. There never was. They both ate at Rich's, the deli next door, virtually every day, finding it cheaper and less bothersome to grab a bagel or egg sandwich for breakfast and a little plastic tray of sushi for lunch or dinner. Two meals a day and then whatever shit came their way. There wasn't a whole lot of order to the way they lived, the two of them, barely friends even now after a month and a half. Pixie wore a white ribbed beater without a bra and a pair of sweatpants that said NAVY on the ass. Her tits were small, never grew after eighth grade, just little buds. She had cut off the hems of the sweatpants, and they were four inches above her ankles. The book landed next to the oversized infantry-looking bag she had picked up in New Jersey. She ran her hands up her arms, fingering the tiny raised scars that traveled like mouse footprints up toward her shoulders. She picked at a scab above her left elbow.

The last month of her senior year in high school, John Rollins, who she called John the Baptist because he still went to church, had felt her scars with the tips of his fingers while they lay on the sculpted carpet of some kid's family room in some house in Fair Oaks in a drunken haze, and then slid his chin down her arm and traced the little transgressions with his tongue; when his mouth met hers again, she'd felt the swerve of sex-love begin to lead her into another *pro-mis-cu-ous* relationship. The lead singer of Korn got baptized in the Jordan River and someone had dropped a camera. The camera snapped a picture all on its own when it hit the ground, and the picture it took—it was later discovered—was of a white dove winging into the air above the water just like when Saint John baptized Jesus. She'd read this somewhere. That's what she needed, a camera to come to life and take a picture of her—only she would be all white like a dove and food would taste like honey.

"Fucking hot," she moaned and slowly stood up, pulling on a long-sleeved shirt before opening her door all the way. The kitchen was there, it *was* her bedroom door almost, a little cubby of an alcove with a twelve-by-twelve-inch section of yellowing laminate for a countertop next to a fridge with as much room as a medicine cabinet. Contact paper with a pattern of tiny pink and teal flowers covered the small area of exposed wall above the counter. There was a tear along one side where someone had started to peel it off. Noel stood next to the two working burners of the quarter-sized stove, elbow stuck out while she concentrated on slowly pressing the handle down on a coffee press. This was her thing.

Noel looked up. "Coffee?"

"Yeah, sure. . . ." Pixie ran a hand up through her hair and scratched at her scalp. Her short black hair shifted to the right as she did this.

Noel's bag was packed with her notebooks and whatever else she took with her to campus and sat neatly next to the front door. Things were subject to Noel. Things respected her.

"Was I reading a book last night? Like a Duane Reade thing? Something you would pick up when you were buying emery boards and toothpaste? I was out with Keith, I think. I lost him in the crowd."

"You just went to bed. An emery board, you mean like a nail file?"

"Nothing's ringing a bell," Pixie said, going to the little fridge to open it and stare at what she knew would be nothing. There was an open can of Diet Pepsi. They didn't even have a half gallon of milk. She was unusually hungry.

"Where were you last night?" Noel said.

"Starlights. Betty Carlton was playing. She's going to bust into the mainstream soon though. I'm sure of it. Then I'll hate her. Someone said the same label that has Nora Jones is considering her."

Noel rinsed out a second mug. "I feel like whenever there's an up-and-coming talent, there's always a rumor that the same label as Nora Jones wants to sign them. Keith's the guy you were with Monday?"

"I guess. Yeah, you met Keith. I want Betty Carlton's voice," Pixie said. "It's like an angel's. Or a bird's. An angel or a bird that's smoked a lot of cigarettes—it has that Demi Moore raspy thing. I could be in love with Demi Moore."

"Demi Moore doesn't have a raspy voice."

"Yeah, she does."

"I saw the flyers for Peggy Carlton all over campus."

"*Betty* Carlton. Cigarettes don't make my voice raspy. I wonder if there's any other way to get that. Men fall in love with women with raspy voices. Boys fall in love . . . even if you don't sing. But if you have a raspy voice and can hit a couple notes, then you can sing."

Noel handed her a mug of coffee. "Tell me what you think, it's from Indonesia. My mom bought it. I think our kitchen upset her. She bought the coffee and ten cans of soup." Noel opened one of two mostly empty cupboards to show her a row of chicken noodle and tomato. "Sometimes she can be domestic, actually."

"It's okay," Pixie said, referring to the coffee. "It's a little strong. So, this book. What the hell?"

"The Duane Reade book?"

"I never saw it before. I don't know where the hell it came from. Half of a fucking book . . ."

"Where is it?"

Pixie went and picked up *Final Approach* from her floor and tossed it to Noel who turned it over and flipped through the pages.

"It was in my hands when I woke up."

"It's the *other* half that's interesting," Noel said, and read out loud, "*Clayton palmed her breast while the white light of the television flickered in the corner of the room.* Nice. Where the other half of the book is—this is what you need to know."

"A dude."

"Of course."

"I was at the Betty Carlton concert. . . . I was in the front row. . . . Oh, I was drumming. Someone handed me drumsticks and I stood next to the stage and drummed on it. A guy with a mandolin handed me drumsticks and I played the hell out of them. Shit. I think I was pretty good, too."

"What did you drink?" Noel continued to flip through the pages.

"Three or four glasses of red wine and a Xany. At least. It was a crap day."

"If you're imagining it's a guy, you'd hope to see something a little more—you know, literary. Not to be a snob, but it says here, *"crumpled in his white-knuckled hand was the airline ticket, his ticket to freedom."* Noel turned the page, *"Never again would he question his first instincts."*

"If I'm imagining a man, I should hope for a guy who reads *Finnegan's Wake*? Fuck that, this guy's got it together. He's secure. He enjoys a good cliffhanger. He wears double-breasted suits."

"Actually, I kind of hate double-breasted suits."

"Yeah," Pixie said, "They're good providers though—men who wear them. My dad's a shit provider. This isn't exactly how my counselor put it, but it's what she felt was important for me to know. I see a counselor every Thursday because it makes me feel like maybe I'm not dead. You should know this about me, I guess. That I see a counselor, not that I feel like I'm dead. Everyone feels like they're dead, some just manage it better. Fathers mess you up good, she says—my counselor. Mothers are irritating, but fathers mess you up good. I'm planning on marrying a woman. But I don't like them yet. I need to work on that."

"You're at an Ivy . . . I mean, you're a success, right?" Noel said.

"800 verbal. 800 math . . . and a kick-ass essay."

"Geeze, you slipped right in."

"K-Y Jelly," Pixie said, "but you *do* know Columbia has plenty of us. The Completely and Entirely Fucked Up."

Noel began to gather together her things and then sat down across from Pixie on their one legless stuffed chair that was angled into the corner of the room.

Pixie said, "I wrote the essay on the idea that self-inflicted harm often becomes predominant in those with high intelligence, or people who are thoughtful slash—pun intended, ha ha—sensitive, which implies a certain type of intelligence anyway. A lot of people wouldn't agree. I wrote that people who hurt themselves are close to truth in a way that messes with them, thus the SI, self-infliction, thus the hurting themselves. Anorexics just want to be pure. They want all the shit out. And they *are* full of shit."

Noel looked at her. "And you got in."

"Go figure, but you know it was well written."

Noel was silent for a moment and then stood up. "I have a class. We'll find that guy," she said, "the guy with the book. I'm pretty sure he's a tool though." She walked toward the door and then turned back around. "It's been good . . . you know, talkin'." She hooked her elbow, made a fist, and swung it in front of her in an exaggerated *gung-ho* motion as a half joke.

When she closed the door, Pixie wished that Noel had just let things sit without pointing and saying in effect—*thank you for sharing.* It was like saying thank you after sex. Fucking stupid and pointless. They could've been friends if she'd just kept her mouth shut.

For all of the street dirt and odor of rubbish—it's always rubbish in New York, not garbage—it was surprising how well the city maintained its reputation. People forgave the city its bile-flavored alleys and overloaded dumpsters. People moved in and became its progeny—siblings littered the place. Fighting, jealous, birth-ordered, and predestined, sometimes empathic siblings. When this fresh new batch of inhabitants, the first-year college students, packed up their bedding sets and matching area rugs, cell phones, and laptops, they brought with them a smokeless innocence and exploratory vanity, moving swiftly from coffee shop to subway stop in elongated strides, elbows out, tunneling through the dreck of encrusted tile walls on the 1 train and then up for air at 116th or Christopher Street. They were burrowing animals looking to copulate. Few left the city without at least a thumb-sized moment of indistinct abandon, a woozy late-night return home in a cab, an unfamiliar warmth inches away in the sheets, and then a sad morning of not so much regret as dull anti-amazement in the wake of what ends up as nothing. She hated New York. Really. She hated it.

Sick of catching glimpses of herself reflected in the store windows, Noel moved to the other side of the sidewalk. Pixie and her half book had made what was most likely going to be a boring day into something with substance to think about. Some days you wake up and there's a morsel of something that can carry you through a dull morning.

The auditorium for French Lit 101 had already filled up when Noel arrived. She found a seat near the back next to a guy who snorted up congestion in a long draw of mucus as she sat down. She pulled out her notebook and stared at the page, trying not to think about the guy. In front of her a woman—at least fifty—rummaged through a large canvas bag on the floor next to her seat, pulled out a small case, and put on a pair of glasses. The lecture began, as usual, with Dr. Moore standing in front of the wide, black, chalk-stained board with his hands sunk deep into his jean pockets. He allowed himself a slow tilting forward and back on his heels as he silently surveyed the room of students. Sizing them up first thing in the morning was his way of attempting to bring them to life. The silence worked, and students would reposition themselves in the hard chairs, pull out pens, sip from travel mugs, uncomfortable. The lecture that day was on *Tartuffe*.

"*Tartuffe*," he said slowly, swinging forward and then back before removing a hand from one of his pockets and picking up a stump of chalk. "Satire." He scratched the word on the board in slightly exaggerated movements, the soft clicks of the chalk animating each letter, and stood back as though to admire. "Was satire born from comedy or comedy born from satire?" He stared at his scribbled word thoughtfully and continued, "Is Molière, one of the great fathers of comedy, angry?" He coughed. "Let me say it this way. What is the role that anger plays in satire? What is the role that anger plays in comedy? If we answer these questions, we perhaps will begin to see if it served as an inspiration to Molière writing *Tartuffe*. We all know that the church—the Roman Catholic Church—was scared. The Catholic Church was jealous. The Reformation was a great threat, and. . . ."

The older woman sitting in front of Noel turned the page of a spiral notebook and quickly wrote something down. There was a page missing from Noel's used copy of *Tartuffe*. A thin river of ripped paper remained snug in the thin binding. It occurred to Noel that Pixie might have been lying about the paperback she found in her hands that morning—it actually makes more sense that a disturbed girl who intentionally cuts herself would find some odd satisfaction in making up an interesting story. Nobody sleeps holding on to something. The book would have fallen out of her hand. She also kept a bunch of twenty-dollar bills and a paper towel with a note to herself thumbtacked to her bulletin board. The note started out, *I'm going to go to school in New York City*. Twenty-dollar bills hid the rest of the note.

Dr. Moore had grown silent again. "So," he finally said, "it is with great pleasure that I introduce our guest here today," more silence to add effect and then a nod to the woman in front of Noel with the spiral notebook, "Dr. Fran Silverman, author of *Molière, Wit, Anger, and the Depravity of the Catholic Church*."

The woman stood, turned to gather together her notes, and caught Noel's eye. Noel smiled kindly. When she reached the front of the room, she was apologetic. "First off, I'm afraid I need to make a slight correction on the title of my most recent book. It is titled *Molière, Wit, Anger, and the Depravity of the Roman Catholic Church in the Seventeenth Century*. Those last two words are important." She smiled and aimed the eraser of her pencil toward Dr. Moore for a moment in playful chastisement. He nodded and laughed approvingly.

Noel looked down at the few notes she had taken so far and began to shade in a cylinder she had drawn using one of the binder holes as a circular end. She drew the empty seat of Dr. Fran Silverman, including graffiti scratched into the backrest that said, *buy low, sell hi.* Dr. Fran Silverman was not as interesting as Dr. Moore. The class began to stir, and Noel looked toward the front of the room, feigning attention.

"I don't think that Molière's response—in effect—in his play is unprecedented. In fact, what else is going on at that time? Literarily, I mean?" Dr. Silverman looked over the class and then paused at Noel, mistaking her expression as an eagerness to enter into discussion. "Who else," this time speaking directly to Noel and nodding in a way that would make no comment from her either rude or stupid, "responded in this way?" There was a silence as Noel's expression of interest quickly faded into one of poorly concealed confusion.

"I, uh . . . in the seventeenth century?"

Dr. Silverman folded her arms and looked at the floor as though in thought and nodded, expecting Noel to enlighten. Silence. Dr. Moore stepped forward and began something of a rescue, throwing out a string of words. "Well," Noel heard him saying, "before the Reformation. . . ."

On the way back to the apartment, Noel stopped and bought a Suzy Q for comfort, licking the edges of cream before wolfing the thing down. Dr. Moore had saved her. Dr. Moore—Mr. Profoundly Silent—had saved her with a string of words.

She wanted to go home to Trinity. Weed the garden. Eat her father's chili. See that her mom was okay. Mess around at the Stop-n-Shop. Talk to Owen. She wanted to sit by the Abenaki and talk to Owen.

9.

Margie: shag carpet and a silver mooneye

The Nethercotts lived on a steep street that made its way up from the main part of town, Maple Avenue. Everything in the town seemed to leak down toward Maple Avenue, the Stop-n-Shop where the kids hung out, situated on the corner of Sixth and Maple, aglow in its fluorescent hum with reruns of special offers—"2-Liter Bottles of Mountain Dew, Diet Pepsi: 89¢"—pasted on a quarter section of the window, the small parking lot arousing an adolescent instinct within the mysteries of a milky dusk. Alongside Maple, its sidekick, the Abenaki river that in heavy rains, like a great bottleneck of water, cut through the town sloughing off mud from its edges with the pure violence of it before it emptied into Weekeepeemee Lake.

Margie did not like the sun. It glared, and was an insistent reminder of her inability to experience light the way that other people seemed to experience it. She had no aptitude for it, and when it was shining brightly she felt terribly unreal. Ten sunny days in a row and she would walk outside only to feel like rubber, a migrating itch beneath her skin that would never take her attempts to scratch it away. She walked the short brick path to the garden shed and began to pull broken pots out of a wooden cabinet and pile them on the cement floor, inspecting them for chips. Her hands were shaking a little bit. There was a gritty film of dust and dirt everywhere—the two painted-shut windows, one slightly cleared of the grime in a small arc where she had taken a wet paper towel to the glass last spring and then lost interest when the dirt didn't wipe off easily. There was a bucket of garden tools, a ripped bag of topsoil infiltrated with the sparkle of Miracle Grow granules. Sometimes she imagined her body shrinking with cancer from things like pesticides, her bones becoming brittle while her mind maintained its course, and here, in her infirmed state, in some bleak bedroom with half a glass of lukewarm water at her bedside, she assumed she would finally answer for herself all of those questions that were so infinitely difficult and that never completely left her mind. She'd been procrastinating for years. A black swath of the topsoil was on the floor next to the bag. Margie kicked it with the rubber toe of her shoe and it spread out further on the floor.

She picked up the pots and walked slowly through the overgrown garden to a set of garbage cans on the side of the house. Nick was inside with a patient. Squinting in the sun, she looked toward the front of the house and saw James O'Neil at the road; his pug, Chrissy, was sniffing the base of a young dogwood tree held up with rubber-covered wires. He looked at the house. He tugged the leash, still looking up, turned, and walked away.

Up in her studio, Margie could hear the mumble of voices below her, a distinct Nick sentence—Nick's deep voice with an inflection that she knew signaled the end of a session. The screech of a chair moving across the floor. She heard what she thought sounded like a woman's cough. She set two pairs of stretcher sticks—four feet by six feet—and extra sticks for support on the floor and sat down with her staple gun.

She wouldn't need an easel. She wasn't sure that her body would cooperate with such a large project, but the expanse appealed to her right now, as though she could make up for her present fragility with the sheer size of the undertaking. She wasn't even sure what she would paint—just anticipated the stages—the gesso, the large soft brush. The murmurs beneath her grew slightly louder. There was another cough. She tucked the canvas over the stretcher sticks and shot two staples into the wood. Her hands ached so much.

She anticipated the expanse of the canvas like a string of perforated tickets to a carnival. The horizon included tinsel music and lights, although she didn't know yet what she would paint. She inched a large mirror into position in the studio. The mirror was salvaged from her grandfather's studio. It was heavy and had originally been secured to the back of a door, a beveled edge, a few small chips. Margie rested it against the wall and then stood back, breathing heavily. It reflected the ceiling light, a light she had installed for function rather than form, an ugly thing that had five halogen bulbs at the ends of moveable extensions. She always tried to paint by natural light—the one skylight angled over the attic floor, but by late afternoon its effect would fade to a before-dinner dullness and Margie would either have to work with the ceiling light or quit for the day. She pulled a cart that was cluttered with paint tubes, brushes, and crumpled wax paper across the floor to where she stood looking at the canvas. She reached out a hand and ran her fingers down the surface. As she did this, the mirror caught the action, her elbow reflected momentarily as a triangular, flesh-colored movement. The door to the attic opened. Nick held the doorknob, his chest concave, folded forward, Margie thought, as though he was somehow restraining himself.

It wasn't so much Nick's looks that had made Margie, back in college, come and sit on the little square of blue carpet in his dorm room, but the way that he looked at people, like they interested him or he saw something in them that other people couldn't see. There was a strange girl who lived on their floor—she always wore a scarf on her head tied in the back like a pirate, as though she'd lost her hair to chemotherapy, but in fact, she was healthy. The girl pulled her books from class to class in a small metal cart and smiled constantly. Margie caught Nick staring at her one day, and she could tell it was fascination, not gall.

Nick was the resident advisor and got into the habit of leaning into the doorjamb of Margie's open door, talking to her while she sat on her bottom bunk bed with a book and notes on her lap. He asked her questions and listened to her answers, staring into the middle distance and nodding. The first time they had sex, it was right there on her bed in her room, as though Nick had been inching his way over to her from day one: it was a beautiful day. Bottom bunk, casement window open, loud Frisbee game outside, Nick's hair caught in under-mesh of upper bunk, a shove and some kissing and a wide muscular back. The fashion at the time for boys was hair very short on the sides, a good bit still on top, and Nick was a boy, just that. The thrill was significant. That night lying in bed, Margie had stared at the little clump of his leftover hair hanging from her roommate's mattress and wondered at how contained the whole thing was, even as the cells inside her womb had already begun to split.

Noel was born that June, and seven months after that Nick and Margie were married. Margie wore her grandmother's tea-length knit brocade wedding dress and Nick wore a suit and tie. Anna, Margie's best friend at the time, held the baby in the back of the little Quaker meeting house, jiggling her on one hip to quiet her from cooing while Nick and Margie said their vows. The cooing only made the moment more profound, Margie and Nick holding hands and repeating their words, all while Noel babbled and smiled in the back, fingering Anna's chin and grabbing at her necklace. It was very inspiring. And when Nick and Margie finally turned and started walking down the aisle as a married couple, they both had picked up the pace to get to Noel, grabbing her and lifting her up in the air, at which point the congregation broke into applause.

At seven months, Noel's smile already had the hint of what would become a thumbprint-sized dimple on one side of her face. And while so many babies begin life with the proportioned features and laughing smiles that yank the hearts of their mothers, only to slowly fall away as they grow, every year Noel grew into a richer, more unique beauty. Now, at eighteen, her full lips took over her face when she smiled, pressing in her dimple and lighting up the hazel of her eyes, as though her auburn hair and wide lips and perfect little dimple were reversed arrows guiding people's gazes to her.

Margie had experienced her own blocky Midwestern youth—the 1970s squirming around the bicentennial and scratchy Vietnam and Nixon's brass-born peace fingers shot into the violet air of Washington, DC—the strange TV war informing some things but then receding completely out of view. When she was nine, her mother died of a brain embolism. She died on the living-room couch, either the evening before Margie found her or during the night, there was no way to know. Margie had woken up that morning and realized that it was already late and she needed to hurry to get ready for school.

She put on her orange velour jumpsuit with the zipper front—she remembers it so clearly—and took a few minutes to gather together her folders and a homework assignment she had completed the night before. The assignment had read: either draw or cut out from magazines at least five different species that belong to a genus. Margie thought "genus" was a typo, and when she carefully drew and colored in five different types of fish, she corrected it to read "genius." Her fish looked good. One of them was a silver Mooneye. Her silver crayon just seemed gray, so she had used glitter. The Mooneye had a large black eye and sharp bottom teeth and she exaggerated both, so that the fish had a strict underbite and the eye looked hollow.

When she came downstairs she could tell immediately that her mother was on the couch, sick probably, with one of her headaches. The couch faced the opposite direction, toward the front window, and her mother's hair and part of her forehead were visible on the arm, where a throw pillow propped her up just a little. Margie went to the kitchen and looked around for her lunch that was usually set out for her on the counter.

"Mom? Where's my lunch?"

She opened the refrigerator and looked in.

"Mom?"

She was starting to worry she would be late for school.

"Mom, where's my lunch? Mom?"

Frustrated because she would be late for school, Margie darted around the kitchen looking for her lunch, and one of the kitchen chairs next to the fridge hit the wall and slid to the linoleum floor. After setting the chair upright again, she went back into the living room and around the couch. Her mother's face was turned toward the picture window, and her chin looked limp, as though it had somehow detached from the rest of her face and was still in place only because of her skin. The morning light from the window made her look pale. Her eyes were closed. Margie hesitated, as though somehow aware that continuing forward with the day would only prove painful, put a hand on her mother's shoulder, and shook her. It felt like the part of the human body that makes it possible for legs to turn and elbows to bend, something like a warm juice but not even necessarily blood, was missing or had turned hard. There was no give. When she shook her mother's shoulder, her arm moved with it and then suddenly slid down to hang above the floor. Two of her fingers hit the carpet and bent, the knuckles half buried in the yellow shag. It was at this point that Margie felt herself fade back into an unidentifiable haze. Static. It was the moment of impact, the way that in a car accident a moment will slow and turn black as though to spare someone the effect of that memory.

Margie did not kill her mother. She knew this. But as that day folded itself like a fan, leaving whole sections of time obliterated, she was less than cognizant and would forever be at a loss to explain it. What was circumstantial and what was her fault. She had been angry when she couldn't find her lunch. She was afraid of being late. Did she cause her mother to die, and if she caused her mother to die, then did she have something to do with her grandfather dying? Because he didn't die until she moved in with him. She could not grasp an equation that sat in her periphery. Probability that her mother might have died, and then, subsequently, her grandfather, as the result of something she did or didn't do, or even—to be fully honest—just thought: P(G/A)=P(F/A)P(M/F)P(G/M). There was an equation for everything. The scattered physical pain and the pall of her mind that were constantly tugging her out of alignment could sometimes feel like proof that she was responsible. Certain illnesses reek of a sovereign retribution, even though she wasn't even sure she believed in God.

SHE WOULD NOT USE GESSO. She squeezed a thumbprint of Burnt Umber onto a piece of pallet paper and squirted the spot with linseed oil. "What do you think?" she said in monotone, and looked into the leaning mirror with its distorted reflection of Nick, legs fat and gargantuan, hand on doorknob, torso narrowing up to a pinch where his shoulders and head seemed a trillion miles away.

10.

Nick: on the mental capacity of those thereby endowed

Major Affective Disorders are not diagnosed if the disturbance is due to an Organic Mental Disorder, but Organic Mental Disorders come with their own challenges as far as diagnosis. *Everyone*, absolutely *everyone*, wants their spouse diagnosed with a bipolar disorder. Medicine cabinets all over America are filled with Seroquel and Abilify, these only after Paxil layers on the twenty pounds or fails to do its business. The root of all evil isn't money but the tenuous state of the human mind, whatever the human mind is. Nick preferred his sessions with his pain patients. Physical pain being a more measurable thing, less dubious and more precise. Somehow reassuring. Last night, when he had gotten up to go to the bathroom he'd noticed that Margie was awake and staring at the ceiling. She didn't even turn her head when he crawled back into bed.

Joe and Carly challenged Nick. It was important for him to continue to practice traditional psychotherapy, but it was a strain to treat a patient you didn't like. *Really* did. not. like. Nick braved his sessions with the

Carlinos by scheduling them near the end of the day, when he could justify a glass or two of Merlot once they left. Carly wore tight jeans and high heels, her wide hips central to every movement, as though puppet strings were attached to hipbones, tugging them up and forward and then off to the side depending on the conversation at hand. Her posture rearranged as frantically as her personality, fingers flailing about in almost involuntary motion. Joe had no choice but to keep quiet. He understood the danger in opening his mouth—danger, not because it would encourage Carly in any way, but danger in that once he began to say *anything* about how he felt or how his wife affected him, he might not be able to stop and could fly into a long-suppressed rage and tear the overbleached junk from his wife's head in one enormous reach of his thick Italian arms. To avoid this, Joe kept his profile low, rarely saying anything more contentious than, "Come on now, Carly." This is how Nick evaluated the Carlinos and, frankly, he couldn't assess the couple fairly anymore. His notes on his yellow legal pad were a conglomeration of lines from this notation or that notation, quotes that came to his mind, an occasional doodle, or references to the DSM, page whatever. It didn't matter anymore—long ago he had diagnosed Carly with BITCH and felt he needed to loyally stand by Joe, if not to help him, then at least to prevent any serious harm. Divorce, apparently, was not an option for these hardcore Catholics. Nick was a shitty psychotherapist and he knew it.

"It's not like I ask you to change much, Joe," Carly said that afternoon, responding to Nick's suggestion that Joe might need more time to process some of her complaints. "When's the last time I had you change the way you run that freakin' store? You run it like it's still freakin' 1984 for god's sake. Look at Starbucks, look at *Panera's*," she said, hitting his knee with two manicured fingernails to get his attention and pronouncing *Panera's* with a curl of the upper lip, pink-blossom lipstick swelling momentarily in disgust and then receding, leaving a smudge on one of her teeth. "This is our competition, Joe, *this* is our competition. Our competition isn't Vincent's anymore. They don't sell stuff anymore—it's not *1984* for god*sssssssss*ake."

Carly reached over and slapped Nick on the knee to make sure he was paying attention. "He's depressed, Nick," she said, leaning forward. "I mean, he's a smart man. He was when I married him. I remember, I thought he was *sooo* smart." She squinted her eyes as she said "sooo," and shrugged.

Nick said, "Let's take some time right now to specifically go through some of the things you've been addressing here, Carly."

Carly began pushing at her cuticles.

"It may be that for both of you to move forward, you may need to. . . ."

She looked up. "What I need to do, Nick, is stop being such a pushover. I've been a pushover all my life, Nick, this is what I am. I'm *timid* and it's gotten me nowhere. I was the shyest, the *shyest* kid in grade school. . . . I don't know why self-esteem came so hard for me. Well, no, that's not true. I *do* know," Carly pressed her index finger down on Nick's desk for effect. "I felt like I understood a world that no one else did." Tears welled in her eyes. "It was a very . . . very lonely place to be."

Nick looked at his notes. He had doodled a collection of boxes in the shape of a pyramid. One box was blackened in. Next to the boxes he had written, *oh dear god*, and then scratched it out heavily. Joe was stretched out in his chair with his arms crossed and his chin down. He glanced up and caught Nick's eye. Nick did his best to communicate for that one small moment his compassion for the old Italian man.

After the Carlinos left, Nick spent fifteen minutes looking over his notes and revisiting their earlier files for the outside chance that he might be able to perceive a new pattern of behavior. He had suggested an antidepressant be prescribed for Carly, standard Sertraline, but after one month of the little cream-colored pill, she had only grown more contentious and irked, claiming the pill made her gain weight. He tucked the Carlinos' folder back in the file cabinet, closed the drawer, and sat down again at his desk.

He could hear Margie upstairs, her soft steps across the studio floor. When she sat on her stool, there was the familiar creaking—the telltale sound of Margie at work, back straight, chin high, her brush damp with color and hovering ten inches away from the canvas. She would pause like that sometimes for a full minute before she started to paint. When she painted, she always surveyed the progress with her eyes angled to the left, a habit that she had developed as a child because of a slight muscular weakness in her right eye.

Nick went upstairs and stood in the doorway of the studio. Margie had begun to apply paint to an enormous canvas. She wore her smock. Her canvas was too big, like she was trying to prove something. She looked at the mirror leaning against the wall, spotted him, and turned around.

"It's four-thirty," he said. "Take a break?"

"What do you think? This is new for me."

"It's very big."

"This," she pointed at the ceiling with the wrong end of her brush, "is the light. I've never painted the light before. I'm tired of faces."

"The ceiling light."

"I'm serious. I'm tired of people, I'm just painting whatever."

"I'm tired of people too," Nick said, leaning back against the wall with his hands in his pockets. He looked around the room at her things, sketches thumbtacked to the walls, empty coffee cans, clippings from art magazines, a few of Noel's paintings from her senior art class—a still life of garlic, two lemons, and a green bottle, and another still life of a crumpled piece of paper next to a Diet Pepsi can.

11.

Noel: original things

Light came up early, plumbing the old house for secret spots but always hitting the same ones—through the kitchen window and running smack into the stainless-steel sink, a flank of it hitting the Norelco coffeemaker and then the old wooden table, in the bedrooms nothing but ghostly movements at drawn curtains and shades, the Persian carpet—the really worn one—soaking it up within blooms of magenta and greens and peaches as though it were absorbing a spill. Her dad sat in the wingback chair in sweats, the *New York Times* in front of him.

"I don't have a vocabulary for these things," he said over the newspaper to Noel, recrossing his legs in the other direction. "I don't understand how this works—getting up with a microphone in front of a number of people with nothing to say, just, what? Rhymes? Do you begin with the rhymes in mind? A subject?"

Noel picked up her laptop and knelt down next to her father. She clicked on a link and turned the screen toward Nick. "Owen, it's Owen. Watch." YouTube. Owen in a dark T-shirt and knit hat pulled low over his forehead, sitting on stairs in a hallway, drywall studded with paint and a brightness that hinted at skylights. *This is for the soul searchers. / This is for the songwriter who feels like who he is doesn't fill the space for who he was meant to be. . . .*

"You begin with the rhythm," Noel said. "At least I do, the rhythm and a cool outfit. I'm sort of a bore to look at so I try to dress in an interesting way." On the screen, Owen moved his hands in a circle and stretched his thin torso left for dramatic effect as he spoke.

"You're not a bore to look at."

"I don't know, some days. Some days I am."

This is for the poet who writes a thousand lines and keeps them to herself because nobody deserves to hear them. . . .

"For me it's hard not to sing, but it's not about singing, it's about the words. I think it needs to be always on the verge of singing, kind of, but never an actual song."

When Nick had helped move Noel's things into the walkup, it had been after a day of auditorium announcements, lines for box lunches, tours, and email sign-ups. There were fresh pamphlets with photos of the library at night. It had all produced a terrific buzz for Nick, and he went around the little apartment like a gerbil sniffing a new cage. The cracked window with the sense of traffic slipping through it in wafts of engine drone and honking made Trinity, from that perspective, seem like nothing but a late-midcentury photo op with its near silence and little bridge crossing the Abenaki River that was buried in layers of asphalt, gummy tar, and ancient 7-Up tabs pressed down like jimmies into dough.

Pixie had arrived a day after Noel. Two large plastic bins with red lids half popping off, full of things: towels, hangers, framed pictures, a small fan fashioned in the shape of a spider web. There was a little purple plastic spider stuck on the web, and when the fan was on, the spider spinned into a thick circular black line.

Nick and Noel watched Owen walk off of the little screen on YouTube. Noel shut the computer and stood up. "I mean, sometimes you forget what you had planned on saying, but then it doesn't really matter. Whatever inspires you. That's exactly what it's about—not being picky, perfect, all that iambic crap. But definitely about passion, you know, *soul.*" She took her computer, went to the couch, sat down, and opened it up again. "It's like Jazz, only spoken and not played. Don't you think Owen's good, though?" she looked at her screen and began to type something.

"Fabulous," Nick said.

"Look at all the likes he's got. . . ."

Nick started to pick up the paper again and then hesitated. "Hey, sweetheart?"

Noel looked up.

"What do you know? About mom. I assume everything; that you and your friends have talked about everything . . . by now."

"I don't know. . . ." She shrugged. "Nothing atypical, I guess."

"Hmmm. . . ."

"I wish," Noel slowly closed the laptop again, "that there was a blood test so that I could say, I don't know, Mom has, I don't know, Rupert Murdoff disease or something like that. Something where I could say it's a really hard disease but she's handling it wonderfully and all of that . . . she's very brave." Noel shrugged.

"The mind is complicated, Noel. It's the MS—and it *is* official now, she has MS, and she *is* brave. It's also the chemicals in her brain."

"Neurotransmitters," Noel said, and started to bite at her thumbnail. "So it's *not* fibromyalgia? Oh, right, that was last month. . . ."

Margie came downstairs and into the living room. She searched a bookcase for something, touching the spines with her finger. Noel went back to her computer and Nick picked up his paper again. Margie pulled a book from a shelf and opened it as though to confirm it was the one she was looking for. "You *aren't* a bore to look at," she said to Noel, and left the room.

She would drive Noel back to school. Driving felt good with its constant anticipation—approaching something. She would clear her head and focus on her daughter. She was peaceful behind the wheel of a car, where things through the windshield were constantly growing larger. They still had the minivan. Noel had learned to drive in it, back straight, leaning toward the windshield with hyper-alert eyes focused on the road ahead. Owen had been in the back seat more than once when Noel had braved the narrow roads of Trinity with Margie in the passenger seat, every once in a while looking up and pointing something out to her daughter. Owen's presence had been helpful—it kept Margie and Noel from arguing. Noel would be stressed but also try to be funny. "You think I don't know that, beeeeeeetttchhh?" Noel would say loudly when Margie pointed out that she could go right at a red light. A car honking behind them.

"People are S.O.B.'s and you are an angel," Owen would say from the back seat after someone honked at her.

Margie drove the van slower than usual over the crest of Manheim Road. She had no desire to drive quickly in light of the longer two-hour trip to New York. It was the short distances that tempted her to drive fast. Noel was writing in a notebook.

"Let's go to the bakery when we get there," Margie said.

"Sure."

"I want a fresh croissant, they're horrible in Trinity. I want one that's flaky and warm. I'll buy you lots of baked goods. Cupcakes and bagels and cream cheese."

"Mom, they'll go bad. Pixie doesn't eat anything."

"I feel like buying stuff."

"I mean, if it will make you feel good . . . go for it." Noel looked up from her notebook.

"It's not about me, though."

"You're driving me back to school. Then we'll go to the bakery, okay, Mom?"

"Okay," Margie smiled as though satisfied, "then it's a plan."

There was a silence.

"We can go to dinner at that Mediterranean place on Amsterdam," she continued, "and then stop in Housing Works. I found the greatest table in there last time—remember that? It was just so damned big. There's always great clothes. All the rich women dump all their last-year stuff. In Trinity, last-year stuff is next-year stuff. It's very easy to stay ahead in Trinity. Even though it's just hours away from New York . . . that's always puzzled me, how rural things get, how fast—when leaving New York—the towns grow rural."

There was another silence.

"It is a little strange," Noel said, and began to text someone.

"That's a hard word to say . . . *rural* . . . *rural* . . ." Margie repeated, and turned her head away from Noel so that she wouldn't see that she was beginning to tear up. She tried to focus on something else, the road, but it didn't help and more tears began to form. She tried to sniff them back quietly.

"Mom?"

Margie ran a hand across one cheek.

"Are you crying?"

She shook her head.

"Bullshit. Yes, you are."

She took the palm of her hand and wiped at both of her eyes. "No worries, I'm sorry. I'm just," she gave her last words a British accent, *"feeling a bit emotional at the moment."*

"Mom, let it go. You have MS; that's a big deal, right?"

"I'm a shithead." She wiped her face again.

Noel shrugged. "Yeah, I guess so. Isn't everyone?"

"No, not you."

"No, I am, I just handle it better. I don't care so much." She rolled down her window and stuck her arm out into the wind, angling her hand like an airplane wing so that it floated up and down. Margie rolled her own window down and adjusted the rearview mirror, using her sleeve to wipe the surface clean.

JUST BEFORE THE EXIT TO THE INTERSTATE, the road dipped down and there were orange lines and lettering spray-painted onto the asphalt—arrows indicating where, at the crest of the hill, a fatal motorcycle accident had occurred two weeks earlier. The tragedy was written into the asphalt—paint lines and circled areas indicating where bits of motorcycle debris had fallen. Follow the trail of a blood path to stretcher lowered to pavement and lifted. . . . At the top of the hill there is an emptiness, a midlevel sky before the crest and then the momentary expanse of complete silence before the biker hit, at full speed, the rear of a stopped truck and flew tucked up and forward into a white oblivion of death. Margie wondered about the last thing he saw—the scraggly evergreen tree at the side of the road, the bare sky, the shock of the truck—metal, chrome, taillights blinking once, perhaps twice if they had time, like a wince inside a momentary world of fetal-shaped trauma.

Noel leaned against the back of the seat. It was sort of good to go back to school. She had gone to a poetry slam held near St. John the Divine in some back room with a small stage and a broken podium, two spotlights screwed to a ceiling and angled toward the stage. She had gone to the slam with a new friend from her art history class, Rhonda, a smart girl (of course) with a soft, kind look about her. With her chin up to see over the heads of people, Noel had watched with Rhonda from the back of the room, letting the voice coming from the stage flood into her mind in a catch of staccato rhythms:

Wise says the woman in the corner shack
Make what you got and then you give it ***back***
Play the game (stomp, stomp, palms forward, face down, and then sweeping back in a swimming motion)
With the rest
Tease me, tease me
You make your coffee with the radio on
While the stiff in the store with the mannequin arm
Gives a nod to the lady, to the lady. . . .

Freestyle. Noel felt the natural loop of rubbing movement that the old minivan made traveling at fifty miles per hour or faster, some sort of a swift *shwee shwee* pattern, and silently tried to come up with words to match. She ended up with what sounded like a nursery rhyme. *When the hand strikes twelve / you have to look at the time / and it will give you a rhyme / can't believe that it's time. . . .* Shit that's bad.

Coming in from the west, they found the George Washington Bridge clogged with traffic, and they idled behind a linen delivery truck, waiting for the tollbooths to come into view. A man on a bicycle weaved through the traffic to get to the bridge. He wore a small backpack with a blinking reflector.

"Someone's going to hit him," Margie said, remembering the spray-painted asphalt on Manheim as they'd left Trinity. Entering the city, as it always did, made some of her balkiest emotions even more palpable; the slow but continuing increase of sound—squeaking brakes, jackhammers, the loud clunk of some far-off steel hitting steel—created a tinge of growing anxiety that matched the faulty workings of her own brain.

"They always make it. This is New York."

"Do you not like it here?"

"I don't love it here."

"I think New York has to grow on you," Margie said hesitantly. "You either start out loving it and then it begins to irritate you, or you start out hating it and then you begin to find you kind of like it. New York is a great place to reminisce about. Always better as a memory."

"I like it." Noel said. She rested her bare feet on the already scuffed dashboard. "I *imagined* that it would be wonderful, which I guess is sort of like remembering it better than it really is."

The linen truck kicked to life and spouted a fresh cloud of exhaust. They inched forward. "I'm sure I'll be happy that I *went* to college here."

An ambulance came up from behind, overwhelming them with the whine of the siren. It gave two loud mechanical-sounding honks, and cars tried to angle to the side to make room, but stopped short with no place to go. The ambulance inched ahead and then, finding a run of space, went quickly through the tollbooths. Margie could see two paramedics in the back window preparing things. One of them pulled out a thin plastic hose and held it up. Noel went back to freestyling a poem in her mind. *We got the bridge up ahead that's covered in metal / give me two hours and I'll make you peddle / give you a medal. . . .* Crapshit. That's all she was good for.

Out of the tollbooths, the traffic remained gridlocked. Up ahead there were two stopped cars with blinkers on. The ambulance was parked, its lights in a virtual spin, back doors open. A gaggle of people, a man in a business suit with a cell phone to his ear, and two cops stood half out of view looking bored and distant. When their minivan inched forward, Noel and Margie could see the guy who had been on the bike, his backpack an arm's length away. He had one knee up and was sweeping it back and forth in a silent movement of pain or confusion. They looked at him as they passed. Blood trickled out of his ears into a sticky mess of hair and more blood that stained the pavement. The reflector on the backpack continued to blink.

In the brisk shelter of impending dusk, mother and daughter stroll down Columbus Avenue, glancing into windows and diverting their eyes from odd people as they approach—the old and haggard, and those fit perfectly to the edges of Manhattan: a woman with a facelift that worked out well and also somehow didn't; a mother and young boy pushing an empty stroller; dogs—mastiffs; the heads of lapdogs sticking out of bags. There are noises: the thick and watery sound of luggage wheels on pavement; a voice, then two voices, bites from other lives that sit on top of the brain and never pass through, just singular and isolated. They go into a store called The Wharf and look at clothing. The mother holds a pair of pants up to her daughter's slim waist. The pants are wide in the legs and hit the floor with a fold. They listen and then try not to listen as an angry customer, a woman, tries to return an item and becomes obscene with a saleswoman. The customer says, "*The Fuck*," and then says it again, "*The Fuck you sayin'*." The mother thinks to herself that there are two ways to say "what the fuck." There is the kinder, "what the," and then the fiercer "the fuck." Both serve the same purpose more or less, she thinks: the one way, with "fuck" hanging out and dangling appropriately for inside the packed and adjective-insensitive volume-cranked city, the other, "what the" heavy with its implications, somehow, counterintuitively, even more direct and potent. These are the idioms of cities, of places where people are exposed to people in ways that they shouldn't be.

They buy a different pair of pants—jeans—and walk out of the store into what has become night. With the dark comes the sense that the honking taxis are even louder and there is a new conversation among the people. Visibility changes. The senses relax ever so much. A man approaches the two women. He has on a wool hat with snips of tangled and greasy gray hair sticking out from beneath it. He is damnation and he is salvation, but has no idea how heavy he is. He works his hands into anxious little circles against one another, rubbing his palms together in an effort to think or an effort to not think.

"You miss got two dollahs?" Margie looks at him while Noel pushes past, running a hand down her mother's back to encourage her forward. The man sees Margie and responds to something, raising his voice, "Jus a few dollahs, miss, jus for mah baby." The women keep walking.

"Stop looking so much," Noel says.

"I'm not looking."

"Yes you are. You always look."

As it grows darker, they pass a silent image projected onto the windowless side of a building: A girl sits in a chair. Between her and the viewer is a sheet of Plexiglas. She stands up. She walks to the foggy Plexiglas, takes a black marker, and scrawls *WHO CARES*, which appears backwards, in mirror image. She steps away, sits back down, and holds the wrong end of the marker to her lips in thought. A loop, the whole scene repeats itself. She stands up, writes on the glass, sits down, the marker to her lips in thought. Stands up, writes, sits, marker to her lips in thought, marker to her lips, marker to her lips. The video loop continues as Margie and Noel walk. It's a soft luminesce in their tiny section of city. They continue down 81st Street to Amsterdam, dodging a new flux of people up from a subway station.

Back in the apartment, Noel and her mother took turns blowing up an air mattress. Margie held the air valve pinched between her fingers and blew. Noel pulled the mattress up and away to try to encourage it to inflate.

"You know the sheets are going to just slip off, right?" Noel said.

Margie held up one finger while she finished exhaling. "This one isn't supposed to do that. It has special grippy stuff and a tight elastic cover. I'll be fine."

"Just let me sleep out here. It's not good for you. You need a lot of rest and stuff."

"I'll be fine. I feel okay." She handed the valve over to Noel. "I'll crash early and you can go out and do whatever you do on Friday nights."

"Not much really. I'm not like that about college."

Margie stretched an arm out and then began to massage one of her hands. She grimaced.

"You all right?"

She got up. "I'm *fine*," she said, and then curled her hands down on themselves and limped with one foot turned in. She went to the counter and feigned picking up a glass with the back of her hands.

"That's not funny, Mom."

"No, it's me being pissed."

Margie had trouble sleeping. It was so different. At home the few cars going by at night would swing their light shadows slowly across the ceiling like white fingers and then speed up when they hit the wall, flying down the plaster to disappear. Here, there was no rhythm to the noise. Trucks loose on their chassis hit rough spots on the road and jumped, clanking like they were filled with thick chains. The various sirens were strong and insistent and of a pitch that stung her ears. She heard voices, sometimes clearly. A woman laughed loudly, *ha ha ha ha!* A man was angry. You wouldn't say that to Mike, he said, and then repeated in a growl, *you wouldn't!* Margie realized that her jaw was tense and she consciously relaxed it, letting her chin drop just a little. She tried not to think.

THE APARTMENT DOOR BANGED against a chair and woke Margie up. She heard a sliding, and then, "Fuck." Something fell into the sink and shattered. She could see someone go into the second bedroom and push the door. It stayed open a foot. There was some sort of moaning, and Noel came out of her room. "Sorry, Mom," she said, and opened her roommate's door to peek in. "You okay?" she whispered. There was a moan. Noel went into the room and then came out. She quietly shut the door behind her, making sure that it closed all the way.

The next morning Noel helped her mom let the air out of the mattress. They rolled it up together, pressing down to deflate it. Margie got her things together, gave Noel a hug, kissed her, and left. She was tired. It would be a long drive home.

12.

Owen: bling bling 54

If there was one thing Owen knew, it was that Richard Wilber was right. About everything. It was scripture. And even if he didn't always use "god" as a proper noun, he was as close to Jesus as anyone on this hellish earth ever got. No one read verse anymore, and that was fine, but he found himself holding back when he wanted so bad to reference some line, or something. He had been obsessed with Eliot after reading *Little Gidding*. He read it to Noel. But then he read *The Waste Land* and it was so shitty (not in a bad poem way, but in a sad way) Eliot died for Owen. It wasn't until recently that he thought of the two poems as bookends. He wanted to talk about these things, but other than with Noel—and he wondered if she was just patronizing him—when he did he always ended up feeling like a pretentious ass. Even at school, even in one of his literature classes, he felt like an ass when he brought stuff up.

When he was sixteen, after seeing a documentary on Studio 54, he had talked Jason into sneaking into 54 Below. You took an elevator down, under where Studio 54 used to be. It was awfully civil. No one bothered with them. Owen wanted to hear Maas Johnson, who at the time was king of scat, at least that's what Owen thought. He imagined Johnson sticking in a few words—like from a Richard Wilbur poem—maybe allowing a word to come out from his palms as he hit certain odd syllables, and those who wanted to understand would understand. They would be parables. That's how Wilbur should be read, like scat: *At just that crux of time when she is made / So beautiful that she or time must fade.* "Crux" would make a good scat word. He loved poems that rhymed.

Was he the only one who thought Noel was beautiful? It seemed like it, although adults appeared to acknowledge it. She didn't straighten her hair, or wear any makeup as far as he could tell. She didn't put pictures of herself on Facebook, although sometimes her friends put pictures of her up, and it drove him nuts, like she was being violated. Especially when they were out doing some stupid college thing. Once, in high school, she had taken a selfie and held the camera up above her head and made those fish lips, looking half sideways, like she was a porn star. It was a joke of course, but still he hated it.

Twice, he'd thought about her at night while he was in bed, and fought it and fought it, but then all at once, like an impulse, he'd given in. Afterward his sorrow was one of the deepest things he'd ever felt. She wasn't even there, he hadn't asked her, and even though the whole act was born out of loneliness, afterward the absence of her made his loneliness hover for days. It was a horrible experience.

Dressing up in some ridiculous bling and winging around a dance floor was safer than love.

13.

Etta: escritorio means desk

The year that Etta and Edward were married it was discovered that Pastor Richards and his assistant, Denise Wagner, had been *sleeping together.* This was very difficult for Etta. She had felt a kinship with the man, a clarity that had caused her to be bold in her pursuit of maturity and godliness.

Three streets up the hill from the Nethercotts, Etta unpacked groceries. Two enormous boxes of Bisquick that she liked to have on hand. She had a recipe. . . . She missed having Tyler at home, coming home with a car full of his friends, all young men with lovely personalities. They all played soccer. When Etta was young it was baseball. The recipe was for tiny pizzas, make your own. She liked to set out bowls of cheese and tomato sauce and pepperoni, mushrooms, green peppers, sometimes even sautéed chicken strips, for the boys to assemble themselves and then munch on after a game.

Etta reached into a paper bag for a little plastic container of Molly McButter, a cholesterol-free topping that Edward liked to have on his popcorn. Edward was always worrying about his cholesterol. She pulled down a pot with a glass lid that she used to make real popcorn. She had strong feelings about microwave popcorn. She poured a puddle of canola oil in the bottom of the pan, set two kernels sizzling, and put the lid on. When they popped, she rained a cup full of kernels loudly into the oil and stood at the stove jiggling the pot over the electric coils, her arm waggling a bit of excess fat with the motion that reached her rear, turning it into a wad of thinly clad flesh smacking left and right in tiny movements. The sound of popping corn dulled and the kettle filled, popping less and less, the lid rising above the pot. Etta laughed to herself and reached to grab a large plastic bowl. She could stand to lose a little weight.

All these years of making popcorn for her husband. The very first thing she'd made after they moved into their little apartment. She hadn't known how to cook yet, really. They were so young. The notes that Edward had sent her back when she was at Briarcliff College had been so direct but so sweet—there was a polite ignorance. His letters had arrived on Fridays usually. Most of the students retreated back to their Westchester homes or out to Long Island, but Etta liked to take a train into the city in the spring and fall months when the light remained good, tucking her handbag under one arm and strolling past the infinity of shallow steps at the Metropolitan Museum of Art or the wide cement courtyard of Lincoln Center. She imagined wonderful things happening at those places. And here she was now, her own little life as an artist. She already had twenty orders for Christmas and it wasn't even Thanksgiving yet.

She and Edward first met in grade school. He had been just a farm boy, really, growing up next to that old overgrown apple orchard, Highland Orchards, and spending his fall days after school driving the tractor with the wagon full of city people: kids, mothers, fathers. Now they wore dark glasses and had water bottles hanging from leather belts and fleece jackets as though riding in a tractor through orchards and pumpkin fields on a brisk fall day required its own athletic gear. The grandparents wore special sun-blocking canvas hats ordered from the back pages of highbrow magazines like the *Atlantic Monthly* and the *New Yorker*. When Edward was young—still thirteen or so—the owner of the orchard had made him dress in a white Easter Bunny costume and greet the children out in the orchard. Etta had seen him once; she went into the little store where they sold the cider and doughnuts to purchase some fresh apple butter for her mother—this was long before New York and Briarcliff College and the letters—and there he was, Edward, in his white bunny suit. Pink nose. Pink ears. It took him a moment to recognize her, but when he did he ducked out. He was like a rabbit that sees the gardener, slipping around the corner so fast Etta caught just one quick glimpse of the fat cottony tail of his costume and then nothing but the cold cement floor of the cider mill. Etta always laughed when she remembered this. He was this adolescent bunny scared to death and hopping away. Sometimes, now, she still called him her little Bunny.

And then after Briarcliff, when she first went with him to that church he used to go to off of Route 17—Marymount Church, and entering the brand-new building with the wide glass doors and friendly people with name tags lined up to greet people, Etta had felt a sort of excitement, one that she couldn't quite distinguish from similar feelings she'd had as a child. The feeling transported her back to a place that was entirely different than the church, a place at home when she was young, nights when her mother, sitting on the edge of the bed, would pull the covers up beneath her chin. Do kids still get tucked in at night? When she entered Marymount Church she felt *tucked in*, she finally realized. She would never forget this. It is what made her pay attention to Pastor Richards in the first place. She liked the way he told self-deprecating jokes. Three months later she was baptized in a white choir robe (swimming suit underneath) in the baptismal hidden under a platform at the front of the church. She spoke into a microphone with the pastor standing next to her in waist-deep water, one arm on her shoulder, looking at her with a smile as he held the microphone up to her face in broad expectation. She cried for the shortest moment, a hiccup really, a faint stall midsentence, and she saw the faces of the congregation tilt ever so slightly, soft smiles, kind looks. They were truly happy for her. Pastor Richards took her backwards into the warm baptismal while she held her nose. She came up from the water to the sound of a million hands clapping. It was a roar. It was exciting. It was the beginning of her life.

Over the next few years the pastor continued with his lighthearted sermons and self-directed jokes, even going so far as to drive his small motorbike into the sanctuary to stunned faces and scattered laughter, the growl and putter of a motor eager to launch, forcing fingers into ears. Laughter. More laughter. Only Jerry Richards would do this, the congregation proudly thought. More gunning of the engine.

When they were married in the church, they hung ribbons of white chintz around the end of each pew. It was a nervous beginning for two young kids. Edward was so clean he looked foreign, and Etta had stuffed manicured toes into heels that painfully squished her feet so much she'd wondered about the state her delicate bones would be in on their wedding night. Not the time to be dependent on Tylenol. There would be no birth control. Children are a blessing from the Lord. *Blessed is the man who fills his quiver with them!* When was there ever a parent who in the end wished they had had *fewer* children? Who rejects what the Lord provides? This was their point of view back then, when Christianity was a simple thing and their God could be packaged and grasped and handed neatly to other people. On the windowsills of the church Etta had made sure that there were hurricanes lit with white candles. She had been nervous about candles and wax and mostly that they would be extinguished by an open door or a breeze. It was superstitious of her, she realized now. In the end they only had Tyler. A wonderful blessing he was, yes. One blessing. One arrow for their empty quiver.

It was all so tragic. The motorcycle, the roar and grind of the engine, in the end was forthright about Pastor Richards, prophetic really. Pride had drowned out the Holy Spirit, and the congregation had gotten the two mixed up anyway.

The telephone rang and Etta reached to pick it up, Molly McButter in one hand. She tucked the receiver between her shoulder and chin and sprinkled the popcorn. It was Christine from across the street.

"Escritorio," Christine said.

"Hello?"

"Escritorio," Christine repeated. "It's the only word he knows. This is what Mrs. Hernandez says. This is Larry's response to anything she asks him on *Manic Mondays*, as she calls them—the day every word in class has to be spoken in Spanish. Oh, Escritorio and *Manuel.* Manuel is the Spanish name he's given himself."

"Escritorio means desk," Etta said.

"I am aware of that."

"Have you talked to him?" Etta turned around and leaned against the counter.

"Tonight. After dinner. I'm making Mark sit with us. Larry needs to know that this *matters* to his father."

"*Does* it Matter to Mark?"

"Yes. Of course," Christine said, "he just never says anything. I *HATE* his passivity."

"Perhaps you should talk just with Mark first? Before you sit down with Larry? Remember, Mark is an I S T J." Etta tended to categorize people by the Myers Briggs type indicator. Once she had said to a friend of Edward's, "My J-ness is getting in the way of your P-ness," and then turned red with embarrassment as she realized what had come out of her mouth.

"I just hung up with Mary Sommerfeld," Christine said, changing the subject. "She told me she was worried about Margie Nethercott."

"She doesn't even know Margie Nethercott."

"She said she saw Margie down next to the lake today and then she saw her head into the woods. She said she looked disturbed."

"That's ridiculous."

"It's just that she was next to the lake," Christine said. "Mary was concerned that she was roaming around next to the lake."

"She's got to think, Christine. What would you need to do if you were her? I don't think walking by herself means she's going to go harm herself. Margie's husband's a psychologist. I'm sure he's on top of everything." It's not that Etta entirely hated Mary Sommerfeld; after all, the woman was surrounded by palpable loneliness. It seemed to leak out of her corners in the form of misplacing intimacy by forcing herself into other people's lives. If she wasn't going to create space for friendships by really caring for people, what else could she do but encroach and gossip? One or the other. Maybe that's why the antidepressants are everywhere. Everyone needs intimacy so they offer up gossip, which is hate, really, hoping to wrangle some kind of not-aloneness, which makes the thing they really need to get and give—love—disappear with TMZ and CNN and everything. She read this somewhere. These thoughts she had. Mary Sommerfeld. It didn't make sense to hate her but still she did. It's awful, and Lord, I'm so sorry, help me to love her.

"Mary said her husband might be part of the problem. She might not feel comfortable telling people if Nick is somehow abusing her. Apparently she spent some time with them after the whole thing happened."

Edward's green Subaru pulled into the driveway. Etta looked out the kitchen window. "Margie doesn't strike me as a person easily intimidated. She had a moment of. . . . she was, for just a moment, unhinged. People need to let it go now . . ."

"Well, her grandfather wasn't normal either," Christine said. "I remember crazy Mr. Baldwin sitting out in front of that old garage smoking his cigarettes. We used to walk past him on the way home from school. He would look at us. He always seemed so angry. He actually scared me."

"Mary doesn't need to worry about Margie. She's just sensitive. Things bother her. Things that probably *should* bother her, bother her." Outside, Edward shut the car door. "Edward's home. I'm going to go. I'll be praying . . . for Larry and Spanish, I mean."

14.

Margie: adjusting for dimension

There's a weeping beech tree on the south side of the river that split into three sometime in its youth, each trunk growing out and away, almost level to the ground as though each section was determined to spread out and take over one-third of the town. One hot summer when she was young, Margie had spent a few days painting the tree. For a while wires attached from trunk to trunk kept it from splitting until they popped and sprung, the beech giving way to gravity and volume, its three trunks continuing to inch out imperceptibly until it was left to fight on its own the slow decomposition spreading from damp ground to bark to wood pulp already taken over by the sorts of insects that pinch their meat and sigh, tiny things that emasculate nature, turning growth to rot. Now the area was overgrown and forgotten, a few steel cables imitating branches looping out within the green mess of leaves and weeds. Margie would never paint it again.

She forgot the name of her clients from Bridgetown and so defaulted to calling them the Bridgestones—part Flinstones, part Mapquest. The dog was an easy paint-in—Irish setters all looking more or less the same. The children were something else. She had worked from a photograph up to a point but needed a sitting in daylight to get a few things right. The grandmother and her two grandchildren, a girl and a boy, showed up, children with twin iPod gadgets—Phones or Touches or something—twin white cords winding up their sleeves and around their shirt collars to lodge in carefully cleaned, waxless ears. The portrait was to be a gift for their mother, so it had been hard to work out a sitting without her knowing about it.

When Margie had worked from a photograph of the children, she had imagined their lives, something she did unintentionally with everyone she painted. She wasn't trying to do this, it just happened—they needed personalities and it was like an internal fight, a pull and tug, to come up with a satisfying backstory for her models. By the time she was done with a work, the subject usually fell within the borders of her subconscious judgments. She liked them or she didn't.

The children didn't look up when Margie said hello. The grandmother was especially friendly.

"Well, I'm glad you didn't need to have the dog here too. The kids have their little games, but I'm afraid Shelly wouldn't have been very easy to keep still," the grandmother joked helplessly.

Margie led them up to her studio and showed them to the platform with the chair. She had taken the original pictures at noon, and it was two o'clock now, but her purpose in having them sit was more for dimension. She was having trouble foreshortening the girl's left leg. Foreshortening was difficult from photographs. It relied on hue. She had them take off their shoes and socks—the grandmother wanted them barefoot in the painting, probably inspired by a Pinterest image. Margie went to work arranging the children as they were in the photograph. The girl was to sit on the floor with one leg forward. She put her legs where she was told and looked back down at her phone. Margie gently picked up the girl's leg and moved it left to a spot marked with blue painter's tape. The girl looked up.

Margie said, "Just a few adjustments." She held a damp brush in her right hand. The girl bent her knee a little as she pressed the left side of her tiny screen.

"Keep your leg out, Megan. Where the artist wants it." Mrs. Bridgestone laughed nervously. Megan straightened it out again. Margie sat on her stool and looked at what she had already painted. Megan's foot was faint and intentionally directionless. She had reserved corrections for the sitting. The girl swiped something on her phone and her leg jerked to the left. Margie stood up and gently pulled her foot to correct the position.

"Megan, you've got to keep your leg straight for the lady," Mrs. Bridgestone said, this time firmly.

"Just . . . one . . . more . . . second," Megan said, looking intently at the screen, and then looking up. She smiled too sweetly, rested the phone in her lap, and leaned back hard, pressing the back of her brother's legs against the legs of the chair.

"Quit it, Megan!" Jeremy said.

"Jeremy, stop!" Mrs. Bridgestone said. "Just be still and then we can go home."

Megan gave an extra jab to Jeremy's shins with her elbow. He kicked her back and it moved her leg out of place.

"Jeremy! I said *stop!*" Mrs. Bridgestone headed toward the platform to move her granddaughter's leg back into position. Margie looked at her, incredulous at witnessing the favoritism the woman showed her granddaughter.

The leg was too far to the right and had to be readjusted. Again. The sun. Margie glanced up through the skylight. It might play a part.

The grandmother pointed a finger at the children. "This is it. Not once more. We will finish this and then we will leave."

Margie stood next to the canvas and blocked in the foreshortened leg and foot one last time, working as fast as she could. She used a wash and it dripped significantly. By 3:30 she had what she needed and walked the Bridgestones to the door, grandmother cheerful, excited, willing to come back again if necessary.

WITH TRINITY'S LATEST GRADUATING senior class off and running—universities mostly, a few trade schools, and one boy, Mike Rococco, managing his parents' pizza shop, the town temporarily lost a bit of its hubris, the first few football games scantily attended, the parking lot of the Stop-n-Shop clear of the usual hand-me-down Toyotas and minivans and Jason Vanderwaal's ugly orange moped with the chipping paint that he habitually leaned next to the fence like a discarded piece of fruit. There was a deflated sense to the place that slowly disappeared as Trinity's next class of seniors dug their heels in and took over, personalities exploding in social blooms of seven or eight, the momentum powered by imagined outrageous freedoms of adulthood finally taking hold and producing the flux and then advances that the class of two thousand whatever naturally produced. They stood in the cold Stop-n-Shop parking lot and ground their cigarettes into the pavement, mouths exhaling a fog of smoke or breath.

Margie always drank a glass of wine before bed. She finished the portrait for the Bridgestones whose name ended up being the O'Hannans, a name that Margie was surprised she hadn't been able to remember. Her failure to remember names and dates alarmed her. She began writing the names of her clients in pencil on the stretcher sticks. Nick kept his clients like prisoners in his first-floor office, listening to them drag their sorrows across the space between them until they had tied regret and anger into unpenetrable knots. They each had a way of possessing their clients, Margie thought; for her it was in the balance of oil and color with the ghost of graphite faintly visible on the pale canvas behind it. Nick's possessing was braver and more absolute; dictums formed by education and authority, he kept his files neat and clean and the order eventually waylaid the nature of the person's psyche, giving way to theories and practices, things that doubled over on themselves and became deceptive. Noel was similar in manner but had a sense of nourishment about her. If nothing else, simple evolution was bound to reform the quirks she inherited from her parents, at least to some extent.

Margie watched the sun sink from lintel to windowsill through the wavy antique glass. She still tried to walk in the evenings and then earlier after the time change, before it became dark. She took off her painting smock and went downstairs to pour herself a glass of red wine.

When she came into the kitchen, Nick was rinsing out a cereal bowl in the sink. He scraped at the edges of it with a spoon. "These shouldn't sit all day. I can't get the crap off," he said.

"Sorry. I wasn't thinking."

"Don't worry about it."

"No. Really, I mean it—I shouldn't do that. It was inconsiderate."

"It's not that big of a deal."

"I wasn't thinking."

"Margie. . . ."

"Shut up, Nick."

"Margie. . . ."

She sat down at the table, put her head in her hands. "Just *shut up*."

Coat your life with enough play, and it's quite possible to drown out the thin murmurs of indecision and despondency. Swing. This is how the child copes. This is how the adult ignores. We become less and less and less, beginning with macaroni and cheese and a little apartment next to the college and growing into scores of furniture, linens, and electronic devices. A trip to Cancun. Oh, *snap*.

15.

Pixie: Xanax, Trip Tickets, and a demon in the making

When Pixie smiled or laughed, which wasn't often, her eyes narrowed bottom up, which made them appear to sparkle and could be deceptive, implying a joy that wasn't there. She opened what was left of the paperback and stood it up on her dresser. It fell over. She stood it up again. It would be an icon to her singularity, blood and spit and ignorance and all. There wasn't much she understood, and she should not expect this to change. She would ease up and stop all medicating. The book would be her reminder. Last night she'd dug a triangle of skin from the space between her index finger and thumb. The dry blood shiny. She'd always been high-functioning, but things were catching up to her and she could see in herself the same inclinations that at first pestered and then took over the stupid girls in high school who used. Drama and then unhealthy attachments and then certain words, like there was a language all its own for those with medicated faculties, words like *sick* for good, and *down* for up. Words that were messed with and then turned on themselves. A certain juxtaposition within each one. The evil for the evil. College wasn't proving to be the miracle she had hoped for. The only way out for her was the George Washington Bridge, and once over, you had to pay a toll to get back in. She would endure the long moments called days in her Harlem of life and try her best. Yeah. Fuck.

Part of her was not in the mood for the crash bang of Starlights. Tinnitus was messing with her ears and her sleep had been fitful at best, even with the residual Xanies from two nights ago still padding her brain. But the noise or the people—both—instinctively drew her out of the little one-and-a-half bedroom and quarter-size kitchen apartment and back onto the streets. She would stay sober tonight.

The ATM was busy. A man with a mastiff stood to one side tucking bills into his wallet as two and then three people bent down to pet the dog and touch its enormous paws. Pixie slowed at the corner, timing her pace so that she wouldn't have to stand long at the intersection, the flashing yellow cabs arching around the turn, pressing swaths of invisible city air toward her torso. She wore a sweater—it would be too warm, she knew, once at Starlights, but the temperature that evening had the briskness, finally, of fall, and Pixie liked her sweaters. The one she wore was brown and had buttons almost the size of teacups, with hand-painted circus scenes. Very eighties. There was a trapeze artist and an elephant. Her unusual clothing choices reflected a boredom she felt with the shrinking size of the world. It was a phenomenon she couldn't come to terms with—the radicalization of clothing and music and literature—each creative push a new attempt at enlarging the hopelessly shrinking human globe. The last one hundred years especially. The Bloomsbury Group? The Beats? She should start her own group: Anthropological Misfits is the name that came to mind. But then it would only be her.

Starlights was abuzz with the anticipated arrival of queer poet Melvin Hobbs, who was to read from his just-released collection of poems called *Enter Here.* The *Kirkus Review* had called the collection *a formidable and brave entrance into the most remarkable and essential elements of contemporary English language.* The poems used offensive sexual terms and unabashedly solicited wide-faced responses from the reader with the intention of doing a Martha Stewart thing with poetry—doling it out to the masses, the young, the old, the rich, the poor. There would be consumers walking around Walmart with *Enter Here* tucked under one arm, ignorant of the title's connotations but eager to dip once more into the highbrow theatre of tastefully disguised erotica.

The line into the bar was a conglomeration of sweatered and tight-shirted femininity peppered with granules of male—heads generally higher in the crowd, balder, grayer even. Everyone moved within their conversations, a foot forward and then a long pause, a smoke or a few weightless words with the guy next to you. Pixie waited in line and looked for Keith. He was from East London and appreciated her unusual buttons and broaches and bulbous-like character, even—she suspected—the raised pattern of scars on her bare arms, momentarily visible when they were matching fireball or tequila shots, a cuff riding up one forearm.

She saw him at the railing, standing on the ramp up to the double doors into Starlights. He was with a small girl in a long feathered dress—yellow—who was talking to him, fast, like she needed something. The dress made out of feathers made Pixie hate the enormous painted buttons on her own sweater.

"Keith!" she called to him with an arm half raised and made her way forward toward the ramp. "Ello love," she said, imitating his accent and frowning. She kissed him on the cheek.

"Pixie girl!" Keith said. He smelled of something. "This is," he looked toward feather girl and paused, pointing a finger into the air as though at a name written in the space between them.

"Maddy," the girl said, obviously interrupted. Keith seemed to have no clue what she had been talking about.

"Hi," Pixie said.

"This, here," Keith said to Maddy, "is my friend Pixie girl."

"Pixie," Pixie said. "Vodka tonight, Keith?"

"You don't know that. Vodka has no scent, love." Keith took an interesting-looking flask out of his breast pocket and unscrewed the cap, holding it up to her nose. The flask was covered with a wire mesh and small canvas straps weaved in and through the wire like fortified ribbons. He held it up in the air for the girls to admire. "Soho," he said, "a place called *wantitback*, one word. Tit is right in the middle," he winked, "but this is not why I like the place, although it would be reasonable for it to be. The wires keep cold drinks cold and hot drinks hot, that's what the tag said. Ey gote some cool stoof." He exaggerated his accent for Pixie and kissed her, this time on the lips, a slight stumble after.

Feather girl, Pixie could tell, wanted to continue what she had been saying to Keith when she had walked up, but seemed to realize his interest was now on Pixie and directed her attention elsewhere. The girl looked out at the crowd and fingered a long beaded necklace that hung from her neck all the way to her waist.

Melvin Hobbs stood on the stage and chewed two pieces of Nicorette. He took them out of his pocket while the audience waited, pressed two white squares out from their little slab of foil, and slipped them into his mouth. He returned the rest of the gum to his pocket and picked up *Enter Here*, flipping through the thin book.

Keith had his arm around Pixie and kissed her again. "Pixie love," he said again.

"Shut up, Keith," she said.

He dropped his arm from her waist, "Boot ye gote me eart, love," he said.

Pixie could see Maddy, feather dress, up near the stage holding her cell phone out for a picture. She couldn't tell if she was taking the picture of the poet or herself. Hobbs placed a knuckle to his lips and began:

"the day that came like a fast-ball,
sore down at my throat when I saw you approach.
Your fist, I thought, might hurl me toward
infinity, had I not. . . ."

James Comenzo and The Trip Tickets began to take the stage while Hobbs read his final poem. They placed guitars on stands and silently bent down to connect electric pulses, flip switches, run a hand over quiet frets. Hobbs had become more animated as he read, and opened fire one last time on the audience, drawing his shoulders back and then heaving them forward, hunched toward the mike, spewing out the last line as a string of exhaled words collected in one long inhaled breath. The words hurried over the darkened room and settled empty on the ignorant heads. Pixie scanned the crowd. Smart phones. Stupid people. Alexander Pope wrote *An Essay on Man* and it felt like Hobbs and Pope were colliding here in a hellhole called Starlights. The contemporary world was quite a thing. What would Pixie have been like if she'd lived when Alexander Pope was writing poems? God, what would she have been addicted to in 1710? She would have found something. Hobbs wrapped up with a double-tiered cough and a quick nod of thanks.

Pixie and Keith sat in a small booth. Keith cupped an empty wine glass between his hands. He flicked the glass with his finger and leaned toward it, putting an ear to the rim. "It's there," he said, referring to the effect of his finger flicking the glass. "It's not even a noise so much—a slight . . . a slight vibration. Like a doggy whistle."

An electric whine from a poorly supervised mike arched into the room. There was a lot of noise after Hobbs left the stage.

"I hate the way people read poetry," Pixie said, and then, referring to the wine glass, "It's too loud in here. You can't *hear* anything."

"That's my point. I *feel* it." Keith reached across the small table and flicked a glass of wine Pixie had decided she would only take a few sips of. "It's the small things that have the biggest effect." He flicked her glass again and took her hand in his, pressing it to the glass. "Especially when there's a lot of noise."

She pulled her hand away. "Stop it."

The small band warmed up, walking toward each other and strumming and then backing away again after new adjustments. Pixie knew little about the band. A girl pulled three cowbells from behind a speaker and set them on the edge of the stage. The crowd had dispersed a little, and the remaining people seemed to anticipate the music as they looked up at the commotion of instruments. Keith had grown sober.

"You ever heard of Blue Jack?" Keith said.

"Blue Jack sounds like a race horse."

"It's a drug."

"It sounds like a racehorse. If it's a drug, I guess that's the point."

"It's a drug."

"A racy drug. A *fast* drug," Pixie said, rolling her eyes.

"It was intended as an extended pain reliever/motivation increaser. Sort of a cross between OxyContin and Zoloft. You get it after hospital in the UK, like after you get your appendix out. It's awesome. It lasts a week. It stays in your system for a week. The idea is that it shouldn't have the same addictive qualities as just a narcotic. The time-release capsule regulates the amount that goes into your system. The pain reliever does its thing first and then gives way to the antidepressant—they overlap. And then the antidepressant sets you gently back down where you started before the operation. They give it to you at hospital—you don't go home with a prescription or anything."

"And they call it Blue Jack?"

"It's Blue Jack on the street."

"Yes. Good." Pixie finished her glass of wine. The Xanax was almost completely out of her system by now and she was ready to bite the buttons off of her own sweater. Kill the thought. Rip the cords from the The Trip Ticket's guitars and use them to strangle anyone who says the word *sweet.* "This is what I need—another drug to add to the *ple-thor-a* of them already crowding my medicine cabinet—or my bucket. I don't have a medicine cabinet."

"That's just it—it doesn't make you want more. It's like a narcotic with built-in self-control. You're Samson with long hair." Keith reached into his front pocket and pulled out a baggie, unwrapped a few small Tylenol-looking capsules.

"Fucking hell, Keith. I don't need that shit."

"No, Pix, it's not like that. It's like the opposite of that. It makes you sharp and then you're fine. You can sleep, you can eat, you can wake up. . . . I took it and read *Swann's Way* and remembered everything for my Proust class."

James Comenzo and The Trip Tickets began a quiet riff. The girl with the cowbells wore a purple crêpe dress with gold plastic coins sewn onto the hem and was leaning down, handing out wooden instruments to eager fans in the front row. Her dress wafted into the small crowd and then receded. She had a ponytail and her hair was starting to gray.

"I've been using *Time Regained* to go to sleep," Pixie said. "It's better than Ambien. It sits on my bedside table. My bedside crate. I don't have a bedside table." She watched as three girls next to the stage took instruments and bent over laughing. They held them up to each other and rattled them. "I'm sick of the word 'rhetoric.'"

"I remembered *everything*, Pixie."

"Do you ever read drugstore shit? Books with titles like *The Manturian Principle* or *The Avenger's Folly*?"

"On a flight home I read a biography of Dolly Parton. A thick wad of newsprint. I enjoyed it *immensely*." Keith smiled widely.

"You're an asshole."

16.

Owen and Noel: a canticle

There was this thing that Owen had realized a year ago when he and Noel were once again in the process of breaking up. They always broke up when the weather had grown monotonous. He wouldn't have realized this except that one night as he was trying to fall asleep, it occurred to him that every time they gave way to whatever it was that still attracted them to each other and kissed, or held hands, suddenly *aware*, the weather had changed. And not changed in an incremental way, but in a cold front moving in, snowstorm, flash flood, heat wave kind of way. He hadn't yet figured out why. Perhaps it was because during these times they happened to spend time together: flash floods tending to require calls to friends, heat waves trips to the lake, snowstorms, of course, because people get bored inside with the streets not cleared yet and need a place to go, a place they can head off toward, pulling on boots, scarves, ski jackets, and high-step through the snow drifts toward some kind of adventure.

They were still just kids. All of them. And stupid, really. Wisdom was knowing how stupid you are, Owen thought. But then he didn't feel stupid. Not most of the time, and if he thought about it too much, it became a circular thing that kept him awake another hour, at least. He liked Gordon, honestly, and it made him feel inferior that he wasn't a malcontent about it the way Noel seemed to be about Columbia. It had intimidated him at first, her getting into Columbia and then actually going there—not just the school but New York City. You had to be smart to live there. Of course this wasn't true, but it was true in the way that people with French or British accents are smarter. Sometimes he felt like such a young bastard, like all the other guys his age, it was inevitable. If you were a dude in your early twenties, you were a bastard. All you ever thought about was girls, and you were a bastard.

Everyone had said he should apply to Juilliard, he would get in for sure, probably a scholarship. But Juilliard seemed so wrong. For him anyway. It was for jazz musicians, not folk. And the *name*—when people asked him where he went to college he would have had to say *Juilliard*, like some sort of bastard, and he wasn't willing to do that. He wasn't willing to do a lot of things, really, things he could possibly fail at. He'd gone to Juilliard's website enough times, four clicks to get to the application requirements, quite a long process, and it really was possible he could have gotten in. But what if he didn't? He knew this about himself—that he was afraid of stuff he could fail at. Going to Gordon was more than safe, and not dating, not falling in love, with Noel was safe. He was safe now in his dorm room with a weak flurry of snow out his window, Brad, his roommate, at lacrosse practice, and two papers to write that would not only be easy, but almost fun. The papers were for English Lit and psychology. He went to his desk and got his laptop. He pushed a few pillows up on the headboard of his bed, leaned back, opened up the computer, and typed *Influences of the Symbolist Movement in The Waste Land.* This, he realized and almost rolled his eyes, was a boring title. He would go back and change it, but then sometimes boring was good.

When her mother left, Noel felt unusually sad. Sometimes she wondered if Pixie, with her twisted mess of a life, tracked in some sort of hate to the apartment. Like it could get stuck to your shoe. She'd never had so much contempt for someone and yet also attraction. She was curious. After her mother left, she had gone into Pixie's room and looked around, refraining from opening a drawer or fingering through a stack of papers on her bed, but just barely. It was idiotic that she'd even thought of it, of going into her room.

The day was flat. One class that was not a challenge or of any interest to her, and then just a short review of a classmate's paper. Maybe that would be interesting. She could tell when another student was trying too hard, and it drove her nuts. Owen would understand that, not that he would never try too hard himself, but he would own up to it at least. Two nights ago, while her mother was still here, she'd had a dream about him that was still in her head even though she kept trying to disregard it. It was so weird because Jason was there, probably because he was always there in real life, like an itch or something. She wanted to like Jason, and she kind of did, more so if she was around him, which didn't make sense either. It was the opposite with Owen. When he was far away she could feel an intense physical attraction to him.

In the dream he was walking down the street to the bridge, and there was a rope that hung out over the water and the rope was tied to a rock in the water (obviously an image influenced by her mother's stuff), but the rope could swing even though it was tied to the rock. Jason was in the periphery (of course), standing on another rock somewhere, but she couldn't really see him. Owen was like this, god, what the heck, *man*, and she felt her insides turning crazy because she wanted him to touch her. He was going to take care of her, or was taking care of her. Like a dad would, but he was most certainly not a dad, and he made her feel so beautiful. The bridge was all silvery from rain. What the hell was the matter with her? Why would she have a dream like that? She decided to call him. He answered, and he seemed happy she called.

"Hey, what's up?"

"Nothing really, just felt like calling. I'm bored. What are you doing?"

"Two papers today. I have the title for the first one. It's an excellent title, but it's dull. I don't know if I would ever want to read the paper. Nah, I wouldn't read it."

"Which is?"

"*Influences of the Symbolist Movement in The Waste Land.*"

"Ha, yeah, that's bad."

"I'm staring at it now. I've been staring at it for five minutes."

"If you just start writing, it will go away and you'll write and then you'll go back to it and come up with something better."

"Think so?"

"Yes, absolutely. I had a dream about you."

"I like that."

"Why?"

"Uh, it's a guy thing. We're bastards. Every one of us."

"It wasn't that kind of dream."

"Shit, that sucks."

"It was in Trinity at the bridge. Jason was there too."

"Of course he was."

"Ha ha, that's what I thought. Not in the dream, but after."

"So, was I looking pretty good?"

"Actually. . . ."

There was a silence. "Noel," Owen hesitated, "so it was that kind of dream?"

"No, I told you, it wasn't."

"Sorry."

"Can you just pay attention?" Noel said.

"Sorry. Go ahead."

Noel suddenly felt foolish for bringing it up. "I don't know, you were going to take care of something." She found herself stopping short of saying "me." *You were going to take care of me.*

"What was it? What was I going to do?"

"I don't know, I never found out. The dream ended. Anyway, I don't even know why I told you. I guess because I'm bored. You should go back to your paper."

"Yeah, I guess so. You should ask your dad what it means . . . That's a joke."

"I know it's a joke." A stupid joke, she thought to herself. "Okay, well, go write. Good luck." They hung up.

17.

Margie: sex by number

Margie was working on holding back emotions that seemed to press from the base of her neck forward, like a fat hand or a surge of adrenaline that was somehow off and felt more like a mucusy confusion than energy. She was aware—because Nick had mentioned it to her—that her feelings tended to show up on her face quickly, sometimes before she even acknowledged them.

Sometimes when she thought of her half-hearted dip in the lake, she was not upset. Her spasms of irrational, possibly menstruation-induced folly seemed years away. She worked her newest project like a construction worker guiding beams on a skyscraper, ignorant of the height at which she performed and the depth to which she could fall. Her canvas covered half the wall. She had arranged a step system in front of the painting—chairs of different sizes, two step stools, a stepladder. She carried her wood palette with her, thumb tucked through the hole like some early Paris artist. The darker tone of the wood provided contrast for the oils. Margie couldn't keep up with her thoughts. There were the colors on her palette and then there were the anticipated colors that appeared on the canvas when placed together. Skin was *everything*. Like prisms, it carried every living color, it seemed to her. She stepped back from the canvas and took one more long look.

She kept the original ceiling light that she had hesitantly sketched in with a wash, but you couldn't tell what it was anymore. She remembered Nick standing at the door as she painted it. She was looking into the angled mirror, and Nick had been there in the mirror too, watching her. She had ignored him as she painted the light, his presence more auditory than anything else as she focused on the shades and tones of the ugly angled thing hanging from the ceiling. It was a spider, and it sparkled like eyes were in the legs.

The painting had evolved into skin. And it was about color. There were turns and curves and horizontals and diagonals, but they were more the effect of color than line. The shapes were either irrelevant or essential, she didn't know yet. There were suggestions of body parts. No penises because that was just stupid. All the penises in art these days drove her nuts. It was like artists kept going back to the most conscious, surface images instead of things that needed to be revealed in a new way. Half the population is already spending about half of every day thinking about penises in all their various forms. Such a cheap way to draw attention. So dull and average. Margie stared at the canvas. As soon as she felt like a shape was taking the form of something, anything, she worked at decreasing the suggestion, moving depth and lines into apathetic contours that disclosed nothing. This was very hard to do and it made her clench her jaw as she poked around with the brush, beating out the definition of a line or increasing depth with cerulean blue buried deep within muddy color until it was as close to black as she could get it. The only certain thing in the painting was where the light source was. Eleven o'clock from behind her. Its cast was clear even if what it fell on was not.

When Etta visited, she hadn't commented on any of Margie's oil portraits; her attention was on the figure drawings tacked to the wall and then also on the photo of Chris Burden. Margie couldn't help but feel as though she had somehow contaminated her. There was an innocence. She had eventually walked to the large painting, stood an arm's length away and tilted her head to the right. Later, Etta called Margie to ask about painting classes. They would meet at the Art Center next week, in the afternoon before the evening sessions began. Nick had been up to the attic once more after that first time when she had just begun the painting, and he seemed pleased. He had nodded and then taken a few more steps back, folded his arms, and kept nodding. He took a picture with his phone. She didn't want it to matter what he thought, and when she worked she always imagined that it didn't, owning whatever it was she was working on, going so far as to take a brush to an unexpected place where it could feel a little bit like rebellion.

Before the end of the day when she had gone in the lake, Nick had made a point of apologizing for his display of anger when she was in the bath. His anger, he told her while leaning forward in the living room chair, elbows on his knees, fingers in a knot above the carpet, was justified, but not his display. *I should not have thrown the toothbrush.* He didn't throw the toothbrush, Margie remembered, he had swiped it off the counter, but she didn't bother to make the correction. Nick had leaned back again in his chair and contemplated her. And then he had gone to her on the couch and kissed her head like a baby. It felt mechanical and contrived.

Margie moved a bucket of gesso to the side and carefully climbed halfway up the stepladder. Her balance was off, and she pressed a palm against a blank part of the canvas to steady herself. She slowly straightened up and stared at the section in front of her. As much as the work was about color, she did not—she definitely did not—want to allow the colors to remain isolated only to be integrated when standing back a bit and perhaps even squinting. Way too stylized. There would be a lot of blending, and this was even harder in light of her desire to keep the shapes ambiguous. The front door closed downstairs. Margie could feel her muscles tightening. She tried to stretch one of her arms by crossing it in front of her and holding it with her other hand. As she did this, her brush hit the canvas, taking out a carefully blended area that she had worked on that morning. She quickly leaned back, away from the painting to spare any more damage, lost her balance, and fell off of the stepladder. Her elbows hit the floor and her hip banged into the legs of her largest easel, causing it to slide a few inches and her hip to sting with sudden pain.

She lay there and stared at the ceiling, her brush still in her hand. Downstairs, voices rose and fell. Someone laughed. She threw the brush at the painting. The brush hit the wall, barely grazing the canvas. She didn't even have enough strength to hit the fucking canvas.

WHEN NICK ATE BROCCOLI he left the stems untouched. He picked each piece up with his fork and turned it as it entered his mouth, as though a certain spiral motion was key to getting at the important part of the vegetable.

"The Carlinos are on vacation—in Mexico," he said. "They won't be around for a month."

Margie stared at her own food. "Halleluiah?"

"Halleluiah. But we'll have some work—I'm sure—when they return."

"*If* they return," Margie said. "Maybe he'll finally crack."

"He won't. He's passive-aggressive but he's got a good heart."

"I'm mean," Margie said. She moved her food around with her fork. "I'm not very nice, am I?"

"No one's truly nice. Especially if they're not feeling well."

"Well . . . that's very nice of you, I guess, . . . to say. Trying to make me feel better."

They ate their dinner.

"I love you, Margie, you know that, right?

"Yes, of course. I know that."

Margie preferred to shower in the evenings, getting the paint off of her hands and sometimes face and climbing into bed clean—Nick faithfully changed the sheets every two weeks. The steamy mirror above the sink was just a haze of herself, and she appreciated the symbolic implications for a moment before taking a towel and swiping a broad arc of clarity across the surface. There was something disturbing about seeing herself naked in the mirror. A pattern of folds. Not that she was overweight—she wasn't—in fact it was perhaps just that: not enough filler to keep things propped up. Her medium-sized breasts sagged down and out, leaving the slight rumple of her stomach muscles beneath lengthy stretch marks left over from her one pregnancy, to carry the eye down to a crotch that, give or take a little trim, could act as husky hippy girl or effete inamorata. It was a body meant for the self-portrait—the intimations of the physical providing salt and oil for the life beneath. It was a paint-by-number body. She could hang herself on a wall of the Metropolitan and hold her own.

Margie pulled on her robe, tied it, and ran a hand through her wet hair. Nick was already in bed. He was lying on top of the covers reading a magazine. Margie went to him in her robe, naked underneath. She stood next to the bed and handed him one end of the terrycloth sash. She turned off the light. She could do this.

"I'm not really sure that I will be able to look. I was praying for a female."

"You won't have any problem," Margie said to Etta. "Maybe at first, but then you'll just be drawing him."

The man dropped his robe and stepped up on a platform covered in a purple sheet. He looked to Margie for direction. "Something simple," she said. "Stand, maybe just place one hand on your hip." She imitated a pose for him.

They were in the back room of the Trinity Art Center. There were two other women there with easels. One had a box of pastel pieces, and the other—a woman wearing a pink scarf over what likely was a bald head—used a china pencil. She kept pausing and unwrapping the tip. She dropped the curly bits of paper at the foot of her easel.

Etta had yet to look up. She rearranged her charcoal and sharpened a pencil. She clumsily flipped over to a new sheet of newsprint, the previous one having not been touched. Margie stood next to her, pointed at the model, and drew an invisible line in the air from his shoulders down to his ankles. "Here," she said, encouraging Etta to look up, "this is a simple line. Start here and pull it down. Use your shoulder. Give yourself a focal point."

Etta took her pencil and hesitantly drew a curved line down the left side of the newsprint. She drew a circle for the head and then began to draw in the model's feet; focused, intense, she drew one foot—five toes, began the other one. "Okay," Margie said, "let's leave this page." She reached over and flipped the paper to a new one. Etta stood with her pencil waiting for directions. "I want you to draw the entire figure in thirty seconds. I'll tell you when to stop."

"Are you kidding?"

"Not at all." Margie looked at the clock above the door. "Okay, begin."

Etta drew.

THANKSGIVING BEGAN TO FILL EMPTY corners of Trinity. A precursor to Christmas, the holiday helped to initiate the rearranging that became so crucial those weeks before December, when clothing and food and toys and decorations would need extra space and swags of faux-pine garland would dipå from corner to corner of doorways and counters and baking isles, filling the helplessly cold and blank outdoors with the internal substitution of greens, reds, and golds.

Center Bank had turkey heads made out of construction paper lining the large window on Maple Avenue. Each turkey represented an employee. The employee's name was written in red crayon. Silence in the town extended from hill to hill, the *fishurr . . . fishurrr . . .* of Route 84 audible only at the peak of Fifth Street, where Mary Sommerfeld's house helped to define the edge of Trinity with a privacy fence and a long line of azalea bushes at the outer edge of her two acres of property. Homes kept their warmth to themselves, boilers feeding heat into kitchens and living rooms like hot breath into cupped hands, a bit of warmth seeping out at the windowsills like heat out of the knuckles.

The temperatures grew increasingly cold and helped to ease the gossip. While phone calls still made their rounds, the cold weather was a natural social barricade that prevented those less acquainted with each other from sharing tits or tats. Mary Sommerfeld remained in her home at the top of Fifth, silently exercising her ruminations into slander. Margie provided enough of a topic to last a year. It was like a year of provisions, food stored in silos to get through the winter. She had not seen Margie Nethercott for weeks, and Margie Nethercott, it appeared, was becoming a shut-in and Etta of all people was trying to help, to minister to her, but it looked like it was *Etta* who was being ministered to more than anything . . . etc., etc., etc., etc. She sat at her small kitchen table with her yellow wall phone that she had replaced in the nineties. She called whoever she thought might be interested; she went to her overheated living room with the window that looked out over the town and perused her magazines: *Oprah*, *Martha Stewart*, *Country Living*.

The college kids would arrive—Tyler and Owen and Noel Nethercott and the twin Freeman girls who lived on the other side of the river in a small house with an awkward addition, and a handful of others who had somehow remained latent through high school and ducked out without fanfare to little state schools and trade schools—soon for Thanksgiving break. The younger children, the kindergarteners and grade-schoolers, peppered the mornings with their high-pitched voices in the cold air as they waited on corners for school buses. The lake and then the river began to ice over—the Abenaki maintaining scabby holes in solid ice, the fast-moving water that rushed up visible for a moment and then secreted down again beneath frosty rime. With an ear trained to the river, if you were close enough, it was possible to catch the sound of the water flowing beneath the ice, a soft and constant sound of movement compared to the *fishurr . . . fishurrr . . .* of Route 84. The school buses came and gathered the children, and then there was silence.

18.

Pixie: bleed

If Pixie came home with Noel, Thanksgiving break would take a completely different form. Miriam, no doubt, would love Pixie and find gigantic similarities between them. They could get their tongues pierced or share Miriam's stash of *Prom Weed*, as she called the crystal flute glass that she kept on her dresser, her memento of Senior Prom, hash mixed with who knew what else. Noel was sure that Miriam's taste in music would appeal to Pixie and prompt her toward even greater feats of calculated rebellion. Andrew Bird, The Cribs, The Blakes, The Black Lips. Harder bands always use the definite article. The lead singer of The Black Lips came on stage naked and ate credit cards. He fell into mosh pits naked, genitals at a swing, and people spread out rather than caught him, afraid to touch his junk. Bruised and battered, he ate more credit cards. Oh, the randomness. Miriam and Pixie could touch the bare tips of each other's fingers peeking out from their open finger gloves, stick out their pierced tongues, and scream for more music. Soul Soul Sisters.

Noel rented a car. Pixie had not been planning on going home. She had no plans, which appeared to bother her little. When Noel invited her to come home with her, she said, “Sure,” without hesitancy but with a tone of expected boredom, and Noel, surprised and unsettled, said, “Great” and “It will be great to have you, so glad you’re coming.” And whatnot. Noel packed as light as she could, two sweaters and a pair of jeans. She still had things in her closet at home. Her boots were there, stacked on a box of half-used yarn from her knitting days. The car was a Rent-a-Lemon or something and had an armrest that was ripped up in the middle as though it had been searched via pocketknife for dope. Stains and cigarette holes were like dark constellations, gathered in clumps across the interior in a faux-leather galaxy.

In the car, Beyoncé threw syllables at them, *all the sin gle la dies / all the single ladies. . . .*

“Sorry,” Noel said, “I guess it’s Z100. There’s just a radio.”

“I love Beyoncé.”

Noel laughed.

“I’m serious,” Pixie said flatly. She tilted her head back against the headrest and closed her eyes.

THEY WERE QUIET MOST OF THE TRIP. When they hit Route 17, Pixie opened up the glove compartment and bent forward looking for something.

“You got a fuse or two in here for me?” she said.

“A fuse?”

“A cigarette. I could use a little friend—you know, wow, but then right, I’m quitting. I keep forgetting. I’m addicted to something I don’t even like. It goes with my . . . ” she paused, “personality. . . . I could take bites out of the seat cushions. All I’ve had is half a Xany this morning." Pixie leaned her head back again. "It's not helping. When I breathe it feels like a lot of little breaths, like when you swim too long and have chlorine in your lungs."

"That's from chlorine? I always wondered. . . . Pixie, do you seriously—are you gonna be okay?"

"I'm not that bad. I sound like I'm on heroin."

Noel looked in the rearview mirror and signaled to change lanes. They passed a large truck that said *Richard & Son.*

"*Rrrgh, frigging shit,*" Pixie made a growling sound, clenched her fists, and pounded the dashboard once, but she was holding back.

"What is it, just the Xanax?"

"*Rrhhrrrgggg,* everything. In the city I walk. A lot. Big steps. This way there's a progress."

"Maybe you *should* smoke. . . . They'll have a cure for cancer by the time it matters."

"You know it's more than the Xanax, all the medicine cabinet shit. Oxy, oxy, oxy, toxins. I could smoke a fucking pine tree right now. I thought this would be good, this trip. I see you as very holistic." She looked over at Noel. "I was surprised when you weren't a vegetarian. Oh, *fucking crap,* my teeth feel all tingly and shit like they do when I'm in an elevator."

"I can pull over. . . ."

"No," Pixie lifted her butt off the seat and dug into her front pocket. She pulled something tiny out between her finger and thumb. "It's less than half a Xanax. I've been saving it." She put it in her mouth and made a grimace, trying to move it further to the back of her tongue. "Something that's been so good to me and it tastes like I'm licking a fucking hubcap."

"A cigarette maybe would be the lesser of two evils. . . ."

"I don't like to fail, although I'm experienced at it."

Noel switched lanes again and signaled to exit. "Actually, we're not that far." She looked over at Pixie. "We'll keep you busy, okay? We'll walk and everything, like you do in the city. And, you know, my dad's a shrink, he's got connections . . . ," she said, half serious.

"I'm fine. I'm just complaining. This isn't a huge thing or anything. That hubcap tasted good though." Pixie rested her head back again and looked out the window. "I can't believe you live here. It's like Rivendale."

Silence.

"*Lord of the Rings*," Pixie said.

"I know."

They drove ten miles longer on Route 86, made their way down Maple, and turned right.

When they got out of the car, Pixie dug down in her other pocket in the unlikely chance she'd find more Xanax and felt something else. She pulled it out and looked at it carefully. It was the blue jack pill Keith had given her.

"Fuck," she said.

"What?"

"I don't know, just . . . *fuck*." She shoved the pill back into her pocket. *Fuck*, she repeated to herself.

THAT NIGHT, PIXIE SAT ON THE COLD FLOOR of the guestroom in a sweatshirt and leggings. The tall windows bothered her, even with the shades drawn, so she sat down under the windowsill, facing the opposite direction. There was a streak of light from a streetlight that poked through one side of the shade where it failed to block the window. It had begun to snow . . . thin, wispy snow that didn't stick. She could feel a waft of cold air coming through the glass and it felt good.

Sleep was not an issue, meaning that it wouldn't happen so there was no point in trying or hoping for it. She hadn't even bothered to pull down the covers on the bed. The bedspread was ivory-colored and had a hem of tassels that hung a few inches above the floor. She could make out a fist-sized dust bunny. A perfect home with a perfect little ball of dirt.

She began to feel cold and hugged legs with her arms.

She ran her hands up under the sleeves of her sweatshirt, and the tips of her fingers touched her scars. Sometimes she allowed herself the usual pattern of thought: a line, a bump, a peeling away of a scab, scratch, and then something sharp and precise. The best ones were when she went deep enough with the razor to cause the skin to actually split, not just make a tiny red line of blood. She hadn't brought any razors, intentionally. The deeper the cut, the wider the skin would separate, and then sometimes you could see fat. Just a little bit. She would pinch the wound together and then release, so that it would pull apart. She kept butterfly bandages for when she did this. It was the blood that was the relief, it had to be because if it didn't bleed, she was disappointed.

It was fucking cold. Pixie stood up and pulled off the bedspread and wrapped it around herself. She sat on the bed and looked at the outline of light where the shade didn't quite cover the window. Her jeans were lying on a stuffed chair in the corner of the room. She got them and sat down again, letting the bedspread fall from her shoulders. She patted the pockets and then reached into them looking for the pill in the tiny plastic bag. She pulled it out and held it up in the dim light. It was a capsule, so she knew she could snort it, or better, cook it. She tucked the pill back into the pocket of her jeans.

There was a deep whir from the electric clock next to the bed when the numbers changed. It was an old-fashioned one with physical numbers that flipped, something like they had at Urban Outfitters.

She leaned back on the pillow and shut her eyes, hugging the jeans to her chest.

THANKSGIVING FELT UNDERDEVELOPED in the Nethercott house compared to when Pixie had been to Thanksgiving in Camden. She'd been to her aunt's twice, and remembered boxes of pies stacked on the microwave and casseroles. There was a turkey too. The dining room was just for the alcohol. A large cooler of beer. Vodka, whiskey, and rum, plus sodas on the dining-room table. She had mixed her first drink when she was around eleven, there in the dining room, and her dad's friends had laughed as she poured. When she took a sip, it hurt, and her eyes watered, but her dad laughed and everyone was watching so she took another drink only this time bigger. She had to go to the bathroom to pour it down the drain, but she still remembers the initial spin she felt, like there was a heavy ball in her head that rolled like a barrel on a ship every time she tilted her head.

Nick was in charge of the turkey and took great care in pressing stuffing into the cavity and tying it with string. He rinsed his hands and then dried them on a towel and opened the oven door. Noel and Pixie sat at the kitchen table dipping pretzel sticks into honey mustard sauce.

"It's not a big bird. It should be ready by three," he said, slipping the roasting pan into the oven.

"Do you remember when you cooked it upside down and it ended up tasting really good?" Noel said, while she chewed a pretzel.

"I remember it always tasting really good. . . . "

"No, you put it in upside down and it ended up tasting even better. You don't remember that?"

"Vaguely," Nick said.

"Yeah, it looked really gross, but it tasted good."

"Is mom up yet?" Nick said.

"Mm-hmm, I heard her."

Pixie took a tiny bite off the end of a pretzel. "What's the deal with men and meat?" she half whispered to herself.

Margie came into the kitchen dressed for the day. She wore a gray turtleneck and had her hair pulled back and twisted into a clip. She went to the cabinet over the cooktop and pulled out two prescription bottles. She tried to open one, pressing down on the cap with her palm, gave up, and handed it to Nick, who quickly opened it and handed it back.

Noel glanced at Pixie.

"I'm glad you could come up with Noel, Pixie," Margie said after she had taken her pills.

"Yeah, no," Pixie said, "I didn't really have anything anyway." She had circles under her eyes.

"Where's your family from?" Nick said.

"My dad. He's from New Brunswick."

"Does he have plans?"

"I don't know."

"He should have come up too," Margie said.

Pixie laughed as she stuck her pretzel in the mustard sauce again.

Noel straightened her fork next to her plate. Pixie sat across from her and her mom was to her left. Pixie kept taking sips of wine and then setting the glass down and then sitting back in her chair as though it hadn't occurred to her to actually eat the food on her plate. Margie rearranged her cloth napkin on her lap. She held it up and folded it neatly and then placed it carefully back on her lap. Her mother was still pretty in a Meryl Streep sort of way. Margie spooned two small servings of cranberry sauce onto her plate.

"The last time I was in New Jersey was when Noel was in fifth grade. There was a field trip," Margie said, pushing the cranberries away from the other food. She wanted to go back to bed; everything made her tired and she'd been napping daily, sometimes twice. Nick was leaning forward, looking for a piece of dark meat on the serving platter. The way his shirtsleeves were pushed above his elbows made her want to sleep even more. He was all about work.

"Oh, yeah, the Statue of Liberty, and then Ellis Island, of course," Noel said. "I actually think about Ellis Island a lot, it made an impression on me for some reason. It was a foggy day, the towers were still there—you could see them through the fog. Weird, just the tops of them."

"You wrote a report," Margie said. "It was about how you couldn't find 'Nethercott' on the immigrant wall."

Noel got up and went into the kitchen and came out with a basket. "You forgot the rolls, Mom." She set them on the table. "So did you have the obligatory Ellis Island field trip?" she asked Pixie.

Pixie straightened up in her chair and reached for her wine glass again. "Yeah. My dad, my dad was . . . ," she took a drink of wine, "um, working near there when we went. Kind of ironic."

"How so?" Nick said.

"I didn't understand irony yet, I mean I felt it, but I didn't know that's what it was."

"How do you *feel* irony?" Noel said.

"I don't know."

"How was it ironic?" Nick said.

"The pictures." Pixie finished her glass of wine and looked around as though for more. "All of those old photographs with the dirty children and shit and lost mothers sitting on their trunks of stuff." Noel got up and went into the kitchen, half rolling her eyes. Irony's not a feeling. She came out with the wine bottle. Pixie continued, "It was one of those things that happens when you're a kid. I thought I would find myself in the pictures." She fingered a small ring in her bottom lip. "My dad was working nearby so that added to everything."

"Ellis Island is supposed to help people feel connected, help them understand where they came from, things like that," Nick said.

"Right." Pixie shrugged.

Noel filled Pixie's glass with more wine before sitting back down.

After dinner Nick made a fire in the living room. Pixie gulped down what was left of two glasses of wine sitting on the kitchen counter. She went to the bathroom, put the seat down on the toilet, and sat down. There was a medicine cabinet. She stood up and opened it and began to look through. Advil, Excedrin, floss, and a razor . . . the plastic disposable kind. Pink.

Pixie moved the razor over the scars of her arm as though shaving. The blades were embedded in the plastic and she couldn't get them out. She tried to find an edge and moved the razor from side to side. It made a few nicks but that was all. She went back to the cabinet and found some nail clippers, sat down, and went to work on her arm, trying to drag a deep line into her skin. The bathroom was small and had a drop ceiling. Eventually, the blood came but it was minor and pathetic. She dug harder. Someone turned on music, Brahms, *A German Requiem*, and it made her laugh. "Ha," she said out loud, and tilted her head back as though to laugh louder. She thought about waiting to really go at the cut—until the music got to that part where it eases up and kind of takes your hand. Of all of the times she had done this, this time was the most visible to herself. She had never been so determined to stop, and here she was never so fully engaged. Once again, with blood. She was able to get a decent amount coming out of the cut. She took two fingers and swiped at the wound, getting as much blood on them as possible, held her hand up, and watched the blood from her fingers drip thinly into the creases between her thumb and palm. She wadded up some toilet paper and held it to her arm, watching it spread into the tissue. She would need one of her Band-Aids.

When Pixie reached the top of the stairs, still holding the toilet paper to her arm, Margie was standing at an open linen closet looking for something. They saw each other and were startled. Margie glanced down at Pixie's arm. Pixie went into the guestroom and shut the door.

19.

Owen and Pixie: hanging trees and ice without borders

Owen reached around his back and pulled his guitar strap tight over his shoulder. He ran through the blues scale, b3, b5, b7. . . .

The group sat in Jason Vanderwaal's half-finished walkout basement. Two knotty pine walls had a light coat of white paint on them and the knotholes showed through like oblong vertical coffee rings. The boiler furnace was in one corner and blasted on with a click and a whir every ten minutes or so. The door to the outside was fit into a cement block wall that had white powder coating the base where it met the floor and it looked diseased. Pixie sat on an enormous beige couch with curved arms and a tear across the seat cushion. She fingered the rip, pulling the edge up and then pressing it back down. It was snowing hard outside. They could see it coming down through the window of the basement door.

"Tell me what you think," Owen said. "It's from a scene in *Passport* where they have this group of people from the nursing home sitting with all these high school kids at dinner. I mean, it's not from the movie itself. It's the scene—it made me think of the song. I watched the movie and then came up with the lyrics. I wanna know what you guys think. *Passport*'s incredible if you haven't seen it. It's directed by Tim Wisneski. He has this habit of sucking butterscotch candy while he directs. He just folds his hands and stops and thinks for a long time and everyone just waits for him to stop sucking his candy and tell them something. I read about it in *Rolling Stone*. Very, very low budget and all that. I read the article."

"The movie probably smells like butterscotch," Miriam said. "When he watches it, I mean. It probably smells like butterscotch to him. I hate that smell."

"There *is* something about smell," Noel said. "But yeah, that's pretty weird, Miriam. You're just weird."

"So, Owen, go for it." Jason looked bored and was leaning back against the base of the couch next to where Pixie sat pulling at the cushion.

Owen said, "The scene in *Passport*, with old people and kids all stuck together eating dinner. . . ."

Miriam was folding a piece of paper into a tiny square and cutting shapes into it with a pair of dull lefty scissors with padded rubber handles. White triangles fell to her lap. "So now we are inspired by movies not life. Movies inspire us, life does not."

"*Passport*'s a good movie," Pixie said, still fiddling with the rip. Her sweater sleeve was pulled almost completely over her hand so that the rip on the couch was hidden beneath the cuff.

"Our *lives* are just movies now," Noel said dramatically and looked at Miriam. "I haven't seen the movie."

Pixie looked at her. "You should." She looked tired. Her eyelids were heavy.

Jocelyn held a remote and was flipping through the muted channels of a small TV in the corner of the basement. "Just sing the damn song, Owen," she said, pausing on a scene of a man filmed inside a robotic alligator. The man looked fearful. The camera was inside the alligator and was angled toward the front of the contraption so that it was possible to see out through a slit in what looked like a cardboard mouth. There was a real alligator three yards away. It raised its head up to crest the water, nostrils gleaming. Jocelyn had gotten her hair highlighted before she returned home and she played with it now, tucking a bundle of it behind an ear and then smoothing her hand down to the ends as though the touch of her hand would familiarize herself with the color change.

Owen looked down and began with a few chords.

"*I saw the white spot on your back. . . .*" He strayed from the pitch slightly—hitting each note twice within each word, his voice wavering effectively in the middle. It was a simple song, but it swelled beneath him. It lasted for a little while, not quite long enough, and then it was over.

When he finished singing they were all looking at him. He glanced down again at the frets and added a small voiced, "*hhmmmnnn . . .*" and the song ended.

"Fuck." Pixie said, abandoning her tugging on the arm of the chair.

"That was beautiful," Noel said. "I might cry." She reached out and touched Owen's knee. He nodded, smiling. Miriam unfolded her piece of paper and held up the snowflake. She handed it to him as a gift.

THE SNOW KEPT FALLING. Large wet flakes stuck to objects. Sticks received an inch or two hedge of powder like thin slices of cake. There were objects that looked odd with the buildup of snow, a quiet submission of form—thin iron railings, fence posts, an upside-down ceramic planter next to Jason's back door. The group made their way down the street, a sloppy collection of weather-resistant attire parceled out among them. Noel wore Jason's father's hunting cap, an orange thing with a camouflage rim. Pixie had declined a pair of boots with fur trim. She half walked and half slid in her little rubber Rocket Dog shoes on the steep road, involuntarily jerking one arm or the other out to keep her balance.

The muffling effect of the snow brought a new intensity to Trinity. Distractions were minimized and a few coughs by Miriam sounded as though they had come down from the gray sky with the snow. The group's heightened sensitivity to sight, smell, and sound included an unusual responsiveness to each other—the way sexiness will sometimes float around a room. Noel looked over at Owen, who was looking at his feet as he slid a few yards and then back into a hesitant jog. Owen looked up as though he had felt her gaze, and they held each other's eyes for a moment. Owen smiled at her. Pixie continued sliding and tiny-stepping her way down the hill ahead of everyone, her rubber shoes plowing the fresh film of snow into a minor wake. She reached down into her pocket and touched the plastic baggie with the tiny bump of the Blue Jack pill and felt it tingle in her fingers.

"We don't have hills like this where I . . ." she almost lost her balance, "come from," she said, but no one could hear her.

WHEN THEY GOT TO THE ABENAKI, it had completely given way to the early winter, rushing muffled under the confines of ice and the riverbank working to hold it back. The water ran fast. The iceless sections of flowing water left portions of the river exposed and then hid again beneath jutting sheets of thick ice that grew out from the banks and rocks and conglomerations of jammed logs and sticks. A large fallen tree—roots visible and dying, still grabbing at the earth like stretched-out fingers—reached halfway across the Abenaki, its trunk forking into two large branches that lay on a tiny island covered by fresh snow.

Owen stepped onto the tree and held a hand out to Noel. She climbed up and slid around him, crossing sideways while hanging onto his hand, sidestepping over it slowly and kicking snow off the tree and into the water with her forward-moving foot. Owen held her hand tightly, and she jerked forward twice but kept her balance. When they got to the island in the middle of the river, she bent down and pulled a sheet of ice up from the edge of the water, ran her tongue over it and made a face.

Jason was back in the woods kicking at something on the ground. He reached down and pulled up a deer antler and hit it against a tree to get the snow off. "Let the wild rumpus start!" he yelled, and held the antler above his head like a torch.

Pixie, startled, turned, smiled slightly, and yelled, "THERE WERE SSOME BUILDINGS . . . THERE WERE THESE . . . REALLY TALL BUILDINGS, AND THEY COULD . . . WALK. THEN THERE WERE SOME VAMPIRES. AND ONE OF THE VAMPIRES . . . BIT THE TALLESST BUILDING, AND HIS FANGS BROKE OFF. THEN ALL HIS OTHER TEETH FELL OUT. THEN HE STAR . . . TED CRYING. AND THEN, AAALL THE OTHER VAMPIRESS . . . SSAID, 'WHY ARE YOU CRYING, WEREN'T THOSE JUS YOUR

BABY TEETH?' AN HE SAID, 'NO. THOSE WERE MY GROWN-UP TEETH!' AND THE VAMPIRES KNEW HE COULDN'T BE A VAMPIRE ANYMORE, SO THEY LEF . . . T HIM. THE END." Pixie then reached one leg out over the water and pulled herself onto a large rock near the riverbank.

"Okay," Jason said. "That was interesting."

"Maurice Sendak, *Where the Wild Things Are*," Owen said half to himself. Noel still held her piece of ice.

Miriam pulled the string out of her hoodie and went to Jason. She made him hold the antler on the top of his head while she took the string and wrapped it first around the antler, and then under his chin, twice, to secure it. She had to pull hard so that there was enough string, and it cut into the flesh near his ear. "Ouch," he said. They both walked over to the riverbank, Miriam looking up at the antler, pleased that it was staying put.

Jason got up on the tree and crossed quickly, in a half run. The antler tilted heavily to the right and he reached up to straighten it. Pixie climbed onto the thickest part of the tree, near the roots, and grabbed hold of them to stand up. She started to pull up and lost her grip. She tried again, this time hugging the roots with her arms, and slowly stood up. She looked down at her shoes, smiled slightly, and then walked forward, hands halfway out, eyes concentrating on the air in front of her as she tried to keep balanced. The muscles in her body jerked with her movements. She was aware of a tightening of her jaw and realized that all of her movements were slower than she intended. She grew embarrassed. Up ahead, Noel held the sheet of ice to her face. A fog of auburn hair. Pixie tried to focus on the slick bark beneath her. Skid of the rocket dogs, the river seemed to laugh, and the teenagers fingered their hats and pieces of ice, and the little quarter-sized Xany and bleeding cut and the gin she'd found that morning in Jason's house failed her, leaving any leftover control to her shoes, the wind, and the movement of river beneath her. She slowly spun and slipped, arms jerking up to the sky, and fell hard onto the tree. She straddled the trunk.

"*Fuck!*" she said, laughing, and looked up at the others. One of her shoes toed the water, and the force of the current pulled her leg under up to her calf. She laughed again and pushed herself up to a sitting position. "*Fuck*, shit, that's ass cold," she said, and suddenly slipped, half tugged by the water—in one untranslatable moment while the others watched—completely off the tree. Pixie glanced up at Noel as she fell, her chopped black hair jolting to the left with the unexpected movement, her pale face giving way to a flicker of fear as her leg, her waist, then her whole body caught in the current and slid under and downstream in one surreal moment, a flash of black jacket and pale skin and then nothing.

THERE WAS AN OPEN WHITE-LIKE AIR above the river, a glut of cold molecules buzzing indifferently before and after Pixie was sucked under. The water continued to mumble and surge, its strength growing no more and no less with a girl in a black jacket lodged somewhere within its persistent gush like a too big bite of bread. A split in the trees seen from thousands of feet above would have revealed only a gray ribbony wetness within a white tree-studded land, winding south toward some enormous sea fed from rivers and rivers and rivers like arteries toward a heart. Pixie was a fading print, a slowing muscle, the scars on her arms shrinking steadily to merge with the pale of her numb white skin.

Fifty feet downstream, thick ice spread out from a group of large rocks and debris, and it was here that Pixie, moving swiftly with the current, was pulled under one last time and then stuck, the visible scene just a darkness beneath a portion of thick ice, one denim-clad leg pressed awkwardly upward by the current into the cold air, water splitting at the shin, one rubber shoe shuddering in the energy of surging water. There was a vastness that felt somehow close-up as the group stood there, as though they had just come out of a raunchy movie theatre and it was staring them in the eyes like a mother.

ETTA HEARD THE SIRENS as she pulled into the driveway with a trunk-load of good deals. A four-pack of Lysol toilet cleaner, apple cider—two half gallons shrink-wrapped together—a six-pack of athletic socks for Edward. He was always wearing his outside, even in the winter—just to take out the garbage, of course. She put the new things away, separating the toilet cleaners and putting two spray bottles in each bathroom. It felt good to be stocked up. A trip into town was now a trip into Walmart, abundant fluorescents and white canyon ceilings, the edges of aisles fading into shelves of *stuff*, Etta thought, layered patches of price tags half rubbed off on travel mugs and notebooks, hair coloring and Rubbermaid, but that is where the deals are. She went to the sink, rinsed out her morning coffee mug, and filled it with the leftover dregs from the coffeemaker. She put it in the microwave, pressed 50 and then "power," and opened up her date book as the oven stirred into its initial beaming hum.

The sirens grew louder and then seemed to fade only to strengthen one last time before quitting with a jerk of high-pitched sound. Etta looked out the kitchen window but could see nothing. She hoped everything was okay and whispered a thin prayer. The snow had begun to ease up. When the phone rang, it was Christine.

"Are you still going to POTS this afternoon?" Parents of Teens met once a month at the Methodist church. Christine and Etta had been going on and off for five years and were now the unofficial leaders. Each with one teenager successfully deposited at a university made the rest of the group look to the two women for helpful tips and cautions. With the group's devotion, Etta had realized that she and Christine had developed the habit of speaking more favorably about their sons, Tyler and Larry, than was warranted. One stated success led to another stated success until the big picture was tainted with idealized study habits and family bonding times, scenes hard to replicate in the honest-to-God world of burgeoning adulthood. The other mothers sat in the circle with Etta and Christine in the little church library, trusting them, wide-eyed and desperate, glancing at the outdated children's books and videos with pictures of animated donkeys and Peters and Jesus's, wishing to all hell they had plucked out the Power Ranger videos from the VHS when their kids were still young, and taken them to the park or baked homemade bread. There were emergency visitors to the POTS meetings—couples at times with a child kicked out of school in a flurry of disciplinary meetings and adolescent showdowns. Etta and Christine did their best. They cared about these kids, they wanted to help.

"I was hoping to get a little painting done, but one of us should be there."

"I can go."

"No. You know, let's go. We should go—I'll pick you up. The snow's pretty much stopped.

The church was on the other side of town. Etta and Christine drove down toward Maple with slow caution, Etta pumping the brakes and tensing her lips in an effort to maintain control. She turned left onto Maple with nothing but a half skid in the opposite direction, and they both breathed a sigh of relief.

"This ice is going to kill the road. The potholes will be enormous. We got the ice . . . and then the salt . . . ," Etta said in monotone, slowing for an uncertain patch of slushy salt/ice. They turned left and crossed over the Abenaki; the guardrails of the flat section of road that traversed the river were piled with fresh snow. Christine lowered her window and tilted her head toward the outside, taking a deep breath. A few thick flakes came through the window before she closed it again.

THE FRIENDS GATHERED DOWNSTREAM from Pixie at both sides of the river like parents at the bottom of a slide, half expecting her to quickly dislodge and pop back up so they could pull her out, take her inside to the warmth, laugh half-heartedly. They looked at each other. They looked at the dark form of Pixie beneath the ice. The movement of the current made her appear to be trembling.

Owen stepped out onto the rocks, and Noel grabbed the hem of his coat to stop him. He reached around with his hand and swatted her away. The rocks were barely visible beneath the ice and rushing water. He placed a foot on one of them and it slid off, breaking through ice. He let the water gush over his shoe, before trying to find another rock to step on. He started to fall and grabbed at another half-submerged rock. His shoulder hit the water and one arm sunk in before he could catch himself and get back up to a standing position.

Jocelyn covered her mouth with both of her hands and moved her face into a silent cry. She began to whine in a high-pitched voice.

Miriam tried to explain to a 911 operator where they were. "It's after the Stop-n-Shop, where the road comes to a T, I think. No. It's where Maple Avenue curves toward the river. *Please.* Just *please, please* hurry. . . ."

PLEASE. DON'T. GIVE. UP. Please. Don't. Give. Up. It was all Noel could do to maintain some sense of control—to silently breathe these words each time the EMT sunk down on Pixie's chest, his own face upward, not even looking at the girl as he focused on the force of his hands pressing down on her. Pixie lay there like rubber, less than blue—absent of color so that you had to feel sorry for the EMT really, it was so obvious that there was nothing that could be done. Still the guy kept pressing down on her. She had been under the water for almost forty minutes. It had been ten minutes before the ambulance arrived, and then at least another twenty before they had been able to safely dislodge her from the heavy current, her jacket floating out like a thick, tar-covered cape as finally her limbs, torso, hair, slack head and neck, had been gathered together and pulled from the icy water, a rubbery jointless mass. Jason stood on the side holding tight to a line they had used for the rescue. The antlers had fallen flat on his head. One point dipped over one of his eyes, and he absentmindedly repositioned it to one side so he could see. Pixie's black hair was barely out of the water when the EMT began to pound on her chest. It had seemed so hopeless until he started CPR. When he started CPR they thought maybe there was a chance, so Noel began with the only help she could give—Please. Don't. Give. Up. Please. Don't. Give. Up. Silently to herself. Behind her stood Owen, the massive discharge of snow and angst from the Heavens leaning into both of them like a large, slow mammal.

But she was dead. It was just so obvious that she was dead.

20.

Owen and Noel: diving

There's a purchase that's made, a freedom from boredom bought, within the mind of people associated closely with tragedy but not bound to the soul of the victim. Noel cared for Pixie but she was no sister. The girl was studded with piercings and split open at the seams.

When they got to the hospital, the glass doors slid open and the group slipped in behind the stretcher and the paramedics who pounded and ran and held up plastic tubing, yelling orders and turning a corner into an area with red electrical sockets and waiting nurses.

For a moment, it looked like Pixie turned her head. She opened her mouth, "Ahmsa," she seemed to say. "Ahmsa, ahmsa." The room became alive with new energy, a man got right in her face and lifted her eyelids, shining a pen light into them. The group stood back watching, anxious.

"She said something," Jocelyn said through her fingers. Her hand had remained on or near her mouth ever since Pixie had fallen into the river.

"She was moaning," Jason said, scratching at his leg with the antler that he now held in his hand. The string from the hoodie was still looped around his neck.

The nurses and at least one doctor continued to work quickly, pulling out equipment, slipping needles into her veins. Medical tape and plastic tubes. Someone gently pushed the group back.

Owen had one hand on Noel's shoulder. "I think she said, 'I'm sorry,'" he said, and pulled Noel close. "It sounded like she said, 'I'm sorry.'"

"I think it was just air coming out of her." Noel welcomed Owen's arm and leaned in.

They ran a line into her femoral artery. She was unresponsive. They wheeled her into another room and attached her to a heart-lung machine, a contraption as big as a small backhoe, but delicate, like the inside of a mouth.

A nurse led Owen, Noel, Miriam, Jocelyn, and Jason to a small waiting room without any windows. Miriam flipped through a copy of *Good Housekeeping*. She kept pausing and tilting her head back and sighing. Noel had been trying to get hold of Pixie's father. She tried the school academic advisor under Pixie's last name, got voicemail, and left a message. Finally, a doctor came into the room and pulled a chair away from the wall so that he could sit closer to the group.

"We have her on the heart-lung machine and we've got a pulse," he said, somewhat pleased. He rested his elbows on his knees.

"That's good, right?" Miriam said, looking over at Noel.

"What does the heart-lung machine do?" Owen said.

"I don't know how to get her father. I can't get hold of her father," Noel said.

The doctor sat up straight. "The heart-lung machine will slowly warm her. Sometimes if a person is under very cold water for quite some time, it's possible to warm the body slowly, and it's unlikely, but sometimes damage can be minimal. The water has to be very cold, and it's highly unlikely, but it has happened. We're giving it a shot."

"Okay?" Noel said, and Owen reached over and put a hand on her back. "What are you saying? That she'll be able to, what, do you mean she could just be a vegetable?"

"I mean she might *not* be in a completely vegetative state. The heart-lung machine will slowly warm her. Sometimes, rarely, the results are surprisingly good. When submerged in cold water, the human body has the capability to slow itself down, like hibernation, so that the systems aren't damaged."

"So she could come out okay?" Miriam said.

"I'm saying she might come out with some function. There's a very small chance. There's a phenomenon called the Mammalian Diving Reflex. What I'm saying is that it's good that the water was cold. It was very good. The cold water may have saved her."

"The water killed her," Miriam said. "The cold water is what, like, killed her. . . ."

"She is alive, she has a pulse," the doctor said. "There's some reason to be hopeful." He stood up and moved the chair back to the wall. "I'm going to have someone come in to help you kids find her parents."

Rubber turned to skin again, a pulse, but still Pixie lay dormant.

MARGIE FOLLOWED NOEL down the hall of the Critical Care Unit. Unlike most people, hospitals didn't bother her. They were real in their urgency, and when she went through the sliding glass doors of a hospital, she could feel herself engage, as though there was a point to everything. The smells felt rich to her, somehow claiming their own property of space; a vase of roses, a warm, plastic tray from food service, and antiseptics left a careful, light touch on everything, like a magical dust with the ability to transform. Large, sliding glass doors separated the rooms from the hallway, and some of the curtains were left open, exposing the patients, most of whom were elderly and entirely unaware. Every room Margie glanced into had an elderly patient. It was mostly quiet except for intermittent beeps from medical equipment or conversations among hospital personnel who didn't appear to have any inclination to keep quiet. Every patient Margie saw blended with the deep blue shadows of the sheets that covered them and the cold metal bars that guarded them from falling out of the beds. All of the human colors were cold. Skin bordered on gray, and white medical tape patched forearms and faces like plugs put there to keep whatever life was left inside.

The doors to Pixie's room were slid open, and there was a nurse next to the bed. She lifted a bag filled with fluid and hung it on another hook, sliding a cart aside to reach one of the small monitors. She adjusted something on the screen. Noel sat down in a chair under the window, and Margie stood next to the bed.

"Is everything the same?" Noel asked the nurse.

"She's doing fine. Nothing new to report. The doctor saw her this morning, he'd like to see her blood pressure come up."

"Can she hear us?"

"We don't know. The CT scan was inconclusive. It showed some activity but that doesn't necessarily mean much."

Margie gently lifted Pixie's wrist. It was covered with tape and wires. Her finger was pinched by a black thermometer and it glowed, turning the tip of her finger translucent and red. Long, white cuffs wrapped both of her shins and slowly inflated and then released. Hospitals were so different now, like they approached perfection but then were unable to grasp some key thing, ingredient for life, cell biology, something Margie would never understand. At what point should humans give up? A brain aneurism is entirely unpredictable. Blood would do its own thing: proceed, turn, flush out, carry a clog of mucus freely down one path only to catch on an artery wall, dig in, and begin to bulge with the pressure of a beating heart. *The doctor would like to see her blood pressure come up.*

Margie looked at the tiny scars on Pixie's arm. There was a Band-Aid on her forearm that was peeled halfway off.

"Owen's on his way over," Noel said. She stood up and looked out the window for his car. "I'm gonna go down to the lobby."

Margie nodded. "I'll stay here." She repositioned the thin blanket across Pixie's waist, leaving the bottom of her legs with the cuffs exposed. After Noel left, she reached up and touched Pixie's forehead, smoothing what hair she had away from her face. Someone had removed the rings from her lips, and the holes were shrunken but still visible. Margie let the back of her hand rest on Pixie's cheek for a moment. Her skin was warmer than it looked.

When Noel came back with Owen and also Jason, Jocelyn, and Miriam, Margie decided to leave. Sometimes Noel's friends energized her and their conversations and thought processes were interesting, but she was engrossed in thoughts of Pixie and didn't want them to decay, as though something sacred were in danger of being ruined, so she left.

JOCELYN AND JASON HUNG BACK just inside the glass doors like they might get contaminated. The hospital was a familiar place for Owen. Scoliosis had been handed down to him through his mother's side of the family. The men were cursed with it. Left without pins and braces and rods, with time the Meenan men's spines would have bent until their torsos were almost parallel to the ground, and then like a final sadness, the vertebrae would have twisted, flipping their face and shoulders upward, toward the sky. If they could walk at all, they would have looked like gnarled knuckles, buckled over and lurching forward in movements not unlike the jerking motion of a lizard coupled with the long, shouldered movements of a giraffe, and for generations Meenan men had submitted to more and more sophisticated attempts to halt the inevitable atrophy. By the time Owen was thirteen and it was obvious—both because of his pain and the way that one of his hips rode a good two or three inches higher than the other—that he had inherited the Meenan predilection for bent backs, he underwent treatment that included a brace at night, a rod inserted next to his spine, and a cast. All of this took one and a half years to complete. Owen understood needles and catheters and the twilight of being only half present.

And here was a girl with plastic veins entering her skin in private areas, a cascade of her own dreams perhaps flooding a half-frozen brain, surrounded by people who didn't know her except to judge and muse about the lines up the insides of her arms. Owen had had a morphine drip for over a week, and it had forced him into a state where he saw the people moving about him with evil covering them. Their mouths were wide and full of blood. Even now, he still refused to think of it as a dream. Owen leaned against the hospital wall and closed his eyes. He often thought that the pain of that experience somehow substituted for typical adolescence in his life. Being in the hospital now, it surprised him how much he felt like an authority, either because of his experience, or more likely—and this rang true to him—because he was not sick and the people here were. The healthy and young (but not too young) would always be the authority. He owned something, his friends owned something, that so many people on the earth don't: youth. And of course with their youth came the blessed ignorance of their own eventual old age. Even as he was cognizant of this, it didn't diminish his optimism.

Jason flipped the channels of the TV. "Why do they have TVs here? No one can watch them, they're all asleep, or unconscious anyway." He moved under the screen and looked up. "It's been two days. What father takes two days to get to his daughter in a hospital?"

"I feel so responsible," Jocelyn said. She had been saying this more or less since the ambulance had pulled up to the Abenaki.

"Please stop saying that." Miriam stood next to the wide glass window. She placed her palm flat against it to feel its coolness. "When I think of someone being in a vegetative state, I have a hard time not picturing an actual vegetable. A cross between a carrot and broccoli. And maybe even a little bit of onion."

"Queen of non sequiturs," Jason said, rolling his eyes.

"That's not a non sequitur," Miriam said. "It's like the opposite of a non sequitur."

Owen sat down on the other side of Pixie's bed. "She more than likely is listening to this whole conversation. Every word."

"If she's listening to it, she won't remember it," Jason said, reaching up with the remote and pointing it at the screen until it went black.

"Can you guys please stop?" Noel said, "because that would be helpful for me right now. I can't even find her mother. I don't know if she even has a mother. Her father had no idea she was even up here. He had no idea who I was. Her father sounds like an asshole, honestly. One-word sentences."

"She can probably hear you," Owen reminded her.

"It's been two days," Jason repeated. "She already knows he's an asshole."

White tape covered Pixie's mouth. A tube went from her mouth to a machine, and the mechanical pumping produced an audible suck that sent its rhythms into the hospital room like the rhythm of a needle on a sewing machine, stitching together monitor, IV drip, metal cart, and blood-pressure cuff. The nurse continued to come quietly and leave, but it didn't appear there was much to do. When a machine continued to beep she came in, pressed a screen, and the beeping went away. Noel touched Pixie's arm through the white sheet and sat down, pulling her chair closer to the bed.

Nick had cancelled his appointments yesterday to be with Noel and her friends and as a result was doing double duty today, back-to-back appointments. The kids had left for the hospital at ten, and Margie was expecting Pixie's father sometime in the afternoon. He would come home with Noel after visiting Pixie in the hospital. Margie straightened the kitchen and made her way up to the studio. She glanced at herself in the mirror, looking for some sort of a clue as to where she should be—her emotions, her physical state. She took out her ponytail and redoubled the elastic over her thick hair, looking at the newspaper clipping of Burden above her table. The blood trickling down Burden's arm looked obnoxiously symbolic to her right now. She reached up as though to touch the picture but then didn't.

Etta's pile of charcoal drawings lay on the floor next to the window. Her figures were mostly too soft—zero angles—and this puzzled Margie. It was a phenomenon that occurred frequently with inexperienced artists, and it seemed to her that it was because of some fear, that somehow the angles and turns that were the reality of the human figure required a certain commitment that beginning artists shied away from. Confidence swam different currents in people. Margie doubted the breath from her lungs, but she could make stuff happen with a nub of charcoal.

She heard a car door open and shut.

It was sunny and cold outside. Pixie's father would have had the lonesome drive winding up Route 17 from New Jersey, Margie thought, and by the time the low buildings and houses of Trinity appeared in the windshield, his mind would be working through hours of images—trailer parks, rubber-roofed diners, sloping woods with the occasional remains of large appliances leaning and rusted next to stumps and sick-looking pine trees. By the time he arrived at the hospital, his thoughts would have already had to wrap around the recesses of filth lining Route 23 and then 17, and by the time he got to their house Margie imagined the man arriving with a depression fueled by more than just his daughter's physical state, if that even bothered him. Noel called from downstairs, "Mom, we're here!" Margie heard the front door close and footsteps into the kitchen.

21.

Pete: a bald man in a navy blazer

When Margie went downstairs, Pixie's father had already removed his coat and handed it to Noel, who stood with it draped over one arm. He wore a navy blazer and tie. His graying hair was cut short and neat, a slick side part too close to one ear gave way to a thin comb-over. He ran his palm over the top of his balding head, following the direction of reassigned hair before he stuck out his hand toward Margie. "Pete, Pete Ammon," he said, bobbing his head up and down.

Margie went to the teakettle while Noel and Pete sat down at the table. She poured the leftover water into the sink and refilled it, letting the water get too high. She poured some out before setting it on the stove and turning on the burner. She grabbed a sponge and wiped the counter, unsure of what to say.

Pete drummed his fingers on the table and looked around the kitchen. "So did you say you're her roommate?"

Margie pulled some mugs out of a cabinet and set them on the table.

"Yeah," Noel said quietly. She looked at her mom, pleading with her eyes.

Margie sat down across from Pete. "Did you talk to the doctors?"

"I talked to the doctor. Yes."

The three of them sat cupping their empty mugs with their hands. Noel took three tea bags from a box on the table, unwrapped them, and placed them in the mugs.

"Pixie." Pete said. "Pete was supposed to be her name. She was a boy, we thought, before she was born." The teakettle started to whistle and Margie got up. "We went ahead and called her Pete anyway, and put it on the birth certificate and everything because her mom thought that would be funny, but people started calling her Pixie—the nurses did—prolly 'cause she was so small. She was premature and didn't do so well at first. We thought she might die." He stood up and took off his blazer and hung it over the back of the chair, hiked his pants up before sitting back down. His pants were roomy and wide, and not quite long enough. Margie poured the hot water into the mugs.

No one said anything. Pete picked at something in his ear and nodded his head again.

Noel watched him. "I'm really sorry," she said. "Nothing should have happened, it wasn't a big deal. She was trying to run across the tree and she slipped. It was icy."

"Pixie . . . Pixie," he said again, "she could of gotten in trouble doing anything. It's an irony she gets into trouble doing something, just walking across a river. . . . She's no innocent girl. No disrespect, she's just always been a hard girl, and I mean that in the way that it sounds—she just don't always see things like other people. She was always smarter than me, back when she was just a little girl. It's why her mother didn't stay, I think. She'd come back like she thought she could come back and dress her girl up in pink after all, and then there she'd be, Pixie hating her—no pink for her, just back in her little room with her notepads and books and she never talked. She didn't like us too much."

"How did she look to you?" Margie asked. "In the hospital?" She was anxious for Nick to finish his last session.

"She looked like a girl with a hose in her mouth, that's for sure. It's funny. I saw her once like that, with a friend, a funnel, one of those car funnels in her mouth, like for oil, in her mouth and her friend pouring a can of Coors down. It goes to your brain quicker that way. The doctor says she's not the same, but her mind might not be dead like she looks. If she's not the same, that's prolly a good thing. She'll wake up and go back to that school, I know it though."

There was a skim of saliva at Pete's mouth that caused curdles of spit to form at the corners and stretch when he talked. The state of his skin, its tough wintered redness, to Margie seemed foundational to the rest of his life. A house with puckered aluminum siding, a rusted propane grill, maybe even a mobile home—Margie thought, but that was too easy. A double wide? One with an actual foundation and a deck off the front porch. She heard Nick's door open. It was three o'clock.

AT THE HOSPITAL, Pete sat next to Pixie with his elbows on his knees, hands clasped, and stared at her. Nick and Margie talked with one of the doctors. "We're encouraged that her pupils are contracting to light. There's some extensor posturing, no edema . . . no swelling. You must understand, of course, there is no story to tell yet—we warmed her, she's alive, but the outcome isn't yet known. If it weren't for her pupils contracting, let me be honest with you, I would have suggested we take her off life support."

Pete stared at his daughter.

The doctor looked over at Pixie lying in bed. "That she's alive at all is a miracle."

PETE DECIDED TO STAY. In Hardboro, across the river and one town over, there was an Extended Stay with a Boston Market next door. Blue and white paper snowflakes were taped to the windows. A touch of glitter. At the lower left corner of the glass, next to the entrance, was an image of a large mug with a creamy whipped top. Words took the place of steam and curled up from the topping, *Home is where the honey is*, and then, *Introducing Boston Market's new spiced honey cider.* Pete parked in the lot for the Extended Stay with the hood of his green Ford Taurus facing the restaurant. When he got out of the car he thought he could hear the faint sound of the river down the road. That, or faint traffic from Route 84. A group of kids were standing next to the doors. One boy took a lit cigarette and went at a kid wearing a knit hat that said, "Etnies." The kid in the hat ducked the cigarette and laughed.

22.

Owen and Noel:
streetlight with music

A week after Pixie's accident, Noel looked out the window of a Greyhound bus. The rent-a-wreck car had been left at a gas station where somebody was supposed to use it to get to some other school in some other state. Someone had thumbed a backwards "FUCK" on the dirty glass of the bus window, correctly visible for the outside world. Underneath it, two lines like waves and then a handprint, the bottom half smeared into nothing. She wiped it away with her cuff. It had started to rain. Pockmarks began to appear in the melting snow like finger holes. There was nothing any of them could do, the doctor had made clear, and still she felt like an accomplice to murder. She would go back to her and Pixie's apartment. Back to her and Pixie's apartment. What the hell.

Last night Owen had stopped by the house. Noel had been doing her laundry. Small piles of folded clothes were on the kitchen table. The scent of perfumed dryer sheets. The kitchen light was the only light on in the house and it had turned the house into a cave, a place where she could have her small, lit area and keep her thoughts in the immediate space around her. There in the cave the rest of the world was not so full of power after all; she could manage in the kitchen with her laundry to fold and the light on and the hum of the dryer down the hall the only thing that hinted at the world beyond. It was a small life after all, she was beginning to realize. In high school, when Friday nights are the closest thing to freedom, the horizon is extensive, so much so that it can be a little terrifying, but here, not even one semester into college and the realization of the immediate world was hitting Noel with a thud that could make her dizzy. Her mom and dad had gone to bed, and the dishwasher had settled into its own unique hum before hitting the high pitch of the rinse cycle. It was a comforting cocoon of domesticity, this cave, and Noel sunk into it like a narcotic. New York City loomed and wavered, offering something like a hot salsa—you want it so freaking bad and it goes down okay but bites the hell out of you once it's there. The quiet knock on the front door didn't startle her, only made her heart skip a beat in a hopeful sort of way, as though she had been expecting him.

They sat in the dark living room on the couch, knees and shoulders touching, a streetlight shooting a harsh, too-white light through the front window and onto the wormy reds and golds of the Persian carpet. Noel fingered the fringe of a throw pillow that she held tucked on her lap. Owen took his iPod out of his front pocket and held it, relaxing down into the couch. He rested the back of his head on the pillows. The clock on the mantle ticked in a little two-step, each sound two syllables. They spoke quietly.

"I'm not going to sleep tonight," Owen said, "I've already decided."

"You will. When it's three AM you will." Noel leaned back too.

"Miriam's upset. She called on my way over."

"I'll call her in the morning." Noel turned her head and looked out the window. The streetlight mimicked the moon, but it was deceitful, stretching across the yard, climbing a snow-covered shrub and then hitting the windowsill and carpet before giving way to the darkness of the room. The memory of the moon on her quilt as a child was something that had been with her for years. Counterpoint—that's what quilts were sometimes called. So strange. She leaned on Owen's shoulder and he put his hand on her knee. The clock ticked. He unwound the earphones of his iPod and went through the songs.

"Here," he said, and reached over and put one of the buds in Noel's right ear. "Old times." He put the other one in his left ear. *Fistful of Love*, by Antony and the Johnsons. They let their heads rest together as Antony's voice warbled, "*I need someone to take care of me . . . when I die, when I die. . . .*"

"I feel like we're in middle school," Noel said.

"I know, it feels that way. It's so awesome."

23.

Margie, Nick, Etta, and Edward: a dead kitten and dinner for four

Margie's mother had killed a kitten when she was five. Backing out of the driveway in the station wagon, they had both heard the beginning of a squeal, nothing more than a chirp that abruptly silenced. The kitten's intestines had popped from the skin, white and bulbous and half soaked in blood. Her mother had used a shovel to get the remains into a plastic bag. Margie had held the bag open.

Such are the ways of growth, she thought. You glide along a set course and then an incident with an unfamiliar severity that heightens emotional sensation trespasses, packing a moment with vividness, and then when that vividness diminishes, you're left with less than when you started.

So the mother leans the shovel against the garage door and pumps the day like a handshake, a busy and necessary interference, nods to the event, scarf wrapped around her hair sprayed into a dark berm.

The driveway was gravel, and when her mother had walked to the end of it with the plastic bag so that she could lift the lid of the aluminum garbage can and drop the dead weight of the kitten in, her steps had made the usual sound, a familiar one, half of a crunch per foot, and then the clang of the aluminum lid.

NICK PIECED TOGETHER THE PARTS of the food processor, something that Margie used little. Nick defaulted to it whenever he cooked, pulling it out to chop the smallest onion or half a green pepper. Etta and Edward would be coming for dinner. They had asked Pete too, but he said, *No thank you, I really appreciate it, no thank you.* Nick wore his white apron—folded down, just around his waist. He fit the large double blade down onto the notched shaft of the Cuisinart, pulled it out again, and scraped at something with his fingernail.

Margie had taken the leaf out of the dining-room table and was pushing the remaining sections of the table back together again. She leaned into one side, pressing until the wood slid forward. There was a loud clang from the kitchen. "*Shit*," she heard Nick say.

When they arrived, Etta was wearing black slacks and a black turtleneck sweater. Around her neck on a silver chain hung a knobby turquoise rock. She wore a large ring on one of her fingers that matched. It was a little much, but somehow it made Margie happy.

Nick shoved up his sleeve to shake Edward's hand, *So glad you could make it*, and went back to the stove. Sometimes Margie assumed haught when there was none—Nick giving his opinion of Etta after first meeting her, striking him as sweet, wholehearted. And then after Margie responded to his comment about Etta with a small shake of her head: "How," Nick wanted to know, "does someone take an adjective such as 'wholehearted' to be pejorative?" As he cooked, every once in a while he turned his head and threw a comment over his shoulder. Edward leaned against the kitchen table with a glass of wine and talked about having a kid in college. Margie took Etta into the living room where they sat down.

Nick wiped his hands on his apron and pulled a pan from the oven. Four salmon filets. He stirred a cream sauce on the stove. Butter and flour roux, capers, and white wine. "So Margie's got Etta doing a little figure drawing down at the art center."

"Etta loves Margie," Edward said. "Don't know why she does the art with her though. She's got plenty going already with her tomatoes and now this landscape. I'm not crazy about it, to tell you the truth, her latest painting, of houses on the hill—it's mostly the roofs, you can't really see much else. She's always done so well with the tomatoes. Sells them like hotcakes. Now she wants to paint people. . . ."

"I'm sure any work she does down at the center will only help her improve as an artist."

Edward took a sip of wine and stared thoughtfully at the floor for a moment. "Let me ask you something, Nick. Do you mind if I ask you something?"

"Of course."

"How do you feel about this figure drawing stuff? With Margie, I mean. They use males and females, right?"

Nick turned around and leaned back against the counter. "Go with Etta down to the center once or twice," he said. "Watch her sketch. It's a very benign situation. Women, men, it's all about shape and form, foreshortening, things like that. If it's bothering you, you should go to class with her."

"Just don't see why she can't draw me, you know?" Nick looked at him. "She's got this great hunk a male flesh walking around right under her nose, heh heh." Edward grabbed a chunk of his midsection with his hands and jiggled it.

"I'm sure she'd love to draw you too—probably wouldn't get more than an outline done before abandoning the thing." Nick winked and turned back to his cooking. "Go take a peek at Margie's studio upstairs," Nick threw over his shoulder. "Go on up. I'll get this on the table."

When Edward came back down, Etta followed Margie into the dining room, necklace swaying to the right as she came around the corner. "Thank you, Nick," Margie said. "Thanks." She gave him a kiss.

Nick looked at Edward. "Well, what'd you think?"

Edward cleared his throat and glanced away. "It was interesting. I'm," he looked at Margie, "not an artist. I don't understand this stuff, I guess. I don't understand art."

The four of them sat down and scooted their chairs up to the table. There were steaming salmon filets with capers in a ceramic dish and a green salad. Margie had washed and dried the lettuce that morning using a salad spinner. She had stared out the window above the kitchen counter and turned the little plastic knob, mouth tense, elbows and hands forcing the movement. Her hands ached the rest of the day. They still ached now.

"This looks delicious," Etta said, sitting up straight and unfolding her napkin onto her lap.

"There's not much to understand, really," Margie said. "People think art is more complicated than it is. It's about monitoring your emotions, experience the art, and then figure out what it's doing and why. And sometimes it's just pretty."

Nick looked up from his plate. "Since when? You're disregarding a lot, Margie."

"Like what?"

"Uh, history, social statements, previous works, the people who create it. How about performance art?"

"Since when is performance art not about how it makes you feel?"

"So art is really just there to make us happy, sad, excited, bored? Margie, all of those feelings exist because you 'understand' the art. It takes a little bit of knowledge, even research."

Margie shrugged, "Sure, I guess so. I mean, Grandma Moses makes your point well, doesn't she?" She smirked just the tiniest bit. And then sarcastically, "We all know she felt strongly about her causes. . . ."

"Oh," Etta chimed in, "I honestly don't know what her work is about. But it's lovely, I've always admired it." She laughed a little.

"You admire it because it makes you happy, Etta. It's pretty. It makes you happy because a woman in her nineties painted pretty pictures." Margie cut into her salmon with the edge of her fork.

"And here," Nick said, "you prove my point perfectly. We know that Grandma Moses painted when she was very old, that her art should have stayed in the back of the drugstore. There's something profound about how people love something so simple."

Edward laughed. "Well, this conversation is most certainly proving my point earlier, that I don't understand art." He laughed again, "Over my head completely," and made a quick swipe with his hand over the top of his own head to demonstrate.

Nick stood up and poured more wine into Margie's and Edward's almost-empty glasses. He raised the bottle as he poured, making an unusually long stream with the wine. Margie shook her head and said, "Seriously, Nick?" It was hard to tell if she was incredulous about the way he was pouring the wine or their conversation.

The conversation turned to Pixie. Chairs creaked and the evening headed toward night.

"It is wonderful that you were able to be here for Pete," Etta said, fingering the turquoise rock of her necklace. "I'm sure you know how to deal with this sort of thing," she said to Nick.

Nick objected even as he delicately slipped in his opinions regarding different forms of grief and the best ways to reassure and support. They talked and Etta laughed now and then, and Edward told a story about trying to surprise Etta on their anniversary and overzealously pruning her bushes into an eternity without flowers or color. Nick put a piece of salmon in his mouth. He slid the fork in upside down and a caper fell onto his shirt. He picked it off and placed it on the edge of his plate.

Later that evening, when they were cleaning up, Nick said, "Margie, you want to be simple, but you're not. You're not, and you never will be."

Down state, deep in the mouth of the river, the Abenaki, already blended with Feldspar Brook, Opalescent River, and finally Hudson, mighty and braided, join like friends and move together toward the land of salt, where water is a mirage and the ships float on acid, alive for a moment but destined to disappear with eternity.

24.

Pixie: sights, lights, and a birthday party

Pixie—if Pixie existed at all—hesitated, aware that her own volition was questionable at best. The white sheets were heavy but at the same time responsible for releasing her to the ceiling. Everything that touched her, counterintuitively given the lightness of her being, was dead weight. *She* was heavier—like ten times heavier—but then here she was flipped face down and rising to the ceiling tiles of the room like she could swim the air. The bare skin of her exposed back between the two ties of her gown brushed the coarse foam of the tile ceiling. She felt the cold strip of the metal grid that supported the tiles. Her gown sagged beneath her. The thing was, the noises were gone. Everything was silent. No voices. No rumbling of carts down the hallway. Absolutely nothing. *Nothing.* On the bed lay herself, breathing tube, IV drip, blood-pressure cuff, now wrapped around an arm (it was presently doing its thing but without the usual noise which compounded the silence), greasy hair half flayed off to one side, and then her dull, anti-expression, as though someone had shoved all the medical apparatus into her when she had just then been letting go, capturing her in half death. Pixie scanned the room from above, looking for a light, a tunnel, some unknown relative to offer her a hand in welcome—some way out—but found none. She grew anxious, turning even, in an awkward way as though trying to turn on the dirt floor of a crawl space with six inches of clearance above her. Her head brushed a tile and lifted it up for a moment. There was nothing. Just silence and the hospital room. And then, in a panic, she began to open her mouth as though to scream, and even though she knew nothing would come out, she felt a sense of pressure that intensified to the point of physical pain. It was like a blood-pressure cuff was wrapped, not just around her body, but around her heart and her mind. The tightening continued to the point of being unbearable, and then suddenly it released.

Everything became magnificent. There was no more haze and no more audible or visual confusion. She was in a new place, and things were crisp, not crisp like they are on a clear, fall day, but crisp because there was everything to back it up—to back up the clarity, because that's what it was, clarity. She had entered reality. There was fullness, and depth, and intimacy, and she thought-talked. There were people, but they weren't strangers, they were the opposite of strangers, and she thought-talked with them and it was better than language, it *was* language—it was *real* language. She somehow moved forward but time did not exist.

Then she saw it, although there was no "then," because there was no time. She saw what seemed to be all of the truth, standing—existing—right with her. And it knew her. No, not "it" but him—even her, for he was definitely personal. There was love and it was good. Everything was about to mean something. It was natural revelation, as walking down a wooded path with sun streaming through the trees is natural revelation, and you can almost put a finger on it, what it is, that beauty, that close brush with perfection, only here with Pixie the natural revelation was stronger, more infinite and close to the answer. He. But he was more than. And he loved her. Everything was about to mean something, just about to, but a darkness that was hideous began from behind her, just a prick, a touch to her ankle, and crept forward somehow faster than was possible, and like a sweeping movement, still without time, it took over everything behind her and the truth that was in front of her, that she was about to perceive, was immediately beyond where she was. Now there were places and she was in a place and the place that was a fierce darkness from behind left only a crack of light, and she shoved her hand—not a ghost's hand, but her very real, physical hand—forward to preserve a small, infinitesimal amount of light, and she opened her mouth. . . .

but nothing came out. She was trembling and looked down at her stupid-looking face lying in the bed beneath her and tried to get back to her body. Lower herself, kick her feet, and then only when she became still, she somehow managed to sink slowly, as long as she remained still, until she was right there, face-to-face with herself almost,

there,

just

a little bit

lower,

yes. Now. She relaxed even more, turned, aligned, and there, okay. The blood-pressure cuff hissed audibly again, easing its grip on her arm. Down the hall people singing, *Happy birthday to you, happy birthday to you. . . .*

PART TWO

Babette looked up from her eggs
and hash browns and said to me with
a quiet intensity, "Life is good, Jack."

—DON DELILLO, *WHITE NOISE*

25.

Noel and Keith and Owen:
city smells and a pill called Blue Jack

Walking south on Amsterdam one unseasonably warm morning in March, Noel spotted Keith, Pixie's friend from first semester, sitting at one of the tables in front of Maximillian's, a local bakery and coffee shop. At first she didn't recognize him by his face, but he was wearing the same scarf as when Pixie had first introduced the two of them. She remembered it because it had struck her as oddly feminine—baby blue, probably cashmere—and then everything else about him was so *college guy.* There was a middle-aged man who wore a kilt and walked down Columbus every morning around 9:30, his upper half in a suit—Noel sometimes spotted him on her way to class on Tuesdays. The man was so perfectly, perfectly out of place, and it killed Noel that she was so profoundly normal next to people like him.

Keith was alone at the table sipping from something in a cardboard sleeve. She thought it was Keith, she was pretty sure. She had only met him once. She passed him, got to the corner, turned around, and went back.

"Keith?" she said, as she approached the table.

He looked up.

"Keith, right?"

He nodded, "Yes," a little confused.

"I'm Pixie's friend, Pixie Ammon's friend. Her roommate. Do you remember me?" She stuck out a hand, "Noel."

"My god, yes, yes," he shook her hand, "I remember you. Starlights. I haven't seen Pixie in ages."

Noel stood there for a moment as though deciding what to do.

Keith pushed a chair toward her, "Sit. I haven't seen Pixie in ages," he repeated.

Noel sat down. A gutter was dripping water on a metal table behind Keith. The water pooled and nudged the edge, forming a membrane and threatening to spill off.

"Pixie, what a girl—I'm afraid she was a bit mad at me last time we saw each other. I tried ringing her and gave up. Not the first time that's happened to me . . . I was a bit of an ass. I was a drunk arse. Very inconsiderate." He took a sip of his drink. The blue scarf hung longer on one side and was about to slide into his lap. "You two still roommates? Did she even make it through that first semester? I know she wasn't sure. . . ."

"Yeah, it's been difficult for Pixie." Noel rubbed self-consciously at one eye.

"God, no. Tell me she isn't using again. I was such a stupid ass. I gave her something the last time I saw her. The next morning I prayed she'd just flush it. I prayed actually—I prayed out loud, I really did. I never pray. I just felt so fucking guilty." Keith shook his head slowly and fingered the cardboard on his cup. "She was a fun girl just coming out of it and I was a bloody ass."

"I don't know what you gave her, but I don't think she was, like clean or anything—at least you know, completely clean or anything anyway. I honestly didn't know her that well even though we were roommates."

"So she left school? Is she back in Jersey?"

Noel told him what had happened, how Pixie had fallen into the river. He leaned one elbow on the table and rested his forehead in his palm. He shut his eyes and then looked up at Noel like she didn't know everything, shaking his head as though he was waiting for her to finish so that he could fill in the details to a story that he, just right then, had begun to piece together. "Christ," he said, "Oh, Christ . . ." The blue scarf finally fell into his lap and he picked it up, absentmindedly wrapping it around one hand, still shaking his head. The dripping from the gutter drain behind him eased up.

"I think Pete, her father—he's sort of an interesting man—just thinks she's going to wake up and everything will be back to normal," Noel said. "He's still up there, in some rented room now it's been so long. She's in long-term care. A residence. Cheaper than New Jersey, apparently. I've been to the place and it's depressing as hell."

Keith ran both hands through his hair and looked up at the sky, frozen for a moment with his hands behind his neck. "I gave her Blue Jack the last time I saw her."

"Blue Jack?"

"Black oil. Blue Jack's basically really pure heroin, really."

"Okay."

"But in pill form. You could swallow it, or you could open it up and snort it. Or if you were really fucked up, you could shoot it. Either way, it's way too pure. Like it's condensed. It's not safe."

"Okay, why? Do you think that's why she was acting weird before she fell?"

"She warned me. She said, 'Keith, I don't need this shit.'"

The angle at which the sun hit the red banners hanging in front of the Metropolitan Museum of Art caused them to flash pink, a squint of weak color, like it was all too much—being outside in the city, with the sky right there, exposed. Bland and impersonal. Noel stepped awkwardly up the stairs, too many of them, knees working double-time. She smelled the sweet, roasted peanuts from a vendor and tried to shrug off the smell. She had grown to hate peanuts, they were everywhere, even the sight of one of the little oily paper bags made her turn away. It was a city thing. If she was at home, she would like them. Up from the subway looking forward to some real air, and you get peanuts. It was a slovenly smell, it slowed her down the way a full stomach can slow you down, a stomach that's overinhabited, fed too much beef or weed so that the eyes grow hazy and the shoulders begin to slump.

It was the crispness of the museum as much as the art that made Noel visit so frequently. *Clean. Man-made cleanliness.* Even the bathrooms. Free clean bathrooms with her student ID. She always felt the ever-so-slight coolness of a breeze, imagined or not, while inside. It was good sleeping weather in the Metropolitan Museum of Art. She always ended up in the same room, staring at the same painting. Sometimes it took her an hour to get there, sometimes fifteen minutes, but it was inevitable.

She went to the modern section and stared at a Rothko. She wandered into a new retrospective of Francis Bacon. Last month was the Frida Kahlo exhibit. Kahlo would have made a great dictator—her face was like propaganda. It was everywhere. Noel's part in Pixie's life was something that troubled her and also did not trouble her, and this in and of itself troubled her terribly. This dichotomy. Was there always a need to assign responsibility? People felt comforted somehow when responsibility was assigned, as though it would prevent further loss, or maybe not even, as though there was some retroactive justice, some dividing of good and bad. There was always that butterfly-effect thing. Anything could be responsible; Pixie brushing her teeth a certain way one March morning when she was five, led to Pixie falling into Abenaki River when she was twenty—or nineteen, who even knew how old she was?

Noel went to the American Abstraction galleries, found her great-grandfather's painting, and sat down on the floor. The painting was of an avocado and a lemon. It was large and rectangular, and the avocado was the most beautiful avocado Noel had ever seen. Split in half, the large dark seed had a residue of green in sections where the fruit of the thing hadn't been completely scraped off. The light in that part of the painting made everything about it beautiful. From the avocado, moving right, the shapes somehow changed and the light dulled as the paint transferred the eye to a crudely painted lemon. The lemon was clearly a lemon, but it had been left bare and indistinct, pasted on. It was amazing how he had painted that transition. Noel sometimes wondered if her grandfather had intended the painting to mock Warhol. The first time she came to the Met by herself to look at the painting, she had brought a sketchbook, thinking she needed a reason to stare at a painting for so long, but she no longer bothered. She sat down, crossed her legs, and stared at the painting as though some kind of speaking would happen. When poet Franz Wright had first showed his famous poet father some of his poetry, his father had said, "Welcome to hell." And then Fitzgerald: *So we beat on, boats against the current, borne back ceaselessly into the past.* Since middle school Noel had never been able to get that line out of her head. She wished she could write a sentence like that, but she knew she never would. At any rate, she wasn't headed to hell like Franz Wright was. She would never write like that.

A boy of about seven or eight lay stomach-down on a bench under an enormous black-and-white Motherwell, chin resting at the edge as he traced an imaginary line on the polished concrete floor. His mother (presumably) and a young girl, probably the boy's sister, were looking at a painting, and the woman was explaining some relationship—some *organic relationship*.

Noel's phone buzzed. She'd been texting with Owen all day. Trying to best each other with colloquialisms. It began with Owen: *yo ur like so sick come visit*

I'm down

soon

soon

They had split the day, texting and real life, eyes up and to the side, thumbs jumping around their keypads. It was a game they played. There had been two long gaps in the banter, forty minutes while Noel talked with Keith and half an hour while Owen watched a large woman outline midcentury American literature on a white board, discussing as she went the impact and relationship each work had on the culture at large. Noel didn't tell Owen she'd met up with Keith.

She left the museum, headed across the park and up Amsterdam toward her apartment. She avoided Pixie's room—she had collected Pixie's things from the rest of the apartment and sequestered them in the little bedroom. An assortment of items lay under Pixie's black bulletin board—she had painted it black their first night in the apartment together. Noel refused to use any of her stuff, going so far as to clean her old coffeemaker and set it on the floor in Pixie's room. Noel smelled the roasting lamb that turned in the window of The Parthenon two stores down, next to Rich's. Sometimes, on a dark day, flaming plates of saganaki were visible from the street, waiters circling the flaming cheese squeezing lemons to put the fire out.

One of the things that had almost kept Owen from going to Gordon at all was this chapel requirement. It wasn't actually a requirement, but if you went, it contributed to your overall GPA, which seemed to him to defeat the purpose. If being Christian is about *grace given to you*, then sitting in an auditorium listening to someone only because it will hike up your GPA is a contradiction—the wrong reasons cancel out the right ones. The righteous thing would be to stay in his room, but he wanted the extra points, so here he was. He signed his name on the *manifest* as he liked to think of it, and found a seat.

The guy started talking. He was dressed all in hemp. A striped Baja hoodie. Dreadlocks. The whole bit. Owen tried to relax and like the guy. He really wanted to. He wasn't in the mood to battle some deep-seated hate today, especially because the message would almost surely be about loving people more. So far, chapel was plus one point for the GPA, but then minus one for his obligatory rather than eager attendance, and another for the hate plus guilt he found himself struggling with as Dude prepared to explain how important it was to love people, *not just people like yourself, but other people.* Owen anticipated what he was about to hear and started getting irritated, but then settled into his chair, opened a notebook, and tried to focus. The music was last, and it was pure crap even though he had to admit it could be earnest.

He wasn't thinking about Thanksgiving anymore, at least compared with before, when he'd first returned to campus. When he first came back, he couldn't get it out of his mind, going over and over it again, remembering different details each time. It was interesting to him that he never had thoughts of "if only" that so many people seem to struggle with. When his mind wandered to that afternoon, he kept thinking about the rock that his foot had slipped off of. If his foot hadn't slipped off, and he'd made his way out to Pixie, and been able to grab her and pull her up, she still would have been unconscious, and at that point, the ambulance wouldn't have arrived yet and she'd have been another ten or twenty minutes out of the cold water before getting to the hospital and put on the machine. The transfer needed to be quick: frozen body to heart-lung machine. It was probably good he hadn't gotten to her earlier. It always bothered him when people, after some near tragedy, a car accident or something, said things like, *At least Jen wasn't in the car, she was planning on it, but decided not to go.* If Jen decided to go, the accident would likely never have happened. Events are subject to the tiniest moments. As much time as it would have taken Jenny to put on her seat belt was enough time to cause the semitruck to merge onto the interstate three seconds earlier and never hit the car to begin with. We think we're so in control.

Dude had taken the microphone off the podium and was now at the edge of the stage: *The meaning of life* **is** *love. Roll up your sleeves. Dig a well!* He yelled the last sentence.

So everyone is well fed, Owen couldn't help thinking, and has plenty of fresh water, and then there's an earthquake, and half the town dies. *Little Gidding* had been in the back of his mind all week. He wished he could write something so good and put it to music: *Who then devised the torment? Love. / Love is the unfamiliar Name / Behind the hands that wove / The intolerable shirt of flame / Which human power cannot remove. / We only live, only suspire / Consumed by either fire or fire.*

He'd rather be writing about the Symbolist Movement than sitting in chapel. It made a lot more sense.

26.

Pete

Pete's girlfriend Sophia's bad mouth had never bothered him, really. Even if it wasn't the way a woman should talk. It was as familiar as his own chest. Now, with Sophia in New Jersey and Pixie here, all of a sudden it mattered that Pixie never liked her to begin with. He should have listened to Pixie.

He liked to visit her early in the day and then go back and light his candles before he ate something and turned on the TV.

Pete sat next to the hospital bed with his wrist on the metal guard, one finger touching a puckered section of sheet. Pixie had been turned and bathed earlier that morning, and was tucked in neatly, the shape of her body visible under the white sheets, like a hospital death, the way that people must die in hospitals, without a bad smell. One of the women who worked at the center liked Pete and talked to him. No one else did, except people from the town when they came to visit, which wasn't very much anymore. And Etta, she still came and she always brought flowers.

New Brunswick, where Pete and Pixie had lived, was bordered by cemeteries that were just left alone. Garbage was in those places—

paper cups were on top of tombstones like people had forgotten about their drinks because of their sadness, or because a widow or son or daughter put down their coffee to pull out the overgrown grass tucked around the stone that the wide industrial lawnmowers hadn't gotten. The cups left on the stones had cold coffee, stale and curdling, mossy cream. Their apartment was above Grove Pizza, a small restaurant with three red booths. The heat from the ovens downstairs turned their little living room nice and warm in the winter, but humid and hot in the summer—the old 5,000 BTU window unit carving a path of cool four or five feet into the room and then giving way to the heat. Pixie used to sit in that few feet of space for hours reading while Pete was working. Seven years, eight years old, ever since her mother left, she just read since they couldn't get reception on the TV. He lost touch with Pixie after that. That's when she went off on her own and he would just see her in the mornings and every once in a while at night if he came home early.

Pete knew he was lucky because of the injury he got when he was working on a rusting tress of the Verrazano Bridge and his grinder slipped and smacked into his left knee, carving out a thick line the size of a hot dog into his thigh. He'd been careless, working too quickly, and left his helmet up a second too long, getting a glimpse of the white arc before realizing his mistake and yanking his helmet down, grinder looking for skin, and then, yeah, straight through the canvas and into his thigh, and all this because he was afraid of the light. He was always afraid of arc eye, the grating sandiness in his eyes that, twice, had kept him up all night. It took less than a half a second of looking at the arc without your helmet and, *motherfucker*, you were fine until night, when everything came together and you reaped what you sowed. It was like invisible thumbs were pressing sand in your eyes. A wad of gauze around his leg and eyes like asphalt, the night of the accident he'd stared at the ceiling until the garbage trucks came, turning left at the intersection and into the Grand Union parking lot, beep, beep, beep, like eye drops into the morning, backing up and heading south again on Route 1.

He was lucky because this happened a week after Pixie left for school. She left him a note on a piece of paper towel on the table in the little kitchen that said where she was going and left an address and said that she wasn't sure when she'd be back. He looked in her room after he found the note, and it was pretty much just her mattress and the little bookcase with all her paperbacks. And the dirty window with her socks stuck in the crack between the two panes to keep out the cold.

When he started to get paid because of the injury and he was home and he wasn't going out after work, he wanted to send Pixie money. He wrapped it, mostly twenty-dollar bills, in a paper towel, the same one that she wrote the note on because he couldn't find another one. He had to do exercises because of his leg. The doctor said there was nerve damage. Now, in Trinity, the checks for his leg came to a post box at the post office on Fern Hill Road. Down the road a little farther was a church that looked like a warehouse except for a steeple made of plastic PVC.

After Pixie had her accident he kind of felt like all of a sudden he could only hear her now, when she couldn't actually talk. In New Jersey, the loud semitrucks on the Turnpike had so much exhaust, and then the planes whining as they landed in Newark, forced them to add stuff to make the noise go away, and so Pete drank. In Trinity, when he saw Pixie for the first time after the accident, he wanted to lift her hand and put it on his lips, like a kiss, and he actually did it. If she had been able to look back at him, he wouldn't of done it. He knew.

Once, after leaving the rehabilitation center, he tried to go to the church on Fern Hill Road. He got into the first part of the church where there were a few chairs and a table like a waiting room, but then the other doors were locked. The building could use a good welder; its vinyl corners weren't barely stuck together. He'd of run a bead around the building like a good shot of Elmer's glue—it would be strong in the seams after he got to it. Once the seams were tight, you wouldn't be able to budge it.

Sometimes he thought about becoming religious.

27.

Margie and Etta:

one half orange juice, one half fear

Margie could not feel her toes, she swore to God she could not feel her toes. You focus too long on something . . . She was on the couch with her feet up on the armrest. Nick was exasperated. He told his wife to sit up, they weren't getting any blood to them. Twenty minutes later and she still couldn't feel her toes. It had started that morning when she took a swig of orange juice and felt the cool liquid slide down one side of her throat—*one side of my throat*, she kept saying, holding her neck and kneading it in an attempt to get a response. From there things became more pronounced: fingers tingling, hot flashes on patches of skin, and then her toes. When you're looking at a future with such uncertainty, clusters of MS oddities become something like a precursor to fear—a heightened inquisitiveness that, once fully realized, has no other direction to go but down, or not down really. Margie's image of fear was more one of *off into the expanse*. It was a disappearing image. Fear *was* not knowing. As Nick sometimes said, most fear can be traced to some emptiness, some missing element of knowledge, which she guessed was in some ways right.

Margie tried to drift off to sleep. She remembered running, in 1979, so fast. 1979 had a haze of speed around it. It was a whirlwind of discolored images—in retrospect perhaps taken from reexperienced old TV commercials: Pepsi, Breck girls, Slinky, Hot Wheels—so many colors, but all faded to pastels as though the only way to view the past was via the Panasonic console TV in the den, sun coming through the sliding glass doors and hitting the screen, oak veneer, and dial for the channels. Now there were Instagram filters. No need to remember anything. Regardless, she ran fast when she was young. There were streetlights and backyards and pavement, and it was before cars locked themselves and it was when phones rang. Back then her muscles hadn't turned on her yet—they were fine-tuned and agreeable. She loved her body back then.

"My toes feel like beetles. They feel crisp, like they're going to dry up and fall off."

Nick pulled the coffee table away from the couch and put a pillow on it. He lifted her feet onto the pillow. "Now try to sit up too. It will pass, it always does."

"So far . . . If I *knew* it would always go away, I would be okay. I need to get my mind off of it—off of my toes. And off of my throat." She ran a hand up her neck.

Outside thick rain shot pellet holes into what was left of old crusty snow, an occasional flat ping when the rain would hit the window. There would be no leaving the house today. Nick moved around the room with a slump to his back, as though the ceiling was about two feet lower than it really was.

Etta walked down to the Nethercotts', the steep decline making her knees ache by the time she reached the house. It was such a wet day. The rain had stopped, and what remained were rivulets of water leaking from under shrinking packs of icy snow that lined the sidewalk, ice melting bottom up. There was a sweetness in the air that promised spring, a warmth at the edges of the day that energized and motivated and called out the people to reinhabit, go forth, and multiply. Etta would have moments when she felt such a sense of purpose in the mighty world—the sky a pink cheek, the mountains lungs, every movement a confirmation of humanity, *of man made in God's image*. Oh, dear Lord in Heaven, have mercy on me, she thought. The glory of the Lord is so very big.

Today she would go to her friend. Margie was having some difficult symptoms, she had noted offhandedly in an email, and Etta felt she could somehow be a manifestation of the love of God for her friend, sit with her, talk with her, read to her. In one hand she held a paper bag with five warm apple fritters wrapped in foil. In the other, an interesting little book she had come across in the used bookstore, *Miss Lonelyhearts & the Day of the Locust*, odd and artsy—she'd flipped through the pages. Something Margie would probably like. What an obscure little thing the book was, hidden away in the back of the Second Reading bookstore under Novellas, next to the flimsy paperback travel guides, lost in the overabundance of published books. It was a terrible black-and-white cover—probably why she'd never heard of it. It appeared almost mimeographed, if there was such a thing, a mimeographed book. Regardless, it would be nice to sit with Margie and read. She was tired today, she had said in an email, didn't have enough energy to drink her orange juice.

Etta knocked on the front door, shifting the fritters to the other hand. Nick opened it looking at his feet, kicking at the little gray rug that was bunching up under the door.

"Etta."

"Hello, Nick. I come bearing gifts—apple fritters actually." She held the paper bag out. "Twice I tried the recipe. This time it worked out. Last time ended up with a melted rubber spatula and grease splatters all over the kitchen." She laughed.

"So kind. . . ." Nick smiled and looked in the bag.

"Is Margie okay? I'm a little worried."

"Yeah," Nick turned toward the living room and Etta followed him. "It's a bad day but we've had them before. She'll be glad to see you."

Margie was sunk into the couch, feet in white socks propped on the coffee table. Her head was tilted back and her eyes were closed. "It's my friend Etta," she said groggily, not bothering to open her eyes. "Do you have any idea how sick it is to feel liquid go down one side of your throat? It's sick. I'm half a person. Something very disturbing about being half a person, Etta—very disturbing indeed."

Nick stood there for a moment while Etta moved some cushions aside so she could sit next to Margie. Etta perplexed him.

"I have a book to read to you. Do you want me to read to you? Oh, and apple fritters. They're very yummy."

"How do apple fritters taste on one side of the throat?"

"You're probably fine now, I'm sure the sensation's passed," Nick said.

"I'm afraid to find out. Afraid. Give me pain over *sensations* any day."

"Oh, Margie," Etta touched her knee, "I'm so sorry. . . ."

"It is shit. It's shit." She lifted her head and opened her eyes. "Sorry about the vulgar language. What book are you going to read to me?"

Etta held up *Miss Lonelyhearts*.

"Nathanael West?" Margie laughed out loud, "Ha, ha, ha, ha, ha, *Soul of Miss L glorify me*, ha, ha, ha, ha. . . ."

"You've read it?" Etta was taken aback. Nick shuffled around, smiled a little bit, and left the room.

"Dear Miss Lonelyhearts, I am writing you because as of eight o'clock this morning I can only feel things on one side of my throat," Margie said. "I'm sorry, it's ironic, that's all. Appropriate though—terribly appropriate. I love Nathanael West. It's an unusual book and a wonderful choice, Etta. I do feel sorry for myself. Forgive me, please forgive me. I don't mean to be rude. You're so kind. You're really, really kind. You really are."

Dear Miss Lonelyhearts—

I am in such pain I don't know what to do sometimes I think I will kill myself my kidneys hurt so much. . . .

28.

Margie: back up for just a sec

When Margie was almost ten, she found a soiled sanitary napkin and a high school gym uniform—a one-piece unit masquerading as two, elastic at the waist, stripes on top and solid blue for the shorts—in the bushes next to the field where the wild grapes were. The grapes were green and sour and somehow wonderfully different from grocery-store grapes. They almost popped when you put them into your mouth. A sideways sweetness. Her mother had been dead for seven months when she found the sanitary napkin. She still acted the same, she was still Margie, and it surprised her. Breakfast in the morning. She stayed at school during lunch period. That was different. She used to walk home for lunch, staring at the cracks in the sidewalk and trying to set a pace that would correspond to the flat sections of concrete, and her mother would have something warmed up from the night before. There was a tightness now, to her life, very ordered, a little bit of a choking sensation that was barely detectible except sometimes when she was in bed at night. She did miss her mother, she would tell herself, and sometimes force herself to cry. It felt good to cry.

She went to the field to sit on a large mound of grass and pick the vines for grapes. Bees hovered over the white clover, and the Midwestern heat magnified the sound of cicadas, their slow zipping hums overlapping each other.

The sanitary napkin and the gym uniform were visible from where she sat. She spotted the blue, went to investigate, and recoiled when she saw the napkin sticking out from under the uniform. She'd heard of rape, and somehow, to her nine-year-old mind, she translated her discovery into a *rape scene.* Margie imagined the girl of the pad and uniform dead and gone, underwater—buried halfway in mud, in a suitcase, the trunk of a car, dirty blonde hair this way and that.

There was a boy, Robbie, who sometimes appeared back then. He was older and Margie remembered him from his earlier appearances, on a bike next to the curb, a group of boys. Basketball, and then in the field with golf clubs and plastic balls, shocking them into the air, whacking them baseball-style, and then with skateboards in the cul-de-sac. Now he had a way about him that interested Margie, as though he might be looking at her in his peripheral vision only to ignore her when she was in full view. He was skinny but his joints were getting big, knees so much more complicated, and elbows that jutted as though to break the skin, the way boys get before the rest of them catches up. Robbie showed up the day she saw the rape scene. He had a plastic bag, a few empty beer cans weighing it down. Schlitz, Coors. He had a collection. She instinctively tried to keep him from seeing the blue uniform and napkin, walking away from it and talking to him so that he might follow her.

"We have tons of beer cans in our garage if you want some more."

"I'm looking for a flat top," he said, not looking up. He swiped his foot out in front of him, back and forth like a metal detector.

"We have those." She watched as he headed away from the area of the gym uniform.

"I doubt it. They're hard to find and they're worth, like, twenty bucks." He hadn't looked at her yet. He bent down and picked up a pink Tab can, drained it, threw it into the weeds behind him. She felt somehow dominant for a moment, trying to head him away from the pad and uniform. In the end the boy was hardly interested in evidence of any rape scene or anything else for that matter, picking his way through the tall grass in search of his beer cans. He looked at her once, barely, and Margie wondered if she had only imagined his sideways glances, if they had been there only because she had wanted them to be there. She wondered if this was just the way of girls and maybe it never stopped, the imagining, as though boys were always looking in the grass for something and then they grew into fathers and set their aluminum cans in carefully stacked pyramids in paneled dens, and girls kept waiting for them to look at them but they wouldn't, at least not really, not in the eyes.

The rest of her year at the age of nine, and then turning ten, she was—however young—changing. The ever-so-slight twin buds on her chest. Her father always looking right through her. They ate breakfast. She went to school. He went to work. She came home. He came home. They ate dinner. He watched TV. She went to bed. He went to bed.

Ten, eleven, twelve, thirteen. All of them disasters. She was a troubled girl, poor thing, her mother had died. All that makeup. She moved to Trinity.

29.

Etta and Margie:

more from lonelyhearts

Margie stared at a little figure on the upper shelf of the bookcase. The figure was a sandy-looking Buddha-like character, a cloak around its shoulders, mild knowledgeable smile. The figure was from Nick's graduate-school days. She didn't know where it had come from. As she stared at it, her vision began to swarm with sparklettes and the periphery became milky.

> *I am kind of ashamed to write to you because a man like me don't take stock in things like that but my wife told me you were a man and not some dopey woman so I thought I would write to you after reading your answer to Disillusioned. I am a cripple forty-one years of age. . . .*

Etta's face was down close to the page, her thumb ready to turn to the next one. She would read normally and then slow down, taking in the words—pausing as though to process—before proceeding on. Her voice was soothing, and Margie, when she stopped staring at the sandy Buddha, closed her eyes to listen to the dips and drawls of Etta's voice, fastening her mind's eye on a dark line of audio-text, something that mimicked a musical stanza, the line carrying some kind of life in it when Etta shifted from dialogue back to prose.

Beyond Etta's voice was the immediate *sh-sh-sh-sh* sound of the disc-shaped Hammacher Schlemmer noise machine coming from the hallway outside Nick's door. The noise was intended to camouflage the goings-on in his office, mix with any great revelations or perfunctory evidence regarding the *Internal Lives of People.* Nick was in there with Carly, and Margie had sensed a sob or two leak past the Hammacher Schlemmer, derailing her concentration on *Miss Lonelyhearts.* Etta was reading faster now, and louder, flying through the gospel according to Shrike. She looked up, stared into the middle distance, and continued reading.

Carly, Margie was pretty sure, was a sobbing mess behind that door. She could almost see the door physically thumping out with bitterness, as though there was a creature of the Jurassic Park sort on the other side. She imagined Nick leaning back in his chair, deterring his loathing by fingering inconsequential areas of his body—running a hand along the back of his neck, picking at an eyebrow, stopping to observe the thick cuticle of a thumb.

Etta's voice came in and out of Margie's concentration but remained comforting. The two women imprinted the couch, the decades-old feather cushions submitting to the weight of their bodies. Margie tilted her head back and closed her eyes. She heard the low *sh-sh* of the noise machine, discerned a compulsory wail leak out from beneath the door of Nick's office, a moan, a hiccup, and most of all Etta's voice, soft, determined, honorable—*They both rolled part of the way down the stairs*, she read out loud, and then looked up, her eyes glistening with tears.

30.

Noel and Owen:

babies, and embryos

Summer was just around the corner and things were beginning to wrap up. Noel's communication with Owen remained text. *ur gone b my bff?* And in light of this, nothing was to be taken seriously. A paper valentine heart made for a friend. They texted to go to this or that YouTube video or Facebook post or look at this and, no way, check this out. They left web videos on each other's Facebook pages, *Bow wow wow, yippee yo yippe yay. . . .* Syncing low-res videos taken with their phones with C-grade music for comic effect. All nonsense, but then the moment things began to change. Owen texts: *only 1 letter diff betwn us L or W. Owen, Noel. Dude, we like the same grl. u b my gf?*

He called her after that. Noel was in the kitchen working at the little half stove, trying to get one of the burners to light. Click, click, click, and then nothing but the wiry smell of gas.

"Seriously."

This was all Owen said when she picked up her phone. The smell of gas became noxious. She put her phone on speaker and set it on the counter. She turned the burner off. "I like texting, though," she said. She opened the front door of the apartment to let the smell out. "It's like we're robots and there are no consequences."

"Exactly. This is why we should be together."

"But that would be irresponsible, us being robots. It's like that movie. . . ."

"We're very compatible. My thumbs hurt which means I must be crazy about you."

"You're always so meta. *I must be crazy about you.* Either you are or you're not."

Noel picked her phone back up and turned off the speaker. "Do you ever leave a book like you leave a movie, sort of stunned? I think it's an indicator of success, not just the success of the book, but of the reader too, like how successful the person was in engaging with it. There's a responsibility that belongs to the consumer. Movies engage us like they're real life, and then we come out of the theatre, not just blinking, but like there's a coat of plastic over everything. Things are less real, not more real. Movies make life seem so inconsequential, good movies do anyway. And then those good movies leave the theatres and shrink—physically shrink, if you think about it—onto your little screens at home and before long they're on your iPhone and you watch them at the same time you're half listening to a lecture in Psych 101. Can you imagine watching *It's a Beautiful Life* during Psych 101? How do you engage? But then you wouldn't have that plastic feeling when it's over, you would just close your notepad and talk to people as you left and you wouldn't think anything more about the boy riding in the tank and then seeing his mother. I finished a book last night that made me feel stunned when I closed it, like a good movie. I was a responsible consumer. It's a new book and very short—*It's Me*, it's called. It's about a guy who thinks he's a dung beetle—but it's not like Kafka or anything. He rolls shit around. . . . I mean real shit, poop. He rolls poop around. Weird, but it stunned me. It was all allegory. Obviously. Like a *Pilgrim's Progress* sort of thing." Noel had given up on the burner and was leaning back against the counter. "You can't multitask when you're reading something like that. There must be so many reasons why people are stupid."

"*Pilgrim's Progress* has plagued me for years," Owen said. "I'm way too much like Christian—almost in a boring way. There are times when I feel like if I look up, I'm going to physically see a valley or a hill or a river, and then I'll be looking around for Faith. Maybe you're Faith, Noel, maybe that's why we should be together. This is why we're so compatible. You are a freak, definitely, but I understand everything you've been saying."

"I'm a freak. . . ."

"Yes, but I mean that as a compliment."

Noel tried the burner again. Click, click, click . . . "My thumbs hurt too, but I think we should have more in common besides just understanding each other. I think we should both be determined to stop the Japanese whaling boats, for instance, or donate a month of our time to measure the thickness of ice floes in the North Atlantic. You're anti-abortion for example. . . ."

"And you're pro-death. . . ."

There was a silence.

"Wow, Owen. Wow. *Christian*, that was nice."

"That was stupid. You're right. I'm sorry. You're not pro-death and taken literally we're both pro-life. I'm anti-abortion, usually, but I'm not even sure. I could actually be pro-choice depending on the circumstances."

"This is a conversation for the nineties; it's moot so let's just drop it. But like I said, I don't think we have enough in common." Noel slammed a pot down on the burner, bent down, and looked for a flame, click, click, click. . . . "I mean, I don't know, whatever. I gotta go."

31.

Noel and Keith:

explosions in the sky

It would rain. The sky had grown deeper between the tree branches toward the south end of the park, which struck a chord with the green leaves, making them darker. Dark skies and dark leaves herald a shift in the weather as air currents go off in separate directions to bond with California wind and strange airstreams originating somewhere north of Maine. But before the rain was an expansive cool that blew across the park, turning leaves underside up, their lighter sides flashing pale in the darkening afternoon. The coolness fingered through people's hair, rounded their necks, settled nowhere. It was a perfect evening except for the possibility of the rain. Noel entered the park at 72nd Street and walked down toward the Bandshell, ignoring the boys with their bike taxis circling at a slow pedal looking to catch her eye and offer a ride. She stopped at the pond to watch the last few boaters heading in. The park was dotted with groups of people slowly funneling toward the area of the old stone Bandshell and around the corner to SummerStage, where Explosions in the Sky was due to begin playing at 5:30. The fact that she was alone had unexpectedly turned out to be all-good, giving her time to muse or not muse, it didn't really matter, just being alone and out of the apartment was so liberating right now, exams almost over, half of the students already having left for home, wherever that was. She was an enigma—all these people and all this time alone, the more surrounded she was, the more she longed for zero conversation and zero knowledge of those around her. Their lives were for her to imagine and nothing more. If she did see someone she knew, she would turn away, she decided. She did not want to see a familiar hat or face or anything. If she recognized a soul it would only be her own tonight. She hoped to lie on the ground outside the little amphitheater, look into the sky, and listen. She would make up words to go with the music.

When it began to rain the drops were large and heavy, thick and audible as they hit the pavement. The leaves shuddered. As Noel walked passed the Bandshell, she noticed that people were beginning to form groups, as though the rain was a tragedy and they needed the comfort of each other. The rain grew harder. One group had an orange poncho and they tried to spread it above their heads, pulling at the edges, their foggy dark hair visible through the thin wet plastic. They laughed and bunched up, pressing into each other. Thunder. And then the sky opened and there were sheets of rain—Noel looked for cover and headed toward a shade tent that SummerStage had set up for ticket sales. People were already huddled under it, those at the edges covering their heads with newspaper or handbags for added protection. The rain quickly soaked through Noel's thin T-shirt and camisole. She found a spot halfway under the tent and tentatively shuffled in further. People moved, crammed, made room. Some laughed. *Shit's got some piss comin' down. . . .*

A girl with a bag made out of a tire held it up, "Look what I get for being green. What the hell, repurpose a tire as a hat, not a freakin' purse!" Her friends laughed. Some guy lit a cigarette, and a few people made a point of looking at him—one girl held a fist to her mouth and coughed twice. The guy with the cigarette inched to the edge of the group and blew his smoke out into the rain. It was Keith.

At first Noel looked down and turned away, but then felt stupid for being false—in light of the rain she wasn't going to be able to lie down on the lawn and look at the sky and listen to Explosions anyway. She pulled her clinging shirt away from her cold skin. "Keith," she said, because he was right next to her by now. He looked at her mid-smoke.

"Noel! Get out of here . . . hey, you an Explosions fan, eh?"

Noel smiled and nodded twice, two long chin-out emphatic nods.

"We keep running into each other."

"I'm not stalking you, I swear."

"Ah, what's to stalk anyway? This skinny dweeb?" He grabbed a pinch of his thin arm and then flicked himself in the bicep with a finger. A large drop of water fell from is chin. "Funny I should run into you again in this monumental megalopolis. Fuckin' day though, eh?"

"I was going to lie on the lawn, I don't have tickets."

"A true fan. I like that you like Explosions in the Sky."

"And I you, Keith." Noel smiled and, feeling awkward, began to rummage in her purse for nothing. The rain lightened, a strong gust of wind and then more rain, either from the trees or the sky, it was hard to tell. The die-hards who had remained in line during the downpour began to move forward as the gate was opened, shuffling ahead as they held umbrellas, jackets, purses, above their heads.

Keith looked over at the line. "General admission and a *deluge* of water." Noel realized he was emphasizing his accent just like he had with Pixie when she first met him at Starlights.

"Well, it's certainly not worth it for me," she said, peering out at the sky as if it would reveal information on its intentions. Her signal she planned to leave when the rain stopped.

Keith nodded toward the queue of people. "They're a bit crazy, I think."

"Don't you have a ticket?"

"I wouldn't stand in the rain for three hours to hear Mozart himself with a bunch of slimy wet people. What do you think the chances of selling a ticket right now are?"

"If the rain lets up, good. But then if the rain lets up, you don't want to sell it, do you?"

"Ah, the skies are not trustworthy tonight. They're teasing us, I'm sure. If it stops, it's just for a laugh—the buggers 'ill let loose again as we're waiting for the second set. What do you say for a cup of coffee? Better yet, wine?"

"I'm nineteen."

"Back in the day I was nineteen. I know just the place."

They walked out of the park and up to 81st Street. Keith led Noel to a small place called Bugout, down a set of stairs, tucked in the basement of a brownstone. There were dusty-colored paper lanterns and scrappy wooden beams that had chalk writing all over them. They sat down in a small booth. Above their heads it said in white chalk, *Wake Up!* Someone had thumbtacked a Polaroid of a girl's face to one of the beams. The girl was wide-eyed and smiling with her mouth wide open so that she looked crazy.

"On me," Keith said, pushing a menu to her side of the table.

"Oh, like a date?" Noel said, as she looked down at the laminated menu.

"Right," Keith winked at her. "Good riddance, *Explosions*, let's have some real fireworks, heh. . . ."

Noel looked at him.

"I don't mean, of course . . . but then it is a Nicholas Sparks sort of evening," he said, and waved a hand at her. "Oh, shut up. I'm an ass, we'll leave it at that."

"I haven't read any of those books. Are they any good?"

"I imagine so. Probably on airplanes they are."

A waitress came over to take their drink orders. Keith said, "Two house merlots and we'll order in a sec."

"IDs please?"

"Fuck." Keith reached into his wallet for his license. "One house merlot, and a *big* glass. Fuck, give me the whole bottle." He looked at Noel, "Yes, like I said, a true ass. I'm sorry about that."

They ordered an asparagus dip with flatbread and sat in the booth with the one glass of wine between them so Noel could take sips. Keith refilled. "It's like communion," he said, and held the glass to her lips. She smiled and her dimple made her whole face light up.

"I've never done drugs," Noel said.

"Wine isn't a drug." Keith pulled the glass away, half serious. "What? You don't drink?"

Noel laughed. "No, not that. I've never even smoked weed. Don't share that with anyone. Don't know why I'm baring my soul like this."

"That's really sweet. I like that."

Noel shrugged.

"So you're a virgin, too?"

Noel broke off a piece of flatbread.

"That's not my business," Keith said, and downed the last of the wine. "That's none of my business. Geeze, look at me."

The wine warmed Noel. She felt the front of her shirt. It was almost dry.

They walked toward Broadway, a great chasm of darkness above their heads where the tops of the buildings appeared to bend in from their low perspective, almost an arc of simple facades, as though the buildings would either eventually touch or continue to steer away from each other, vastly different, off into different boroughs, states, countries.

Keith had a slight pop to his walk, as though a hip had dislocated and not quite made it back to where it belonged. It was an agreeable rhythm, one that added spirit to his frame—it seemed a British peculiarity, his mismatched sides, as Keith was, most of all, from London. Noel allowed herself a wide range of thought as the wine had temporarily hit that spot of insufficiency that she usually felt and padded it with meaning and interest. The expanse of concrete sidewalk and miniature courtyards with wrought-iron fences, stairs up, stairs down, bags of garbage, broken fire hydrants that had a certain bareness to them so that it was obvious they were dry, missing something. The rain had completely stopped and the cool breeze was back. Keith's hand brushed hers as they walked, and he went back to it without looking at her and held it lightly in his own.

"You're on Amsterdam and what?" Keith said as they came to the corner.

"Down, it's 75th. Follow the smell of the gyros." She let go of his hand. "You don't need to walk me. It was fun hanging out."

"I'll walk you. I like you. I want to walk you because I like you."

"Okay," she shrugged. "Sure, all right." They turned on Amsterdam.

"I want to know how Pixie's doing."

"Wish I had something to tell you. She's in long-term care. She has a feeding tube. It's what we all fear will happen, you know, to ourselves? Some people think she feels stuff, other people say she doesn't. Doctors have no clue—they know far less than we ever thought. Where she is, the rehabilitation center, is pretty awful. Her dad, Pete, visits her. He's turned out to be sort of a good guy, I guess. I like him. I mean, he's definitely not quite right, but I don't know what the trouble between them was. He visits her every day, I think. Nobody tells him what we're all thinking—that he should let her go. I don't even know if the thought has occurred to him. Even after the doctors talk to him, I don't think he gets it. I was up there two weeks ago, and it's like there's been a culling; all the people who cared so much at first, they don't think it's worth it—that she'll die, that Pete needs to realize what's going on, that he's wasting his money, or the state's money, or whoever pays for stuff like that. The last time I visited her it was a month after it happened—December, maybe January. Winter break."

"I should visit."

"Why?"

"Pixie, she would visit me, I think."

"The drugs, that you gave her. That still bothers you?"

"No. Yes. It's just that the last time I saw her, I wasn't being good. I don't want her to remember me that way. Silly."

"Yeah, it is. Silly. But you could visit her if you want. Pete maybe would like someone else to visit. It's hard to say. He keeps to himself, has a room, and then I don't know, just sort of hangs around and visits her. He lights candles at night. A spiritual thing, I guess. People at first tried to have him over and stuff. I mean, it's not like people don't care anymore. Miriam and I are going to visit when I get back—Miriam and Owen and me. Some friends of mine. They were there when it happened. We were all there."

"Shit."

"Yeah."

They reached The Parthenon and stood in front of the window with the slow-turning slab of lamb, heat lamp angled at it so that it emitted a reddish glow. Keith bent down and kissed her goodbye, a soft kiss on the lips that hesitated perfectly. He ran his hand down her arm. He pulled away, looked her in the eyes, cupped her chin in his hands and kissed her again. "You're very lovely," he said. Noel half smiled and cocked her head slightly to one side. Deep inside the restaurant a small fire erupted on a plate of saganaki balanced on a waiter's arm. "*Opaah!*" they heard from behind the glass. Clapping.

32.

Margie and Etta:
mechanics of a wipeout

Etta climbed the stairs to Margie's studio with her wooden box of oil paints. She had carefully packed them up, pressed a piece of foam on top to keep them from shifting, brushes on top of that. She was a neat person. She always had been. Thankfully, though, other people's messes didn't bother her. Order was an established part of her life that she viewed as sort of the way she interacted with things. She would have made a terrific secretary. Being in Margie's home was an adventure, the books, the thumbtacks left on the walls. Oh, and *specimens*, of all things—things like the skull of a squirrel and hawk feathers, like an old national park museum. There was an x-ray of Noel's broken fibula when she was ten, split clear through, tacked up on the wall of the landing up to the attic. Etta had touched it once as she passed by, and it was dusty; her finger made a line of clarity on the plastic sheet, so she had pulled a sleeve up to cover her hand and wiped the rest of the x-ray. Clean and shiny. There.

Margie was having a good week. She was on her stool at the large painting she had begun when she was at work doing the Bridgestone children. The ceiling light she had initially painted had evolved into what looked like a metalwork of ovens. So odd. The canvas was an enormous room, pinks and grays, and the wiring of the light was up at the ceiling and then somehow descended into ductwork—crisp and defined—with grommets connecting elbows of metal and then moving, Escher-like, into something like potbellied stoves and around corners to bond with a new color or form that was hard to interpret. There were areas of great representation, even though it would be hard to say exactly what it was that they were. The preciseness of color and form into overlapping mixtures of new colors was stunning. Margie's back was unnaturally straight as she reached up and left, guiding a fat camel-hair brush smoothly around the corner of something that had the shape of a small propane tank and the colors of dented nickel but then left much to be interpreted. Margie was feeling really good. She was very excited, and she was in that sweet spot where her painting was talking to her.

"Margie, that's wonderful," Etta said, standing back and staring at it.

"You think? I'm beginning to like it. Until a week ago I thought it sucked. I had left it alone for a long time, but I got over that. I think there's always a moment when you hate your work—if it's going to be a good piece, anyway—and you want to take a knife to it, but then if you can get over that, it can end up being something you really love. Maybe because you hated it so much and had to fight for it. Who knows."

"I really like it."

"Maybe I'll give it to you when it's finished."

There was a silence.

Margie turned halfway around and looked at Etta. "I'm joking."

Etta quickly recovered and smiled. "Just hard to imagine where we'd hang it."

Margie swished her brush in a can. "Let's get you set up," she said, and began covering a small table with a dark brown cloth. She set a pewter pitcher on the cloth and then an orange, and a white dish next to the orange. She took three stems of fake daisies from a coffee can on the floor and put them in the pitcher. "Find a spot," she said, and nodded toward an easel. Etta began moving the easel around the still life as she eyed the table, finally settling on a place where light from the window was behind her and to the right. Margie took a small canvas that had been leaning against the wall and put it on the easel. "Start with burnt sienna," she said. "Mix the linseed with quite a bit of the turpenoid, try half and half to start. Oh, and shake up the linseed and turpenoid—make it a third, actually."

Etta obediently covered her canvas with the dull color. Ed would so not like this. "Noel must be coming home soon," she said as she painted. Margie was back on her stool working on the propane-tank thing. It was beginning to have skin tones. More and more.

"Friday. We can't wait. She was home a lot that first month, at first with Pixie, to visit Pixie . . . but now it's been a while, it will be different to have her home for the summer."

"Have you visited Pixie?"

"Yes. I've been a few times. I run into Pete, though, sometimes . . . he talks so little."

"I saw him last week. He seemed worn out." Etta finished covering the canvas and turned toward Margie. "Done. Now what?"

"Now you sketch everything in. Use the burnt sienna plain. Dark. But mix it with the linseed a little."

"I'm scared."

"Go on. Big strokes, none of your tight little pencil sketch stuff. Take it all in the shoulder. Paint with your shoulder."

"Now I *am* scared. What do you mean, paint with your shoulder?"

"The movement, it should come from your shoulder—not so much your wrist or fingers."

Etta stared at the canvas.

"Come on. Then you get to do the wipeout, it's the best part. Hurry up, let's go." Margie waved her brush in the air.

Etta took a step backward and straightened her arm, touching the tip of her brush to the painting. "This is so *scary*," she said.

Even with Margie's repeated prodding, Etta could not sketch out the still life quickly. She took the paint thick on the tip of her brush, practically hugged the painting, and leaned into it like she was writing a letter. Margie placed her hands on Etta's shoulders and gently moved her back, away from the canvas.

"Use your shoulder."

"I don't really get that. How do I use my shoulder?"

"The movement, let the movement originate from your shoulder."

Etta painted her lines, stepped back, painted more lines. The pitcher, the bowl, the daisies.

"Okay, fine. Now," Margie handed her a cloth, "wipe off the lighter areas. Look at the pitcher. Where you see light, wipe out the paint."

Etta dragged the cloth along the edge of her sketch of the pitcher. "Wow. Neat."

"See? See the depth?" Margie said. "Keep going. . . ."

33.

Owen: the path

The compelling nature of tunes like this was a mystery. The combination of everything—the melody, the chord progression, the mood, the poetry. All of it created a vibe beyond words. The right amount of repetition, the right amount of surprise . . . there's something infectious in it, it's some kind of magical spell. Epic songs communicate more than the sum of their parts.

Owen loved Leonard Cohen. He couldn't stop loving "Hallelujah" no matter how hard he tried, and on his own—by himself—he had strummed out his own cover of it like two thousand other people. It was embarrassing. He waited till the house was empty before he played. Of course he thought of Noel. Of course. Once, when he was alone on his bed leaning against the wall, he'd played it almost like he'd composed the thing himself, belted it out, made a true fit of passion out of it. It was a thing, the song. It would always be. Like a card you could hand to people, compact and simple, and then they open it and there's something handwritten that's real. Someday, Hallmark will probably make one of those cards that plays a horrible, barely recognizable song when you open it up and it will play "Hallelujah." Then, finally, maybe, he'll never sing it again. Maybe.

It fascinated him how Cohen was able to turn a biblical story into something profane and yet sounding like it was ordered from Heaven. Now Cohen is old and thin, but his face still looks the same. Maybe his songs somehow preserved it—like the sadness of them, counterintuitively, keeps away the bitterness that usually presses faces down, forces a slightly protruding chin further out, caves in cheeks. But he knows Cohen was as confused and searching as anyone, spiritually, even though he probably wouldn't have said so. "Hallelujah," as far as the lyrics, was messed up, but—still—the chord progression, the melody.

Seriously, God, what is this world you've put me in?

THE SOCCER TEAM WAS PRACTICING. The field was a raised plateau so that the spring melt had muddied only the few sloping feet around it. At this point, the team was just messing around, kicking the ball up, catching it on their knees, getting their shoulders under it and using their heads to pass it off to a teammate. Owen walked past the field with his hands in his pockets. It was still cold. He had never been good at the team sports, probably had something to do with feeling responsible for the rest of the team. Afraid of how his own mistakes would affect others. This is how he lived his life, and it carried too much weight as it was. He knew somehow he'd played a part in keeping his friends away from pills, weed even—Miriam's prom weed notwithstanding. You're a good man, Charlie Brown. Probably the only kid his age in America who didn't play soccer. If he wanted recreation, it was of the solitary sort. Hiking, kayaking, leaving people behind, way behind, so he couldn't hear their sorrows and want to make them go away—or feel the need to make them go away. If he kayaked or hiked, stuff could echo in his ears for a while but then the water or the woods would take over. He needed to take time away, go up a mountain. With all of the praise he got for being Owen, he was likely the most selfish one of all, just very, very good at appearing otherwise. Sometimes leaving the dorm for even a short walk gave him perspective.

He passed the field and headed up a set of stairs to a parking lot and across to the woods where there was a trailhead. It would be muddy, but he had worn his hiking boots and didn't care anyway. He wouldn't run into anybody this early in the spring. He had already started to warm up and unzipped his jacket.

There was no phone in his pocket. No ear buds or paperback book or even Moleskine. As he began the slow climb up the mountain, he could hear the falls in the distance, louder than usual and full of every drop of water skimming down, like the purpose of the mountain was enriched by the spring melt. It *was* the purpose, taking the water like that. It's what mountains are for. These waterfalls. They've been used as sightseeing destinations and hydrodams and eighth wonders of the world for so long—signs and plaques telling them what's important to notice, the number of gallons of water that flow over them in a day—that there's nothing left for people to wonder about. The awe of them, angling water to just the right places so the force doesn't destroy stuff, villages built in dry areas. As he walked, he stepped over the angled water bars; someone had already set logs into the trail to channel runoff. He felt happy.

As the sound of the falls got closer, he couldn't help thinking about Noel. Pixie was marginal now, only what she had unintentionally brought to Trinity seemed to matter, but even still, she was some kind of hollow, like a darkened hole that people had to deal with or ignore. Hope? But there *was* no hope. What good was there? What made him feel like this? Was it just his personal (so, selfish) desire for Noel? *O happy land where all are kings!* He remembered a Puritan prayer he'd read once and smiled to himself. Maybe he could stay happy.

The path grew narrow, and as he made his way uphill he was grateful for a section with plenty of roots to step on. Below, to the right, he began to see the water through the bare trees. The trees didn't have leaves yet, but the tiniest of buds if you bothered to look. A reddish tint to some of them. Someday, he'll learn the names of trees, the names of birds. He'll be one of those old men who carry around binoculars and speculate about mating patterns. The rush of the falls grew thunderous.

34.

Margie: things we miss

Margie, honestly, had only visited Pixie twice since that first time at the hospital with Noel. This time she decided to go because of an idea she had felt stirring within her as she painted. The idea was that perhaps, maybe, in the same way that Etta faithfully visited Pixie once a week, bringing her flowers and saying a prayer, Margie might have something to add as well. Something to give. She had been feeling so good lately and it made her feel bounteous, the idea of helping someone. The answer, perhaps, was to always be reaching out and helping others in some way, not think about herself, her pain, that unsettledness.

When she came into the room, she noticed that someone had moved a more comfortable chair next to the bed, one that reclined. There was a pillow and a blanket on the chair. Pete must be using it to sleep in. Other than that, nothing much had changed. Etta's flowers this week were tulips. They sat on the deep windowsill next to a vent. She went around to the other side of the bed and sat down in the chair. It was in the reclining position, so she put it back upright and rested her arms on her knees. The nursing home was quieter than the hospital was and the orderlies appeared listless. Too much exposure, Margie thought, numb. The room looked like it should have smelled musty, but it didn't, it smelled like ammonia. There was far less equipment now, just a few necessary lines, no slow-breathing cuffs on her legs. She looked at her. It was easy to imagine Pixie at forty. Sun-damaged skin and smoker's wrinkles. Her short, choppy cut, which presently could have been a stylist's take on couture, would turn to gray and then be dyed and cut and dyed some more, turning brittle from some combination of the same chemicals that made her room smell like super-concentrated pee. But then Pixie was fair, pale really, so no sun damage, or very little anyway. What would it be like to have Pete as a father? He obviously loved her, even if he hadn't as of yet, or maybe just hadn't labeled it until now. If you had a stupid father, who loved you deeply, but did everything wrong, would things still be okay? Is there power in love, regardless of whether it's ever expressed? But Margie wasn't doing much good sitting here musing. She wanted to somehow bless Pixie, as Etta would say, but then she didn't know how to pray. And if she tried, she was certain it would do no good. People pray sometimes when they're scared, but she wasn't scared. She hadn't brought flowers but she'd brought a pin.

Margie leaned closer to the bed and let her wrists rest on the guard. Unlike the metal one at the hospital, this one was made of a tough plastic. Beige. Pixie's head was turned slightly left, away from Margie, having been turned but left like that, her head awkwardly to one side, but her arm was bare and rested tightly next to the guard from her shoulder to her elbow, where her forearm was on the edge of the mattress, free from the sheets and guardrail. Margie could see the scars that began above her wrist, on the inside of her arm, sometimes intersecting each other and most of them raised, just a shade toward blue compared to the rest of her skin. Her hands were in a calm half fist, naturally relaxed. Flat hands were never relaxed, even if they were resting on something. Margie remembered her mother's hand in the shag carpet when she'd found her the morning she died. It wasn't the first time she'd ever thought of it. The image was always there and it didn't really bother her. It was just the way things were. Margie reached out and lifted Pixie's hand, placing it further up on the mattress, next to her thigh. She turned it palm up, so that she could see the scars, and ran her fingers over them, following them up past the inside of her elbow and beneath the sleeve of her hospital gown, where they continued even farther. She pulled up the sleeve, and could see a few elongated scars that began at the top of her shoulder and disappeared, appearing to continue all the way down her back. Someone had bothered to run a comb through her hair, which looked greasy, like she had a man's cut and it had been pressed into place with pomade.

Margie folded her arms on the plastic guard and rested her chin on her hands and looked at Pixie. She began to whisper out loud what she thought would be a prayer but found her voice catching before she could speak. She tried again, but this time before the words came out she began to cry, just a little at first. And then more tears came until her mouth contorted and her eyes turned red and swelled and her nose ran so that she grabbed a box of Kleenex. She didn't stop crying for a long time.

35.

Pete: a lazarus opportunity

Pete had developed an odd habit, a tick, with his eyes. He would open them as wide as he could in an ocular stretch, and then squeeze them shut. This made him appear at first as though something unexpected had hit his cornea, and then when the process was repeated, two times, three times, he took on that internally crazed appearance that's so indicting of the unstable, like he had a mental itch that he was trying to get at through his eyes. It was hard to say if it was the periodic stretching of his eyes, or his resolute conviction that Pixie would "rise from the dead," that caused the people of Trinity to think he was in need of medication. Nick felt that both were incriminating, and after just a short time talking with Pete, decided he should refer him to Dr. Lynch as possibly schizophrenic, or at least as having a schizotypal personality disorder, and the doctor could give him a scrip for Haldol or one of the more recent antipsychotics. It looked like he already had tardive dyskinesia so maybe Seroquel.

Nick had finally convinced Pete to come for dinner. Margie remained upstairs with her painting until the last minute, deepening the negative space with an ochre—something that had become difficult to do as the negative space was, it could be argued, the more she worked on the painting, actually positive space. The ovens were rounded and thick at the corners. Etta's wipeout on the other side of the room, with her awkward, slow initial sketches, caught Margie's eye. She looked back at her own painting. There was a softness to the ovens, the rounded corners a nice contrast to the metal-looking ductwork that took right and left turns and angled down from nowhere back into the belly of something like a stove the color of skin. She listened to Nick in the kitchen and glanced out the window from time to time to check for Pete's car.

When she came downstairs Pete was already in the kitchen sitting at a chair pulled away from the table. He held a glass of beer. Nick gave Margie a look. She'd been late coming down.

"Pete," Margie said, "good to see you. I was just finishing up something."

Pete stood up and smiled nervously and then slipped back into his chair.

"We've been talking," Nick said as he dumped a box of fettuccini into boiling water, "about some of the opinions he's getting from Pixie's doctors . . ."

Margie looked at Pete. "I visited her," she said. "Noel comes home soon and we'll go together. Noel will want to see her."

"Well, that'd be nice. Your friend, Etta, just came to visit. Brought her husband, and some flowers they had. She's been coming all along. Sometimes she prays for Pixie and I appreciate that." Pete widened his eyes and it startled Margie at first. He squeezed them shut. He looked away and then widened them again.

"Religion can really be helpful," Nick said, "helps you feel grounded. There's a lot to be said for religion. God should be a comfort, God doesn't want to scare you." Nick turned down the burner under the fettuccini.

"I light the candles for her."

"He's had different advice from the doctors," Nick said to Margie over his shoulder.

"One of them says let her go," Pete opened his eyes, squeezed them shut. "Go where? That's not up to me, letting her go."

"It's difficult sometimes to think that we might play a role in something this earnest," Nick said.

"Maybe God wants to raise her from the dead."

Nick said, "Well, hmm. . . ."

"What's that to me, if God wants to raise her from the dead?" He shrugged and reached for his beer.

"Sometimes we need to take things as they are . . ."

Pete widened his eyes, squeezed them shut, widened them again.

"Prayer helps us feel in control. . . . It's good for us," Nick said.

"I light the candles. I have a lot of them now. I read a Bible sometimes."

"A great place to start. Try to meditate, center yourself. Do you know what I mean when I say center yourself?"

"I can already feel that. I can feel God, and it makes everything back off." Pete finished the last of his beer and set it down hard on the table.

PETE WENT TO ROSEDALE'S TO MAKE COPIES. Rosedale's was a mailing store where you could register your car or get a notary public or pay a gas bill. There were three parking spaces in front. He had taken a picture of Pixie. He brushed her hair, positioned the camera from above, pressed the button, waited those extra-long seconds for the flash. The camera had cost $39.98 and he had gotten it at Rite Aid. The hard plastic from the packaging fell to the floor next to Pixie's bed. The picture didn't look like her—her face was flat and blank, and it looked like her lips were numb and somehow glued together and would need to be peeled apart before she could talk. After taking the picture, Pete had looked at it and been disappointed. He touched her lips and peeled them apart so that her mouth was open. They fell back together. It was her hair. He carefully took the brush and brushed it over her ear and down the side of her face. Static lifted strands into the air when he finished, and he tried to smooth them down with the palm of his hand. He lifted the camera again, this time keeping it a little to the side. The red dot at his finger lit up, the camera paused, and Pixie's face flashed white with her lips closed and her hair brushed to one side. At Rosedale's, a woman helped him make copies of the photograph.

THE FLYERS WERE EVERYWHERE. *See Pixie Rise!* Black and white. The woman had helped Pete print out the words *See Pixie Rise!* with a thick marker, then copy them all off. Fifty. They were stapled to telephone poles and thumbtacked to bulletin boards in the grocery stores. Taped to benches in the Square next to the tennis courts. Slid under the wipers of cars.

Spring rain eventually puckered the thin paper, and the images of Pixie took on a new hollowness with the folds. The thick handwritten words moved with the pleating of the paper, fattening and then disappearing, the photograph showing a new twist of the girl's jaw or corrugation of her nose. It was nothing but a picture, no more alive than what they were stapled to. Pete went methodically into stores, over to the library, the church, stairwells, bulletin boards, telephone poles, his large hands pressing a staple gun with determined force, as though the pressing itself was love, a way to go backwards.

At the bottom of the flyers it said in small black letters, *July 3, Northeast Rehabilitation Center, 8:00 p.m.* He added three bumps to the cursive *m*, the way they taught him in school.

The white pages lifted at the corners and threatened to become detached. Some did, falling next to curbs, conforming into drains with the rain, clinging to the iron grilles as the paper began its disintegration, softening and then pilling as the pulp began to separate. The hills of Trinity added to the profundity. There was a crying, in a way, the upper streets taking the rain first, sheets of it at times, soaking the papers, pulling at them, and then the rivulets of water draining toward Maple. People picked up the soggy papers and sighed, folded them carefully, and threw them away. There was a respect for the flyers, for Pixie's face, that no one would trespass, a reverence for her father, Pete, who continued to post them. Staple gun, large hands, some barely visible beam of hope as he nodded silently to the people he saw on the street. They tilted their heads, mouths closed, smiled back.

The papers dried in their new rain-generated shape, became almost crisp again, and then the rain would come once more and there the papers would be in the sewer grates, others slowly inching their way down the hills. Miriam said, "The whole town is freaking crying."

July 3 was because it was the day before Independence Day and there would be a natural celebration—a celebration of *liberation*, the day after Pixie rose from the dead. A parade, fireworks, Pete thought. A day for the wonder of what would happen.

36.

Miriam and Pete:

the college kids come home

Miriam had never left, of course, and for this reason she felt the need to feed her peers with the sort of information that would make them feel caught up but at the same time like they hadn't missed much. It was true, they hadn't. Missed much. Trinity was Trinity, the grass was coming up green and thick, the leaves had begun to grow and unfurl. The Abenaki caught hold of spring and ran fast, like a running of the bulls. The water was clearer than ever in the spring.

Pete's apparent decline into pathos and then his surge of hope fed by some Bible verse or something was what people were talking about. In fact, by the time Noel, Owen, Jason, and Jocelyn got home, it was really pretty old news. The flyers were still there—Pete replenished them from time to time—but by now they weren't so precious, people no longer politely picked them up and discretely threw them away. They saw them but they were old and too familiar, and there were other circulars competing now, like the neon orange one, George's Pizza and Subs. And the Stop-n-Shop: Marlboros for the state minimum.

Pete continued to come and go, stretch his eyes and squint, and look around. Etta, and Christine sometimes—every once in a while Margie—still visited Pixie and sat next to her bed for a half hour or so. Once Miriam went. She came with a small glass vase and a single yellow rose and set it on the heating vents next to the wide glass window, where the flower was reflected in a foggy smudge of yellowy color. Pete kept lighting his candles. There were a lot of them in his room now, and at night, when it was dark, it was possible to see the glow—the flicker from them—in the window of the Extended Stay.

When Miriam went to Noel's house, it was after a thunderstorm and the rain was still pinging into the gutters, an unrelenting urge to continue, sky beginning to tighten up but ever so slowly. The windows were halfway open, and the sweet, fresh smell made it through the screens and into the Nethercotts' living room where they sat. Miriam sighed.

"Now that you're done with a year of college and I didn't take even one class, didn't take any tests or anything, does this mean that I'm a year behind you? Like I lost a year of life—the way they say addicts lose whatever time they spend using . . . they get clean and find themselves fourteen again, scared to talk to the opposite sex and stuff?

"Not unless you sat and watched TV all year," Noel said.

"Does Hulu count?"

Noel smiled.

"I think when people get together now," Miriam said, "they should designate a certain spot in the room as the *camera angle*, a place where everyone should think of as the place where the camera is—like there will always be a recording of everything that's going on. Like in *The Office*. It would make everyone more profound, more funny. It would make people more *purposeful*. I think it would be hard to be depressed, or feel depressed, if there was a camera angled on your face all the time. . . ." Miriam paused. "And if someone said something stupid, like say, Jason said something stupid, you could look over at the camera intentionally, like it's interviewing you, the way Jim does with Dwight on *The Office*, and kind of give it a look—like, 'Geez, that guy over there is so stupid.'" Miriam listened to the rain. It had become steady again. "But I kind of hate *The Office*. I love *Arrested Development*. Just watched it twice through. The whole season actually. I have a crush on Michael. I think it's because he takes care of everyone, which means I must see myself in one of the characters—maybe Buster. I don't think I'm Lindsay, I'm just not pretty or slutty enough."

"Some colleges give credit for life experience," Noel said. "You can get three credits for a year doing something different or challenging. They have you write a paper. A pretty long one, though."

Margie came into the room holding her hands away from her sides as though they were on fire. Noel gave her a puzzled look.

"Different and challenging," Miriam said slowly, "those are the key words. I worked at Ace Hardware." She lifted her head when she realized Margie was there. "Hi, Mrs. Nethercott."

"If you can write, you *make* your year into something special," Noel continued. "Key in on some special ingredient of your time there, what you learned from the older people you spent time with and so forth."

"But you can write. I would never use the word *ingredient* in a sentence the way you just did, for example."

"How are you, Miriam?" Margie asked. "I've missed seeing you around."

"Pretty good. Bored, I mean. Pretty crappy to be completely honest. But you," Miriam said, "how are you? With the multiple sclerosis and everything? Is it still bad? I hope you feel better. Than last summer anyway."

"Ha ha," Margie laughed. "I'll never live that down."

"No, I totally get it. I do. I don't mean to bring it up but I totally get it. I'm really sorry."

"Thanks, Miriam. I've missed you. You're always honest. I feel a lot better; I was afraid I'd end up in a wheelchair, and I could. But I'm on new meds and usually I feel okay but some days it's still bad. I've gotten more used to the idea, and besides I feel a lot better."

Noel looked at Margie, "What's up with your hands, Mom?"

"They're swollen."

"They don't look swollen."

"They are, they feel like they are." She held one of them loosely in the other and massaged her own palm. "It's the rain perhaps, the humidity. I had to stop painting." She went to the large living-room window and pushed it up a few more inches using an elbow. Noel got up to help her, shoving it up the rest of the way.

"We're waiting for Owen. We're going over to visit Pixie," Noel said.

"Yes," Margie said. "Do that." She left the room.

Noel looked at Miriam after she left. "You know my mom has chronic depression, right? She has relapses. She can talk about the MS but she never talks about the depression."

"I thought so. I just assumed."

PETE WAS IN THE ROOM WITH A BIBLE, one finger running over the page like it was a recipe and he was about to pause and go get the sugar before he continued. He !ooked up. The three of them silently came in the room.

"Hello, Pete," Owen said quietly, and touched his shoulder before pulling up a chair upholstered in brown vinyl. Pete looked up with his eyes squinted shut.

He stretched them open again. "Hi. Hi. You know Pixie?"

"She's a friend of ours," Owen began. "You don't remember us?" and then stopped short before identifying himself as one of the people with her at the accident.

"You a school friend?"

"Yes," said Noel. "We're roommates. You've had dinner with my parents. Nick and Margie are my parents. I brought some of her things." She held up a plastic bag into which she had put some of Pixie's collectibles from the apartment—a small wooden elephant painted in colorful designs, a large, framed photograph of Malcolm Gladwell . . .

"She is a smart girl," Pete said, "she was always smart."

Miriam took the bag from Noel and began taking things out. She pulled out the picture of Gladwell and silently held it up to Noel, raising her eyebrows. Noel shrugged. Miriam carefully set the photograph on the bedside table, leaning it against the wall. She ran a hand over the front to get the dust off.

"That her boyfriend?" Pete reached for the picture.

"He's a writer," Noel said. "She liked his work, I guess."

"Maybe they were dating."

"She took . . . she got the picture from the journalism building. It was in a hallway or something. Pixie did stuff like that. She took it home and hung it on our wall."

Pete stretched his eyes open.

Owen stood next to the bed and touched Pixie's hand. On the inside of her arm the welts looked like small pasted-on worms. Light worms.

Noel watched Owen touch Pixie. Owen was thin. From the side he was a filament of an S, like a genetic symbol. His concave chest scooped out. Did he have any other choice but to play the guitar and be into folk music? He wasn't made for soccer or computers. History, of course, but then that was his major. . . . He complied with his physical self, it seemed.

"She looks peaceful," Noel said, looking down at Pixie.

"Oh, she is," Pete brushed the back of his hand against her cheek. "I just sit here and I can tell she's peaceful. I read to her. I been reading the Bible." He looked at Pixie softly, like a puppy asleep. "She, she's listening. I didn't always know her before now; it's now that I miss her, you know. Before, I didn't see her too much, and now, now that she's all still and quiet, I come to find out I can't live without her. She was always a reader, Pixie, ever since she was just four or five, couldn't get her away from those books and I just said, okay then. I was so busy with the bridges back then. Then I got this scud injury and here I am with nothing to do but be her pop. So I'm reading to her like it's all she has, because I think it is, all she has for now. I'm reading the Gospel a Saint John." Pete caressed his Bible with the same care that he had caressed Pixie's cheek.

Owen sat down.

"You coming? When we pray for her?"

No one said anything. A woman wearing rose-colored scrubs pushed a metal cart past the open door. Someone yelled to her from down the hall, and she turned and smiled and gave whoever it was the finger.

"We'll be back," Noel said from the foot of the bed. Owen looked at her.

"Just as long as you come back on the Third, all right? July third. You see the posters? I need people here."

"We'll come," Owen said.

"You come back July third." He squinted and opened his eyes. "We can all light the candles and pray. She's expecting you all to be here." He winked, but it was hard to tell if it was intentional.

"We'll be here," Miriam said, "don't worry. July third."

Pete leaned forward and then back again as though anxious. He pressed the Bible to his forehead. “Come back, okay?”

Miriam went to him and put her arms around his shoulders. She hugged him from behind and pressed her face to the top of his head. He smelled of cigarettes. “We’ll be here,” she said.

37.

Margie: ears like broccoli

Margie went to bed for three days. Monday, Tuesday, Wednesday, during which time she imagined the ovens that she had painted opening their doors to her in a cacophony of sound. Cast iron scraping open, the fire—a burning that was more of a warmth than a threat. She imagined her hands in the ovens, heating up in the fires like molten globs of glass.

She lay still on her back because this was the only way she didn't feel pain. The heaviness she felt in her limbs was eased when her physical body was all at the same level, limbs out at forty-five-degree angles like a snow angel. An increased dose of Lyrica had begun to help, plus the anti-depressants, but it was the warming weather, the approaching humidity, the constant itch of imaginary fingers on her skin.

Her ears were numb too. They felt like vegetables, even when she touched them, especially when she touched them. When there is no feeling, that part of your body has to be *something*. Lips become rubber. Ears become broccoli.

She imagined the colors of her palette, a red ochre and a touch of sap green. But she would mix them and the intensity of the pigments would be hidden deep within the oil. . . .

Nick brought her some Masala tea.

She pressed her pillow up on the headboard and inched back almost to a sitting position. "Nick," she said.

He put a paisley cloth napkin on the bedside table and set the mug on top of it. He bent and kissed her on the forehead.

"You brought me chai tea?"

"Chai means tea," he said. "It's like saying 'tea tea.'"

"You brought me tea tea?"

He smiled. "That's weird."

"Sometimes mothers ask their toddlers if they need to go tee tee." Margie said slowly, and reached for the tea before pulling back. "I'm sorry, Nick, it's my hands, they're just, so, heavy. . . ."

Nick picked up the mug and began to blow on the tea to cool it. "It's still too hot anyway."

"What day is it?"

"Wednesday. June 10, I think. Why?"

"I lost track."

Nick took a sip to test the temperature. He started blowing again.

"You are a good man."

"I think so."

"July 3, I want the flare-up to go away by then."

"For the Fourth?"

"For Pete." Margie said. Nick gently guided the mug to her lips. She took a very light sip. "That's nice."

"I have someone in a few minutes." Nick lifted the mug to her lips again.

"I'm such an invalid. I'm sorry you have to go. I'll call Etta, I think I've been alone too much. I need to talk, or listen or something. What day is it?"

"June 10. It's Wednesday."

NICK RODE HIS BICYCLE, a skinny yellow thing, in the evenings after dinner, especially after a hard or disorienting day. The wind on his face helped to straighten things out. It occurred to him that the actual physicality of biking might set his dopamine levels right, align synaptic gaps, or cause surges of brain chemicals that could kick in like vodka to float the end of his day like a wave onto a foamy shore. We are such specimens of pain and comfort. One or the other, never both—always scrambling toward comfort. M. Scott Peck thought much health came with simply eating the part of the cake you liked least, first. For example, you like icing, you save it for the last. But—and here it was hard to understand Peck as a therapist—life for many people is all cake and no icing. All burnt, scabby cake with salt substituted for sugar. Was he saying that it was up to the people who were dealt the bad cards to make the most of things? The unfairness of life. The unfairness of dopamine and norepinephrine and the things that shoved the chemicals this way or that. Recently Nick had been researching his ancestry online. There was a castle in Scotland, he thought he remembered his grandmother say. Donnelly. A surname a few generations back. Margie thought it was silly to look up his ancestry. We all came from oysters anyway, she said, so who cares?

He let the bike glide down the hill toward Maple, where he turned south and began to pedal again. The river was on his right, with the metal railing that was installed in the eighties during the height of Trinity's little economic boom. Was Margie's grandfather still alive then? Now here the town still is, big trees and the river and a wrought-iron railing that reflects a town that had lived once, twice, and now kept on only because of its history. It was a giant loop of survival. What kept Trinity happy? Trinity itself. Nick rounded the bend and stood and pumped for extra power. He passed over the bridge and got a whiff of the fresh water. Was it a smell or a feeling? Nothing in the world like fast-moving fresh water.

He stood again and pedaled hard, cranking down and around as he went up the hill on the other side of the river, the bike leaning slightly left and then right with every turn of the pedals. He would make it work today, make his bike hum, fill his lungs, every shoulder muscle in sync with his legs. He had, if he thought about it, achieved much. So much of life he'd been able to grasp. The road was a little wet and he enjoyed the small-sounding suck that the wheels made. Reason was probably his greatest gift. Lack of reason was responsible for much emotional pollution. . . . Carly Carlino was incapable of following a simple line of reason; her passions curtailed logic. Margie was smart. She was smart. His wife was smart.

The road leveled out and the smell of the tall pines on either side of the two-lane road became dominant in the fresh air, and Nick slowed, let go of the handlebars, and straightened his back. The sun was behind the tops of the trees, sinking west, and the light came through in long hazy slants, so much so that the bike literally sliced through them, lingering for just a touch longer as his speed decreased. He heard a car approaching from the rear and leaned forward again, gripped the handlebars, and began to pedal. The car shifted to the middle of the road and passed him.

The MS hug was a phenomenon during which one felt a tight constriction of the muscles around the stomach area, a fantastic squeeze that could almost be somehow emotionally satisfying, like those first contractions in early labor—a baby's tiny fists knocking at the super-tight uterus. You had to relax into it though, or it could freak you out. Sometimes Margie woke up with the squeeze and inevitably her dreams would have already aligned themselves, attempting to disguise the pressure as an authentic hug or heavy coat around her middle—anything to rationally explain the sensation.

She had been napping, dreaming that a frozen ball of ice was being rolled from side to side over her stomach. Every time the ice rolled over her it left a new film of water that froze and tightened.

Margie pushed herself up in bed and leaned against her pillow. She stretched her legs out and to the sides in a V. Her upper arms were stiff, but the thick, swollen feeling in her hands had disappeared. There was no tingling either. Noel came into the room and sat on the bed. She put her hand on Margie's foot and squeezed it through the covers.

"Hi, baby," Margie said.

"You starting to feel better, Mom?"

"Actually, I might be. I was just thinking I might be. How was your day?"

"We went to see Pete. I mean Pixie, really. Mom, he doesn't seem right. Pete seems worse. Like really strange."

"He's developed a significant tick."

"What does Dad think?"

"He thinks he has schizotypal disorder. He thinks he should be medicated. He hasn't seen him for a while, though, so it's hard to say."

"I mean," Noel said, "he's not dangerous or anything, just weird, and like, disillusioned. You know he wants to have everyone pray? That he thinks Pixie's going to come out of the coma? I mean, there's nothing wrong with praying, but he's so convinced that she's going to come back . . . like on a specific day even."

Margie nodded.

"It's a little weird."

"Yes. I know."

"I can tell Miriam's still really upset. She was so *accommodating* with him. She said we'd all be there, on the Third. Do you know he's pasted flyers all over town?"

"He put those up a while ago."

"They have Pixie's picture on them. She looks so dead . . . she looks awful."

"It is a little shocking."

Noel left the room and the day rolled back into nothing and Margie fell back asleep. She slept through the evening and into the night and when she awoke in the morning her body felt free and her mind felt lucid. She went upstairs and began to paint.

38.

Margie, Etta, Keith, Owen, Noel, Miriam, Jocelyn, Jason:

Devendra Banhart looks like Jesus

Someone egged the Nethercotts' house. No telling who it was. It was more than likely a random act, but one couldn't help wondering—thinking back to anyone who might have something against Nick, or Margie, or even Noel. Margie went to open the curtains of the front window and something that looked like milk was spidered on the glass, a stringy thickness that ran down to the windowsill, where, finally, yellow yolk had hardened and cracked—it looked like one yolk was still intact—like food in the middle of a hot pan.

KEITH HAD RENTED ONE OF THOSE little Manhattan wheels-when-you-need-them cars, and it took him a while to feel comfortable again driving. It was some tiny blue deal, a Hyundai, with a plastic strip of white copy above the bumper that said *wheels when you need them*, and then *needwheels.com*. He drove up the West Side Highway in the right lane, both hands stiff on the steering wheel and his chin lifted an inch or two higher than normal. He had never felt comfortable driving in the States. His first experience was in New Jersey, and the roundabouts there were so poorly designed, and the drivers so hesitant in them, that you couldn't be sure who would do what and what went where. In New Jersey, he'd actually circled a roundabout three times while a car on his right braked and sped and braked and sped past exits, until finally basically careening out of the loop in an angst of speed. Keith had mumbled *stupid-shit* under his breath as he orbited the little patch of grass ringed with a cracked cement curb, until he caught an actual glimpse of *stupid-shit* who turned out to be some elderly lady, an old thing with paper-thin hands and what looked like huge clip-on earrings.

Today he just needed to warm up to the whole driving thing again. He decided against the George Washington Bridge. In Manhattan, the driving didn't intimidate him so much; it was more the oddness, the positions, of things in the car. Even the cup holders were weird, to the right and under something. Foldout contraptions with James Bond sensibilities. Never easy to find. He just needed a few minutes to acclimate. He paid the three-dollar toll to leave the island and headed up the Saw Mill, keeping his distance from a minivan ahead of him with an orange-colored sticker that read, *My Aunt Was Killed by a Drunk Driver*.

MY GRANDFATHER THOUGHT that guilt could be a motivation to paint—to create art," Margie said, enjoying the long reach of her arm, this new sense of hesitant *remission* that she was feeling, almost afraid to exercise it or it would disappear. She was filled with an energy that felt eternal. She talked fast. "He said we work through stuff when we paint, even with commissioned pieces, that somehow we battle our own guilt over things, that maybe it's just in the brushstrokes themselves, but art is always somehow very personal. Never like doing taxes or selling real estate. He painted things half done, you know, so it makes me think he felt guilty about, I don't know, a short life? Something he failed to complete? I know when I paint I can sort of do battle with my work—like there's an attitude, a personification of my work that I need to come to terms with. We're either arguing with each other—the painting and me—or it's submitting nicely, becoming what I want it to be."

"I've always painted tomatoes, so it's hard to see that as anything more . . . ," Etta said. She was beginning to add definition to her wipeout with blue.

"Always empathize with your subject. Very important. Especially in portraiture, but really almost as much with objects. You empathize with the space even, the shapes and the colors. The more you paint, you'll understand this." Margie was feeling very strong. Energetic. The energy.

Margie's painting of the ovens was getting darker, more fragile in its depiction. The negative space was still very specific and well defined, but of such a deepness that it was easy to miss. The lines were sharp, but so similar in tone and texture that the eye could miss them. From off to the side a bit, the oil in the paint shimmered and made the forms easier to interpret. The pipes, the ovens themselves, were not clearly ovens anymore but . . . drawers? Morgue-like shelves? No, that would be stupid. Margie painted fast. She understood more and more clearly that they were to represent heat without its usual manifestation—fire. There would be a lack of light. The importance of this was clear to her as she painted. The pinks had been almost completely snuffed by blues but then blue was a cool color. It was an impossible feat. Funny how she had begun the painting by sketching out the ceiling light in the attic studio. She climbed the stepladder. She climbed down. She stood back as some kind of internal rpms charged up her torso. Now it was just a disfigured roundness, oblong and deep. She clenched her teeth like a baby refusing spinach. Refusing. Energy charged up her torso.

Etta's rounded shoulders hid the painting she was working on. She was such an eager student, so blindly trusting and humble, really. She appeared to know herself—her limits, where her talent stopped and she would need to go the rest of the way, as far as she could get, via hard work. Not a quitter, and it was inspiring to Margie, who was, fundamentally, a quitter. Ha ha. Margie watched Etta squirt more linseed and turpenoid on the palette paper and circle her brush in the paint. The pewter pitcher was beginning to really pop. The rounded edge of the pitcher was still begging for more definition, but it looked like Etta had no intention of abandoning the shape of the reflection anytime soon. She stood too close and ran a thin line onto the surface.

"Remember to back up," Margie said. "back up, back up, back up. . . ."

"It's this one spot. . . ."

"Yes, it's always just this one spot. But this is when you have to *remember* to give some distance between you and the canvas. You don't want to spend all that time perfecting the miniscule reflection of the white dish on the pewter only to find that it's all off and cockeyed and way too big or too small. Fine to paint that close, but at least keep going back to check."

Etta backed up, cocked her head to the side.

A door closed downstairs. "One of these days I'm going to take you to New York. We'll visit the Met and the Museum of Modern Art, the MoMA, and have lunch. You'll love it."

"That sounds intimidating."

"No. Inspiring. There's an installation at MoMA where you go into a room and find you're in the bottom of a pool. You look up and see the surface of the water. There's a ladder."

"I don't know that that will inspire me."

"Not the pool—the pool's just for fun. But other things you would find inspiring. It's a big world out there, Etta."

"I like to think that it's not so big. I like to think that it's all very manageable."

"That doesn't sound very Christian. Doesn't *God* manage everything? And isn't the world really big? I mean the universe?"

"Just being honest. The Christian life is a constant act of giving control to God. Of trusting him with how big the universe is. In fact, I have a book for you to read. It was very helpful to me."

"*Let Go and Let God*?" Margie said, smiling.

Etta blushed. "No, not that one. It's just that, *faith*," Etta made a fist for emphasis with her brush still stuck through a knuckle, "faith is where it all begins and so, well. . . ."

"So we have faith in what we don't see," Margie said, "because if we could see it, it wouldn't be faith."

"Sort of. But then you *can* see it."

"What? The Virgin Mary in the burn patterns on my frying pan?"

"The Virgin Mary's a whole other discussion." Etta let the conversation drop.

"Pixie's friend, Keith, is coming up this evening," Margie said. "Noel says he was pretty close to her, to Pixie. They dated maybe, I think. He'll be staying here and we have nothing to feed him." She went into a small section with a little bit of yellow, watched it disappear onto the canvas, adding the faintest tint of light. "Nothing at all."

THE MOTORING WENT FAIRLY WELL, all things considered. Couldn't find squat on the stations up there until he got closer to Trinity so he kept listening to a mix of Wreckless Eric and Le Loup. Five songs total, over and over. The tall pines on either side of the road, it seemed to him, began to sway with the music as the monotony of the telephone poles and dashes of yellow color on asphalt reached in through the windows, boring him over and over and over in time with the speed of the car.

His original roommate, when he first came to New York, had married a Sri Lankan woman. Matt. The guy was so ordinary it was sort of a statement. Polos and cargo pants with pockets that he actually *put* stuff in. Who knew what, but they definitely had something in them. Of course the Sri Lankan woman was a disappointment. Just another woman. The accent and the saris were fun for a while and then they had a kid and the kid turned out to be fat.

Noel had seemed somewhat taken aback when he told her he would visit, as though she hadn't thought he'd take her up on it. In the end he and Pixie weren't that close—very pretty, though—but somehow he still felt a part of her life. She'd made such a point of getting rid of her old friends who used, going so far as to delete them from her cell, etc., etc. But then here he was sliding a Blue Jack across the table toward her. She had said she was going to definitely make new friends. It was a part of her sobriety.

Keith pressed on the gas for a hill and the Hyundai slowed and kicked into gear, working to keep pace up the incline. Pretty picture, this part of the States. He was looking forward to seeing Noel.

NOEL WAS WEARING A TIGHT T-SHIRT with a large snail on the front. Small tits but they were cute. The spiral shell reached up to one shoulder. The window in the kitchen above the sink was open, and outside you could hear the faint sound of the river. They would meet up with Noel's friends, grab lunch at a little restaurant—Samantha's—and go up to visit Pixie.

Margie had come downstairs to meet Keith with a few swipes of paint still on her forearms. *Excuse my appearance, nice to meet you. It will mean a lot to Pixie's father that you came.*

Noel explained her mother after she went back upstairs. "My mother's an artist—a portrait artist, actually—she does that for a living. But her stuff is actually sort of Alice Neel–like, if she's given the freedom. You know Alice Neel?" Noel looked up. "Midcentury artist—I always think of her as painting musicians, although I'm not sure she ever really did, probably more visual artists. They sit in chairs with bored expressions, her subjects, and wear striped pants and stuff."

"Interesting."

"It is. Sometimes my mom has to do crappy stuff for money, though. Three children under a tree, in front of the family fireplace, hands folded in their laps like an Olan Mills portrait. I think it's hard when she has to paint like that. She can get depressed sometimes . . . she gets happy, she gets sad. . . ."

"I'd like to see them. Her paintings."

"We can go up later. I'll take you up for a look."

Miriam had fallen in love with the guy at the video store, still open after Blockbuster and Hulu and every imaginable streaming propaedeutic movie. He was overweight. "Not *fat* really, but thick and chunky like a good candy bar," she said. "It's all hidden in there, like the fat is on the inside and not hanging off of him. He calls me crazy hair girl." She was sporting a baby-doll cut, with her dyed black bangs cut super short and on an angle. "Like *Amélie*," she had said, referring to one of her favorite movies.

"I don't know his name yet, actually," she said. "I got that nine ninety-five deal, where you always get a movie and can keep it forever until you want another one, so I would see him pretty much every day. I'm pretty sure he loves me too, or lusts me, which for now is probably best anyway. He thinks I'm artsy because of the movies I rent, but now I can only rent indie films and documentaries because I've gotten myself into this box, and I really, actually, wanted to see that film *The Razor's Edge,* even though I know it will be stupid. I'm getting a little sick of the Indie films. I brought home *Requiem for a Dream* and just left it on my dresser next to the Prom Weed for three days, I didn't want to watch it again really. So now I'm living a lie, a total fricking lie."

They were finishing up at Samantha's. Keith had been talkative and described where he was from, satisfying them with a description of the country outside the city with the sheep that would get stuck on the road, and the little *pubs* where he and his friends would drive out to sometimes, and how so many of them just stayed in Wembley and never had any plans of leaving.

Owen was wearing a T-shirt that said, *I take a bath every day.*

THEY LISTENED TO "LITTLE YELLOW SPIDER" by Devendra Banhart as they drove to see Pixie, all of them squished into the Hyundai and laughing, elbows in faces and knees shoved up against the back seats. Miriam had held the CD over Keith's shoulder as she sat behind him in the back seat until he noticed, took it from her, and slid it into the CD player.

"We still use CDs, by the way. This is probably the only mix I've *really* liked from Folk Fag over here," she said, nodding sideways at Owen.

"You're welcome," Owen said.

"Have you seen the music video? Wonderfully strange. They're wearing Indian headdresses and stuff. Kissing. Drinking. Devendra looks like Jesus."

Jocelyn flattened her head against the seat so she could see past Owen to Miriam. "Is that really his name, Devendra?"

"I don't know. I think so."

THE REHABILITATION CENTER was being repointed and the walkways repaired. There were bricklayers with wheelbarrows and sludge. Dried gray up the sides of their jeans. A jackhammer set the parking lot vibrating, and the sun was bright and everything was gathered up into a loud, enormous irritation. Their short thirty-yard walk from the car to the building was miserable, and by the time they were in the hallway they had stopped talking and were rubbing at their temples and tilting their chins up to stretch their necks. Pixie's room was down the hall to the left, and Noel took a moment to drink from a water fountain.

Jason joined them late, having been busy working on his old Torino, a dull blue one that he had inherited from his grandmother of all people and that he was determined to get running again. It hadn't been started in over thirty years. He came through the front doors of the center somewhat enthusiastically and was unprepared for the somber group, *Hey, sup!* His friends were already walking toward Pixie's room, Keith with flowers that had been soaked in dye so that they bloomed bright neon purple and pink.

39.

Owen and Noel:

alpacas in moonlight

Seeking faith while he doubted was the most important thing that Owen ever did. *Oh, Lord, help me in my unbelief.* What was faith if you sought God already knowing him? Trusting him meant trusting he would give you trust. Seeking him meant that you *wanted* him. And if you want him, what god would ever say, *No, I don't want you to want me*? At least not the God he believed in—the God that was, truth be told, starting to matter in every way he could think of. After that, well. He was still seeking, but now he believed. And now that he believed, he knew God would reveal himself in his seeking. What the hell was going on with him? But what about Pixie, and dead mothers, and childhood cancer—always childhood cancer even though adult cancer was just as tragic, kind of. A life cut short is a life cut short but every life is cut short. No one, Owen had begun to believe, should ever die, was *supposed* to die, as crazy as that sounded even to himself. He would never say this to anyone. But death was a true bastard and a prick. Everyone was always trying to eradicate it and for good reason because it wasn't the way things should be.

"There are things about America I love," Keith said, "but the cost of college is not one of them." Jocelyn had just said her parents were worried about paying her tuition the next semester. "I don't think people listen to your generation, quite honestly. Your protests and whatnot don't seem to make much of a bloody difference."

Owen was staring at Keith and it was hard to tell what he was thinking.

THEY WERE SITTING AROUND Miriam's hookah in a section of her mother's garage that had been cleared of stuff, two hoses curled up from the blue-tinted glass and into Jason and Owen's laps, where they took turns inhaling, the sound of the bubbling water adding to the odd quiet of the garage. There was a small tan carpet remnant and an old couch, a coffee table that was splitting down the middle due to moisture, and quite a few pillows. There was a standing fan that slowly turned from side to side, blowing air into the garage. The smoke for the day was strawberry. Miriam was squeezing a fine line of henna from a sparkly tube onto the back of Noel's hand.

"It's a little disrespectful hearing you talk about America like you live here," Miriam said. "You go to college here, right? Or *university*, as you would call it. You wear your wellies and take your satchel to campus in America. Go back if you don't like it."

"Well that's a fine way to welcome the outsider," Keith said. "In the UK we like to say *cheerio*. And it's not a satchel, it's a rucksack."

"Cheerio," Miriam said.

Noel scratched a small drop of the henna off her forearm. "I suppose you're right about our protests not doing much good. Marches, sit-ins. Sometimes they make the news though."

Jason and Jocelyn sat next to each other and were trying to come up with examples of onomatopoeia. "*Repuuulsive*," Jason said, drawing the word out.

"*Repuuulsive*," Joceyln repeated.

'It's like the beginning of a barf," Jason said, "rep*uuul*sive," and gagged for effect. "It comes from the back of your throat. Just like puke."

"I've decided to stop talking about things that I don't know about," Owen said, trying to redirect the conversation. "Really, it's a new resolution. I decided to do this when I overheard a couple of guys in Starbucks at school. Grad students probably. I heard one of them say, 'I'm hard on new moms—they think they're writing great poetry—*that it's transgressive and interesting*, but it's not.' Something like that. *Transgressive and interesting*. It made me want to throw up."

"But they *did* know about poetry obviously," Noel said. "They were teaching it apparently."

Owen took a long hit from the hookah and blew the smoke back over his shoulder. "Yeah, but I guess I thought they sounded so stupid and they were talking about something they knew something about—how totally dumb I must sound when I talk about things I really don't know anything about. It's a bad habit I have. Or maybe the worst thing, like these guys at Starbucks, was that they were so *intense*, like they were far more knowledgeable than they probably were. This is where I fail. I start talking based on very little knowledge, really."

"Then how do we formulate ideas?" Keith said. He was watching Miriam with the henna and didn't look up.

"Think. That's how we formulate them. We first *think* about them and then we talk about them."

"But I think you're talking about the person who blathers on about nothing. Most people, I don't believe, do that so much."

Noel looked up from her hand. "*Everyone* does it. Politicians do it. Artists do it. Being successful has a lot to do with one's ability to *blather.*"

"You're either a good blatherer or a bad blatherer," Miriam mimicked Keith's accent.

"SWEET MOTHER OF GOD!" Jason exclaimed after Keith and Noel left. "What the hell, Mir, you're a real bitch to Keith."

"I don't like him."

"Why the hell not?"

"I just don't."

"Well, it shows."

"I don't care."

Owen stood and stretched, resisting the temptation to add to the conversation.

OWEN AND NOEL DROVE CIRCLES around the town, making their way over the river and up to the alpaca farm. Keith had stayed back at the house and Noel felt at peace with the familiarity of Trinity without Keith, of Owen and her alone in the car. She pushed eject on the CD player and waited. The disk slid slowly out of the slot, and she took it and held it up to the fading light coming through the windshield to see better.

"Beach Music," she read.

"I run out of titles for mixes," Owen said, "but I need to call them something. Music for Fridays, Music for Studying. There's also a Beach Music 2 and Beach Music 3. Very unsatisfying, I know. I hate naming things."

"When's the last time you went to the beach?"

Owen pulled onto a patch of grass next to the gate to the William's farm. An alpaca stood next to the fence, its white fur glowing in the darkening evening. "I think I was in fourth grade. I remember because my mom thought I should collect shells or sand or something and show them to Mrs. Kendricks, my teacher. She wanted me to be a teacher's pet. I hid the little jar of shells in my desk for the rest of the semester. The lid came off and the shells and sand ended up all over my stuff. Mrs. Kendricks made me stay in at recess to clean it all up. Oh, the irony."

"But you still ended up the teacher's pet."

"Don't ever say that again."

"You should embrace your goodness, Owen."

"What is this *goodness* you talk about?"

"I think, I think it's a character thing. I think it's because everyone trusts you." Noel opened a plastic CD case and slid the mix in. She leaned forward and squinted out the window. "We need to pet the alpacas. They do look lonely, don't you think?" she said with the tone of a vintage movie star.

Owen followed Noel to the fence. "I drink. I use certain swear words. . . ."

Noel ran a hand over the alpaca's nose. "He's so patient, like he's been waiting for us all day. That's just it, though, you use *certain* swear words—you have very clear boundaries."

"I sound like a very exciting person. How can you stay away from me?"

"But you are, Owen, you're exciting in a good way. Okay, maybe not exciting, but interesting, which I think is of higher value anyway." She stood on the lower fence rail and reached over to pet the alpaca's neck. "Look, another one." An alpaca came up behind the other one and nudged its side. "I think I need to get one of these. One of these would make me happy. I just know it." She bunched her hair up and pulled it over her shoulders to rest on her back. "I'll ask for one for

Christmas. I'll name it Bee Sting. I don't know why, but I think that needs to be its name. Bee Sting."

Owen stood behind her and put one hand on either side of the fence. Noel stepped down off of the rail and he smelled her hair. She half turned and his breath went into her ear. "Noel, it's always like this for me and you know it, don't you?"

"Yeah." She turned around to face him. "I'm still mad at you about the abortion thing." By now there was a moon. His face looked pale. "The things that work for us work really well, and the things that don't would always—ultimately—I don't know."

"Right." He touched her upper lip with his finger. "I just, shit. *Fuuuuuck*," he said slowly, and leaned forward and kissed her, his finger holding place for his lips. He let his body sink into hers. He held her face in his hands, he touched her hair. He ran his hands down her sides and pressed her to himself.

"Don't say that," she said through the kissing. "I don't like it when you say that word."

WHEN NOEL GOT HOME, Margie was still up. She sat in the living room. She was just staring.

Noel closed the front door quietly.

"Hi, baby," Margie said.

"Hey."

"Keith went to bed already. He said he wanted get up early tomorrow. Everything okay?"

"Yeah," Noel sat down. "It's fine. He's probably anxious to get back. He's going to stick around tomorrow for a bit and then take off. I'm sure we bore him, I mean my friends. Maybe I bore him. I think he was hoping for something, you know, between *us*, but I think it's become clear that ain't gonna happen."

"No?"

"Abundantly clear," Noel said, and slipped out of her light jacket. She folded it and put it over the arm of the couch. "He's perfectly nice and all that, and good looking, but I don't know. . . ."

"Was he with Pixie? Before. . . ."

"I have no idea. I really don't know."

They were both quiet.

"I saw Pixie cut herself," Margie said. She didn't look at Noel, but stared out into the room.

"What? When?"

"Thanksgiving." Margie repositioned herself and looked at Noel. "Well, I didn't actually *see* her do it. I saw her afterward. She was holding something to her arm, where she hurt herself. You know, there was some blood."

"What did you say?"

"I didn't say anything. Should I have? What's to say?"

"I don't know, I guess not. It's just weird. It's sad." Noel got up and took her jacket with her. "I guess I'll go to bed. I should get up when Keith does."

"You do that, *Missy*," Margie said quietly, using her pet name for Noel, one of mock anger that she'd used when Noel was younger.

"You coming?"

"I'll be up soon. I love you."

"Love you too," Noel said, and climbed the stairs to bed.

MARGIE HAD NOT BEEN ONE of those girls who studied herself in the mirror. By the time she had moved in with her grandfather, she was already sick of adolescence and wanted to move on. Her body, however, had yet to catch up with her mind, and when she caught glimpses of herself in the mirror she felt disgust.

The disgust came with the understanding that once the process of adolescence ended, she would have relief. The disgust in herself, she reasoned, would come to an end when her body had finished its journey through the disturbing melee of hormones, moods, and skin irritations that seemed such a fundamental part of a panic that she could feel, like an itch that if let to spread, would actually enter into her and be impossible to relieve.

She wanted to get fat.

But somewhere off in the vast universe it had been decided that this would not be so. Almost systematically, her maturity brought with it a leveling off of everything—like sprinkling glitter on a design drawn in glue, things stuck in certain places, and in the end you couldn't help but stand back and admire what had become of Margie, despite her mother's death, her distant father, all that makeup.

When Margie moved in with her grandfather, he was absorbed in nothing. He seemed to tire quickly of whatever he was working on.

And then she began to sketch. Her grandfather noticed immediately the depth that she was trying to create. She lovingly foreshortened a spoon that she had drawn lying on the little table in their kitchen above the garage, tilting her head and squinting, a soft and delicate movement at her lips as she *looked*, more from her left eye, more from her right eye, trying every possible way of viewing the spoon, as though it was a changing thing that had to be snapped at every angle lest something be missed. What sort of volition makes art? Margie moved as though a large hand was pressing at the base of her neck, pitching her forward into something like a roar of visible possibility.

When they had begun to paint together, the first object was a simple piece of white bread. It had a Warhol feel about it, which suited Margie well at the time. She used charcoal on gray paper, white highlights, and her grandfather talked with her about chiaroscuro as she drew, sitting next to her dabbing at his own painting of the bread until she was finished. His painting, in oil, was never completed, and he leaned it against a wall where it slowly dried.. The colors were muted, as he had wanted to avoid a pop-art feel, and then where the paint ended, his confident lines took over, that ability he had to exaggerate in just the right places, where a corner of a line became so much more than a corner—a decision really, to reverse back on itself or carry forward, only tilted toward a new image, where the actual turn becomes the line of a jaw or a deep recess beneath the ear, a decision that could change a work entirely.

Margie's growth had slowed by then, evened out, settled in. Tall, slim, dark hair that hinted at a responsibility within her. When her grandfather became sick, they didn't talk as much, as though bereaving ahead of time.

From the bread, they went on to paint fruit with bites in them. Margie painted a single peach, a juicy, crystallized bite, then birthday cake (her seventeenth), brie and baguette (not pop art enough for her), so back to bread, sandwiches, this time an Italian hoagie from Stop-n-Shop. Eventually, the subject matter drove her grandfather to paint deeper, fuller, transparent layers. With death almost touchable in front of him, he painted with confidence, everything falling away.

And then when the weather was nice, they opened the garage door. The wood door had insulation stapled to the inside, and when it was opened the yellow fibers hung and bowed above their heads, an occasional tuft loosening and falling on a shoulder or floating to their feet. Sometimes the spiky little bits would drop into the paint and end up embedded somewhere on the canvas. Things shifted quickly near the end, Margie cooking for him, finding him a wheelchair to paint from, helping him climb back up the narrow stairs to the apartment.

Doctor's appointments, bottles of pills on the windowsill, and then the little cloud of fame when the New York people came to watch from the gravel driveway outside the garage.

"I would never have thought things would be like this when I was your age," he had told Margie as she walked slowly up the stairs behind him, steadying him with a palm to his back for security. "Life is hard to predict."

"It's good in a way."

"I don't know," he said, and took another deep breath. "I could think of nicer things."

"I mean it's good we can't predict it. It's good that we don't know."

By the end of that summer, her grandfather was able to paint for only an hour before needing to rest. The people still came, hoping to find the garage door open, but more often than not it was closed, and eventually they stopped coming except to occasionally knock on the little side door under the pretense of asking how he was doing and then if he had his work in any galleries.

He told Margie to keep quiet until . . . for a while, which meant she should not mess with things while he was still around. "Grandma Moses was a racehorse once she died," he said, "$70,000 for a drugstore painting on cardboard. When she first started painting she would have hoped to get five dollars for it."

The first time Margie painted a portrait it was of her grandfather, deep into his sickness, moments—it almost looked like when it was finished—before his death. It was late in the day and he sat in his chair half golden from the sun, half blue from cancer. Really, it was like Alice Neel. Not intentionally, she didn't think, but then she'd seen her paintings and loved them so they might have been in her mind. The colors were intense, and even back then, when Margie had barely begun to paint, she had a way of pulling up the colors from beneath the skin. The paper-thinness of it made the blues and reds and yellows come through. The reality of the weakening life under the skin made the skin nothing but a dull translucent layer, really, something to be pushed aside like a curtain. She saw past the simple mediocre tones and into her grandfather's physical being—his slowing pulse, the ache of blood against artery walls pulsing forward in ever more fragile ways and lessening, so that the blues and grays crept from the edges of him toward what was left of his vitality, down to a dot, a modicum of life somewhere in his center that appeared from time to time as a brief light in his eyes, and Margie would feel a kind of relief wash over her. Layer on layer and then yellow ochre, burnt sienna, cobalt, more cobalt with a touch of alizarin crimson like a quarter into a pond, and the purple spread out, more burnt sienna, bringing it deeper, even more, so that her grandfather was still—even—himself.

40.

Miriam: electronic cigarettes

Sometime around three in the afternoon the feeling became intolerable. It was a premonition of some blankness that could take over, grab her about the face like a cloth napkin soaked in ether and half suffocate her, leaving her just alive enough to experience the squeeze and pressure of a dark slavery that she had first acquiesced to when alone, friendless, and not in her right mind. She would have made a perfect heroin addict—one shot of halleluiah and she would have been all in, rubber tube still dangling from one arm. It was only by some providential grace that her vice was simple nicotine.

Miriam had taken the job after her friends left for college. Wandering the mall alone looking for a new something, anything—some material thing perhaps—that would take the edge off of the emptiness. She had imagined taking a year off of life would be a sort of comma. Two weeks in and she was stuck in what felt more like a strange parenthesis. Her fixation that evening had been shoes and she was looking for something European-like. A strappy leather thing, or reinvention of the Birkenstock. When she passed by the kiosk, she noticed a small cloud of smoke exiting the mouth of a skinny Eastern European kid wearing a shiny black shirt, unbuttoned to his diaphragm. He had instantly sensed her interest and stuck the smokeless cigarette within her eyesight, his thin frame following, so that she would have had to shove him aside to continue walking. Not a smoker, she explained, but there was a "help wanted" sign, and ten dollars an hour for sitting on a stool pretending to inhale steam while she listened to her iPod seemed just the thing right now.

Now, with her friends home, Miriam hid her new addiction in humor, making a little scene of taking it out, inhaling, hitting the stiff electric element against a dish or a coffee mug as though to rid it of ashes. When she inhaled, the little LED light glowed bright, turning something that looked like a dried-up raisin into a facsimile of glowing ash. It was like fake logs in a fake fireplace. She blew the steam out slowly, working her mouth into a small, round opening, as though she knew how to make smoke rings.

"I don't know exactly how we're supposed to act, I only know that we need to be there," Noel said. Keith was standing at the door, hands above his head resting on the molding. He was skinny.

Miriam straightened up in her chair and closed her eyes, looking especially peaceful as she inhaled another lungful of steam.

"I could come back, actually, I've thought about it," Keith said, pulling down the front of his T-shirt, half aware that a bit of pubic hair was visible from his lower-slung jeans. "If you think it would mean anything to Pete. And if she wakes up, shit, I want to be there."

"She's not going to wake up," Jocelyn said. "She's *not* going to freaking wake up."

Keith was leaving soon. Jocelyn, Noel, and Miriam sat at the kitchen table with the remains of Nick's Sunday paper. Miriam had the comics section open and was looking at a new strip by a guy named Buddy Walker. "I can't believe you guys still get these things," she said, referring to the paper. She held her cigarette in the other hand, elbow resting on the table, her wrist pressed out and away as though there was smoke that needed to be rerouted.

"Obscurity has become the new professionalism," she said. "We are so used to so much that nothing is new—even though this has sort of always been true—now it's even more true. Everybody's trying to make something that's not *familiar.* We are now at the point where we'd rather look at a photo of a dirty street curb, we're so tired of sunsets. Look at this comic strip. It has stuff as people; a fire hydrant named Alex, a parking meter named Quinn. The street comes alive when the people disappear. They talk to each other. The parking meter says to the fire hydrant, *you little squirt.* This is how we rest our eyes Sunday morning in between FoxNews.com and the *Huffpost.* It's like a commercial for Fruit Loops and we pay for the stuff."

"Ever read Ecclesiastes?" Keith said. "Nothing new under the sun."

"Oh," Miriam continued, "and more and more shows are cartoons. Cartoons for adults, *The Family Guy, The Simpsons. . . .*"

"Say that again, Keith," Jocelyn interrupted. "Say *Ecclesiastitees.*"

Keith smiled. He took his hands down from the doorjamb and crossed them. He leaned against the wall.

"I would really like to visit you," she said.

Noel was in a weird state that morning. She had woken up early—like four o'clock in the morning. She finally got out of bed and opened the window, focusing until she could hear the river. Listening to the water was something she had done as a child. This was supposed to be an exciting time in life, but here she was waking up at four in the morning so *sad.* She had turned on the light and gone to her closet and sat on the floor and sifted through a box of things she had saved from grade school, which made her even more sad, but she couldn't help it. It was an impulse. She had taken a beaded bracelet she made at a summer day camp and wrapped it around her wrist. She wore the bracelet now.

"Ecclesiastes," Keith said, and winked.

Miriam inhaled steam from her electronic cigarette and shook her head in disapproval.

NOEL HEARD A CAR DOOR SLAM and she knew and hoped it was Owen. When he came into the kitchen they looked at each other, neither of them smiling, just a look that lasted one beat more than usual. He sat down at the table opposite Miriam. Noel fingered her beaded bracelet. "Keith, what are you gonna do after you graduate?" she said, rather lamely.

"Not sure yet. My folks live in Wembley so there's not much to go back to. I've grown to like it here. I mean, I liked it from the start, but I think I like it even more now."

"Oh, makes sense I guess."

"What's Wembley like?" Jocelyn asked.

"Kind of like the Giants' stadium in New Jersey, to be honest. It's where Wembley Stadium is and that's all it's about."

Owen glanced at Noel. She half smiled, stood up, and went into the living room. He followed her and when they were alone he took both of her hands in his and kissed her lightly. "We have the whole summer," he said.

"I know, I've been thinking about that. Do you think this one will stick?"

"I think it will if we listen to the right music."

"You better make the playlist then," Noel said. "Playlists. One playlist will get on our nerves."

"I'm not going to say the L word but I really want to." Owen lifted a strand of her hair and set it back down on her shoulder.

"Not yet. I agree."

"I decided a long time ago not to say the L word until I say the M word."

"What does that mean? I'm confused."

"Never mind."

"No, seriously, what does that mean?" Noel stepped back and looked him in the face.

"Seriously, never mind."

"Okay, whatever, it's good we have all summer to figure this out."

"I won't ask what that means either."

"I'm only saying what you said, Owen."

"I said we have the whole summer. I didn't say we have the whole summer *to figure things out*. I meant that we have the whole summer to be together."

"Is that really what you meant?"

"Yes, it's absolutely what I meant."

"Let's stop talking about it," Noel said. "Things will get crappy already."

"Agreed. Let's stick to kissing because I love that more than anything in the world right now." They kissed. It was always gentle. Noel loved that.

41.

Margie and Etta:

banana bread and lost civilizations

Once eleven o'clock came around, the house was usually in a slow roll, turning, as though to tip windows toward the east. What was left in the coffee pot was burnt to a thick film. Etta came up the stairs to the attic with a loaf of banana bread wrapped in tinfoil. She had had her hair highlighted since the last time Margie had seen her. It was cropped short and angled down from high on the back of her neck to her chin. From the front it was a bit too bulbous, curling under, tight, a perky swing to it that had the effect of punctuating her movements.

A window that had lost its sash weight was propped open with a stick. Margie went to it, tried to raise it higher, pressed the stick into the opening at a higher angle. She walked back to the middle of the room spreading her fingers out, took her elbow in one hand, twisted, stretched, repeated the process with the other side. It was a warm day, and she'd felt her body begin to slow and ache.

"With nuts," Etta held out her banana bread.

Margie took the loaf and held it up to her nose and smelled it. "Mmm . . . if you ever stop cooking for me, I'm going to think you don't like me anymore."

"I wasn't sure about the nuts."

"Baking is—what's that book you talk about?—your *love language*?"

"Yes, sort of. It makes me happy. I give other people what—really—I want."

"I could make you banana bread?"

"Right, but what you want to do is probably talk or help me do things. It's difficult, we try to give other people what we really want, like the guy who tries to fix his wife instead of listening."

"Nick listens."

"Good."

"Sometimes it makes me angry."

"He's a good husband, he wants to help, right?"

"Yes. He is good. He tilts his head and he listens."

"His intentions are good. . . ."

"Very. . . ."

"You're kind of hard on him, Margie."

"It's just, sometimes I feel like a file in his cabinet. A folder under *Dissociative Disorders.* On bad days I'm Sylvia Plath in a bell jar, and when he talks it's like this deep echo coming from the American Psychiatric Association. It marginalizes me. He explains me to me. Thanks for the banana bread though. It smells delicious."

"Sorry about the nuts."

"No, I like nuts," Margie said as she took the easel with Etta's painting and moved it further away from the still life. "I know," she said. "Nick's got a hell of a lot to work with, with me. And when he just gets pissed, like any guy would, it only makes me worse. Angry and all that. I really do belong in a file. How do you stop being obsessed with yourself? Make banana bread? Does that work?"

"I think we're all obsessed with ourselves. Who isn't?"

"Are we worth all the obsession?"

"Probably not. But maybe it helps us get better—improve, well, as people."

The two of them spent an hour painting and then went for a walk, Margie dragging her left leg the tiniest bit to ease a tug that was running up the back of her thigh. Noel and her friends had left the house. Keith's little rented car was gone and so was the minivan. Nick's door was closed when they left, and the Hammacher Schlemmer thing was hissing in the hallway.

They walked down the street toward Maple, Margie slowing even more with the decline to be sure of her footing. It was such a warm afternoon. The stiffness of spring, that leftover part of winter, was gone, and there was a smoothness to the air and the movements of people like it had all been oiled. They stood for a moment at the end of the street so that Margie could rest and watched as a woman with an orange double stroller tried to collapse it as two toddlers stood next to her holding onto her legs. Carlino's, behind the woman, offered family-sized lasagna for $15.99.

By the time they reached Maple and Fifth, Margie was weary. They went to a bench and sat down. One of the old-fashioned globe streetlights that had been installed in the late seventies was broken, a scatter of glass fanned out wide around it, a few shards under the bench where they sat. It seemed there was a constant pushing up that happened somewhere beneath the town, the whole county for that matter. Weeds bloomed green from under cement and brick, a habit of infinitesimally increasing, their very slowness giving them the power and strength they needed. Margie reached down under the bench and pulled up a palm-sized piece of glass from the broken streetlight.

"Were there other people here before us? Did the first Indians come with deer hides strapped to their backs, hoping to farm the land

and make a civilization?" She held up the piece of glass. "In the year 3000, someone will find this deep in the earth and lecture a class on the use of glass bakeware in the twentieth century."

Etta smiled.

"Only the class will be meeting in some sort of a pod. A pod made out of synthetic fibers that stretches so that you can sit anywhere and feel like you're floating in air." Margie stretched her knees straight. "I actually just described the internet, didn't I?"

"I can't even imagine the world existing in one hundred years. The earth would have turned into an oven long before that. Unless we figure out what to do."

"Do you know," Margie said, "that there are people alive right now—babies—who are alive, who will be alive in the year 2110?"

Etta said, "If we figure out what to do about global warming, then we'll probably figure out what to do about aging, right? Maybe *we'll* still be alive."

"Maybe we'll still be alive and look like Angelina Jolie."

Etta laughed. A small red car passed them.

"A synthetic Angelina Jolie," Margie continued. She stood up slowly and walked to a trash can at the corner. "No, that's not true, we'll look like Jenna Jamison. We'll all look like Jenna Jamison. The women will, anyway." She tossed the piece of glass from the streetlight into the garbage.

They continued down the street. "Who's Jenna Jamison?" Etta asked.

42.

Mr. Pete: the dismal swamp

Pete's imagination was leaving him. His thoughts would usually pop into his mind as interesting and different, and then trade places with other interesting thoughts—or on a good day, an even more important thought, one that was really, really good. One that he thought would make him a happy man. But this hadn't been happening so much. He might need more sleep.

Pete felt sick. He lay on his bed in his hotel room widening his eyes now and then, as though trying to take in something more meaningful than the black, two-cup coffeemaker and mini fridge on the other side of the room, but couldn't come up with anything. Until he had Pixie back he could see no help for himself. If Pixie rose from the dead and came out of her coma, then he was not a fool and God was true. But he felt nothing. Worse than nothing, sick. He tried to come up with some faith by rolling over on his stomach and folding his hands together and praying into them. *Oh, Father, dear Jesus, I'll do my part, but here I really need you. I need you and Pixie needs you and you know this. I know you know this, but right now I don't feel nothing.*

He stretched open his eyes and pulled the Bible out of the drawer of the bedside table. It was stiff, like maybe he shouldn't be reading it because it didn't belong to him. He thumbed through the pages and stopped where he imagined the Holy Ghost wanted him to stop. He dropped his finger to the page and read each word carefully. *I repeat, let no one think me foolish. But even if you do, accept me as a fool, so that I too may boast a little.* He didn't know who the Gideons were—that's what the Bible said on it—but he felt close to them.

The hospital had given Pixie's clothes—her possessions—to Pete, like she was already dead. They were in a big, blue, see-through plastic bag with a fold-over flap. He kept the bag on a chair next to the TV. Jeans, a small orange T-shirt, a flannel shirt with a rip on one of the sleeves. There was a chain too, the ends connected with a safety pin. Her shoes. Socks. Earrings. Even an elastic hair band.

Pete rolled back onto his side and stared at the plastic bag. He felt sick. When Pixie was growing up he stayed away, going out to drink after work. Things just happened with Pixie, she got taken care of. There wasn't much he could do for Pixie. She started going to school and then she turned out to be smart.

He took the remote in one hand and turned on the TV. A large white cruise ship was on the screen. Then a close-up of a man about to swing a golf club, and then swinging, and then the ball went into the hole. Pete left the channel on with the sound almost inaudible and closed his eyes. The changing lights from the screen hit his eyelids and he opened them to see the picture. Now the picture was a room with a man in a green chair and a woman in the background, in a kitchen, moving around. Bertolli Frozen Dinners, it said.

Pete slowly sat up and rubbed his eyes, running his hands through his thin hair. He needed to keep thinking about Pixie and July 3. He needed to be ready. He opened his eyes as wide as he could, went to the chair, and picked up the plastic bag. He needed to think hard about her.

He hadn't ever opened it completely. He pulled the plastic flap and dropped what was in it on the bed. He smelled the T-shirt but it meant nothing. Then he picked up each thing, looking for something. He found a dime in the front pocket of the jeans, stuck his hand into the other one, felt a pill and pulled it out. It was large and blue on one side and white on the other. He rubbed it between his fingers and the capsule started to collapse. He smelled his fingers. He touched his tongue on the pill. He heard a small scream and got scared but then realized it was coming from the TV.

43.

Owen and Noel: swimming

"Why is it that in the pictures of Neil Armstrong on the moon, you can see through him?" Miriam sat on the sand adjusting the strap on a pair of Speedo goggles. She wanted to see the bottom of the lake. "He's transparent, gray and transparent, and obviously floating—but we expected that because of no gravity and everything. Are people see-through on the moon?"

"There's gravity on the moon," Jason said in monotone, "just not as much."

She pulled the tight rubber strap over her head and adjusted the little cups over her eyes. The skin of her forehead puckered up painfully. She pulled them off. "Ouch." Jocelyn wasn't at the lake yet. Noel and Owen were hesitantly wading into the mucky water, knees up for every step like there was a lot of mud to get through.

"I never understood," Miriam continued, "why they weren't afraid that—you know—when they jumped like that, that they wouldn't just lose touch with the moon and just float away. Scariest thing in the world, to float away into space. What could be worse? You would just float until you starved to death, I guess."

"No. Until your oxygen ran out," Jason said, "which wouldn't be that long. Going to the moon would be sweet."

"You think that because you have no idea how scary it would be. If you die in space and there is an afterlife, do you get to go? I mean, is Heaven and earth a thing or does it not really matter where you die? Or live?"

"Why don't you think about things that matter, Miriam? Like world hunger or global warming."

"There are already so many people working on those. And don't you think it matters where you go when you die? If you don't think it matters, then you don't believe in an afterlife. But you're afraid to admit this maybe."

"So I should be afraid of space, and I shouldn't be afraid to die."

"Well. In some ways. This is ideal, yes." Miriam worked at the rubber strap of the goggles, trying to lengthen it.

Jason took off his shirt and spread it out on the ground as though to dry. He began to wade into the water. Miriam watched him. She could see Noel and Owen, now almost up to their shoulders in the water. Noel screamed and dunked under the water, she screamed again and it was softened by a breeze that rippled the middle of the lake. Owen dove under and came up on the other side of Noel, tossed his head in a quick slick of water and short hair.

Jocelyn came up behind Miriam and spread a towel on the ground. She sat down, and the two girls looked out over the water at Noel and Owen, at Jason cupping water in his palms and splashing himself. Miriam's hair was a tangled mess on top of her head where the goggles nested half on, half off, the plastic cups angled out like two truncated antennae.

Noel and Owen waded back into shore. Keith had texted Noel when he was back in the city: *thx, btw cool house and friends.*

Now, it felt a little bit like high school was elbowing its way back into their lives. Owen and Noel grimaced as their feet sunk into the sludge of the bottom. Noel shivered and sank back down into the lake, floating her chin, letting the water touch her lips, recede, touch her lips, recede.

THE OTHERS HAD LEFT. Noel dried off with a towel, then Owen. Jason's T-shirt was crumpled into a twisted mass, forgotten on top of the picnic table. They walked toward Owen's car and he opened the door for her, tossing a water bottle that was on the seat into the back and brushing off a few crumbs of a bagel. When he straightened up, Noel was leaning on the car, her stomach flat against the window. She folded her arms on the warm metal roof and rested her chin on her hands.

"For me, the sunny days are the most depressing," she said.

"The sun is supposed to make you less depressed. Vitamin D and all that."

"I like the warmth, though, the roof of your car. It's like a heating pad when you're sick. It's nice after swimming." She made a point of flattening herself to the car even more to extract the heat.

"There are people who wear special glasses to try to get more sun into their brains so that they won't be depressed. You could try those."

"I don't know what it is, it's so bright, so light, it almost feels like I don't fit in. When it's a sunny day it reminds me of strip malls and gas stations. And it makes me depressed."

"I can get depressed on a gray day."

"Gray days are actually kind of comforting to me."

Owen closed the passenger door and leaned against it, facing

Noel, an elbow on the roof. He took a strand of her hair and moved it away so that he could see her better. She glanced at him and narrowed her eyes. "You always do that with my hair."

"My friend Noel," he said.

"Always and forever. I like to kiss you sometimes."

"Being your friend is one of my biggest sacrifices."

"Thank you?"

"So much easier, for me, to stay away."

"That would make me sad."

"And so I'm your friend."

"Forever?"

"Forever," Owen said, and threaded his fingers in hers and kissed them.

She hugged him and he could feel the warmth of her body—sun to car to Noel to Owen. She pressed her ear to his chest.

"You know, don't you?" she said. "That I still feel something?"

"Peace. That's what your name means—peace. Yes, I do know that. Come on, we'll have to give you shock therapy if we don't get you out of this sun." He opened the car door again and she slid in.

44.

Margie and Noel: ovens

Before Margie was officially diagnosed, during that year of MRIs and questions and visits to the neurologist and doctors diagnosing her with depression again and again, she had insulted her kind. One night, coming out of the grocery store, bags of groceries in the trunk, she had pulled up to a stop sign and realized there was a man next to the car who didn't look quite right. He was a crooked shadow in her peripheral vision, walking slowly alongside the car, and she had instinctively locked the doors. Hearing the click of the locks, the man had turned so she could see his face and lunged at her window, curling his hands clawlike as though about to attack and growling loudly—the noise all the more unnerving because it was muffled by her closed window. He turned and continued to walk—the lopsided gait so indicative of MS, a perennial doggie paddle, hands hooked like quotations in front of his chest, one foot turned inward suggesting a movement that would carry him sideways as much as forward, inward, bent, leading into some kind of mediocrity.

The neurologist had not wanted to diagnose her with MS. It was a complicated process and could take over a year and so he had initially attributed her symptoms to the imipramine she took for depression and said it was that and prescribed a different one. He took his big book of drugs and thumbed through the thin pages right in front of her, landing on a section and actually showing it to her—turning the book around so that she could see the listed side effects of imipramine. The MRI had been inconclusive. His waiting room had been crisp and meticulous, as though to prove true all that was said behind the examining-room door, as though organization itself could change things, control things, and bring about good things. Once he diagnosed her with MS her body seemed to relax into it and comply. Symptoms lined up like kids for ice cream, waiting their turn.

Margie was trying to open a box of long-grain wild rice. Nick was waiting in the kitchen for his client, Nancy Torre, to arrive. Nancy Torre fascinated Margie. She had a weak chin and big close-set eyes and thinning hair, but also a certain peace about her. It was hard for Margie to imagine her needing therapy, she seemed so confident, especially in light of her looks, which were so odd that it had to be a challenge not to be negatively affected by them. Her big eyes and small chin, like an upside-down triangle. Strands of brown hair. But maybe Margie had it all wrong, maybe her poor looks were a gift—a freedom, so hopeless that she fell beyond judgment.

She struggled with the box of rice. "The side of the box says to push and pull up to open but it's not working." She scratched at what looked like a perforated part of the cardboard.

Nick said, "I don't read the directions, I just open the box."

"You force things."

He took the box from her and pressed the perforated tab in with his thumb and handed it back to her.

She turned back to the stove. "You force things and then they break."

The house was in its swollen cycle of summer, floorboards thick with humidity and wallpaper coming up at the corners, tempting someone to snag a piece of thick paper between thumb and finger and pull. In his office, Nick had a newer window unit that he religiously kept at seventy-one degrees. The rest of the house could bulk with the heat, but his room with the two bookcases, the large wooden desk, and the Henry Miller chair would forever be seventy-one degrees. Like a pair of selfish lungs, the door would open, the air would flow out, and Nick would close it tightly, only to be opened forty-five minutes later with a smile and a handshake and some half-sober person leaving, emotion hanging in the air so heavy Margie felt like she could touch it. Nick had become proficient at reading the faces of people after a session; it was all in the forehead, different for different ages, but still the interpretation was always in the forehead, which of course affected the eyes, but the very beginning was right there between the eyes like a Hindu woman's bindi.

For Margie, the heat was a terrible thing, thinning out her nerves and any strength that they had melting into the larger viscosity of blood, muscle, bone. She envisioned herself as a girl sometimes, in the summer, tan shoulders and bony mosquito-bitten legs, popping tar bubbles on the street in front of her home. She had sucked in so much summer heat back then, squinting her eyes all the way from June through September.

After Nancy Torre arrived, Margie went to the attic to paint. She turned on a small air conditioner stuffed into the front window and sat down on the floor. Etta's still life was visible in the tall mirror still leaning against the wall. The flowers were still in the can, and the dark sheet that she had taped to the wall as a backdrop had fallen on the floor. Dots of oil paint covered in loose plastic wrap were on the bench next to the easel.

She stared at the lower left corner of her large painting, sitting in a half cross-legged position that stretched her legs in just the right way. She used a brush as thick as her hand and applied the paint in confident strokes into the negative space. She liked it. She finished that section and moved on to the next.

On her way up the stairs, Noel paused at the x-ray of her broken fibula. The sun coming from the little window at the landing gave it the effect of being aged and then also of having some implantation—as though there could be a nail hidden somewhere in the bone, a sliver of white with the hint of a flat head. She'd seen stuff like that before.

Margie was sitting on the floor and had a large brush. She stretched her arm to get at a certain spot.

"This is beautiful, Mom," Noel said and pulled up a stool.

"It feels good to hear that."

"It is. Really. Kind of profound really. It must be. What does it mean?"

"I don't know." There was a pause. She laughed. "No idea whatsoever."

She leaned over to the right and hit a section with a small swipe of the brush. "It was good to begin with something that made me stay away from the figure. I would never do a portrait this large. I'm still not sure what it is. I keep thinking ovens, but that's just me."

"Sylvia Plath."

"Really? Oh."

Noel got off the stool, turned around with her back to the wall, and slid down to sit next to the painting so she could see her mother better.

"It's weird being home. I sort of want you to tuck me in at night and bring me a glass of water. It's weird. Before I left for school I just wanted autonomy. Now I want you to carry me like a baby. I'm homesick. Even when I'm home I'm homesick."

Margie scraped paint off the brush on the palette.

"But then I still can't wait to get back to school, to my apartment."

"I think that's normal. I think it's just hard, leaving home. It's a hard time. I mean, of course you can stay. You don't *have* to leave."

"Yeah, I do. You know that. Maybe everything feels more intense because of Pixie."

"Maybe."

"How are you?" Noel said.

Margie smiled at her daughter.

"Well?"

"I'm fine." She slid over and sat against the wall with Noel, still holding the paintbrush. "I see my issues as a cocktail that consists of a meager dopamine level, PMS or menopausal symptoms—who knows which—MS symptoms, and external factors such as strained relationships, latent mourning, or too much sun. Is that too much information? . . . And just plain foolishness."

Noel looked at her mother. "You don't like the sun?"

"Not really."

"I love you, Mom."

"I love you too." Margie took Noel's head and leaned it on her shoulder and began to stroke her hair. "Really, how on earth did I ever end up with you?"

45.

Pete: the dark corridor

It had been a while since Pete had prayed. He didn't feel guilty as much as stressed. He had some time to make up. It was almost July 3. It was hot. There were people now who needed him—people other than Pixie. They would sometimes come up to him on the street and place a hand on his shoulder and say they were rooting for him, and it made him scared, like he had to get Pixie prayed back to life and it was too late to go back. But what he wanted was for them to pray too. It felt like it all depended on him instead of God. In a way it did, he supposed. Although God had the last say, it says in the Bible that he needed to have faith. He worked at his faith, every morning quoting the Bible to himself kind of like prayer, *Stretch out your hand, stretch out your hand*, he practiced. Mark 3:5. *He stretched it out and his hand was restored.* But Pete knew it wasn't real prayer. He didn't know about real prayer. Took more faith to pray than to just plain gather up and heal yourself, he thought.

Pixie was as pale as ever, although she always had been anyway. She was see-through when she was born, when she came out. All white and you could almost see her veins. So he needed to pray. He needed to pray a lot before July 3. He knew that there would be some people who would come for sure. Etta brought the flowers ever since the accident. When they moved Pixie to the new hospital, the room was already set up. Flowers, a special blanket with a big bear on it. He thought it was Etta. Etta did stuff like that.

Lord God Almighty, maker of Heaven and earth, I'm not religious but I still need help. He had trouble when he prayed because he could go into prayers that the priests say, and then he wouldn't have the words to say what he needed. Those prayers weren't his. *Lord God Almighty, maker of Heaven and earth, maker of all things visible and invisible . . .* and then he would say words like *I beseech thee*, which he was unworthy to use and belonged to a priest anyway. He wasn't a priest. He would start again. *Lord God Almighty, maker of Heaven and earth, please, give ear to my . . .* using words he heard in church, words that were too far away and holy, and he would start again. *Oh, Lord God, please, look at me and see me and don't turn away yet because I have no other choice but to come to you. I don't know anything except that you say you are love and so here I am and I need you to love me and Pixie, because we don't have no other way to live.* And he would trail off just because he was talking to *God*, and he wasn't sure he really was anyway, and if that was true, then he didn't have faith to begin with. But here all these people were depending on him almost like that. And there wasn't a way she would come to herself again if it weren't God's will.

The new hospital room was ugly with fluorescent light, something that scared him out because sometimes it could flicker like there was faulty wiring somewhere. It was like a fish tank, the room was. A silent place. The lights in the ceiling were old, old floor tiles, chipped wood dressers and hospital beds that were old too. The sounds of all the TVs everywhere, voices, jingles, and fancy music, all the nursing home sounds. You had no choice but to be okay with stuff if you wanted to hear, to understand, try to take on some burden for your loved one. There was a fiberglass fountain in the front of the building where the two long hallways met next to the nurse's counter. It was the fountain that was on the brochure, a gray plastic fountain that had a stream of water over a shelf of yellow-stained plastic and then emptied into a little pond with a rock in the middle, and then pumped back up to do it again. The fountain was next to the big foggy window and two doors that opened and shut when you pushed through a wheelchair or stretcher and it didn't make any sound, the fountain didn't. People came and went; their faces were like the fountain. They came and then they went.

Around five every evening there was the smell. And it didn't matter what was for dinner, the smell was always the same, like of white gravy and fruit from a can that left a pool of peach juice. Whatever the meat was, it was cooked in salt and was the big part of the meal. So many people couldn't eat it anyway. It had to be mushed first. Oh, how could the faithful pray, even the food that they ate is a malaise, he thought to himself. The word *malaise* came to him odd and unexpected and he didn't know really what it meant.

ETTA ADMIRED A SWATH of stars and stripes that hung above the entrance of the nursing home. She had been struck by the apathy of the place the first few times she visied Pixie, carts of picked-at food left in the hallway to crust over and shrink in the open air. Empty wheelchairs discarded like grocery carts next to rooms. She didn't think the patients were well cared for.

She held her cluster of red knock-out roses, repositioning them in the glass vase. They weren't ideal, as knock-outs could be leggy, but she had forced them into a forgivable arrangement by pruning and snipping off thorns, sticking them one by one into the water with an eye for continuity and symmetry. Tall in the middle and shorter on the sides.

Pete was in his usual chair and had his leg out—the one with the injury—and he was massaging it with his large hands, digging into the muscle where the chunk had been taken out, or burned out really. He worked his fingers into the cloth of his jeans, kneading his leg.

He had to be careful; there was a sore spot in the middle where the doctor said it was scarred and could seize up into a spasm, and then he couldn't do anything but grit his teeth and wait for it to go away. When Etta came into the room he was bent forward with his mouth closed tight.

"Hello, Pete," Etta said, carefully setting the roses on the dresser next to the previous week's flowers—white daisies from the grocery store that were already browning at the edges.

He sat back up in the chair and watched as she removed the old vase of flowers and threw them out and emptied the water into the sink.

"It's been a good day for her, I think," Pete said. "I think she wanted to smile."

Etta placed her purse on the floor next to a metal chair on the opposite side of the bed and went to Pixie. She leaned over the girl and squinted her eyes as though to envision a sunset in fuller color—orienting the image of Pixie as a complete picture, the way Margie had taught her to stand back from a painting to reorient. "You think she's happy? I think she might be happy today, you're right, Pete. I see something behind those eyes today."

"I called the nurse in this morning because she was tryen to move her mouth. 8:30 this morning like she had planned it and everything. And she just kept trying, I could tell, because of the way the edges of her lips got thin for a little bit. The nurse says it was involuntary, like the way you get a tick in your eyelid. But she didn't care, and I don't think she really wanted anything from Pixie 'cause that would be more work for her. They'd have to rehabilitate her"—he said "rehabilitate" with a firmness on the syllables—"and that means walkin' her down the hallway and feedin' her and wipen her face. I've seen the patients they are rehabilitating and you can tell they don't like it."

Etta gently squeezed Pixie's wrist.

"The first time I came in here," Pete said, "after they moved her, I could tell Pixie didn't like it. It's just a feeling I had, like when the door's left open in the house and you just know it even though you don't see it open and you don't feel air. Something's different. It just is."

"Do you ever read to her?" Etta said, sitting down on the other side of the bed. "Sometimes they hear you. People will wake up and remember things that people—their loved ones—said to them while they were asleep."

"Oh, yeah, I read to her. I read some, but sometimes not out loud."

"I'm sure it doesn't matter how well you read, just that you are there, speaking to her."

The broad fluorescent light of the ceiling flickered once and seemed to grow brighter. Pete glanced up, straightened out his injured leg once more, and pulled his chair closer to Pixie.

"If it were me," Etta said, "I think I would just want to hear your voice. It's the human contact more than anything. Even if she doesn't know what you're saying."

Pete touched the sheet and smoothed it delicately with his large hand. "Hi, Pixie," he said.

Etta smiled.

"I've been thinking about when we pray, July 3, for her. Is it okay not to have a priest here? I mean, you're religious, is it okay if it's just some people praying without a minister?"

"I don't think it matters to God, if that's what you mean."

"I just mean do you think God will answer our prayers even if we don't have a priest?"

"I think he'll either say yes or he'll say no, no matter what."

"He's gonna say yes. I mean, I know I believe that."

46.

Trinity: red white and blue

Owen and Noel and Miriam were having a conversation about sperm donors. Miriam had been having another internal conversation with herself and blurted out one of her thoughts: "If you donate your sperm, aren't you sort of disqualifying yourself from being a sperm donor to begin with?"

Owen was driving and they had pulled over to buy fireworks at Charlie's Explosions, a seasonal tent that went up each June. There were large cellophane bags of bottle rockets and Roman candles, tables with brightly colored cardboard packages, green wicks and cone-shaped containers promising tricolored flames and high-decibel detonations. A young man wearing a hunting hat perused one of the tables, turning over the products to examine them before adding them to a pile next to the register.

"Explain," Noel said in monotone.

"Sparklers!" Miriam was distracted. She picked up a box and shook it. "Sparklers are the only *good* sort of fireworks. Firecrackers are mean and M-80s are deviant."

"Actually," Noel said, "I think I know what you mean. We'd always hear on the news about some older kid who had the firecrackers and M-80s, a lost finger, one eye, one hand . . . the obligatory interview: *If only I had paid attention to safety. . . .*"

"I could never keep track of what was legal and what was illegal," Owen said.

"You would care," Noel looked at him and smiled.

"Geeze, Owen," Miriam added, "you really are *too* good sometimes."

"No, I mean, I used them like any other kid. What the hell, you two? I shouldn't have to defend my good choices as a thirteen-year-old kid, okay. You hung out with me, right?"

"Yes," Noel said, "we did, and you kept us out of trouble. Now, sperm donation. Your point, Miriam?"

"Sperm donors are not a substantially great lot. If a guy donates his sperm, then the fact that he donated his sperm should disqualify him from being a sperm donor, although I realize the problem with this. What sort of emotional constitution or DNA structure would cause someone to throw their progeny around like that? How could you live with yourself knowing that you had a child somewhere, who was alive, who was connected to you in such an intimate way? The fact that you are okay with this means that you are not suited to pass on such a weak emotional or psychological blueprint to the next generation. It's such an obvious problem but I've never heard anyone talk about it."

"The guy just has a greater desire to help someone—to help a man and woman to have a baby. He doesn't see past that," Noel said.

"No, let's be honest," Owen said, "the guy is donating his sperm because he gets a hundred ninety-nine bucks for each squirt. Plus it bolsters his pride to know he qualified. I don't think he thinks past the point of handing over his little plastic cup and getting his check from Mt. Carmel Fertility Clinic or wherever." Miriam had boxes of sparklers in her arms and dropped one. Two more fell on the ground as she was picking it up.

Owen picked them up, handed them to her, and continued, "Is it any different for the guy who gets a woman pregnant the regular way? Few guys are thinking ahead to the baby."

"Physical passion is one thing," Miriam said, "but for two hundred dollars? It takes a certain brainlessness it seems to me. A lopsidedness to your DNA."

"She has a point," Noel said. "Miriam, you have a point. You always have a point."

THERE WASN'T MUCH FANFARE yet regarding the Fourth of July. The town hosted the area's only parade and the best fireworks display within forty-five miles, but Maple Avenue was as yet uninspiring. There were a few shops that had put up flags, and the McDonald's was advertising red, white, or blue ice freezes for fifty cents the whole week leading up to the Fourth, but the rest of the town appeared behind schedule. By the middle of June virtually everyone knew Pixie's father, Pete, was planning a prayer meeting of the sort that could raise the dead and calm the viper. There were members of Trinity Community Church who planned to walk around the nursing care facility and ask for the mercy of God to come upon Pixie and give Pete faith and hope, something to increase Pete's own faith, that he would trust Christ for all things regardless of what the will of God was. Pixie had become the town's own babychild, and she was encased in her little coma like she was swathed in a blanket or some kind of chrysalis. Life was waiting for her somehow. There would be an awakening, if for nothing else than the people's compassion. We are a selfish lot, some of them reasoned. It takes a tragedy like this to remind people of what's really important in life. It was an episode of *Extreme Makeover: Home Edition* or a touch from the Make-a-Wish or Angel Foundation. Good was headed their way and the people hungered for it. They dropped twenty-dollar bills into the offering plate on Sunday and took the time to pick up the garbage that missed the trash, opening doors for each other and nodding, the faces of the people expectant, although no one knew exactly for what. Somehow there was a resonance that Pete stirred up within Trinity, like the town was an enormous bowl and he had let loose a marble that was spinning around deeper and deeper, broadcasting a shrill but deep whir with every revolution.

There was a small group of members from Eastgate Charismatic Church in Corner Junction who had heard about Pixie and had already begun to pray. They made an announcement at the Sunday service. They would pack guitars and amplifiers and carpool to Trinity.

Etta, after visiting Pete, went home to get a casserole into the oven. It was a recipe she'd gotten from Edward's mother before she passed away, a hot dog casserole. Nothing she would serve to anyone but the two of them in light of the main ingredient, but they were, honestly, both nuts about it. She imagined it had appeared one month in the late sixties or early seventies in a copy of *Better Homes*, and here they were forty years later setting the Corning Ware, steaming, on the middle of the table like the kitchen was still shining with linoleum and Formica.

She went to the front window and peered out, expecting Edward to drive up any minute. She turned off the oven and cracked the door open, leaving the casserole in to stay warm. It was still very light out, the sun still above the horizon, just beginning to merge with the line of pine trees in the west. From the porch, the sun seemed to melt on summer evenings, a slow engagement with the horizon and then a faint light, like a visible squeal before it became just that shade of gold over the roofs that hit their living room with a wash, during the summer, always right before Edward came home. Etta had long viewed it as somehow metaphorical, the brightness before Ed, like it was always her first calling to love her husband, a weary man at times, she acknowledged. The back of his suit coat was wrinkled up by the end of the day and his large feet pointed just a little too much out to the sides, but Ed loved her, she knew this, and if she were to stand him up next to George Clooney or Richard Gere, he'd look like a raisin but his heart would beat a thousand times louder. For this she was thankful.

When he came in the door he looked a little blank, like it would take a minute or two to realize where he was and what his next activity would be. Etta went to him and kissed him and took the suit coat he had draped over one arm.

"I went to visit Pixie today," Etta said as she went into the kitchen. "She's the same. Pete thinks she's trying to smile."

Edward ran a hand through his carefully cut short hair. "What did you say to him?"

"I said that maybe she is trying to smile. He sits with her for hours. He would know. I really, really don't like that place. It's awful. There's plastic flowers in the atrium."

"Does Pete seem to mind?"

"I don't think too much. So I guess it shouldn't matter to me either, right? There's not a whole lot to taking care of Pixie. They use the term 'vegetative state,' I've noticed, although I'm not sure that's a term doctors throw around anymore."

Etta pulled the casserole out of the oven and set it on the table. Edward washed his hands in the kitchen sink, using the dish towel to dry them. "What about this prayer thing he wants to do? Who's going to that? They mentioned it in church. Are we going?"

"I should be there. I want to be there. I really like Pete. I've been trying to get him to come to church."

They both sat down and instinctively took each other's hands across the table. "Thank you, Lord," Edward prayed, "for this food, for your love, for Etta, in Jesus's name, amen." He winked at his wife and began to eat, picking at the slices of hot dog with his fork. Sometimes people take pictures of their food, Etta thought.

MARGIE WAS PRETTY SURE she heard music coming from somewhere outside, the way drumbeats sound from far away. That morning she had called Nick's Hammacher Schlemmer noise machine a "hummer," referencing it as something that he perhaps gained status from, the way a Hummer truck will be for a guy in a mid-life crisis, and he didn't think it was amusing. She was trying to be funny. He answered her by directing his response to an unsaid something—a presupposition he had—that in her statement she was referencing resentment she was harboring in light of the amount of time he was with his clients. "Perhaps you don't appreciate the time I spend working because I don't leave the house every morning." He made a point to begin his comment with *perhaps*, perhaps you feel this way because . . . perhaps your feelings reflect a deeper conflict within you that is tied to an anger . . . *perhaps*.

"I thought it was funny, Nick."

"You meant nothing. . . ."

"It was funny."

"Not because you think I tie my work to my self-worth. . . ."

"It was funny because you are the last person who would ever buy a Hummer."

"Not because my counseling practice serves me the way a Hummer serves certain insecure men. . . ."

"Hummer, Hammacher Schlemmer, you don't think that's funny?"

"It's only funny as a double entendre."

"*Perhaps* it bothers you because it's true?" And here Margie gave in. "*Perhaps* you would have laughed if my comment hadn't struck a certain chord?"

"So, yes," Nick had said, "you admit the comment was passive-aggressive."

"Oh, go to crapping hell," Margie said dismissively. "Stop pointing everything out to me," and she walked outside and headed to the potting shed.

47.

Owen: can't decide about the anger thing

Someone finally hung the flags. Eighteen of them total. Every lamppost of the four main blocks of Maple Avenue. Someone on the Trinity Historical Council had insisted on pure cotton, seamed and sewn—nothing synthetic or stamped like the flags they sold at Home Depot—and it had paid off. Looked very principled, Owen thought, the town did, as though herein history was somehow bent and shaped through American hard work and resourcefulness, a serious cadence with the future in mind. The fact that in actuality the town was a small fringe place that finally, in the eighties, had begun to form its own personality relying on its history—a history somewhat invented—bothered no one. The elderly who knew better kept quiet, the community already having evolved in their aging minds into something as brilliant as nostalgia.

It wasn't the fricking life he would have chosen for himself, Trinity. He loved his family but it was a small life they lived. Sometimes gifted people came from small towns, but then everyone made a big deal of the fact that they had small beginnings—small beginnings, ha!—which meant, really, that most gifted people had big beginnings. Why the hell did he care so much? Went against everything he was about, but it was still there.

He wanted to get everyone through this whole Pixie thing, especially Noel, but he didn't know how to get through it himself, so what to do. . . .

Last night.

They fell on the grass together. Her hips. Her jeans.

Goddammit.

Three more days and people would have to deal with Pete and Pixie and Prayer one way or the other. They would either go and offer support or they wouldn't. Everyone knew about it and this was the problem. It was no longer possible to be passive. There was no independent party. If you didn't go, then you either didn't believe in prayer or you didn't care. The only other option was to fake it. And there were those who would.

They were on the grass and they loved each other and they were the only people who had loved or would ever love or understand love, ever, ha. He thought about love. Maybe loving *with* someone made you love each other and that's what the deal was.

He loved in his own way, though, and it was as real as it could be right now. He loved Noel's hair and her smile and her mother and her house and where she went to school. What if she lived in a raised ranch? What if her mom read *People* magazine, or worse, *People* magazine was stacked in the bathroom? What if Noel was going to school to be a hairdresser? What if all of this was true but everything else was the same? It was hard to separate, all of it. All of the way things are—the house, her mother, her school—even her views on abortion. All of this was Noel.

Sympathy.

Empathy.

If she got sick or depressed, would he love her? Not still want to lie on the grass with her, but love her? Maybe real love was only possible with time. That would explain all the divorces. Not enough time together. Maybe real love scares people. Ugly love, the kind where you're sitting in an ugly restaurant staring at the food stuck on your spouse's bottom lip and it's disgusting and you have to decide whether to tell them or not even because you know the next time you eat together the food will be there again? Leave the spouse before you have to deal with this sort of thing.

Divorce is understandable. He didn't think people should write their own wedding vows. They were so temporal. *You made me understand what love is, I love everything about you, the first day we met. . . .* The old tried and true: in sickness and in health till death do us part. Change the language maybe: I will love you even if you get sick and I have to spoon-feed you. I will love you until you die or I die, even if you turn into the worst bitch ever.

Mary Sommerfeld—he thought he might actually hate her—had organized a small area on the nursing home property where people could gather in support of Pete and Pixie. She had a green shade tent she had purchased at Walmart a year earlier for the October Yard Sale that you could assemble with practically the push of a button, and so she made it clear to people that everyone was welcome. There would be a vigil. Candles. An evening moment of silence and perhaps a song or two.

The big question was whether food should be provided. It was an unusual event to say the least, she declared, so there was no precedent. Pizza, while making the youth happy, seemed a little sacrilegious because of its sloppiness. Finger food would be the most appropriate—nothing one needed a fork for. Something to nibble, respectfully. And in the end, who knew how many would come? There was no way to predict who would attend. Eight o'clock. Would people be hungry? Mary Sommerfeld got on the phone and began to make calls. Etta was first on the list. Dependable Etta. She would not call Margie unless Etta thought it appropriate. Margie was in a different orbit altogether, and needed to be forgiven her social inadequacies. It was because of Margie, in part, that the town was rallying around this helpless little girl from New Jersey and her father. After all, she was Margie's daughter's friend.

Etta answered the phone with a bit of breathlessness. Her mind had been somewhere else and, as though she had needed to run to pick up the phone, it took something like physical strength to redirect her thoughts to the sound of the ringing telephone. "Hello?"

"Etta, it's Mary. I have three people who have offered to bring brownies, and I can't seem to get anyone to bring anything substantial. I'm not looking for anything fancy, just cheese and crackers. Everyone wants to bring brownies."

"For what?" Etta didn't understand.

"For the Third. The event for Pixie."

"Event?"

"The vigil. I assumed you were one of the organizers. We've talked about it, Etta. You asked if I planned to come."

"You're planning food?"

"Nothing complicated. It begins at eight o'clock. People will be hungry. I don't think anyone has thought about this. Or, for example, if it will rain. I'm setting up our tent, the one we used for the Yard Sale. It's very easy."

"I don't think it's the sort of thing that needs food. . . ."

"Well, I would like to help."

"I'll be inside with Pete, Mary. I'll be inside praying. That's what it's about. Pete just wants people to pray."

"Of course, we're going to pray. I asked Christine to bring candles—the ones from the Easter service. To show our support. If he looks out the window, he'll see a group of us holding candles. I think it will encourage him. Did you know he has candles in his window at the Extended Stay?"

"Mary, it's not going to be completely dark yet. At eight in the evening."

"The candles are a symbol of our support."

"I'd skip the candles. Go ahead and bring brownies if you want, but I'd skip the candles." Etta was growing irritated.

"I told you, we already have too many people bringing brownies."

"That's fine. Listen," Etta said, "if there's a group of people outside *keeping vigil*, that would be great. Ed will be coming. And Noel and Owen and their friends. So that would be good, sure. Thanks, Mary."

Other towns in other places are skimming through the summer with the usual things—citronella candles, resin Adirondack chairs, and new stainless-steel gas grills—the people sit cigarette-less, eyeing each other's things, and the children do their cartwheels and climb cedar playsets. Towns are barely defined—although people crave definition. Houses breed houses breed Walmarts and Targets; roads are widened—cement islands with patches of green grass and baby trees boosted up with rubber-covered wire and thick wooden spikes. The cars are new and shiny like the gas grills, and children in the back seats watch the signs and wonders flow past.

The Fourth of July is such a defining day, and the people know this so they buy small flags and connect them to their mailboxes. They wear T-shirts with slogans and colors, intimate with each other in their anticipation. The beer is purchased, the fireworks set aside.

48.

Trinity: a pause for confession

On the morning of July 3, Margie crept into Nick's office at 7:30 AM with toast and jam and a cup of tea. Lately, he hadn't been drinking coffee. He was in his old leather chair reading through notes and had a look on his face that resembled a seared piece of meat, like an intentional scar. He looked up.

"I brought you tea. And toast."

"Thank you."

"I'm sorry," Margie said, and handed him the mug.

He blew on the tea.

"I'm sorry."

"All men are defensive. I think it's because we feel responsible. It makes things complicated."

"You help a lot of people, Nick. I really believe in you, and I do want you to solve stuff. But then I also don't want you to try to solve stuff. It's unfair."

Nick looked at her, set his notes on his lap, sighed. "I love you."

"I'm a mess." Margie said.

"No."

"Yes."

Nick touched the hot tea to his lips and shook his head.

"And," Margie continued, "you know this isn't the end of the conversation. We'll have it again, when we're seventy-eight and have those little pillboxes that give you the right pills for each day." She came around the desk, clumsily sat down on his lap as she felt a small jerk hit her torso, and slowly and carefully took the tea from him. She set it down next to the toast. "I can't believe I'm up this early."

Nick wrapped his arms around her.

"I haven't been fair to you," she said. "I'm not always fair." She leaned back into Nick and he readjusted his legs to ease the weight.

"If it's about being fair, that will never happen," Nick said. "In marriage, spouses assume this is the end-all, that everything must be fair and even. We tell our children that life isn't fair, but we demand it of each other."

"*Our* marriage, not marriages over there." She nodded to the empty chairs next to his desk. "Us. You're right, everything you say is right. It's so right it's worth not writing down. You're not a failure." He glanced at the wall, his cabinets, eyes wandered a little like he might have a thought. He did this, looked around distracted. He'd done it for years, when they were dating, when he tried to figure out how to raise Noel on days when she was young and being difficult—*complicated*, he used to say. He *figured out* how to raise Noel and how to have a marriage, how to be married to *her*. Figured out how to be married to her when she was being *complicated*.

"You know what?" He pressed a hand to the small of her back and kissed her. "You're right. I don't always handle things well. You just found out you have MS." And then, hesitantly, "We found out. At times, I'm not a good husband. Etta's a good. . . ."

"Nick, you aren't a failure and I'm a complicated wife, more complicated than most."

Margie suddenly felt like she wanted to hold Nick. She turned on his lap and began to kiss him. He slipped his hands under the elastic waist of her pajamas and felt the soft area below the small of her back. He ran his hands down to her bare hips and then thighs, pulling down the pajamas, leaving her exposed. She reached around and tugged them back up. "You're giving me a plumber's crack," she said, and kissed him again. "A good what?" Margie asked. "Etta's a good what?"

"Etta's grown on me," he said, and pulled her top up to expose her small breasts. He kissed them, and she wrapped her arms tightly around him.

NOEL WOKE TO A TEXT FROM KEITH. He was in Orlando staying with a friend and had just shot a gun for the first time. *I can hold up a gas stn now come w me we get rich.*

She rolled over on her elbows and texted him back: *hows yr aim?*

good

?

actually i'm pretty good

It was already hot in her room. The tall windows were open and there was no breeze coming through. Her floor was covered in clothes. She kicked off the sheet, sat up, and ran her hands through her hair.

big day, she texted. *pray for Pixie*

?

with Pete pray for pixie

of course

Already it felt like an odd day, as though it was possible it would turn on itself and snap back and deflate. . . . She was worried about

Pete already. She got out of bed and began to pick up the clothes scattered around her floor. She grabbed a hanger and pulled a T-shirt that said *grunge is dead* over the wire. She hung the shirt in her closet and picked up a pair of jeans. Her phone rang. It was Owen.

"Owen?"

"Hey."

"Owen, I feel scared. Why do I feel so scared?"

MIRIAM WAS WORKING on a paper sign. It was large. She wasn't sure what it should say and wanted opinions.

"Praise the Lord. Isn't that what they usually say, Christians? Christians always say, 'Praise the Lord.'" She had thick craft paper unrolled on Noel's kitchen table so that it hung down at the edges. She was hovering over a corner of it with a pencil. Owen was leaning against the counter and Noel was squatting in front of the open refrigerator door looking for something.

"I think that's kind of outdated," Owen said. "How about something simple. Pray for Pixie."

"Pray for Pixie seems insincere," Noel said. "Because of the *p*'s. It seems like you just used that because of, you know, *pray* and *Pixie* both start with a *P*. She slid a can of half-used spaghetti sauce further back in the refrigerator and opened a plastic container. She pulled out a carton of orange juice and set it on the counter.

"See Pixie Rise." Miriam said. "It's perfect. It has that old-time carnival or revival meeting feel to it. Like they had in the tents with the sawdust and stuff and the ministers in front and the people all over falling down because of the Holy Ghost."

"You're crazy," Noel said, "you can't write that. When nothing happens, it will just be worse. It's like people will want their money back."

"When nothing happens? What kind of faith is that? If you go into things that way, I assure you, nothing *will* happen. You have no sense of adventure. It's a visible way to trust. *See. Pixie. Rise.* This is what Pete wrote on the flyers, right?"

"Jesus, Miriam, this isn't a game. Pete's a real guy and he wants his daughter back. He needs *people* right now. He needs our support. Our love."

"And this is how I'm supporting him, by making a sign that says what he would want it to say." She sketched out the first letter, a bubble *S* with a little flourish of hearts sprung like a halo over the top. She pulled at the paper so that she could begin the next letter. "Eeee," she said slowly as she drew. "I'll make two *e*'s and put dots in them like eyes looking forward, toward Pixie's future life."

"Miriam, I'm serious. You can't do this. You're being an idiot and the eyes are too much, obviously." Noel tried to grab the pencil from her hand but she pulled it away. "Owen, tell her she can't do this."

Owen didn't say anything.

"Lighten up, Noel," Miriam said. "It's not like she's really dead or anything. A coma is just someone sleeping."

Owen left the room.

THE TOWN SLOWLY GAVE WAY. Even those unacquainted with Pete or Pixie knew something of the situation. The fact that it had involved young people was significant. Older people receive a mild energy from the youth, from talk of the youth, of their car accidents and graffiti and parents' involvement or lack of involvement. Jack Pirelli on Fifth Street and Audrey Donalds above the park sitting in their chairs in their living rooms. Audrey Donalds still had her crown from when she was homecoming queen in the china cabinet in the dining room. The situation moved the day, the story of a girl who had fallen into the river in fall—the river they could hear all day long and even at night if they paid attention. The tragedies of other people's lives, the generationally distant and those unfinished kids on the other side of town. If Jack Pirelli and Audrey Donalds knew anything, it was that even though the sun came up every day, some days it had something to shine on and other days not so much.

Margie lay down on her bed to rest. She heard something like a moan from somewhere deep in the house and closed her eyes.

The town. Take a camera with very high resolution and back up—focus, click—back up—focus, click. We will view the town like an eagle and hover like a rumor. The atmosphere waits for us. From above, lampposts become thick dots, their flags toothpicks with a faint coat of red. The sidewalk is white from a distance, like a gravel path through a miniature train set. The hills we don't pay attention to, they watch but nothing more. The street, Maple Avenue, is light, and could be the river itself if we didn't know better. It turns and bends just a little and almost seems to move but doesn't. It's a shiny day, rooftops the way Etta sees them, reflections. People begin to move. You can see the people from above if you look closely. Because of their shoulders, they're larger than the lampposts; they carry bags and walk, feet punching out in front of them like small dark thumbs, a different lilt to the steps of one compared to another. If we back up any further, they won't be people, so we stay and watch. Focus on the person with the large object, over there next to the parking lot. There is the small beach next to the lake the color of masking tape, like a small section of tape was ripped off and pressed down next to the lake. The little shed that they call a boathouse. The trees are pine near the water and into the air they emit a nostalgic smell, a backwards whisper reminding people that they can't get at something they know is important. There's a disturbance in an area of the town, a gathering—people, we realize, moving around. Something large begins to form and then, between two smudges of out-of-focus green—trees, we understand—there forms a crowd and with the crowd what we know is a banner. The banner appears to us, to the camera, as just a thin dark line that doesn't sway or move because the day is still. The day is still and hot and the people are waiting. The people are like grasshoppers and they wait.

49.

Noel and Owen:

invasion of dazzle

Noel held Owen's hand as they crossed the parking lot. Miriam was standing on a cardboard box that was quickly collapsing, trying to get at the branch of a small tree with a long string of sticky duct tape. She tossed the tape in the air and it barely left her hand. Her sign lay crumpled on the grass and she was worried that it would rip. She tried again, this time pulling the tape apart, and it got stuck to itself. She looked down and tried to yank it off. When Owen and Noel walked up, she was trying to get an edge with her teeth, spitting a tiny fleck of something with her pointed tongue. The box she was standing on was smashed beneath her and she kicked it out of the way.

"You're going in with us, aren't you?" Noel said. She let go of Owen's hand.

"Yeah." Miriam pulled out a long section of the duct tape and began to secure the paper sign to the low branches of the trees. With the length of butcher block paper strung between the trees, the effect was more one of sorrow than optimism, sunk and wrinkled, black marker words barely visible in the paper folds. Miriam walked to the middle of the sign, where it hung low to the ground, and tried to hold it up. See. Pi . . . Rise. She let the section fall and moved to the right to try again. See. . . . xie. Rise. Owen came and stretched the paper higher, using both of his hands.

"Good," Miriam said. "Just like that. Don't move, it's perfect."

He took the top edge of the sign and tried to pull it tight between the trees. It crumpled loudly as he readjusted the edges and held out a hand for Miriam to give him more tape.

"It's just that," Miriam said, "I think this is very much like Pixie would want, a sign, a physical statement. At least that's what I think. She was a bold girl, after all."

A minivan pulled into the parking lot of the rehabilitation center and began to back up to the edge of the grass. Mary Sommerfeld got out and opened the rear door, her fleshy upper arms all a-jiggle with the effort. Two more cars pulled in behind her and a man got out of one and came around to help. He pulled a folding table out of the van and rested it on the grass, taking each leg and tugging it out before turning the table upright. Owen stood back from the sign one more time and then went back and tried to straighten a lower corner that hung loose.

"That's fine," Miriam said, "don't worry about it."

Noel took Owen's hand again.

People began to gather in the parking lot, some holding items covered in plastic or tinfoil. A boy of about twelve had a tower of paper cups that he disconnected and reconnected. He dropped them and they fell apart and he bent to pick them up.

The paper sign had folded over in the middle again. It was hard to read.

Janet from the post office showed up with a box of candles. Jocelyn came with a large plastic garbage bag and began pulling out flattened paper lanterns. She opened up each one and attached a bare hanging bulb inside. She dropped the cords on the grass and looked at the trees for appropriate limbs to hang them from. Her hair was shiny and straightened.

A red, white, and blue plastic tablecloth covered the folding table. A man set a large orange cooler with a spigot on it, at the edge so the spigot hung free. The boy with the cups set them next to the cooler and pressed the spigot. A stream of liquid came out. He removed one of the plastic cups and held it under the spigot and pushed again.

Nick showed up and sat in someone's folding chair.

People talked and milled about and picked food from aluminum trays. Clouds came in and covered the sun, which dropped lower anyway so that the edges of things became less distinct. An old man some people remembered as Mr. Mosteller—who used to hand out pretzels to the kids at the bus stop on the corner of Maple and Fifth—walked right into the folding table, knocking the plastic cooler off and into the grass. People gathered in confusion and picked it up. It grew darker and the small crowd grew larger as it attracted attention. Jocelyn's paper lanterns were hung from the trees on the area of grass next to the parking lot, extension cords pulled across the cement, and their light brought the evening even closer, attracting bugs and people. Cars pulled into the lot and two groups of middle schoolers wandered into the crowd looking for food. Noel looked for her mother. Etta called Margie from her cell, the keypad inches from her face as she dialed.

The windows of the nursing home became reflective in the low, disappearing sun. The monitors in Pixie's room kept track of her blood pressure and heart rate.

50.

Pixie: the faithful

Pixie, in her subconscious cocoon, had been shifting ever so slightly, and in a way Pete was right, she had smiled. Inside there had been a smile a mile wide, although it wasn't clear why. There was no way to perceive her movements; they were as yet undetectable. Four different attendants came in that day to do the usual things—check blood pressure, adjust hanging IV bag. With her cool skin came a certain smell that over the months had settled into her subcutaneous parts, and if you leaned in close, it was hard to separate the smell from the temperature, like one was necessary for the other. But deep in Pixie there continued the movement of blood and the slow, weak thump of a heart so delicate that what would normally be understood as a single event turned into two, three, and four. The opening of a ventricle, slow swish of blood as though deciding whether to enter or leave, and close, a suck and a pop if you can imagine a pop as an elongated process. What happened in her brain was anyone's guess. Smiles. Wonderful mounting moments of lucid thought. Incomplete arcs that held promise but then fell into a wasteland of things cut short.

The TV was on with the volume set low, emitting an aluminum hint of words from the upper corner of the room. Pete sat next to the bed, his back leaning against the same wall from which grew the hoses and plugs. He had stretched his legs forward and crossed them at the ankles, hands fisted together over his crotch as he slept. He was tilted left and half-supported by the guard of the hospital bed, his jaw slack, a breath exiting his mouth that was strong enough to cause his lips to bulge intermittently with each exhale of air. When Etta and Margie came in quietly, and then Noel and Owen, Miriam and then Jocelyn, he dropped his chin even more and then reacted to the sound of the door closing with a quick up-nod, opening his eyes and sitting up straight, startled.

One day and here things were. A cold malfunction of fate and one young soul was dipping toward death. There was no understanding the new state of Pixie. Her personal childhood, the one with the little air conditioner and the filmy window and pizza smell, wasn't lost in the activity that day, just hidden beneath the desire for a miracle, people craning their necks for a purpose where there might be one or there might not. From that cold day that she went into the river to this warm one, much had happened. Her still figure quiet but for the mechanics of the room around her, the beep and hiss, and her father resting his forehead on the bed guard, staring at the white sheet that had a small yellow stain, brown at the edges like the sheet had only been rinsed, not washed.

Margie stood under the TV with her back against the wall and listened. Here she thought that Etta, with her painted tomatoes and her Christian self-help books and her little bob of blonde hair, should be the seer and interpret what was to be interpreted, but she seemed timid and uncertain, going to Pete and leaning down just a little and touching his knee. The small group formed a U around the edges of the room. Outside the large window it was dark except for soft touches of light where the paper lanterns hung next to the parking lot.

The fluorescent room made their eyeballs ache, and their zeal shrank in the unremarkable atmosphere.

There had been a time, once, when Margie had kissed a boy for thirty minutes under her window in the moonlight. It was a dreamy event, the moon at perfect light as though confirming the act, the boy's large hand under her sweatshirt at her bare warm skin. This was youth, and if there had been a lake, they would have taken off their clothes and dived, but it was the Midwest and there were only streets and curbs and small trees.

Pete had an open Bible that he pulled onto his lap from the bedside table. Miss Lonelyhearts would approve, Margie thought, trying to engage, yet feeling tugged into her own past. She focused her eyes on the dark window and tried to imagine the lanterns outside as moons.

Pete stood up and walked to the window. He looked at the gathering of people in the darkening evening. He looked at the lanterns and the shape of the tent and the cars pulled neatly into their spaces. He reached up and pressed a palm to the glass, still holding the Bible. There was a faint sound of music, of guitars, and there were drums. People were singing.

Margie looked at the floor and then out the window, imagining the activity of people and light as far away, on some beach in some other place. The TV, still on, spewed little bits of noise. Owen turned it off.

PRAYER GETS LET LOOSE from a sincerity of soul. Imagine yourself as Pixie, hovering at the ceiling, back brushing against the tiles. You look down. The room is still with thought and reason. You have a choice, you had a choice. Will someone take your hand? Come from the hallway? Lead you? Now? Someone tells a joke that you can't hear. You laugh. A future is forming and you need to engage. There is so much that is not understood, and here you are with a whole lot of it in one of your hands and you know that you can be ignorant if you want. You cannot hear anything, but you can feel it and it's so much clearer that way. The hallway calls to you with an honest light and you realize that it's not a powder coating but real and personal and love, but here are all these people beneath you, heads bowed, trying to call out to the God who would storm the river and pull you into salvation, but they don't know who they pray to. You look at yourself in the bed with your greasy hair and pale skin, lying pious and tucked in like a dead girl, and you think that maybe it's here in the room with the people that you'll finally say yes.

IN THE END IT WASN'T LIKE the movies at all. The fluorescent lights in the ceiling made tiny barely perceptible *zip, zip* sounds, and the night completely overcame the parking lot outside where Owen held Noel in her arms as she cried. The tent was disassembled and the people began to leave, and then they all left and Etta hung back with Pete, praying.

A nurse came and lifted Pixie's wrist and took her pulse. Bored, she repositioned the plastic bag hanging from the hook. She wrote something on a chart.

Etta stood with her hand on Pixie's foot through the sheet. She went forward and kissed her on the forehead. Pete looked up and he was crying. Tears ran down his face.

Years ago, Etta had seen a commemorative book on 9/11. It had images of the planes, the fires, the dust, the horrified faces, the melted items, and abandoned rooms. In the middle of the book was a full-page spread, the grand finale placed like an intermission. There was the man falling through the air, white Brooks Brothers shirt skimming his sides, trousers like water at his shins. There was a book called *Falling Man*, she remembered, that didn't have pictures. She hadn't read it. What a horrible thing, Etta thought.

51.

smoke

It was funny how Miriam had carefully rolled the crumpled brown paper into a floppy tube and stuffed it in the little trunk of her Toyota Celica. Months later, the paper sign could be found in her mother's living room, crushed next to the two old printers and the dried flower wreath with the painted Styrofoam berries that were each in turn splitting their plastic and turning white almost like real living things. The ceiling was ever lower in that house with the rise of detritus from the floor. It was furious growth, latent items closest to the floor smashed into the rust-colored carpet and spilling guts of yarn and paper and beaded things, left to decay like people in diners sipping tea or coffee, floating with the current of history as the upper layer of young things still crackles and snaps and makes it into the story of somebody's life. Miriam sat outside in a white resin chair next to her mother's front door and smoked a Marlboro. Soft and papery, it gave to the shape of her lips and made her feel alive with comfort.

On the other side of town Margie stood on the gravel next to her grandfather's old studio. The painted wood siding had long ago been replaced with cedar that had aged nicely into a gray that contrasted with the bronze plaque with the green patina that said *Lee Bollinger* etched into the metal like he was a Civil War hero. The garage door that used to be white, chipped and crooked, was now a large double-paned window through which could be seen the original easels and paints, tubes set out in neat rows with their ends curling like scorpions. Burnt Umber, Phthalo Blue, Permanent Sap Green. Margie dropped her forehead to the glass and cupped her hands around her face to see clearly. The wheelchair was actually still there, backed against a wall. She imagined her grandfather in it, his thin leather belt high on his stomach the way his generation used to wear them, the bulge of flesh above and below it folding deeply as he leaned into his work. He wasn't talkative and he wasn't affectionate, but he gave Margie what he had. There was a spider web above the wheelchair in the corner of the room. She turned and walked down the street toward home.

The kids would be leaving for school soon and had started one of their fires again. She could smell it coming from the direction of the river. It was too warm for a fire, she thought, but then a breeze lifted the hair on her arms and made her shiver. As she walked down toward Maple, she thought she could see the smoke through the trees on the other side of town but wasn't sure. It could just be clusters of branches. From a distance, they can look gray and hazy, kind of like smoke.

Epilogue

To wake up meant that Pixie would have to push something up to the surface and be able to focus on it. It required a physical cognition that she hadn't used for some time, and so when it was too late to back out, she got up the nerve and let go of what had been so lovingly pulling at her soul and concentrated on her father in the chair with his head bowed wanting to change something but unable to. This helped.

She lifted two fingers. That's all, just the fingers. Nothing. It was all in the eyes, though, she discovered; she was able to open them for a second or two. Big bang for the buck, Pete looked at her, caught his breath, stood up, leaned over the bed, and pushed something. Oh, now we have contact. She opened them once more, caught his eyes, and closed them.

WHAT A GLORIOUS BUSTLE OF LIFE, the little room with the metal bed and synthetic hospital equipment. Nurses don't wear white anymore, they opt for patterns suited, it seemed to Pixie, for their personalities. Mickey and Minnie. Balloons. Was she in a pediatric ward? What the hell happened? Pete put his large warm hand to her cheek and her eyes welled up even though she didn't feel sad or happy, and tears ran down the side of her face and into her ears. The feeling was like zippers opening. She could breathe. She was taped together in various places, needles stuck into her with tubes and juice and lines leading to things. A thin tube ran over one of her thighs and out from under the sheet. The tube grew warm and then cool again. Her mouth, oh, her mouth and her throat, she hadn't thought about her mouth. She was in, she was out, she drifted back down.

THERE WAS A LINE FROM A SONG by Devendra Banhart that kept repeating in Pixie's mind when she awoke again to her father sitting next to her and someone sponging her forehead. *We see things like this,* someone said at least three times, as though it was such an honor and somehow worth bragging about. The song was about something she couldn't quite remember and began, *Let regret end at the start of the day.* The first intentional thought Pixie had was to figure out the song, there was more to it, but all she had was that one line. She needed to get right on that, but with all the activity and then the two doctors—or the one doctor, it was hard to tell— she barely had time to take her first official breath of mortal air. Pete had lost weight. He looked starved, like he'd been eating applesauce for months. The front of his shirt had a stain, and it reminded Pixie of a commercial that has a woman with a bottle of laundry detergent . . . there's some sort of white room and children playing. People detached various things from her body. Somebody, the doctor, or the other one, pulled a lamp on a long metal arm out from the wall. Her father looked at her like he was holding his breath. He bent over and kissed her on the forehead. What the hell was that? There was so much she didn't understand, but in a way it didn't matter. She tried to lift a knee and it moved. Oh, the control, the swell of control. And now the biggest thing, to speak, but she should wait, this, she knew, would take time. It was the consonants she worried about, they would be difficult. Someone ran water into a sink. There was a shadow of people gathered outside the door in the hallway but they didn't talk. One of them came in the room and Pete turned to look. He got up and hugged the shadow and the shadow came to the foot of the bed and then she was very light, it turned out, with a nice head, her hair was bright and curled under, and there was a necklace hanging from her neck and it was almost as though she knew Pixie, the way she stood there and smiled; it wasn't a smirky smile, it was a real one, and Pixie would make a note of this, that the woman with the nice bright hair and the necklace could be trusted. Then she remembered the song; *Let regret end at the start of the day / and don't take no secrets back to your grave / let everyone know, let everyone know.* She slowly folded her arms under the sheet and ran her hands along her upper arms because this is something she used to do, and there they still were, all the scars lined up like words. She felt the soft ridges and played them with her fingers, but even though they were still there, it was like feeling light because that was another world and another life. She remembered the name of the song, "Angelika," it was called, she was pretty sure of this.

Acknowledgments

While many writers like to wait until a manuscript is complete, wrinkles ironed out, adjustments made, before allowing anyone to read it, I am not one of them. My only qualification before handing off a first draft for wise eyes to see is that the story has a beginning, middle, and end, however patched together they might be.

My early readers and encouragers, as well as those who gently let me know the first draft needed a bit of work, include Rick James, Lyn Matejczyk, and Jennifer McNerney, while those who gave it a final read with a happy thumbs-up are David Bennett Thomas and Sarah Arthur. So much gratefulness.

Much-needed cheering for my writing in general came from Dorothy Greco, Sarah Arthur, and John and Lyn Matejczyk. Thank you for helping keep my fingers at the keyboard.

Susan Payne gave me insight into the unique qualities and challenges of multiple sclerosis. Thank you for your transparency. I respect and value you.

I'm grateful for Phil Fox Rose who gave me his honest and insightful thoughts as well as encouragement as he made his way through the final draft, as well as Robert Edmonson, who tackled the sticky business of implementing last minute changes.

Many, many thanks to Sr. Antonia and Molly O'Leary for their oh so important work in making sure that the novel is read and appreciated by many.

And most of all, thank you Rick, Avery, Whitney, and Will. Your unique personalities and thoughtful ideas will never cease to inspire me.

You may also be interested in...

Online Book Group Discussion Guide for *Can You See Anything Now?*
www.paracletepress.com/CanYouSeeAnythingNow

Notes on Orion

A Memoir

978-1-61261-932-3 • $18.99 • Trade paper

COMING 2018

Author Katherine James is no stranger to tragedy. This is a poignant and emotional memoir from the mother of a son who overdoses, but survives. The story of James's son is woven with an eloquent account of her and her husband's determination to help their son and his friends break free from the grip of today's powerful and accessible culture of drugs. This is a story of good and evil, death and life, that tugs at the soul and lays bare the opioid epidemic in America.

Everbloom

Stories of Deeply Rooted and Transformed Lives

Women of Redbud Writers Guild

978-1-612-61933-0 • $18.99 • Trade paper

Be inspired by the transforming power of story.

Through the pain, loss, beauty and redemption in these pages, you will find freedom and the courage to embrace your own story. The women of Redbud know the importance of spiritual shelter, and how easy it becomes to feel alone and misunderstood. In the *Everbloom* collection they offer essays, stories and poetry: intensely personal accounts of transformation, and the journeys to find their own voices. Best of all, they invite you to join them, with writing prompts that encourage a response of honesty, faith and imagination. Accept the invitation: set out on the journey to find your own voice.

"We read to see elements of our own hearts, experiences and stories reflected back to us in the words of others. This collection is just that: stories that help us feel seen, known, and understood. Honestly and beautifully told, this book will keep you in good company along your own journey."

—**Shauna Niequist**, bestselling author of *Present Over Perfect*

Available through your local bookseller or
through Paraclete Press: www.paracletepress.com; 1-800-451-5006